OUR LADY OF INFIDELITY

Also by Jackie Parker

Love Letters to My Fans

OUR LADY OF INFIDELITY

A Novel of Miracles

JACKIE PARKER

Arcade Publishing • New York

First Edition

Arcade Publishing books may be purchased in bulk at special discounts for sales promotion, corporate gifts, fund-raising, or educational purposes. Special editions can also be created to specifications. For details, contact the Special Sales Department, Arcade Publishing, 307 West 36th Street, 11th Floor, New York, NY 10018 or arcade@skyhorsepublishing.com.

Arcade Publishing® is a registered trademark of Skyhorse Publishing, Inc.®, a Delaware corporation.

Visit our website at www.arcadepub.com.

10 9 8 7 6 5 4 3 2 1

Library of Congress Cataloging-in-Publication Data

Parker, Jackie.
Our Lady of Infidelity : a novel of miracles / Jackie Parker.
pages cm
ISBN 978-1-62872-430-1 (hardback)
1. Miracles—Fiction. 2. Spiritual life—Fiction. 3. California—Fiction.
I. Title.
PS3616.A745225O97 2014
813'.6—dc23 2014009096

Cover design by Rain Saukus
Cover photo: Thinkstock

Ebook ISBN: 978-1-62872-474-5

Printed in the United States of America

OUR LADY OF INFIDELITY

PROLOGUE

There is a form of love so beautiful we can hardly stand to be in its presence. Given where we live and what we are, it is simply beyond us. We know that now. But there was a time here in Infidelity, an unbearably hot end of August into September, when we got to taste it. When it tried us out and found us wanting.

It came to us through a child, Luz Reyes, a name that few of us had pronounced, though she lived (along with her mother Josefina Guerra-Reyes) nearly six years at the margins of our lives. First, a few miles up the freeway in a converted garage behind the auto shop belonging to Bryant Platz. And then, later, right among us in one of the stucco bungalows in the hill district, a small brown rise just up from where the church used to be.

Some claim it was not Luz at all who was responsible for what arrived in Infidelity that August the fifteenth. That it was far more complicated than her so-called gift. Right from the start the skeptics among us were casting about for blame, trying to figure who was behind that car wash vision that had us all confounded. They had their pick of candidates.

Walt Adair is usually named first because it was his window—his car wash. Though Walt had mixed feelings about the whole thing right from the start.

Some blame Josefina for not dragging her daughter off that sidewalk right away and giving her a good hard slap. Others say the beauteous Zoe Luedke was the cause. Here one day, gone the next, golden-eyed, graceful, and shy. Hers were the hands that put in the window. Strange hands too, long-fingered, maimed. An accident, some say of that chopped-off finger. *That husband*, the rumormongers whisper.

In the end, most people settle on Father Bill. Never mind that we were ripe for it—what he stirred in us, the hunger for something we had not known was missing. The promise we could not fulfill without him. Though in the blame department we are none of us exempt, because all of us took and most of us got and no one considered what it might cost Luz.

Any way you view it, something happened to a child here and we let it.

The day it started was hot. Summer in the High Desert no one's expecting snow, but this particular August the fifteenth dawned so hot even the Joshua trees woke confused, their gray wooly branches pointing down to the earth instead of up to the impossibly blue and cloudless desert sky.

At least that was the report from the campgrounds ten miles east of here. Strange reports up and down the freeway in Infidelity that day. The dependable griddle at the Infidelity Diner burned everything that touched it—buttermilk pancakes to tuna melts. Tourists in the sliding-door view rooms of the Infidelity Motel awoke to a racket of sand against glass that completely obscured the trio of Joshua trees and the snow-capped San Jacinto peaks they'd paid extra to see.

One hundred and three on the Joshua Freeway and not quite eight. The sun, a molten globe, burned fierce and white. Drivers heading east would speak of the glare. How they had been nearly blinded behind their windshields and had to proceed through Infidelity on faith. Up the steep Joshua grade then headlong into the bowl of it. Just swimming that morning, they all said, with unearthly light.

And Luz Reyes, the child who would become for a while the center of all our lives, steps out of her house in the hill district, 9 Mariposa Lane, headed for Our Lady of Guadalupe and eight o'clock Mass but ends up at the car wash—a long mile away.

There she stands on the sidewalk outside Walt Adair's front office, thick dark braids down her back, her starched yellow dress limp with sweat, new sandals coated with High Desert road dust. *Called*, she will later claim. *Called by what?* She is right out there staring when Walt looks up, checking traffic. Walks out to find her all alone.

"What are you doing, honey?"

No reply.

"What are you looking at?"

She turns her squarish head and faces him, eyes rolled skyward like the answer is up there and she is trying to pull it down. Walt is a dad, he knows the look—she is making something up.

"Big wings."

"Big wings, huh?" He glances into the brilliant empty sky. "What, a hawk?"

"The Quetzal."

"Never heard of it. Did mother bring you down here?"

She shakes her head.

"Does Father Bill know you're here?"

No again.

"Who brought you, Luz? Did you walk off again on those fast little feet?"

Still no reply.

Her cheek is hot as a furnace, and there is something about her smell, Walt says later. Like someone has doused her in rosewater. Sun poisoned. He lifts her up and carries her to his office where it is cool, then sits her on the sofa. Luz drinks some water, lets him wash down her face with a wet paper towel. Then he grabs a handful of ice from his fridge case, slides a cube along her palms and wrists, a trick he remembers from his own kids' fevers. The whole time she's staring across the room—at that crazy window.

"So Luz, how did you get here?"

"A lady told me."

"What lady?"

She closes her eyes and begins to speak—the words he can never bring himself to repeat—floored by what comes at him next, some feeling between thankfulness and ordinary love. But bigger. A lot bigger. *What the hell?* he thinks.

"How 'bout we call your mother."

Then across the room Luz runs, banging out the door, ice cubes flying behind her. This time when Walt tries to lift her from the sidewalk she fights him off. When he cannot reach Josefina by phone, he tries everyone he knows in the hill district, until old Wren Otto drives to the church and calls out Father Bill in the middle of saying Mass.

By the time they arrive—Father Bill and, a little while later, a dozen or so of his faithful—Luz is kneeling on the sidewalk, tears streaming. Enraptured.

Father Bill kneels next to her, covers the top of her head with his hands and tries talking ordinary sense. He cannot bring her back. A good hour he is at it, his black robe still on from Mass soaked through with sweat and reeking. He had thrown up.

Finally, he shouts, "Stop it, Luz!"

Then Luz starts in with the noises, deep in her throat. A few folks fall to their knees. Some start moaning.

"Oh, God no. Please."

"Luz, listen to me, now," Walt says. "No more nonsense. I want you to get up!"

She doesn't.

The sidewalk is hot enough to scramble egg whites. But Luz will not remember the heat, only that suddenly there were green wings above her, the wings of the Quetzal (already extinct in her country and never, of course, seen in the Mojave), the sweet smell of roses and cedar, and a deep coolness before she ceased to see.

Josefina Reyes will recall nothing unusual about the start of that day save for a leftover blueberry waffle. But within herself, Josefina confesses, she had awakened with a certain unreasonable joy. Though she is only one week out of the hospital with the warnings of her doctors still fresh in her ears, she feels perfect, absolutely restored, exactly as she knew she would feel, impending dialysis and incipient uremia be damned. Filled with her old energy.

Right before Luz leaves the house, Josefina kisses her daughter three times on her broad, stony forehead, reminds her to drink one glass of water per hour, to stay off the hot playground at summer school, and repeats the daily injunction: a half-hour of reading will do more for her future than going to Mass.

"Don't waste time saying Rosaries for my health, for my body has already cured me. And no little tricks with your Zoe. No campgrounds, no makeup, even if it is her last day."

Then she brings Luz back through the house to the kitchen and opens the refrigerator to show Luz the syrup she has prepared—one pineapple cored and blended, four ounces of guava paste, a scant cup of sugar.

"See how I slave for your sweet tooth, gordita? Make the refrescas to be cool. *Zoe* scrapes the ice. Listen! You only pour. Don't touch the big knife."

"Ay, Mami, you are hurting my ears. You are so bossy again."

"Be glad. This way you know I'm not dead."

So thrilled is Josefina with the return of her strength that she does not accompany Luz to the front door. She has decided, in the ten minutes she has left before driving to work, to sweep Luz's room and straighten the dog-eared Madonnas of the Centuries that only the most tolerant of nonbelievers would allow her daughter to tape on the walls throughout a four-room house.

As soon as the front door closes behind her, a voice directs Luz to the car wash, urges her a long mile in terrible heat in the wrong direction. Not for a moment does she consider ignoring it, she says later, so kind it is, unfamiliar, yet still, a voice she *knows.*

Josefina herself, driving at a snail's pace through light brilliant and granular as snowfall, passes her own daughter unseeing.

And all of us who are used to the sight of Luz Reyes walking to Mass in her starched yellow dress, the thick dark braids down her back, watch her turn right instead of left at the end of Mariposa Lane, stepping onto the shoulder of the freeway. Yet not one of us opens a window or a door that day to ask where she is going. We did not want to interfere, we said later, for it was clear from the purposefulness of her step that Luz knew exactly where she was headed.

August the fifteenth, the day of Our Lady's Assumption. A coincidence, many of us believed, and perhaps still do, one in a long string of coincidences—or a hoax, venal and cruel. Or something far greater. Who among us can say for sure?

CHAPTER 1

The first time they are together is at Father Bill's table, a Wednesday or a Thursday. No one remembers exactly—a sweltering August night. Father Bill at the head, Josefina seated stiffly to his left, then Luz, head down and hands in her lap so she won't stare. Across from Luz there is Zoe, the creamy skin, the yellow-brown eyes, and other things Luz is dying to look at—like that hand. Next to Zoe Father Bill put Walt, overdressed in his usual blue oxford, amazed that the woman he has been musing on for days has turned up beside him.

The room is plain, nearly empty of furnishings, the not-quite-steady table with a frayed white cloth, six mismatched hard-back chairs and no cushions, and the tall west-facing windows through which the light of High Desert sunset now pours. If only they would look out, the San Jacinto Mountains are turning silky pink just beyond them, but instead they are admiring his food.

Father Bill will say he had no idea what would come of this night. That it is simple gratitude that made him ask Zoe to join him for a meal. What else does he have to give to a stranger (a Samaritan, truly), but his passion for food, his talent to feed? Now he thanks them all for coming and then starts the blessings, first them, then the focaccia, the rosemary chicken, the eggplant parmesan, the broccoli with lemon zest, the frozen cannolis, and two flavors of ice cream that Luz will scoop out for dessert. He thanks his late mother in heaven for the recipes, thanks the fourth ward of the city of Newark, New Jersey, where he was raised,

Italians in row houses, the air thick with garlic and sauce. Thanks his uncle Gerard whose three-meat gravy he was wise enough not to make in such heat, and the province of Calabria, his ancestral home, where even now the men who walk the high cobbled streets have his thick black hair, his narrow-set gray eyes, and munificent, unbalanced tables.

"We are here, Lord, not just to nourish our bodies but to nourish one another."

And then he pours the wine. They follow him as he lifts his glass.

"To Zoe Luedke, hero of the day. The one who rescued me from sunstroke."

Everyone must drink. Luz takes a sip of her orange juice, careful not to dribble, and crunches the ice in her teeth. Josefina thinks of dousing Father Bill with the chilled Chardonnay, which she knows she should not, in her condition, swallow but will just to spite him because she has heard too much already about this *Sewey*. And now here she is seated across from her daughter—what does he know of her—a woman who picks up men in wild shirts on the freeway: a woman who from unearned beauty is no doubt used to too much attention. Look how she flaunts that face—no makeup, such easy smiles. But too tall, too pale, the fine hair that does not hold its color, and the unpronounceable name. *Sewey*—and in the same breath as hero. He is crazy. He is a forty-five-year-old teenager, already half-mad with love.

"And these are my girls. Josefina and Luz Reyes." He says their names properly at least.

"Hose-a-fina and Loose," repeats Zoe, as if she has never heard Spanish.

"Pretty good," says Father Bill, turning to them, "don't you agree?"

Josefina barely nods. She has that look he hates. She could shut down like a tainted clam and spoil the whole meal. Luz feasts her eyes on the stranger, gold in her hair, gold in the brown of her wide, shining eyes. *Zoe*, she says to herself. A gold ocean appears in Luz's mind.

At last now they can eat.

They pass the platters, which are heavy, the same blue misplaced windmill design as the chipped plates that are filling up fast. Luz gets two chicken legs, a large square of eggplant, even the broccoli. She digs right in. She never waits. Josefina watches as if her daughter's eating is a sport and she's the coach, Walt thinks, amused, *Keep going! Good job, mamita*! It is always like this. The child eats; the mother watches. Luz has arrived on first base. Josefina can relax.

Walt helps Zoe to chicken. He is so nervous beside her (the long bare arms, that lovely white neck, and the vulnerable collar bones—his undoing in a woman—such creamy skin), he must focus to hold the heaping platter steady while she reaches, twice, once for a breast, then for a thigh. "There's so much!" she says. "And I'm starved." A sudden rush of joy courses through Walt; her voice affects him like music—so many risings and fallings in so few words. What will he do if she says more than three at a time? "That's good!" booms Walt, "This is the place to be hungry." When she offers to serve him the steaming eggplant, it nearly slides from the spoon onto his perfect blue shirt. They laugh, apologize to each other. On one side of the table the tension breaks.

"So what's the word on *your* car?" Father Bill asks. Zoe has driven to the rectory in Platz's garage loaner, a hulking Dodge Dart.

Zoe swallows her chicken. It is wonderful—so tender (he bastes it every quarter hour in brown butter). "A cracked radiator. Unfixable. Platz says it could take a week before he finds a replacement. A '78 Nova, it's a hard thing to find."

A week, thinks Walt, perhaps even longer.

"What a pity. And mine was only minor, all that steam and just a hose," Father Bill says.

Josefina nudges Luz, who smiles.

"Did someone say something funny?" asks Father Bill.

"No-va," says Luz and gives Zoe the force of her penetrating eyes and a mouth full of eggplant. Josefina wipes the mouth. Luz squirms and continues, "You know Spanish? No va. Does not go."

Zoe slaps her forehead. "Now they tell me!" The minute she does it she realizes she has made a mistake and quickly puts the hand in her lap. Josefina feels sick to her stomach. She turns her head to Father Bill; her thick black hair conceals half her face, her features already obscured by the swelling that makes her look like she has just been roused from a bad sleep. She whispers to Father Bill in Spanish. Father Bill whispers back in kind.

Now they have seen it, Zoe should tell the story of her missing fingertip, which always puts people at ease, but to tell it she will have to speak of her husband and to strangers. She returns to her food, hoping nothing more will be made of the finger, but the table has gone silent.

"Something wrong?" Walt asks.

They are waiting for her to explain.

"An accident at my shop. The most common injury there is for woodworkers." Zoe holds up her hand—missing fingertip and all—for them to see again.

"Does it hurt?" asks Luz.

"Not at all."

Josefina puts her own intact hand on Luz's arm, "Co-may, mamita."

It had happened three years before after an impromptu picnic. The first time she and Michael had made love. *Cold Spring in autumn. Golden oaks and scarlet maples spilling their colors into the blue of Long Lake, air tinged with frost. "I knew it would be like this," Michael says, enfolding Zoe in a blanket. "Like what?" she whispered. "Like home." Lovemaking to scramble the senses. Wine at lunch, forbidden in the wood trade. She'd sliced her finger clean through at the joint on a Grizzly Saw. When he raced to her, the table saw running, eight feet of walnut spun out at the kickback. Michael tore off his shirt, wrapped the finger, retrieved the tip, drove to the hospital berating himself. "Don't fall for me. I'm bad news." Too late, Zoe thought. And then said so. Both of them laughing, giddy with shock and relief. And so it began. Hermit-girl and the man she had loved since high school. After years of aloneness she was finally home.*

"Zoe is a carpenter, Luz. She has a red toolbox," Father Bill explains.

"A cabinetmaker, kitchen cabinets mostly. My shop is very far away. In a place called Cold Spring."

"You know how to use tools?" Luz asks.

"I do."

"Comay," Josefina insists.

"No, because maybe she can give Walt his window!"

"That is not your business. How many times must I say you do not worry for the world!"

"Let's not start on my window. Not tonight, please!" Walt laughs. His smile is genial. The sun creases are white around his deep-set blue eyes, something worn and expectant about his face. At forty-five, his skin has freckled (too many hours on the tennis court—in the old life).

Zoe softens and forgives him for the way he kept her the night she drove the grubby Dart through his car wash. Walt standing in the exit lane wanting to talk, she inside the car in tears, wanting only to leave.

"That window is just waiting for someone to trip over," Father Bill says, picking up his wine glass.

"No one's fallen yet, Father. It's still in one piece."

"You've been lucky."

"It's behind the couch now."

"Is that progress?"

Father Bill laughs at his own little joke and finishes his wine. Even Josefina seems amused. Walt deserves this, he knows. His window, again. These days everything he does takes him long to decide. The design of his wash, one year to come up with, the window he has bought but can't figure where to put, the coupon books he has for months debated if he should offer, these are decisions that do not make themselves. So they laugh at him, the people of Infidelity—who have not much to laugh at, truth be told. Walt is used to it. On the days he's feeling thin-skinned he avoids the diner crowd, or if he can't he ignores their remarks, does not take the bait when it's been tossed. He knows his window was a mistake. He should have returned it right away. A single-glazed horizontal slider bought on sale at Home Depot, all wrong for this hot climate. What was he thinking? He was thinking it would give him a view.

"Well," says Zoe, "I've installed windows."

"I'll keep it in mind. But I'm sure you don't want to work on your vacation. You're at the campgrounds?"

"Yep. Still there."

"And you're a crag rat—a climber?"

She could tell Walt she had come for the sights, for the desert, for the climbing at the campgrounds, which is what she told her customers in Cold Spring, even the ones who knew better. It is fifteen dollars a week at the Joshua Tree Campgrounds and somewhere in the vicinity her husband may be waiting, not for her, but still he may be near.

"Not yet," she says and hopes they're too polite to question her further. "What size is the window?"

"Four by six."

"It would only take a day to install."

"Thanks. I'll think about it."

They go back to eating in silence, Zoe relieved. She has managed to deflect the conversation away from her life and onto Walt's window, which has brought a little levity to the table at least, and who knows—maybe a job. There is no radiator on order at the Infidelity Garage because Zoe is strapped. Four breakdowns of the Nova on her crazy trip west and bills piling up in the Cold Spring post office. Old house. New shop. Expensive equipment. They had taken on too much. Way too fast.

Father Bill urges a little more food on his guests. Who can refuse such tastes even if the body must be stretched to receive them? And besides, it is cooler, have they noticed? They have all ceased to sweat. He opens the second wine with a flourish and a pop. From under Father Bill's wide-flung casements, the cool desert air wafts in like a reasonable neighbor come over to offer relief.

Luz takes a drink of orange juice, looks straight across at Zoe, then pushes back her chair and stands up.

"What's wrong, mamita?" Josefina asks as Luz begins to walk. "Come back. Sit down and finish." Luz does not obey, walking to Zoe, bending close now to whisper, so softly that Zoe must ask her to say it again when she's through. After Luz has whispered for the second time in Zoe's shiny ear, she stays with her hand on that strong, bare white arm.

"You heard it?"

"Yes."

Luz can return to her seat.

At the place where Luz touched her, Zoe feels something rise under her skin and spawn out through her blood, like the bubbles of a thousand silver fish rushing to the surface of a lake. Now she feels it in her shoulder then straight down her spine. Luz is already back to her chair, but Zoe is being run through with lightness, she sees it, how can she? A silver sensation like a stalled AC current is stuck at the base of her neck. She is tipping, falling backward. It is Walt who grabs her chair just in time.

Now Zoe has risen to her feet, quite surprised to find herself upright. Immediately Walt stands up too—"Shall we clear?"—and reaches across for her plate.

Josefina has gone pale. She takes Luz's face in her hands. "Did you say something crazy? What did you tell that woman that no one else could hear?"

"Josefina!" Father Bill says sharply and asks Zoe and Walt to sit down.

"It must be the wine," Zoe says, sorry she has caused such a fuss when already the sensation has passed.

"Or the heat," Walt adds.

Once she is seated, Zoe feels downright foolish.

"Your little girl asked me again to help Walt with his window."

"Because they always laugh at him," Luz says, training those dark eyes at her mother.

"Oh, honey," says Walt.

Now Josefina looks contrite. "Come here, mamita." She pulls Luz onto her lap.

"There, you see? It was harmless." Father Bill puts his hand on the top of Luz's head and holds it long enough for a blessing. "How about it, Walt, shall we clear?"

Luz burrows into her mother's soft breast like an infant. Josefina kisses her forehead, her cheeks; she is kissing Luz's hands. It is too much for Zoe, who averts her eyes.

As the men leave the dining room with the platters and plates, Zoe looks out the window at the darkening mountain, breathes deeply, inhaling the cool rush of sweet night air. It is her own fault she nearly passed out, Zoe thinks. It is Michael's. Or it is the breakdown-plagued trip west. Maybe even the climate, the heat, the dry air. Her dizzy spell had nothing to do with the touch of a child whose mother adores her, who is right now allowing those kisses.

"You like ice cream?" Josefina asks in heavily accented English.

"I do," Zoe says.

"Prepare to wait for it, then." And she laughs, a big careless laugh that is startling. "Because with my daughter serving we will have to be extremely patient."

It is the first time all evening that Josefina has spoken directly to Zoe.

"I have been told I am patient to a fault," Zoe says.

"To a fault? What does it mean?"

"I can be too patient."

"No one can be too patient."

Ah, yes, yes they can. Zoe waited two weeks after Michael left before accepting he had actually gone. She stands at her workbench for hours, days, wrecking her schedule while she waits for the grain of the wood to reveal itself before she will make the first cut. This evening, she will be happy to wait a few minutes for a child to serve ice cream.

Josefina murmurs to Luz, runs her hands down her daughter's thick braid, then leans forward, puts her elbow on the table, and rests her head in her hand. After a few seconds she closes her eyes.

Zoe listens to the men's voices in the kitchen, the clattering of plates and cutlery. A few months ago it would be Michael and Zoe in their kitchen cleaning up, cabinets half-stripped, flooring ripped up, guests for dinner anyway. Now the Cold Spring house bought with such hope is deserted, the unfinished rooms, their shop in the back, empty of life. The slate-gray Hudson moves along without them in the unseen distance.

Outside it is growing dark, the High Desert night sky taking on a blackness whose depth Zoe does not recognize. So many stars it makes her giddy. For three nights she has lost herself watching the desert sky expand under darkness. At night it seems wider even than in the piercing blue day, when it is already so vast she has to stop looking or she's afraid she'll dissolve. How different the sky is in this part of the world, Zoe thinks, as if up to now she has been given only a glimpse of all that is actually there. In a little while she will be unroofed and under it again: the noisy Sheep Meadow campsite, her collapsing two-person tent.

When Walt returns, he does not seem surprised to find Josefina asleep at the table and carefully sets the dessert bowls, a glass of water, and the ice cream scoop before Luz, who looks up and smiles but remains on the lap of her mother. When he returns to his seat, he bends quite close to Zoe, so close she can smell him, clean, the undertone of alcohol on his breath, musk, a familiar cologne. A wash of surprised desire runs through her.

"How are you doing?" Walt asks in a hushed voice, so as not to disturb Josefina.

"Much better, thanks."

"I'd like to explain about the other night."

"Oh," says Zoe. "Really, it's not necessary."

Luz climbs carefully off of her sleeping mother's lap, takes her seat, and watches Zoe reach for her wine glass with that hand. It is a big hand and white. The skin over the missing fingertip perfectly smooth.

From the outside Walt's car wash had looked a little sad, a white forlorn barn dropped down in the desert. A hundred yards off sat Walt in his office (or so she had thought), a small stucco box built so close to the freeway you could walk out the door, follow the path to the sidewalk, and be hit by the wind and the heat from the onrushing cars.

"Don't you think all the lights in the wash are so beautiful?" Luz asks in a whisper.

"I guess so. Yes. They are." Inside the wash there were hundreds of delicate overhead lights that began flashing as soon as she'd entered, then the water rained down in a slow, dreamy whoosh. The lights flickered, grew faint. For a moment it was quiet and dark. Zoe was overcome with a great feeling of peace. The cycle resumed, water pounding, lights brighter, and by the time it was over Zoe could not stop her tears.

"Lots of people break down at my car wash like you did. The lucky ones."

"Lucky ones?" Zoe laughs nervously.

Walt smiles. She thinks he's joking. He does not have the words to convince her he is not. He really is handsome, Zoe thinks, even-featured, *too even*, too well put together, like one of her well-heeled clients. Now the ice cream is here. Father Bill with his green parrot shirt and his self-effacing warmth, wedging two gallons under his chin. When he puts them before Luz, she takes off the tops, dips the scooper into the water glass then into the first container, making a perfect pink round of peppermint ice cream in very slow motion, before easing it into its bowl. Now the water glass to rinse, now the green ice cream: pistachio and soft enough to scoop. Pistachio and peppermint, her favorites that Father Bill always gets for her. She holds up the first yellow bowl like a trophy.

"For Zoe," Luz says. Father Bill hands Zoe the bowl. Josefina opens her eyes and sits back, forcing herself awake.

"I think our guest should start or she'll soon be drinking soup," says Father Bill. "By all means," says Walt. "Okay, here goes," Zoe says as she puts her teaspoon into the pink mound and begins.

When at last the meal is over, the cannoli dish empty, the ice cream a memory, just before they all rise and go out into the cool starry night, Father Bill looks from one to the other appraisingly. Then he smiles.

"What are we waiting for?" asks Luz, breaking the silence. Even Josefina laughs. Then the thanks begin and the offers to clean up; Father Bill, refusing, walks his guests to the door. "We did very well, don't you think?" he asks as if he is not quite sure. "I think we should do this again."

"I'll have you for dinner at the campgrounds," Zoe jokes.

Luz looks from Father Bill to her mother. Walt turns around on the step. "We are going to the campgrounds?" Luz asks.

"Come, mamita," says Josefina, taking Luz's hand and rushing into the dark with barely a whispered goodnight.

After Zoe and Walt say good-bye, walking together to their cars, even after all three of the cars are gone from his parking lot, Father Bill remains on the steps of the rectory, following the lights as they take their separate routes through the dark. How unlucky that the evening has ended with a mention of the campgrounds. Now Josefina won't sleep for worrying.

Tonight she has driven the three short blocks from her blue house to his church, a fine walk but she will not walk in the dark. He has only to look at her face to see that she is having a bad time. She never speaks of it anymore. It is a given. All her symptoms, some physical, some psychological. What is the difference? They persist. He does not go inside until he has followed the lights of Josefina's car up the hill and into the driveway of her house, which he can just about see from the blistered steps of his church.

Then, ignoring the mess in the kitchen, he walks around to his office, opens the screen door, goes to his desk and sits down to begin the night's calls. He calls two priests in the greater Los Angeles diocese in the wealthiest parishes. A mercy call, he explains, on behalf of a parishioner without family or funds who may soon be unable to work, worse, might require an organ donation. Both calls evoke silence, offense. He has overstepped the bounds of charity, it seems. *Since when does charity have bounds?* he wonders. One of the priests asks the parishioner's name. "I'd like to pray for her. Or is it a him?" A delicate matter, Father Bill explains. He cannot give out the name. The calls end badly, with hollow promises.

When he returns to the wreckage of his kitchen, the great heap of dishes piled in his sink cheers him, and he is able to let go the heaviness in his chest. He feels a deep satisfaction about the evening, as if all he could ask of it has been given. Now he stands at his sink below the dismal brown cabinets Zoe Luedke, a maker of cabinets so it turns out, would have dismantled and replaced in less than a day. He looks down at his dishes, looks further, and realizes he cannot see his feet. His belly has grown quite impressive. No wonder Josefina reaches under his shirt and whispers in Spanish, "We have made a miracle, William. You look six months gone." Her touch, he thinks, and wonders if perhaps he will go to her later, though he promised himself he would not. Lately her skin feels different—papery, too dry. She is not drinking water.

He turns on the hot water and pours a liberal quantity of blue dish liquid into the sink, watching the bubbles, then takes up the sponge. Or could it be the detergents that are making Josefina's fingers feel like sandpaper? Does she remember to wear gloves? A woman from a family in which no girl made a bed or washed a dish. Now Josefina is a housekeeper with sandpaper hands. Who would have believed it? And he sighs.

He should be grateful. She takes her medicine. Follows the diet. She works. She sleeps. She is mostly free from fear. And their life together is in many ways beautiful. He has long ago gotten over the guilt of their relation. Now, thanks to a parishioner's bequest, he has been able to give her a house, for a little while at least, until his bishop insists that he sell it. She pays four hundred dollars a month, one-third her salary, but that is more than sufficient. The neighbors do not comment on his visits to the little blue hill district house. Their own houses are dark when he leaves her deep in the night. If they notice, they don't suspect why he is there, or so he likes to tell himself. His parish is insignificant. He has failed to attract many believers to Our Lady of Guadalupe (he knows they call it Our Lady of Infidelity behind his back), knows that he asks too much of those who stay. In his state a small failing parish, perhaps it is just as well. He will soon be gone.

Since his escape from the country of death, he has lost his ambition. He is slow in his brain and his blood. So at forty-five he understands better his few parishioners, whose average age is nearly eighty, and he understands Josefina when she says she is thirty-two plus one hundred. It is because of El Salvador, where you live several lifetimes in a month, if you are lucky, and if you survive, as they did, and she barely, a life lived in safety seems like a dream. He had left a promising career in the Newark parishes, drawn by the call of liberation theology. A rising star in the church, he had given it up after he read the reports, a whole town massacred by its own soldiers, Mozote. Every child, every adult save one. And those who told of it, even in the press of his country, were not believed. "You do not want to get into that mess," his bishop had warned. "There is no profit in it. You can do more here." He could not remain. He was entirely unprepared for El Salvador. Even in the cities they were killing priests, their archbishop, professors, judges, journalists, imprisoned, disappeared. What they could do to a body—Dr. Raphael Reyes, the charismatic professor of biology—his friend.

To their own bodies, his, Josefina's, though nearly eight years have passed, it is still El Salvador. You cannot know so many people who have died and not died in their beds but been killed, and not killed but slaughtered, their corpses dispersed like refuse in the green coffee fields, in the black sands, on the highway, the alleys, impaled on the gates. At the university. You cannot know deaths like that so intimately and be young. The whole sense of hope bleeds out of you when you have lived as they have in El Salvador, him for three scant years. Her country, her family, her losses, too large to count.

And there it is again after such a fine night, El Salvador. A night that arrived with a taste of pure happiness. Even in this moment when his body pretends to know nothing of what he has lived, when his body is light and delicious, despite its new weight, happy to have fed and eaten, satisfied with his little dinner and his guests. How can he know a whole day's joy when so many dead live within him, his friend—more, his brother, Dr. Raphael Reyes, the husband of Josefina, the father Luz has never seen.

But still, lately, ten days to be precise, in spite of El Salvador—*with* El Salvador—he feels joy that arrives to him always as surprise, such a gift. He is walking once more in absolute trust. He accepts every moment, each imperfection, even the half-rotten eggplant with the places he must cut out. With such a small parish, so few to tend, he does not know what else to do when he's like this but cook and invite.

He is grateful most of all that the bad time with Luz has now passed. It is nine weeks since she wandered from school to the desert, that time warp with no explanation. Nine weeks since she speaks of being *called.* Since the beginning of June he has carried his fears for her, asking God to take back what he hopes is only incipient, that gift of the spirit he does not believe in. Blames himself for inciting her fervor with the stories of saints, books about Fatima and Medjugorje, the little girl seers of Garabandal. Let there be nothing unnatural in the being of this child, he asks, just a very small flaw in her brain, a glitch that is right now repairing itself, a chemical gap.

He will do what he tells Luz to do. "Don't think about it. Don't talk about it." The less attention they give it, the better. And soon, God willing, her obsession will fade. She will have no more out-of-time wanderings, no dreams in which the Virgin Mother opens her blue starry robe and calls out her name.

There, he is back to himself. He is washing his dishes, reviewing the happiness of his guests. He covers the rosemary chicken with foil (he has made so much it will last him all week) giving thanks for ten easy nights, ten mornings that have found him in his own narrow bed, waking eager and ravenous—like a pregnant woman, or a happy child.

And for Zoe Luedke, he says thank you for her, her arrival to them out of nowhere, exactly as his dream had foretold it, like the sudden brisk desert wind promising something he senses but does not yet know.

CHAPTER 2

For one week following this night Walt Adair tortures himself over what to do with his window, a question that has plagued him on and off for a year. Installed on the south-facing wall it will give him a fine view of traffic, just as the window next to the entry door on the north lets him see out to the Little San Bernadino Mountains, his modest white barn of a car wash, and the newly clean cars as they come through. But each time Zoe Luedke calls to ask if he's ready for an estimate, instead of saying, "Sure, just come by," he pleads for a little more time.

As much as he'd like to see her again, as surprised as he is just to hear that musical voice, the thought of a window that will let him look out at the traffic makes him vaguely uneasy; he can't quite figure out why. Each night he drives the mile on an unpaved back road to his property, a half-acre site in the desert: two-bedroom adobe, four-foot-tall River Rock fountain, old cactus garden. His only addition, the trailer he bought for his daughter's visits (that in three years she has not stayed in or seen). Before he goes into the house, he turns on the fountain and poses his question to the night: Should he or shouldn't he put in that window? He gets no reply. He has only the counsel of his friend, Father Bill, which has helped Walt before but is not helping now: *If it's before you, it's yours.* You bought the damn window, now put it to work. But he can't.

Twice that week he awakens having dreamed about Zoe, first, as a dim figure moving inside the trailer. The next time she is standing outside it, near the fountain and the cactus, everything glowing with a strange silver light. Her hair, her whole body shimmers as if in first snow. The dreams make him happy but give him no answer, only the sensation that he's seen Zoe Luedke again in the flesh.

Each day he does his chores a little more thoughtfully, replaces half a dozen burned-out pinpoint lights in the ceiling of the wash, flushes the crystal rinse solvent so it runs like clean rain. In the office where he welcomes his customers—the few that come by—he wipes every smudge off the Formica counter behind which he stands. Cleans every spill on the snack bar on the opposite wall, with its urns of freshly brewed coffee and tall piles of cups. Shines up the glass-door refrigerator below with its ample supply of sodas and juice. Vacuums the carpeted floor, slaps the pillows on his vast velvet couch, in front of the wall that might soon hold the window—or not.

So obsessed is Walt with the question of his window he forgets to give several first-timer customers "the talk." More than one customer drives out of the car wash moved by their experience in ways they do not understand.

Still, in a single morning Walt makes the calls he has put off all year and knows what the job of installing his window should cost: one thousand dollars, on average, about four hundred more than he is prepared to spend.

When Father Bill stops by for an afternoon coffee, he sees the couch pushed into the middle of the room, with the window leaning against it and Walt stretched flat beside the south wall, feeling for studs.

"Who are you thinking of hiring?" Father Bill asks. pouring himself an extra large cup, then opening the refrigerator for the stainless steel pitcher of milk.

"No idea. Not sure I am hiring anybody."

"How about Zoe? From what I hear she can use the work."

"Who have you been talking to, Luz?"

"I've been talking to Zoe," says Father Bill.

"What's the problem?" Walt asks.

"That I can't say."

"She's calling me, too," Walt says.

"Really?"

"She's been pretty damn persistent."

"Well, she can use the work."

Walt could recite word for word Father Bill's standard bid to join one who needs serving to one who can serve. A simple exchange for Father Bill, but one that ignores the normal laws of commerce that Walt still tends to respect. "If something is needed and someone can provide, what's the issue? What could possibly stop them from giving?" "Lots of things," Walt usually says. "It's just not that simple." "Ah," Father Bill always says, "but it is."

Walt wishes Father Bill would come at it directly, "Here's what I want you to do," but that's never his way. The priest can be downright elusive. There are things he won't speak of that Walt wonders about but is too polite to put on the table. One day he is going to ask Father Bill about his years in El Salvador. All he will say of that time is that's where he met Josefina. What's the big secret, after all? What does he have to hide? It's not as if Walt asks about their relations. But Walt doesn't like evasion in his friends. And he does not like the sense he's being pushed.

"Well," says Father Bill, then he stands up and hands Walt his mug, "here's something that might help you see the situation more broadly. Zoe can't pay for that radiator. Her car's just sitting up at the garage."

"What's she been using for transportation?"

"The loaner. I helped her work something out with Platz. I'd prefer you don't mention it."

"Who would I tell?"

"In case you hear them talking at the diner."

Father Bill leaves Walt feeling guilty, as if knowing Zoe's short on money he's now obliged to help. But the more Walt muses on the problem, the less inclined he is to call her.

He wonders if putting in the window might even backfire—like the ads he took out in the *High Desert Pennysaver*, and those radio spots last summer, after which business declined. Since then he has come to believe there's a whole other way to get what he wants for his car wash. He has started to see it three, even four times a day—a nice line of traffic headed for his wash—see it quite happily in his mind.

He used to do the same thing with his tennis game and it worked really well with his serve. He'd see the high toss, see the seams of the falling green ball, even feel the Tourna Grip sticky in his palm. And when Ryan was eight and just starting in Little League, his pale freckled arm like a reed, how many evenings did they spend wearing a groove on Gwen's perfect lawn while they worked on the pitch? It was simply a part of their practice, no different from the long toss, teaching his son to see first then throw. Ryan's eyes tightly closed while Walt talked him through every motion. "Don't throw the ball till you've first seen it in the strike zone." It is all dependent on seeing—any athlete can tell you—the whole thing begins in the mind.

In the same way his wash came to him after six months of nothing, this is the way he now see his customers, preexisting, in a sense, already there. On the couch, dozing, an unseen effort goes on within him, half in reverie, half in dream. A riot of drivers speed toward Walt's car wash on their way to the Palms, the Marine base, or back from the Joshua Tree Campgrounds, their cars all covered with fine white grit. And now they are stopping at his blue neon sign, their directionals blinking in red synchrony: right for the west bound, left for the east, and now the dust rises off countless hot hoods, so many cars it stops traffic. How Walt has come to enjoy this.

He no longer questions the method that will bring the Immaculate Autos Experience its success. It's a leap of surpassing illogic, he knows, but nonetheless wholly his. And this is the reason he can't decide to do anything about his window except pick it up and put it back behind his couch, nearly out of sight. Seeing traffic coming at him on the freeway *with his eyes* would betray his process. Those cars will come, are coming, and in the right time. He doesn't need a window to show him. All he needs is to keep to his vision and wait.

The phone rouses him from his dream state, and he gets up from the couch. He picks up the phone, hears his son's voice and his day is made. Walking straight to the coffee machine, the phone cradled in his neck, Walt fills his blue mug, hoping that the call will turn into a conversation. Though any call from his son is so rare, it's already a gift.

"Dad," says Ryan in his newly cracked voice, which pains Walt as a lightning split tree would, the insides exposed, the living wood splintered. "We're in the semi-finals, and they're starting me. We play in the college stadium in Fullerton eleven o'clock on August fifteenth. Can you make it?"

"You bet I can make it. You know I will."

He walks without thinking back to the big gray velvet couch that looks so out of place in this spare, flimsy structure that he calls his office. Then he sits down, puts his feet on the coffee table, and closes his eyes as he listens to Ryan report on the five miles he has picked up on his fastball. How the pitch they have worked on for six years has now taken off with a vengeance.

He might almost be home with his son stretched out next to him, his sweet clean boy-sweat and the skunky mildew odor rising from his bare feet and the size ten sneakers.

This is the family room couch Gwen wanted to toss when she remarried. Cost him four hundred dollars just to have it trucked the seventy miles down and worth every penny. He only has to touch it to remember who he is.

"Here's when I knew, Dad. I was just nailing the zone. It was so easy. It was a joke."

"You got it, Ryan. You own it now."

"I just better not lose it."

"Don't go there. Stay seeing it. See it all the time. It will be there when you need it." What do these words mean, coming from him? "I've just decided something pretty interesting." Where to begin? Not doing something is a little dangerous, he knows, too much like all the not-doing Gwen thinks landed Walt here—away from them all.

"Dad? What is it?"

"Let's wait. I'll tell you at dinner next week. Be good to your mother. Tell Jen to call."

"Is it about you moving back?"

"Back to Newport? No."

In the background he hears the low voice of a man now. He hears his wife calling out a response. David, the new husband to his wife. His son in the room. Walt knew the man. They'd had a nodding acquaintance at the club. Self-satisfied. A jerk on the court. Walt did not like him even then. First serve percentage sixty-two to Walt's forty-eight.

"Next time I see you I'll explain it. And Ryan? Remember, don't rush the arm."

After they say good-bye, a wave of exhaustion washes through Walt Adair. It is not quite ten in the morning, and already he feels he has had a full day. When the door to his office opens, Walt sees a tall woman with long milky legs and a Chinese straw hat.

"You're a lifesaver," she says, as she comes toward him. It is Zoe in work clothes, denim overall shorts, faded blue tee shirt, work boots, and thick yellow socks, her face half hidden in the shadow of the hat. He hardly recognizes her.

"Well, hello," Walt says.

"This could not have come at a better time." Even her lilting voice is different, forced. She takes off the hat and puts it on the coffee table between them. Zoe's face appears drawn and exhausted. It shocks him a little, as if in the week or so since Father Bill's dinner she had suffered some kind of loss.

"Right back," she says.

Then out she goes again returning with a rented sledgehammer, power saw, and four hefty lengths of wood.

"Slow down. What is all this?" Walt asks.

"Wait, there's more. Don't worry. I'm going to put up a little wall of plastic to spare you the dust. Six hundred is fine, by the way. But let me warn you, I haven't done one of these in a while. I'll have to go slow. Right back."

For a moment Walt thinks he has missed a step. Was there a phone call he does not remember? Something he said that led her to think he had agreed to go through with installing the window? All he remembers in this moment is catching her chair as it fell backward, and the silvery haze of his dream.

Once again she returns, this time with a gray plastic crate filled with stuff: tubes of silicone and caulking, boxes of nails. Walt had no idea one window required so much equipment to mount.

"So where exactly do you want it?"

"I was thinking of there." Walt points to the south wall, "But you're a little ahead of yourself."

Give Walt the week, Father Bill had said to her, then show up prepared. If he waffles, don't let him.

"Didn't you tell Father Bill you would do it for six hundred?"

"I only said six hundred was all I would pay."

"That's fine."

"I would pay six hundred if I wanted the window installed, but I don't."

"You've changed your mind?"

"I never made it up. I don't want it done. Never said I did. I have decided against it for sure."

She will have to stand firm now. Walt is waffling. He is waffling big-time. She says nothing. Here she is, ready. Having paid to rent tools, buy materials. All of it right on the floor where he can see it. She puts her hands on her bare thighs, but her touch barely registers, another piece of herself given to the air. She looks at her work boots, white with accumulated Mojave dust. Her skin feels gritty and dry.

Now she will have to find the spark to convince Walt—not her strong point, much more Michael's.

"I don't get it. Father Bill said you agreed."

"It's a misunderstanding. I didn't."

"Oh," says Zoe. *What am I doing here?* she thinks. *Not just here in this car wash, but here? Among strangers. Talking to them. Intruding myself in their lives.* All week driving a loaner she can't even pay for up and down the thirty-mile stretch of freeway between Joshua Tree National Park and the town of Twenty-Nine Palms? To theme motels and RV parks, to bowling alleys, and darkened coffee bars, to an outdoor all-you-can-eat Texas-barbecue joint packed with off-duty Marines from the nearby base, where she has found no trace of Michael, no one who recognizes his photo. All week talking to strangers. She has repeated Michael's name, described his appearance, his airy gait and intense dark eyes, his distinctive candy-crackling voice sometimes saying who he is to her and sometimes, when asked, a lot more. Described as well their Luedke and Payne white van, tempted to take out the flyer that she keeps in her pocket, folded now, its pale lilac bond creased and stained. It has left her depleted. She is already filled up with no's.

Zoe stares at the wall where she should be marking studs, making measurements. Instead she takes the stud finder out of the pocket of her shorts—it has been digging into her hipbone for over an hour—and drops it on the coffee table beside a pile of magazines.

"I've rented tools, bought headers and flashing. They can't be returned."

"Why would you do that without checking with me first?"

Let Father Bill pay for the headers and flashing, Walt thinks, for now he is angry. He knows what has happened, they've set him up, the missing step that Father Bill likes to allow, so the server will step up to the service line. Well, it isn't his serve, no reason for him to walk out to the court. He will try to send her off with some measure of grace and deal with Bill later.

"Would you like a cup of water? I'll help you carry this stuff out."

"I've got water in the car."

"In the car? It'll boil," says Walt.

Zoe sits down. She is not ready to bend to defeat. She lifts the handle of the hammer; the familiar weight steadies her. She has fallen into the hole that is Infidelity, her options dwindling with every hot hour, her ability to resist what is happening to her as well. Six hundred dollars for a job that needs doing. Six hundred dollars to get Platz started on her car. To keep her in the loaner doing what she thought she could do but which now seems insane: looking for Michael in a place she's not even sure he has come to, Michael who does not want to be found. If she can just figure how to make Walt say a simple yes, maybe other yeses will start to descend. Maybe Michael.

Now Walt sits down too, keeping his distance, saying nothing. The nothing continues. Nothing and no, Zoe thinks. They are both mired in silence, the breeding ground for doubt. In a blink Michael would have Walt Adair talking, so happy to put in that window he'd pay more, who knows, maybe the whole thousand. When Zoe digs for the words that Michael would say, she only succeeds in calling up the graceful length of his torso, the disarming smile, enough to unleash him toward her. Now she feels Michael entirely, the sense of his flesh, the smoky deep fragrance that is gone.

"How about taking your car through the wash?" says Walt.

"What car? I'm not driving my car. That's the whole point. I've got the loaner. Platz is about to send the highway patrol to come get me—and it."

Walt laughs nervously but then sees she's not joking. She is drawn and deflated; under whatever tensions she's been living, the beauty of her face has collapsed.

"I thought you had it all worked out with Platz."

"I don't have anything worked out."

"I thought Father Bill said—"

"Yes, well, and I thought Father Bill said you were ready to hire me."

Now Walt is trying to fix her in a life he has no information to build from. He remembers the evening at Father Bill's as a haze of good feeling and overeating and very little else, except when he'd caught her chair. Something elusive had opened inside him in her presence that evening. Now it's closed. What he feels now is a familiar tightness around his chest, a sensation that brings his old life back in a rush. This is how he used to go through each day, in the armor. Why is the armor up now? Right behind the couch he sees the reason, not two feet from them, leaning against the wall. He is simply protecting his window. Its right to stay on the floor.

The office door opens and Walt looks toward it with relief. A customer will make it easier for him to let her go. And go she will, he realizes, he will surely not see her after this. But it is not a customer, it is Bryant Platz.

"I had to be here for it," Platz says and struts to the center of the office, his usual room-conquering walk. He crosses his heavily tattooed arms. On his left arm a concatenated coil of green serpents compete for top snake. His unzipped leather vest is open to the navel, his skin deeply tanned. He looks Zoe over as if she is something for sale.

"I dig your work clothes, kid. Nice leg. So, are we going to get down to it sometime this morning? Some of us have to get back to work. They're waiting across the street for the go."

"What go?" Walt asks.

Zoe is standing, the hammer resting against her thigh. As she picks it up, she can feel its full weight pulling her down. Like her life is pulling her. Nowhere and down. The wall where the window should be is blank and ugly. Such shoddy construction, it would only take a few swings, though if she connects with a stud, it might mean disaster, but she has stepped out of consequence into action. Even the weight of the hammer is her ally; gravity reversing itself as it rises upward from metal through wood and into her grip. She takes four quick strides to the wall, pulls the hammer behind her like a batter about to take on a wild pitch. Platz jumps back.

When the hammer hits wall, she is thinking of Walt, of that stubborn resistance that deserves to be smashed. She is thinking of the absence of Michael. The rage arrives in red force. She has so many reasons to smash through that wall! Out they come like horses through the gate. Walt calls, "Zoe! Zoe! Slow down!" But she is not Zoe, she is nameless—the unstoppable instrument of right action and the correct transfer of six hundred dollars—her arm moving with an abandon she has never allowed in the thirty-one years of her carefully constructed, misfortune-plagued life.

The wallboard yields quickly. Plaster dust and bits of board sail past her like tiny fragments of bone. Soon a three-foot hole has been opened, through which the freeway traffic, the hulking glass front of the diner, and the little hacienda of the Infidelity Motel are now visible. When she puts down the hammer and turns to face Walt, she sees the face of a man hit by something he has never imagined.

I have become Michael, Zoe thinks, I have the power to ruin things.

"I just lost forty bucks on you," Platz says and smacks Walt on the back, "Way to go."

When the first group from the diner comes in to see for themselves, they find Walt on his knees with a hand vacuum, sucking plaster dust off the cushions of that vast velvet couch now smack in the middle of his office. Behind him, through a wall of clear plastic, Zoe picks at the top of the gaping hole with a small, unseen tool, a miner afraid of a cave-in. With her features hidden by goggles, her hair tucked into a cap, she doesn't look much like those rumors they have been hearing ad infinitum at breakfast. She is tall, all right, but entirely lacking in glamour. The reports about her have been exaggerated.

She works hours undoing the damage of her hasty rough opening, measuring and re-measuring from outside and in. Chipping at plaster, shoring up studs. It is hours before she first begins sawing the frame for the header and late afternoon before she pushes aside the plastic sheeting and steps through, walks past the spectators who have camped on the couch to say that the framing is level and square.

"Is that good?" Walt asks.

For the first time in days Zoe laughs. "I'll say. Now I'm going to need help."

"Take your pick," Walt says.

The men on the couch guffaw.

"You," she says pointing at Chico Platz, Platz's stepkid, the only one with a sober expression. The men laugh as Chico looks around. "Me?" Sixteen and bookish, concave chest, arms with no weight. "That's right, you," Zoe says. "Ten dollars an hour—are you game?"

Zoe has done this for years. She knows a good worker, careful eyes, steady hands. No cowboys, thank you.

The foot traffic in his office is something to see, including the people who tell him he's crazy for opening a drive-thru thousand-watt car wash instead of a regular one. But no Father Bill in the throng. No Josefina and Luz.

By the end of the day, in spite of himself, even Walt has joined in the general good feeling. By dint of his decision to put in that window, he has earned Chico Platz fifty dollars and Emily Otto one hundred twenty—the really big bettor in the diner pool. He has brought to an end the subject of yearlong speculation. *Will Walt ever put in that window?* And right now in the hottest hour of the day before the winds and the rare but hoped-for thirty-degree temperature drop of midsummer before a threatened thunderstorm, an event of some note is occurring in a place where not much of note has occurred since Luz Reyes disappeared from school and was found at the campgrounds. There are some who will say it was all because of a beautiful woman, that Walt could never have decided without her. But however it happened, in ten hours or so Walt Adair has managed to revise a three-year reputation. In putting in that window, he has become a new man.

"Take your time," Walt says when Zoe sweeps back the plastic wall and comes out to say she's got a problem with the header. "Take all the time you need. I'm sure you can solve it."

He is loosened by laughter, the sheer number of people who have stopped by his car wash. He even finds himself wondering why he made such a big deal out of something so small and simple. He can look or not look through the window, and if he prefers the traffic of his mind, that's what he will have.

When she's through, he checks it thoroughly, first on the sidewalk and then inside. To his eye it looks perfect. Even and plumb. Aside from the new raw stucco, the window looks quite unremarkable, like something that has always been there. He will show Zoe his gratitude, he thinks. He will at least buy her a dinner.

They are greeted with smiles at the diner, given the best front booth, served by Bobbie herself. They eat cornbread-stuffed chicken breast, a golden-beet salad with poppy seed dressing. They drink a bottle of Bobbie's twelve-dollar best house wine. And they can't take their eyes off the window on the opposite side of the freeway, straining to see it in the headlights of the cars once it has grown dark.

In the end Walt Adair gives Zoe two hundred more than she'd asked and is amazed to see her eyes well up when he hands her the bills. She leaves him then, to drive up to Platz at the garage. *If you need a place to stay I've got an empty trailer just waiting,* he thinks. But too late. She's gone.

When he returns to his office, it is only to attend to his sign, which he has forgotten to turn off. The meal and the wine have made him groggy and he goes inside the office. Under the window is a startling spill of blue, an entirely new phenomenon, the result of the light from his exterior sign coming through the glass and hitting the carpet. The couch is still where he pushed it, in the middle of the room. He takes a six-pack of Sam Adams from the half-fridge under his counter and settles back on the couch, imagining Zoe were there to look at the view with him, the homely but well put-in window, the bonus of blue light awash on the floor. He watches a few cars go by, then finds himself reaching toward Zoe in his mind trying to pull her back. The office is clean now; she had organized a bunch of the watchers and they had gotten up all the plaster dust and splinters of wood. The plastic wall taken down and removed, every last tube of caulk cleared out. She was good. He had enjoyed watching her handle the men. She was used to it, he reminds himself. She has her own shop, "kitchen cabinets mostly," as she'd told them at Father Bill's little dinner.

Now he sees her out on the freeway headed for the garage. She had called Platz and asked him to meet her. She wanted to give him the money that night. He hopes it all goes well with Platz, that he doesn't give her a hard time about the loaner, hopes that she makes it safely to the campgrounds, and that wherever she sleeps, she sleeps well. He thinks of odd jobs he might give her, or others who might need her help. Of the steady way she worked and how much he'd enjoyed it. Now it is late, nearly ten. If he does not get up, he will surely conk out on the couch and ruin his chances for an uninterrupted rest. A few minutes later, he still has not moved. When he hears Zoe call to him, a thrill unfurls in the center of his chest. He goes to the door, glad he has stayed, certain he'll find her standing on his step in the dark, but no one is there.

CHAPTER 3

Though there are many who say when they looked it was even—how plumb the sides, how level the sill, how long the wait as Zoe measured and remeasured, made perfect the header, fiddled for the ninety-fifth time with every detail of the framing before that window went in, and though no one disputes that even the flashing has been hidden exceptionally well, how did they *miss* what was obvious? What they see now they must have failed to see then: Walt's window is crooked. Its upper right corner slants three inches higher than its left.

In the clear light of high desert morning, no one can deny the window in Walt's car wash is a spectacular botch.

"She tricked him. I knew it. So every man of principle is undone by a woman of passion," spouts Platz holding court at the diner in his usual window booth, where the usual breakfast crowd sits. Their faces are upturned, their eggs are congealing; his words are gospel. This is the man who has seen Zoe Luedke strike the first blow to the wall.

"Made no move to stop her. Walt just let her swing." He shows them the motion. "Bam! Bam! Then you know what Walt says? 'What the hell. I guess there's no going back.' That man was played by a woman, just like she tried to play me."

As soon as they've eaten, the diner crowd drives four lanes across to the car wash, illegal U turns be damned. Marches up Walt's walk and into his too chilly office to gawk once again at the strange-angled window—this time from the inside—get their two rotten cents in, and laugh.

But the children of Infidelity are another story entirely. And many Infidelity kids are brought by to see it that day. What a relief such a wrong public thing is, much worse than a letter drawn backward or an out loud reading mistake, or getting caught pinching or punching your sister, or spitting at someone, or losing a toy or a bracelet, or saying bad words to a friend. Or any of the secret humiliations they suffer. Sleep will come easier to the children that night, and for months when an Infidelity child draws a house, one window will decidedly slant.

It's the onslaught of kids (already his biggest fans wash-wise) who bring Walt some relief, their laughter, their pointing, their begging their parents, "Now can we get our car washed?" August the eighth will break records at Immaculate Autos, and his off-kilter window's the cause. By late afternoon, Walt has thrown up his hands, embraced the mistake, and let himself join in the fun.

By then Walt has left three messages for Father Bill and has not yet heard back and is beginning to wonder if the priest is deliberately refusing his calls.

Then Wren and Emily Otto show up for their regular Friday wash. At ninety-three, Wren is surely the best-groomed man in Infidelity, wears a tie every day, always the same kind, Prussian blue silk with fine red stripes. He owns a half-dozen, all the same. "The business of the day is worth dressing for, no matter how hot the weather," Wren had advised Walt when he first arrived in Infidelity. Wren liked Walt's blue cotton oxfords. His wife liked the comment so much she cross-stitched it into a pillow and made one for Walt. He's got it back at the house.

"A human mistake. That was me sixty-two years back," Wren says. "She kept with me, nonetheless."

"Not to mention what you stood for with me."

"She's too modest. Emily was always perfect."

"See how he does? The sad thing is, he believes it. And me with those teeth and that temper? You forget everything in time. Come on honey, let's clean the Cutlass and have us a cry."

And off they go to the wash.

Walt has himself quite a line of customers waiting by the time Father Bill finally calls, and his place is noisy. With a couple of little kids skipping around, Walt is feeling quite good, juggling three things at once, swiping credit cards, trying to delay a first-timer so he can explain the Immaculate Autos experience, and waving to that little red-headed curly-haired on-again off-again friend of Luz's whose name he forgets, to go take her soda, it's free today. The red-headed mother insists on paying for it, sliding a dollar over the counter.

"I'm tied up," he says to Father Bill. He's heard about the window, Walt thinks. He is going to try to make it up to me. Another dinner invitation, maybe and then with a rush, Walt thinks of Zoe beside him at Father Bill's table. How quickly the body forgets. His mind has to remind it she's taken his money for an incompetent job. "I'm having quite a big day."

When Father Bill says he is calling from the hospital, Walt automatically thinks of Luz, rescued from the campgrounds in June. The priest is relaying instructions. Reminding Walt how to get to the hospital. Telling Walt where to meet them. Walt's heartbeat quickens and before he even puts down the phone he is in crisis mode, making plans to close down his car wash while he reviews the route to the High Desert Hospital. Straight down the freeway, no turns. The last time he was there it was early June. He had gone on his own when he heard Luz had been found. The whole town half crazy: *a disappeared child.* No one yet knows how she got to the campgrounds, much less why. If Father Bill or Josefina had found out the answer, they had kept it to themselves.

Right away he calls the Platzs trying to locate Chico. If Walt can get him, he might be able to keep his wash open. If he can't, he will simply tell his customers to come back tomorrow; he must close down the wash.

"Sure," says Bryant's wife, Patty. Chico's here doing nothing. Hang on."

There is rush hour traffic on the freeway by the time Walt leaves the car wash. He waits for the air conditioning to take hold in the Civic. His old driving impatience makes the blood beat in his head as it used to on his daily commute. When he thinks of having just handed over the wash to a seventeen-year-old, he wonders why he didn't just close down, then remembers how busy it was, customers he has not seen in months, some not ever. Father Bill had not even said whether it was Josefina or Luz.

When Walt passes the sign for the campgrounds, he flushes, humiliated. She had to have known it would tilt, he thinks, seeing Zoe's face in his mind's eye. But by the time he gets through Twenty-Nine Palms, he is too focused on what he will find in the hospital to give Zoe more than a passing ill thought. If Josefina's the one who is sick, he may finally learn the reason for her frequent withdrawals. For sometimes as long as a week she just disappears, does not go to work, takes no phone calls. Father Bill takes over with Luz and no explanations. Maybe now he'll find out what's behind all that. He should be above curiosity, thinking solely of Josefina's well being, but he's not. No one knows anything about them. Their past never mentioned, not even to him, the only one in Infidelity who is included in Father Bill's dinners at the rectory.

One night, after too much wine, Josefina had spoken of her student days in El Salvador. She had been a medical student at the university, she said. Walt was shocked, though not because she is unintelligent, simply because it was a revelation that gave him a new way to think of her, one that has left him wanting to know more. Now she cleans houses. Something is wrong. Lots of things, probably. He can't make it fit. Another time, when he mentioned his bankruptcy, she had asked about the scope of his holdings. "Too bad you could not hold on for longer," she said. "Land in a good place is always of value in the long run. My father used to say that. Of course, when he said it I laughed."

He had wanted to ask about her father that night, what he did for a living, even, but she had not offered anything other than that single sentence. He only knows this: Josefina has no more family. Father Bill told him that, but not how it happened. And often when they are together there is Luz sitting at the table, taking everything in.

"All right," he says as he sees the sign for the hospital and then the High Desert Hospital itself. He looks for directions to the parking lot. Why are they so hard to find? God, he hopes it's not Luz. It has to be bad if he's been called.

They are sitting together on a bench in the lobby, where the receptionist in the emergency room suggested he look. He was flustered and could not remember where Father Bill said to meet them. It is a small hospital, unusually quiet, but the lobby seems vast, the floor long and white, the air conditioning a shock to the system. The first thing he notices is her hair, which is wild and undone. He has never seen Luz without the neat braids. The second, when he gets closer, are the droplets of blood on Father Bill's chino pants.

"Ah," says Father Bill and stands up. "Look who's here!" But Luz was expecting Zoe, not Walt. The Felangela, she had said, to take care of me. Father Bill did not understand. "You hardly know her." *I do*, Luz had thought, though she can't explain it. She hears the things about Zoe that her mother and Father Bill say in the night. Zoe looking for her husband everywhere in the desert, driving the big car from the garage. And the things that they don't say. Every night Zoe going back to the campgrounds to sleep.

Luz does not look up. She appears to be holding her own hands, but no, Walt sees, she's got a rosary. He smiles. She lifts her head slightly. He knows those eyes; he has seen her once before when she was afraid like this. When it was she in a bed in this hospital, her face slathered in ointment, her blistered lips white, and everyone stumped. High Desert police, social worker, doctor, mother, and priest all crowded into that room: "Who took you into the campgrounds, Luz? Who made you go?"

Luz should have been at his wash today. She should have been one of the laughing children, bending and twisting to straighten the window in their minds.

His heart is pounding. He is afraid of what Father Bill will tell him. He bends down to touch Luz's foot dangling from the chair, the red sandal that appears quite new. A powerful longing rushes through Walt. He wishes he could hold her. He has nearly forgotten, or perhaps he has not allowed himself to remember the heat and the smallness of his children's bodies, the sweetness of their drenching tears. He would sing to them when they cried. He could not stand their sorrow. It surprises him to feel it still within him, even with this child whom he has never once held. His own children are so far away. If they cry he no longer sees it, their grief subsumed by distance. His children who do not know their own father's house. "Hey, honey," Walt says and gives the foot a squeeze.

"Where is Josefina? What happened?"

Father Bill's gesture is almost imperceptible. Of course. He cannot say. Luz is right there.

"So what do you need? I'm here."

"Yes," says Father Bill, "you made good time."

CHAPTER 4

She cringes at their every touch, even the nurse who has tried several times to reassure her. These hands are danger, Josefina's body knows. It reacts automatically to any strange touch, as if she were still in the Ilopango, waiting for the colonel and the ones in dark glasses, waiting for the wires and knives.

They take the clothes from her; they look. She hears their questions and knows that she is in a hospital, a safe place, knows because she has been to a hospital before and learned safety there.

"How did you get these?"

Ah, they are looking at her. Let them believe some deranged lover has left such scars on her breasts and her thighs. Let them think her body bears the marks of some senseless crime.

Do they want to hear the history of her country? Of theirs? How else can she answer, and if she does will they think she is crazy? That she has invented such horrors? Each mark is deliberate. Those who did it to her were *taught.* She will have to give history; she will have to give politics. Where to start? Perhaps with the battle in her own family that went on seven years. She is fourteen. Esperanza, her little sister, just eight, nearly choking on a fish bone because Josefina and her father are once again fighting, and in the middle of dinner. He is red-faced; Josefina is outraged. Their mother's mild cries are ignored. Three times she claps her manicured hands. Their voices insult the carved oaken table that has been in his family for centuries at which no daughter dared raise her voice. From the mud that has dried in the soles of her shoes, her father has discovered her crime. "You are doing that damned work with the campesinos. You are going again with the communist priests who will get us all killed."

"Papi, I am teaching poor people to read!"

The nurse tries again. William pleads to Josefina in Spanish, "Let her give you the shot. It will be easier."

Now she will try to pull herself back. Her arms and her legs are quaking, the cold running through her like ice. And still she sees clearly those men who she knows are not here in the cubicle of the High Desert Hospital, but who appeared in her mind the same as the ambulance in her driveway, the siren, their noiseless white cars. Here they come in dark glasses—those known to her and those unknown—the faces that devour the homely white face of her nurse. If she can wait now. If she can stay in her skin. If she can think of her daughter and do nothing, in time it will pass.

The nurse says something to Father Bill. All she can hear are her last words, "advanced states."

In what way has Josefina advanced?

"We are also dealing with her post-traumatic stress."

Josefina picks out Father Bill's words from among the voices that are clamoring within and around her, two people and Luz, her eyes tell her now. Two people and Luz are in her room. She hears Father Bill give the words that are as solid for her as the bed table the nurse has pushed to the wall. Beside it stands her post-traumatic stress, a cabinet of steel, the secrets it holds locked inside the drawers. Nothing within it can save her. Her body does not know where she is.

Outside the drawn green curtains, beyond the white door, another voice teases through. Ah, she thinks, she is coming out of it. This is how she emerges. She pulls herself upward by sound. Now she takes a breath, the air nauseating, thick with spoiling flesh, antiseptic, unwholesome food. The throbbing in her head dulled but present. She can hear Luz's little voice, even over the respirator in the cubicle of the dying woman to her left, and over the drone of the television, the voice of the far patient she has not seen. Who is it that Luz is speaking with outside the door? Is it the woman that Josefina dreads? The one who has been here to see Josefina one time already, the same woman, the same large white teeth? The one who the hospital sent to study her daughter (and her) when Luz was found in the campgrounds after she ran from her school in the spring? The intruder who came to their house, with papers and questions? But the voice that is mixing with Luz's is a man's voice, kind and familiar. Ah yes, now she has it. Outside the room with her daughter is Walt.

"Okay!" Josefina calls out, and pushes herself into a sitting position, a truce more with herself than with the long-faced nurse. It will take hours, maybe days for the faces to depart. For the cabinet to diminish, four drawers then two, someone to remove it completely, ah, all those files. Still, if she does not assert herself in its presence, this nurse will shoot her so full of the Demerol she will tell everything, they will know what she is, know where her friends are, and then all will be lost. "Ah," she says and tries to smile. This is the easy part; this is simply the needle for sleep. If she shakes, she will shake. If she is flooded with the images of those men and their cars, she will try not to scream. If Esperanza chokes on a codfish bone, her mother will rise from the chair just in time. Josefina's little daughter is here now. Her daughter, Luz, seven years old. She is outside the door. The child in her womb who survived every wire and knife and has grown into life.

But now the nurse is talking quite fast, and Josefina cannot follow. Always the English is difficult when she begins the return to her senses. Another unsafe boundary she must cross.

"As soon as he gets your results, the doctor will visit. He will explain the procedure. And later the anesthetist will come by and let you know what to expect." William tells her in Spanish, her William, whom the others call Father Bill. She answers in kind.

"You can't send me an anesthetist now?"

William laughs. This is good. She can joke. She is coming back.

"Where will they put it?"

The nurse does not touch her. At last even this long-faced nurse is catching on. She points to the place in her chest, a six-inch tubing will soon be embedded in Josefina's flesh, as if she needed one more mark of disfigurement, but this is what will save her for the dialysis. She looks at where the object will be. The object she won't be able to hide from her daughter, nor from her employers who put up with her absences because she is good, because she loves their cold marble houses, the way they echo like wonderful tombs. Her mother must stay seated. She is rising in protest. The pearls at her neck, her best gray silk suit. "Were I not dead, I could not have survived to see you so shamed." Ah, her mother has retained her humor. From a house where no girl ever cooked a meal or made a bed, Josefina, the medical student has become quite an expert at cleaning. She knows just the right cleanser for the marble, half measures of vinegar and water for wood, and how to give shine to the tile. It is wonderful actually, a relief, she has found. She wishes she were on her knees now, on the marble, circling the floor.

"Okay," says the nurse. "We'll send someone to clean you."

"I can't take a chower?"

"What did she say?"

"She wants a shower."

"Not yet. Right now let's stay with a sponge bath."

"And now," says Josefina, "Can I please have my daughter?"

"You're sure?" asks William, *her* William, whose flesh tastes faintly of cumin, whose mouth kisses her scars.

Oh, but he has been worried, now she can see it, see him, his tired face. Josefina holds out her hand. She knows just how to rouse him, every place that he loves to be touched. "Please, give me Luz. Tell her that I am here only for tests."

"All right," he says, then goes to get Luz.

* * *

Luz stands by the bed and looks at her mother, who is smiling but weakly, her arms held out but not high, a bad smell, strong medicines, something sweet and disgusting like licking blood. When Luz goes into her mother's neck, her feet on the floor, she stops up her nose and her mouth, as if she is drowning.

"Why did you fall?" Luz asks to the neck. "Why did the ambulance take you? Why didn't you go in the car?"

"We will soon know. Now they will give me the tests."

"Will you sleep in the hospital?"

"Yes."

"How many days?"

"Two or three," says Josefina.

"Probably three," says William.

"Can I?" Luz whispers, her knee already on the mattress. Even with the smell, she can be close to her mother.

"Ah, yes." Josefina says, as she tries to shift her body on the bed to make room for Luz.

"No, honey," says the nurse as Luz climbs onto the bed. "Sit in the chair."

"Come here, mamita," says Josefina ignoring the nurse. "See? I don't break."

The nurse looms down, "We'd really prefer if she sat in the chair. Lose, do you hear me?"

"Luz," Josefina corrects.

"I'll share my chair with you Luz," Walt Adair says.

Walt, thinks Josefina. So focused has she been on her daughter she has not even seen him there.

"She is fine here with me," says Josefina.

The nurse sighs softly, opens the curtain, and leaves.

"No one brushed my hair," Josefina says and gives Walt an embarrassed smile, "Or my daughter's. And I am sorry if I stink."

"I'm very glad to be called," Walt says. He is honored. This woman, this child. To be summoned at such a time. The smell in the room is making him nauseous, an overlay of urine as if she were drenched in it.

"The Felangela can brush me when she comes," Luz says, picking her head up and smoothing her mother's wild hair. "She does it so slow. She makes pictures come into my mind."

"What are you saying, mamita? The Felangela has never brushed your hair."

Walt wishes he understood Spanish. The words are musical, it distracts him for a moment, from the odor. In his other life, it was a thing he abhorred. The sounds of the language. Spanish. The bilingual state of California. These people, he would say to Gwen, why don't they learn our language? "So we can have workers," she replied.

"Already you are imagining you have found someone to brush hair better than me?" Josefina says, this time in English.

"No!" says Luz.

"Should I go?" asks Walt, "I could wait outside if you like."

"They are sending in someone to clean me," says Josefina. "William, do you want to go out for a coffee with Walt? Luz can eat ice cream."

"I don't want to go out when they come to clean you," says Luz.

"Maybe La Felangela will come for you." Josefina says.

La Felangela? Walt has never heard Josefina speak to her daughter like this. He has heard her disparage Our Lady of Guadalupe. She has joked with him about the little saints Luz collects by the dozens, like Ryan's action figures, Jen's Barbies. Now Josefina is talking to Luz about angels?

"I'll leave you three for a minute. Be right outside, Luz," he says. Walt goes out through the drapes, then out into the hall. He feels sick. He does not like how she looks, the dark yellow cast of her skin, the vague swelling of her face, the thick rancid smell of her flesh. It doesn't look good. His heart is pounding. Something very wrong, he can feel it. In the hallway where dinner carts clatter unseen, the smell of boiled potatoes and fish. Now Walt is beginning to feel unsteady and chilled. A young girl goes into Josefina's room with a pan and a sponge. Luz's voice comes through the door. Father Bill's deep calming bass, no doubt urging her to leave. All of them now speaking Spanish. Luz is going to give Walt quite a time.

Finally, Father Bill comes out. Luz is holding his hand. "Let's get this child something to eat."

"No," says Luz.

"We have a girl who needs dinner, and do you know what else? Who will turn on the lights at the church? The people are coming for the meeting. I don't want them to think I forgot."

"From the Feast?" asks Luz.

"Yes. Who will do it? How about you and Walt?"

"No!'

"The fifteenth is almost here for us. There's a lot to do."

"Ah," says Walt, who has figured it out. "The Feast of the Assumption. Remember last year, Luz?"

Yes, she remembers. She has been counting the days. But she has been counting them wrong. Mami is in the hospital. She should not have wished the days to pass quickly. She should have wished them instead to stay slow, so slow that this day, with Mami in the hospital by ambulance, would never have come.

The Feast of the Assumption, thinks Walt, always too hot, always those tables outside in back of the church, with the frosting melting off the cakes, the crocks of bad chili, the bingo over the speaker system, those sad carnival rides, the kids with red faces in the ball-jumping pen. Walt always skips it. The dog days of high desert summer. The families. Especially, he thinks, the families. This year he will have a legitimate excuse: he will be with his own family, in a restaurant, if it all goes well, and before that in the stadium of Fullerton College, watching his son, starting pitcher in the league semifinals. He will not have to deal with the Feast of the Assumption. Though Walt would like to say something to Father Bill about his assumptions regarding Zoe Luedke. That she was honest. That she was competent. He'd like to say right now how wrong his friend was to foist her upon him, and what he, Walt, is stuck with and publicly, but that will wait. Josefina is suffering, from what he doesn't yet know, and he has been called here for Luz. It would be unseemly to bring up his window.

Now Father Bill is bending to Luz, his voice rising softly in a question.

"La Felangela," Luz replies.

"Walt is here now. He came all the way here just for you."

Luz nods and stands with her back to the wall, gazing at the fluorescent ceiling lights as the men walk away to talk. Even without her lips moving, she has learned she can pray.

"We're going to need help for the next couple of days. Someone to watch Luz overnight. Two, three nights at the most. I can cover the days pretty well. She has summer school till nearly three," Father Bill says.

"Of course," Walt says. He is inspecting the Father's clerical shirt. Hard to see blood on the black. If Josefina trusts Walt with Luz, how can he refuse? In fact, he is touched. And actually he realizes, it's good. Luz has been to his home several times. She loves to walk barefoot through the water and over the stones in his River Rock fountain, to put her hand under the water as it spills out of the mouth of the trout. She has played in the little white trailer he had furnished so carefully for Jen. For Ryan, there's a room in his house. Luz could stay there if she preferred. If she doesn't mind sleeping in a bed with sheets and quilt printed with bats, gloves, balls, and the red haloed LA Angels insignia, waking up to the photos of Hall of Fame pitchers—Dizzy Dean through Don Sutton. Perhaps when Luz is away from the hospital, she will be more receptive to him. He agrees to take her.

But Luz has ideas of her own.

"I want to only sleep here in the hospital."

"Honey you can't. You know that," Father Bill says.

"Then let me come back after I eat."

When the nurse comes out of the room, Luz races inside. They catch the door as it swings. Behind the curtains the sounds of two televisions are competing, the cubicles now smell of boiled potatoes and fish, but Josefina looks clean. She wears a brave smile, and her dark hair lies freshly combed against her skin with its yellow dark cast, its smell like a mistaken perfume, thick in the air.

After discussion in two languages they all agree Walt will stay with Luz at the blue house. But first he will take her to the diner.

"I don't want you to be alone in the hospital, Mami."

"Alone? I have all the nurses and doctors who are here for my help. I have Father Bill. You go for eating with Walt. Oh, they have taken my money."

"I'll give them money to eat," Father Bill says.

"That's fine, don't worry, Father, I'll get this," says Walt.

Now Luz burrows in her mother's neck whispering.

"No, Luz. For my help we have many smart doctors like you will be when you are grown. She wants to light candles in the church."

"Only turn on the porch lights for the people who are coming to the meeting, then straight to the diner, Lucy Luz," says Father Bill.

"We turn on the porch light then go straight to the diner," Walt says. "Agreed?" Luz looks at him but does not reply. The diner—the last place Walt wants to be tonight—though it is late and perhaps most of the regulars will have left. Still he knows Bobbie will not let him off easy. He will have to swallow his pride for Luz's sake. Let them say what they will about his window or his manhood. Let them think what they want about how he'd been hoodwinked by Zoe. Because right now this evening and until Josefina is well, the main thing is Josefina and Luz.

But the diner is nearly empty; the regulars have long since gone home. Two solitary strangers sit at opposite ends of the counter, finishing their meals. Bobbie looks up from the cash register and comes out to greet Walt and Luz with transparent false cheer, leads them to a window booth and takes their order.

By the time their meals are served, the strangers have left. Luz eats her meal, chicken strips and fries. Walt indulges himself in a beer and a burger, piling on onions, tomatoes and lettuce, along with copious amounts of ketchup and mustard. They eat in silence looking down at their food. When he asks Luz if she wants dessert, she says yes. Walt signals to Bobbie. Luz orders strawberry pie.

"So where's your friend Zoe?" Bobbie asks Walt when she comes back one final time to give him the check. Walt says nothing.

Luz looks up from her strawberry pie. "We don't know," says Luz. "Maybe looking for her husband."

"Who?" says Walt.

"Michael," Luz says, and drinks a long swallow of juice, then puts down her glass, running her tongue over her lips.

Walt looks at Bobbie. "Who?"

"Her husband," says Luz.

"How do you know this?" Bobbie asks. Now this is a choice piece of gossip.

"From Mami and Father Bill talking. She looks for him in the mountains, in the deserts, and maybe the sea. And every place where the carpenters work."

Bobbie gets up, smiling. "Well, what do you know?"

Walt puts on his best poker face to disguise his ignorance, no less his pride. His mouth has gone dry.

Outside the diner Luz stops in the middle of the dark parking lot and looks up at Walt. "Are you taking me to see the window now?"

"What?"

"Is it a surprise for me that now you have your window?"

He has nearly forgotten it was Luz who first brought up the subject the night of their dinner at Father Bill's.

Walt is tired and not a little ashamed. He needs no more reminders of Zoe. Still, he can surely indulge Luz this. In the Civic they wait for the traffic to pass, then make a U turn across the freeway and enter the wash. Habit leads him to his parking spot at the rear of the office; the path to the sidewalk is hard to see in spite of the clarity of the night, the profusion of summer stars. Walt takes Luz's hand and she lets him.

When they get to the window it looks perfect, as if it has suddenly corrected itself. Walt does not know what to make of the thing. Quiet gathers around Luz like a thin dusky powder, and, for a while, she simply stands there looking. When he bends to her, though, he sees she is crying and reaches to smooth back her hair, "Luz, I'm so sorry. I promise you Mami will be well," though he shouldn't be promising. He knows nothing, not even what's wrong; still the words form themselves without thought.

When he tries to get her to return to the car and go home she refuses, a flash of stubbornness that surprises him. When she begins to speak, he can't tell what she's saying. It's all Spanish. He lets her be like this for several minutes. Then he insists, reminding her that it's late.

"Luz," he says when she does not respond, and kneels to her. "I hate to see you so sad. Let me take you home."

"I am not sad," she says. Then Luz reaches out and touches Walt's face, looks deep into his eyes. He wonders how it is that she is looking at him like that, as if he, and not she, is the one who is sad. And suddenly it is not Luz's face that he sees before him. It is a woman's face, such beautiful strong features, he thinks, such an expression—a woman powerful and kind, Native American, or perhaps some other indigenous female. It happens so quickly his mind cannot grasp it, his eyes far ahead of his brain. A powerful joy fills his chest. Now Luz is Luz again and she is speaking and Walt is grappling with the gap.

"You are going to be very happy from all the business," she says.

"What business?"

"When the people all come to your car wash."

"That's what I'm waiting for, honey. Let's hope it happens soon."

"It will," she says.

CHAPTER 5

Father Bill and Zoe stand in the harsh light of the hospital entrance. He reaches for her hands as if it is she who is going to need comforting. "Chronic *renal disease, irreversible*," he explains. Zoe says "Huh!" and takes back her hands. "If Josefina had a sister, a brother, but no," he goes on, "Josefina has no one but Luz. No money, no insurance. She is only thirty-two. A transplant would save her. Her chances for transplant are nil. Nil," he repeats. There, at last, it is out of him, witnessed by one who barely knows them, knows nothing of their past or the complicated deceptions of their lives.

Stripped of its meaning the word sounds like music to Zoe, the name of something wonderful, a rare silver plant. *Nil* cannot mean death, that Luz will be motherless and fatherless both—that vibrant Josefina, only a year older than Zoe, a woman she hardly knows, is at her life's end.

Now Zoe's own life falls from her as surely as the shakes fall from the trunk of the hemlock, thick and intact and ready to be used in a whole new way, her life layered onto theirs.

"Isn't there anything they can do?"

"We are going to put her on dialysis. We are going to go through the transplant registry. We will do whatever they say to do. That may buy us time. And we are going to keep the truth from Luz for as long as we can."

He has omitted any mention of prayer. Even she, who has had no experience of it, has the urge to ask something, this starry profusion above them to shift just a little. Though she knows that only the desperate talk to stars. Only the helpless think their lives have been marked out by fate. Zoe looks up at the desert night sky. Too many, she thinks. Father Bill looks up with her. The sky that usually gives him such solace is again the sky of El Salvador, the same one under which all the sorrows on earth have been told.

"We need someone to stay with Luz now. Three, four days at the most is what they're saying it will take to get her stabilized. And Luz has been asking for you."

"To stay with Luz?"

"Yes."

"Starting when?"

"Right now. We'll pay you. No, Josefina insists." Josefina who does not trust. Who does not even like Zoe, he thinks. Why has she picked Zoe for Luz? Luz cannot stay with the Platz's who have known her since she was three. Patty Platz who would welcome Luz with her house filled with diversions, all Tommy's toys. The pool, Josefina says. The swimming pool with its danger of drowning, and Luz cannot swim. Only Zoe. Zoe in the blue house. Luz in her own bed. You, William, close. It is the least he can give them, the one Luz asks for. A great deal to ask of a stranger, but she is no longer that. He has given her this secret.

Zoe feels the cold night air on her back, along her arms. She's not the right one for this. She has never taken care of a child. Should she say so? But, she thinks, ashamed of the thought, they need help and she could really use the money.

"I'm sorry. I have made you a party to this."

"Don't be sorry for that, please," says Zoe. "Will you tell me what to do with Luz? What she needs? I'm not exactly experienced with children."

He laughs. He, who has struggled for months with this question: what to do with Luz.

"Yes, I'll tell you. When we get to the house you can write it all down."

"Okay. That will be good." A book of instructions for Luz.

"We can start talking in the car. Do you mind if we take mine? Once you two are settled I need to come back. I'll have Platz and Chico drive down here and bring the Dart to the house for you. You'll need it in the morning."

They have no one, thinks Zoe. He must be all that they have. When they are close to his car, he gives her the keys and asks her to drive. On the ride to the house he leans back on the headrest and closes his eyes and says nothing more until they reach the hill district, when he suddenly sits up. "Turn here," he says at the rise. Small stucco houses line both sides of the street, separated by concrete driveways. Halfway up he says, "Here," and points to a house indistinguishable from the others except for its pale blue color, bars on the windows. All along the curb there are weeds, three feet tall, moving in the night air like miniature wheat.

"Wait, please," Father Bill says after Zoe has turned off the engine. "I need a minute." They remain in the darkened driveway, the car windows rolled down to the cold night air. In this way they begin to hear it. A sound like the beating of hands on the skin of a drum. And then through the lighted front window they can see Luz's dark head rushing past, and then they hear Walt's voice calling her name.

CHAPTER 6

Father Bill is out of the car in an instant. He is running up the walk, fishing for the house keys in his pocket. He must open three locks before he can see inside to her. There is Walt standing helpless, Luz speeding down the hall past the calendar Madonnas, one for each month of the year. Father Bill moves in quickly past Walt, yet lets Luz run on ahead, into Josefina's bedroom. His heart hammers hard and he panics, unable to remember what to do to bring her back.

The social worker had said, "Hold her, wrap your arms around her so she cannot move. Show her she is safe." He is afraid to put a hand on her; any human touch might push her over the edge. But now Luz stands in the doorway staring past him. Then she races down the hall again. "Whoa!" says Zoe, as Luz rushes past Father Bill and throws her arms around Zoe's waist. Zoe Luedke with her yellow-brown eyes and strong white arms and her missing fingertip. *The Felangela* who has given her the window. Who has given the gift.

"How long has she been like this?" Father Bill asks Walt.

"A half hour, maybe less. I was sure she was sleeping. And then she was up and running through the house. I don't like what I saw of those feet."

"Luz," says Father Bill gently, but she won't go to him. She is still dressed in the clothes of the day.

"You came back." Luz says, looking far up at the shining white face of Zoe, the Felangela.

"Yes, I did."

"Is she all right?" murmurs Walt.

"Luz, look at me, please," Father Bill commands. "Mami is sleeping. She is feeling a little better."

Luz does not look at Father Bill. She clings to Zoe like a chimp to its mother.

Isn't it unnatural, Zoe wonders, for a child to take so quickly to a stranger? Remembering the experience at Father Bill's dinner, the way that she felt when Luz touched her arm, for a moment, looking down at Luz, Zoe is afraid. When she turns to Walt Adair, he looks away.

"Can you come to the couch and let Zoe sit down?"

"No," says Luz.

"It's okay," says Zoe, patting Luz on the head,

"Maybe," says Father Bill, "Zoe can help wash your face."

"Shall we do that?" asks Zoe.

Very quickly Luz is washed, her teeth brushed, she is in her summer pajamas, saying goodnight. She does not want to talk to her friend, Father Bill. She takes Zoe's hands, dragging her from the living room.

Luz can sleep now. She will ask for a dream, though she already has more than she's asked for. Once again Our Lady has given her a visit. But how did She know to come on the same day that Mami was taken to the hospital by ambulance?

"Rest well, honey," says Walt. "It will be okay."

Yes, thinks Luz. The window is in. The Felangela is here. Our Lady is coming and soon.

Luz walks with Zoe into her white room with its white canopy, lace curtains, and four white pillows.

"How lovely," says Zoe, the canopy has gold butterflies, tiny flowers of gold that glint in the dark. Luz turns on a lamp and climbs into bed. Above her toy shelf her best writing has been displayed, her best second-grade work, a Tortoise Report with twenty-seven true facts and several accompanying photos. "You can read it," says Luz.

Zoe turns back to Luz. "Let's wait till tomorrow. Father Bill needs to talk to me now. He's going to tell me all about Y-O-U."

"All right, but stay with me just a little while," says Luz.

Zoe sits down at the foot of Luz's bed. "Okay," she whispers. "Do you want the light on?"

"Not now, Walt," Father Bill's voice insists. "Can't it wait?" And then the voices grow soft.

By the time Zoe has left Luz and come into the living room, Walt has gone. Father Bill is alone on the couch, his legs stretched straight out before him, his hands over his prominent stomach. "She settled down pretty well," Zoe says softly.

"You see? You are just what she needs." Then he stands up. He does not trust it. He goes to Luz's room and looks in. The room is dark. Luz is silent. "Are you asleep?" he says. Luz does not answer. He goes back to the living room, finishes a whiskey, and has a second. Zoe declines the whiskey but accepts a beer. When Zoe reminds him he was going to give her a list, he goes into the kitchen, finds a pad and a pencil, and hands them to her, sits down beside her, and dictates Luz's routine. Zoe is grateful, though a little surprised at how well he knows Luz's life. She can't help but wonder, is it possible that Father Bill is also the father of Luz?

For nearly an hour Father Bill waits with his heart in his mouth, but Luz does not wake. There are no outcries; the odor of sanctity, thick as rosewater, fails to materialize. It will be fine, he tells himself. Luz has had a shock. He has to be careful what he lets himself think. "Dissociative Disorder," he repeats over and over like a prayer, the social worker's name for it. He has never seen an ecstatic. He is not even certain he believes in such things. He prefers not to deal with the mystical strain of his faith, suspect to him as to most. Too dangerous. Too hard to control. Revelation in the light of reason, that is the teaching of his Church. His as well. There, he is calmer. "If there's something you think you can't handle tonight or tomorrow, just call me at the hospital," he says, leaning across Zoe to write down the numbers on top of the list. "Just ask them to find me. Don't hesitate."

"Yes," says Zoe, "Thanks. I will. That makes me feel a lot better."

Zoe who knows nothing. Who has never been alone with a child, let alone a child like Luz.

When Father Bill leaves, Zoe has a moment of panic. There is a child in her care. A strange child at that. There is a list, so much to do just to step into the day. There is Josefina in the High Desert Hospital, whose chances for transplant are nil. Zoe picks up the list, the dry reassurance of paper. She will read it and read it, study the bathroom, open cupboards, search for towels, for sheets, memorize the kitchen, try to remember where everything is, rehearse the day that's to come. In this way she will prepare for the morning, deluding herself that she can.

CHAPTER 7

At last Zoe lies down on the brown couch, slips off her white cotton trousers, slips the pale green sheet under and around her, and closes her eyes. All night she skirts the edge of sleep, watching the desert sky change color: black to indigo to ash. Watching through the barred windows as the blue-white summer stars fade out.

The house of Josefina and Luz Reyes is well guarded, but from what, Zoe wonders as she sits up. What would a thief take? The house is spare, scarcely furnished. The brown couch, a nondescript end table beside it, a small television in the corner on an old metal stand that Zoe will not turn on lest she wake Luz. But Luz does not stir. In spite of all she has been through and seen, Luz's sleep is unbroken. It is Zoe who is awake.

Now Zoe stands up and goes barefoot into the kitchen, feeling her way in the dark to the counter and a small shaded lamp, switching it on. The light it gives off makes the kitchen feel golden and intimate, smoothing the uneven walls, which are thick with old layers of paint. There are red plates and colorful mugs, a small shiny pot on the drain board, and a pile of clean yellow cloths folded on the counter beside an immaculate gas stove. She goes to the refrigerator and pours some milk into the pot, heats the milk, then pours it into a mug and sits down at the table—its chrome legs polished to a high silver sheen—sipping her milk. It's a lovely room at night. A small island of safety that Josefina has made. But Josefina is not safe. Zoe sees her lying sleepless in her hospital bed, displaced in her body, with what unthinkable fears? Soon Zoe is fighting off grief for a woman she hardly knows. She will have to be able to hide it by morning or Luz will know everything without being told. *Josefina,* Zoe thinks, and tries to see only her name. Before her on the table is the list that will guide her through the fast-approaching day. How can she possibly manage it all? She will start now. And so, at three in the morning Zoe decides she will make Luz's lunch. Back to the refrigerator, which is full of fat plastic tubs. She opens the largest, searching for the sweet corn tamales, finds plump blue-green peppers stuffed with cheese in a thick red sauce. *The food of the dead,* thinks Zoe, before she can stop herself. She has only four hours to shut down her mind.

In the next tub she finds the tamales. Then in the cabinets to the right of the sink, the small plastic containers with bright colored tops, the little red boxes of raisins, the Yoo-hoos, the brown sacks and napkins. The kitchen is well organized; her task is quite easy. Now Zoe slides all the items into the sack and folds down the edge, Luz's summer school lunch is complete. Feeling satisfied, she puts the sack on the top shelf of the refrigerator next to the milk, washes the tamale tub, and goes to the back door and peers through the glass. Through it she can see the gutters hanging loose from the mountings of the neighbor's roof and wonders who lives there, and what she could charge to fix them. And then Zoe remembers Walt's window. Was it just yesterday she installed it? The whole thing seems dreamy, something she has done ages ago or did not do at all, a thing she imagined. It has been weeks since she has been able to work fully absorbed, without once thinking of Michael, she realizes. And how happy Walt was in the end, and how generous. (And what was wrong with him this evening that he was so cold?) Even Chico Platz surprised himself. In spite of his awkwardness, his thin chest and arms, he was an excellent helper, careful—a good eye. She was glad that she chose him. A good job all around.

And now here she stands in the middle of the night, wide awake in Josefina Reyes' bright kitchen. Zoe let into the home of a stranger, a stranger's child in her care—the child of a woman whose life Zoe can't let herself feel. She picks up the list, to see what is next: all these enormous small tasks.

Number two on the list: iron the yellow dress Luz will wear to Mass. There it is, hanging on the back door of the kitchen, waiting. Only Zoe doesn't know the first thing about ironing. Michael irons. He has been ironing since he was twelve. He irons. She watches. It charms her. Though Michael has never ironed a little girl's dress. There is no little dress in their Cold Spring house. No little girl. No Michael. No her. Okay, thinks Zoe, this is bad. If she lets herself go there, she will never sleep at all.

At this point if she were home, she would go straight to the shower. In the first days when Michael left she would shower two or sometimes three times a day, and one awful Sunday she stopped counting after six. But the campground where she has been for nearly a week has no showers, only a couple of outdoor faucets with long lines of strangers, the disarmingly frank talk of half-naked climbers. She drives to the faucets at night and washes in the dark when she is certain to be alone. Several times on the road, in various motel shower stalls, Michael's heartbeat had come to her, the powerful thrum of it insisting itself through her own. Now she waits for it to come back, but it has not found her. Not in the campgrounds. She waits, too, for his touch, some living sense of him. She can hardly feel herself, her body halved without the hands that have touched it into pleasure. Her skin seems papery even under water. Her nipples harden obediently but the small softness of her breasts, the forthright shoulders feel as if they belong to a strange other. The answering voice of herself is gone, her body a thing apart. Even the soft zones of the flesh, her inner thighs, the sweet envelope of her vulva, the tensile petals of her vagina have become like little independent isles. Recognizable, familiar beauties of her woman-ness, distant and stilled.

Zoe puts her empty mug in the sink, rinses it. The yellow dress can wait until morning. She takes one final look around the kitchen, then reaches to turn off the lamp. *Nothing,* she thinks, *I would change nothing in this room. I would not even sand down the walls.*

Three hours later, Zoe is awakened by Luz looming over her, a curtain of thick black hair, solemn black eyes. Zoe's heart races ahead. She picks up her watch from the floor beside Luz's bare brown foot. It is only 6:30. Luz steps back.

"Do you remember why I'm here?" Zoe asks, undoing the sheet and struggling to sit up.

"Tell me," says Luz.

"Because your mother is in the hospital."

"Let's call her right now."

"It's too early. We'll do it as soon as you get home from school." Breakfast, eight o'clock Mass, then Luz goes on the nine o'clock summer school bus. She will return home at two-forty-five, Zoe thinks.

Luz regards her silently, a staring presence in pale blue summer pajamas. "Why else?" Luz asks hoarsely.

"Why else what?" Zoe replies.

". . . are you here?"

"I don't know." Zoe pauses, wonders herself. "Because you asked for me?"

Luz looks at Zoe appraisingly. "And from Our Lady," she says.

"What lady?"

"You can say it."

"Luz, what do you mean?"

Luz bends in close once again, putting her hand on the couch near Zoe's thigh, her dark hair brushing Zoe's cheek, her breath metallic. "Our Lady that sent you for the window."

"What lady? No lady sent me. Walt gave me a job. He paid me money."

Luz looks into Zoe's eyes to make sure she is telling the truth. She reaches for Zoe's arm. But right away Zoe is on her feet, a long white body in tiny underpants and the tee shirt she wore when she came to Luz in the night.

"Where are your pajamas?" asks Luz.

"In the campgrounds with the rest of my stuff," says Zoe, and slips on her cotton slacks. "At some point I'll have to go get them."

Luz's heart beats fast. She has been waiting for the way to be shown. Here it is—and through pajamas. She walks to the bathroom, shutting the door behind her. Her heart races so hard it hurts. Luz brushes her teeth—very hard, until white tiny bubbles cover her mouth. She looks very hard into her own dark eyes, the eyes of her father, Dr. Raphael Reyes, her mother says. Sometimes she can see things when she does this. Sometimes she sees people, other eyes, faces, her own face changing. But always Mami is in the blue house knocking on the door of the bathroom saying, *Hurry I'll be late for my work.* The knocking that makes everything stop.

Now Zoe waits outside the bathroom trying to remain calm. Is it Luz? Is it her? She had that falling sensation again, and just as Luz touched her. A spawn of silver fish in her blood. Zoe listens to the sound of water running in the sink, then the flush of the toilet. She counts the Madonnas scotch-taped to the wall where she leans, waiting for Luz, one Madonna for each month. Quite an array. She recognizes a couple of famous paintings in the line-up: Michelangelo's *Holy Family*, Da Vinci's *Madonna of the Rocks*. This vivid one near her she has never seen. She peers down to read its title: *Estoy Contigo* by an artist named Rosa M, bright blues and reds, a strong simple figure, Rosa M's Madonna (if she *is* a Madonna), the yellow sun like a child's. From their height, from the way they are taped, Zoe knows who put these Madonnas on the wall. Oh, thinks Zoe, Not *a lady*, Our Lady. *Our Lady that sent you for the window?* Is that what Luz thinks—Our Lady brought *Zoe?* And brought her to put in Walt's window? Why would Luz believe such a thing? The answer is not on her list.

It has grown quiet in the bathroom. Zoe wonders what could possibly be going on. She knocks on the door. She calls out Luz's name. Luz does not respond. Where on her list does it tell her how long Luz can stay in the bathroom?

"Honey," she says, "I'd like to shower."

The door opens; Luz comes out, white toothpaste marks around her mouth. "You can," Luz says. "Do you know how to work it?"

"Yes, thanks."

Luz goes into her room and closes the door, turning the lock so it clicks. Not on the list: can or can't Luz lock her door?

All through breakfast or what passes for it, while Zoe wrestles with the iron, trying not to mangle the yellow dress—or at least not to burn it—Luz sits in her summer pajamas caught in the net of her thoughts, her blueberry waffle hardly eaten, her orange juice undrunk.

"Three days and Mami will be home. Do you have a calendar? We can mark them off," Zoe says.

"We have *The Madonnas of the Centuries*, but not the right years. We are waiting for a new calendar from my school."

"Maybe we can make our own three-day calendar when you come back from summer school. That's how fast those days are going to go. One. Two. Three."

Luz does not look convinced.

When Zoe hands Luz the yellow dress, Luz says nothing about the creases, the splotches of water the size of Rosa M's sun. She goes into her room and comes out in the dress, hairbrush in hand.

"Mami does the braids in my room."

* * *

Zoe sits on the edge of the bed the better to brush Luz's hair. Under the filmy white canopy with the winking gold shapes, each sewn by Josefina to keep in the good dreams and send away bad.

First Zoe brushes Luz's hair to get out all the knots, her left hand on Luz's head to keep it still. Zoe brushes so slowly that pictures come into Luz's mind.

"What beautiful shining hair," Zoe says.

In her mind Luz can see the white hand resting on her head like a flower with one broken petal.

Now Luz takes the rosary from her sock drawer where she keeps it to be safe, holding it out for Zoe to touch, Zoe's long finger caressing one of the pale green beads. The broken finger from the other hand stays in her lap, holding the brush. "Look carefully," says Luz as she shows Zoe the faces carved on the beads, a man's then a woman's, a woman's then a man's. They are looking into each other's eyes.

"Oh," says Zoe, who wonders if they are the faces of lovers. "How soft the stones are. Where did it come from?"

"Esperanza."

"Who is that?"

"The little sister of my mother." Happiness comes to Luz by surprise because she could say it out loud. "Esperanza Guerra." Happiness comes again. Already this morning Our Lady is giving many surprises to her heart. "Mi tia. You know what that means?"

"Tell me."

"My aunt."

"You have an aunt in El Salvador?" Zoe asks.

Don't talk about it. Luz shrugs then looks up at Zoe. "In El Salvador we don't have anyone."

"Where did they go?"

"We lost all the family there."

Luz has said what she should not.

"I'm so sorry," says Zoe, but Luz has walked away.

How is such a thing possible, Zoe wonders, as she stands up, to lose all the family? Does this mean they have no one at all? Then Zoe remembers Father Bill's words: *No living relative but Luz.*

Now Zoe looks at her watch. Where has the time gone? They must hurry or they will be late for Mass. No time for items five through nine on the list. Zoe hurries Luz to the door. Zoe has forgotten the sunscreen. The lunch. The summer school clothes so Luz can change in the car before she gets on the bus. And Luz has forgotten her backpack, her books. But Luz does not care. She will not go to summer school today. She will stay all day with Zoe and then later, because of Zoe's pajamas, Our Lady will show them the way to the campgrounds.

* * *

To get ready for Mass Luz must try not to notice the Mariposa Lane houses or think who lives in them. Luz must not think of the world, must not wonder about what happens to the people in the houses or how the Felangela has come to walk beside her with Mami taken to the hospital by ambulance, Mami down on the floor with her eyes closed not hearing, and then with that bad smell. Must say the name of her church, Our Lady of Guadalupe. Of the man Juan Diego who gave Our Lady of Guadalupe the roses that are red and can bloom in the winter, even in snow. Luz must not tell the story of Juan Diego. Must not think of Our Lady with roses under her robe. Must not think must not feel. Not the heat of the sun, which already is hot and shines on her everywhere, even on her feet through the cut out parts of her sandals.

Must not remember how it has burned her once and can burn her again, or how the Felangela has forgotten the sunscreen and balm. Must not think too much of the Felangela and her finger, so close Luz could touch it, so close Luz can smell the soap on her skin from the shower. Luz must not lick her lips, must not worry that they will once again burn. Must not count the splits on the tar of the road, must not count the cars or say whose they are. Must not see her mother on the floor of the kitchen. Must not hear the ambulance. Must not remember Mami's bad smell.

Must count the steps of the church.

"We made it," says Zoe.

Luz looks up through the strong rays of the sun. She can hardly see the Felangela's face.

"Did you have a first holy communion?" Luz asks.

"No."

"That's all right. He doesn't care. Everyone can stay."

CHAPTER 8

It's a church, Zoe thinks, as she follows Luz up the blistered front steps through the heavy wood door. *A church*, as if she were expecting something else. The outside is modest to say the least, with a simple spire and a pea-green wood frame—wrong material for this climate, and it is not doing well. But inside the entry it is cool and soothing, a plain vaulted ceiling, a floor of dark slate, the old mahogany pews with their sweet rich smell, the rows of red votives where Luz goes and lights her own candle. Zoe watches, afraid Luz will burn herself, but Luz knows exactly what to do, candle to candle, hers is lit. Then she says a prayer, a soft murmuring sound, quickly finished. "Will you sit with me?" Luz asks.

"Go ahead. I'll find a seat in the back," Zoe says. Luz goes quickly down the center aisle in her creased yellow dress and her crooked braids to the first row. The only child present, Zoe observes. Zoe looks down at her clothes, suddenly embarrassed by her filmy white slacks wrinkled and spotted with tamale sauce, the white tee shirt, which she had slept in.

There are only a dozen people this morning for Father Bill's eight o'clock Mass, in the pews close to the altar, some on their knees, some seated, all women, casually dressed, though their heads are covered and bowed. Zoe sits down in a back pew and breathes in the silence and the rich smell of old wood, runs her hand over the worn mahogany of the bench, comforting, smooth. She wonders briefly at its history then takes another deep breath. She closes her eyes.

When she opens them, there is Father Bill making his way to the altar, everything about him a surprise: the robe, his stride, weighted and slow. She has seen the man in his other life. She has not seen the man as this. He looks out at his congregation, at his brave Luz. If she were closer, Zoe would see his eyes.

He can't say the words. He can't lift the cup. He is ambushed by the enormity of an undeserved grace. How does such grace persist? He tends it so carelessly, and its fruits are given anyway, so abundant, so sweet. The souls of his congregants beckoning him toward them, even in his time of despair.

When the vision appears—when they're all struck crazy by the bizarre visitations they think they can see in that car wash window—Zoe will remember the feeling that had come to her when she first saw Father Bill at the altar, a sweetness so great she had wanted to get up and run out of the church. And only for Luz's sake, in case Luz had turned to make sure Zoe was there, had she stayed.

CHAPTER 9

It is decided on the steps of Our Lady of Guadalupe before Father Bill returns to the hospital and the two pots of marigolds that Zoe had not even noticed shrivel to a powder in the heat that Luz Reyes can stay home from summer school. Who could put a child on the summer school bus without lunch, without her books, a child who is crying such tears?

"And what will you do all day?" asks Father Bill.

Luz wipes her eyes, looks at Zoe.

"Don't worry about us," Zoe says. "We'll be fine."

"When can we go to the campgrounds?" Luz asks, as soon as they are back at the house.

"In two hours," Zoe says, already drained by the heat.

Luz goes to her room and closes the door. The house grows quiet. Zoe sits down on the brown couch. The heat of the day walks through the walls and takes over. She gets up and tries to force open the windows. Six inches is all she can manage. The windows are held shut by guards. Bars and guards. Not one air conditioner. She does the few breakfast dishes, picks up a magazine written in Spanish, flops on the couch unable to keep her eyes open, feels herself drifting off. She wakes with a start, the house still, the air weighted with heat, looks at her watch. An hour has passed. When she goes to the door of Luz's room and listens, she hears nothing. "Luz?" Zoe calls. There is no reply. She feels the panic rising within. Luz has escaped! Zoe calls out again, turns the knob, but the door is locked. "Luz!" A long pause and then she hears footsteps. Luz opens the door.

"Is it time to go to the campgrounds?"

Luz has changed into shorts and a tee shirt, her face lightly glazed with sweat. The bare wooden floor is strewn with little figurines, coloring books and crayons spread out on the unmade bed. "Not yet. Promise me, Luz," says Zoe, stepping into the room, "You won't lock the door again."

"Okay."

"Can I come in? You were going to read me your tortoise facts."

"You read," says Luz. "I already know it."

Zoe steps past the toys on the floor and goes to the wall. "Facts about the Mojave Tortoise." Luz sits down on the floor. "Number one. Never pick up a tortoise. It could pee. That's a fact, really?"

"Yes," says Luz, looking up. "It would get scared. Then it would pee."

"I see," says Zoe, noting the red check next to the fact, noting all twenty-seven red checks.

"If it pees it will die," says Luz. "Read."

"Fact number two, the tortoise walks slow. Interesting." By the time she has come to the twenty-seventh fact, Zoe's mouth is dry as cardboard, but she is definitely enlightened. The Mojave tortoise is quite a little creature. It can hug, chat, knock over other tortoises, though only the boy tortoises do that, and somehow in a way that Luz does not remember, it can also save water.

"Did you see one in the campgrounds?" Luz asks, as Zoe settles down on the floor next to Luz and stretches out her long legs. "Fact number three," Zoe quotes, "the tortoise spends almost all of its life in its burrow. So no, I have not seen one yet."

"You will," says Luz. "When you take me. You will see many. They always come to me. I don't know why. Here."

She has handed Zoe a figurine.

"What is this?" asks Zoe.

"This is Our Lady of Fatima," says Luz, then hands Zoe another. "This is Our Lady of Perpetual Help."

Five-inch plaster saints, these are her toys? No wonder she's obsessed, Zoe thinks.

"Our Lady of the Miraculous. Isn't she pretty?" asks Luz.

"Gorgeous. I love the blue robe. Did Mami buy them for you?"

"No," says Luz. "We found the box from the lady who gave Father Billy the house. Mami said throw them out."

"Wait, a lady gave Father Bill this house?"

"Yes, because she died. But she was very old. And she used to give me yellow candy after Mass, but I didn't eat them because they were sour."

"Were they lemon drops?"

"Yes. Here, this one is a man. Take him." And Luz hands Zoe a handsome winged figure. Then she grins.

To see such a smile on the face of this child lightens the burden of the day. I only need to play with her, Zoe thinks. Just hang out with Luz on the floor and play with her saints and try not to pass out from the heat.

"Do you know who you have?" Luz asks.

"I have no idea."

"He is the one who carries the souls to heaven. Now do you know him?"

"Sorry, I don't."

"His name is Saint Michael."

"Saint Michael. What do you know? After he takes them to heaven, what does he do?"

"He gets more souls and brings them."

"Nice job," Zoe says.

Luz takes Saint Michael from Zoe's hand and replaces it with another winged figure. "Raf-ay-elllll! I love him," Luz shouts, hugging the little man to her chest. Then she gives Zoe the Holy Family, three figures that have been fused into one.

"And this," says Luz before Zoe can even admire the tiny child or reach again for the winged Michael, en route to heaven while Zoe's Michael has left her in hell, "this is Saint Lucy. The one that gets Mami really angry that I hide."

Zoe says nothing, though she thinks Lucy is cute.

"Do you think they are stories or are they real?" Luz asks, looking appraisingly at Zoe so close beside her she can feel the heat of her flesh and smell the sharp sweat smell that is not like her mother's.

"I like stories," says Zoe.

"Because they are real."

"I guess. In a way, so touché."

"What is touché?" says Luz.

"It's French."

"Oh," says Luz, reaching for another figure. "So is she. Bernadette, from Lourdes, France." She holds up a pretty long-haired saint with a small rosy mouth and a lovely silver dress, albeit plaster.

Later Luz will put her communion veil on Zoe's head, with its crown of little seed pearls. She will show Zoe her white gloves, the dress like a little bride's, and her communion album of gold-bordered white leather, the first photo taken on the steps of Our Lady of Guadalupe, fat pink peonies in the planting box beside them. Josefina is unsmiling, an obviously reluctant celebrant. Luz is in full white regalia, grinning big. And there is one photograph with all three of them, Luz in the middle, Father Bill looking proud. *My girls*, thinks Zoe. Isn't that what he'd called them when he invited her to share a meal at the rectory? "My girls will be there," he had said. "I'd like them to meet you." Does Father Bill know that one of his girls is obsessed?

"Do you know Father Bill a long time?" Zoe asks, having coaxed Luz into the kitchen to drink and to have an early lunch. She takes out the paper bag from the refrigerator where she had forgotten it that morning and puts the cold tamales on a plate, stands the raisin box beside it, chilled solid as brick.

"I know Father Bill from before I was born," Luz says, taking a bite of tamale. Zoe's own stomach is growling. She goes back to the refrigerator and takes out the peppers she had seen the previous night. Josefina's food, Zoe thinks guiltily.

"From before you were born, that's impossible," Zoe says, as she puts the peppers on a plate and brings them to the table.

Luz gets up and goes out of the kitchen, returning with a framed newspaper article written in Spanish, the article that has been folded many times over and is already yellowed.

"Where did you get this?"

"From Mami's room."

The paper is *El Diario de Hoy*, the date, 18 Agosto 1987. Above the text is the photograph of a man with Luz's dark eyes and broad, stony forehead, an intense expression. The photograph has captured him in the midst of speaking, as if he is exhorting a crowd. "Dr. Raphael Reyes," says Luz. Zoe makes out the words. *Universidad de El Salvador, muerto con veinte otros.*

"This is my father. Dr. Raphael Reyes. Not a doctor. A teacher in the college. Do you like his face?"

"Yes, very much. I think you look like him."

"Yes. And Father Bill knew him too. Father Bill was a priest and a teacher in my country but for the poor people with Mami. People who could not read."

"Oh, I see. And they were all friends?"

"Teachers and friends in my country."

Where you lost all the family, Zoe thinks, *but why?* Zoe wonders but does not ask. "So that's how Father Bill knew you before you were born?"

"Yes," says Luz. "We have to put it right back now."

Zoe helps Luz replace the photograph on the nail above the small white dresser in Josefina's tiny bedroom, the bed unmade, a sheet tossed on the floor, the closet flung open, a wrong acrid odor permeating the air. She has walked into lives of people she cannot fathom, some who are living, some who have already died.

"When will they call me?" Luz asks once they have returned to the kitchen. She sits at the table but does not touch the second tamale.

"Soon, honey, I'm sure. Try to eat a little. You must be hungry. You hardly ate breakfast."

"Now will we go to the campground?"

"Let's wait until it gets cooler. Four-thirty or five."

When the phone call comes, Zoe is sitting at the kitchen table trying to decipher a Spanish language magazine, drowsy with heat and three hours of sleep, wishing she could nap. Luz is back in her room. Zoe calls out her name, but Luz does not appear.

"I think she is sleeping," Zoe says to Father Bill.

"She doesn't sleep in the middle of the day," he says abruptly. "Go and see what she's doing."

It is in the bathroom that Zoe finds Luz. Zoe has to open the door with her credit card, sliding it under the lock. Luz jumps off the edge of the tub where she has been perched, staring into the mirror.

"Didn't you hear the telephone? Didn't you hear me calling?"

"No," says Luz thickly.

And for the first time Zoe smells the scent, the too-sweet aroma of roses.

CHAPTER 10

When Luz puts her ear to the phone, she hears her mother saying her name. It sounds like Josefina is speaking from under deep water.

"Why are you talking so soft?"

"The medicines do this. For making me tired. They say I must sleep. You ate?"

"Yes," says Luz, "but just one tamale. What is wrong with you? Why did you fall down?"

"We don't know yet. They are testing my blood, mamita. They are testing my everything. They are giving me medicine. Soon I'll be home. Do not worry. I will come to you soon."

"She talked soft," Luz says to Zoe after she puts down the phone.

"The tests must be making her tired."

"I will be quiet. When she comes home, I'll let her keep sleeping."

You are already quiet, Luz Reyes, thinks Zoe. "Why don't we go to the campgrounds?"

"No," says Luz as she heads out of the kitchen.

"Where are you going?"

"I have to do something."

"What?" Zoe asks.

"Something for Mami."

"I want to see it. Don't leave me alone in the kitchen."

Luz turns. "You are lonely? Come to my room. I will show you."

How can Zoe object to the prayer cards? To the Joyful and Sorrowful Mysteries, not to mention the Luminous Ones? To the little system Luz shows her in secret and teaches her to say? Ten days of these magic Rosaries for someone in need.

"Is that what you have been doing when you lock the door?" Zoe asks. "Have you been saying Rosaries for Mami?"

"Yes," says Luz. "But don't tell Father Bill. He doesn't want me to do it too much."

Ah, Zoe thinks.

"Do you want to say it for Michael?"

"Saint Michael?"

"Your Michael," says Luz as she strokes Zoe's hand.

"Who told you I had a Michael?"

Luz looks down at the floor. "I hear everything they say, Mami and Father Bill." Zoe puts her hand on Luz's neck, the fingers long and cool. "The ones that disappear need every prayer," says Luz.

"The ones that disappear?"

"Ask deep," Luz says, "with your body. I will show you."

A Glorious Mystery for Wednesday. A Luminous One for tomorrow, very long, very involved, Zoe thinks. Still, it makes Luz so happy to say it. And Zoe will not be with Luz for long. Why should she not help Luz endure what is here in the moment and the unspeakable thing that is to come? *The ones who disappear need every prayer.* And the ones who remain. She says a Glorious Mystery for Michael. A Luminous one for herself.

When they have finished, Zoe can smell it distinctly, a sweet thick scent rising off of Luz's skin. "Are you wearing your mother's perfume?"

"Perfume?" asks Luz.

"Don't think I can't smell it. It's coming from you." Zoe says nuzzling Luz in the neck.

Luz laughs. A small crackling fire of a laugh. Luz throws back her head.

"Don't tell Father Bill what you smell."

"Is it his?"

"He doesn't wear perfume."

"Where did you get it?"

Luz shrugs.

"If you took it from Mami, you have to put it right back."

"Okay," says Luz getting up from the floor and walking to her dresser, "when you go back to the kitchen."

"Are you kicking me out?"

"You are funny."

"Well, are you?"

"Yes!" says Luz.

"Remember, don't lock the door."

Zoe goes back to the kitchen and does the few lunch dishes. She hears Luz walking to her mother's bedroom. She hears the door open and close and then suddenly Luz's running feet as she comes flying back to the kitchen.

"What is it?" asks Zoe,

Luz stands with her hands pressed against her ears, her face contorted.

"What's wrong, Luz? Did you hurt yourself?"

"Mozote," is all she can say.

But Zoe has never heard of Mozote. And Luz, who has told too many secrets already, is unable to explain.

CHAPTER 11

That night, instead of telling Father Bill her concerns about Luz, Zoe ends up trying to cheer him (and maybe herself) by saying how well Luz is doing, how helpful the list is, neglecting to mention the peculiar rose smell, the endless Rosaries, the locked doors, the family in El Salvador Luz has told her about who are gone. After their phone call, Zoe lies exhausted on the brown couch in the same tee shirt and pants she has worn for two days. Tomorrow she will get to the campgrounds and retrieve her clothes.

Right now she should get up and go through the house and look for the source of that smell, which lingers. Or maybe it's grown. But she is unable to move, her body heavy with their sorrow and the sickly sweet smell with no source.

Searching her own house day after day after Michael left, looking for she did not know what—love notes with which to wound herself—Zoe had come upon a lilac flyer hidden in Michael's sock drawer, ***Pilgrims Unite for a Great Event***, it read. Below was a hand-drawn map. This must be a joke, she had thought: the Mojave, the Joshua Tree Campgrounds, a black dot the size of a dime due east of the campgrounds. **Join us in an uprising of spirit, a congregation of joy.** It was the kind of thing she and Michael might make fun of. But Michael had been in the Mojave, she remembered. It was where he had learned he had a gift for wood.

He had come to her shop looking for work. She had not talked to him since high school. Thirty-two, a wanderer, no profession. Son of a respected doctor, his father's shame. He had been on four continents by then. Zoe had never gone further than Maine, third generation woodworker. Her own shop by thirty. The only woman in the wood trade for miles. Michael was driving a school bus, coaching youth hockey at the Ice House in Rhinebeck. She had glimpsed him one night at the locals' hangout, alone at the bar. Seen him early one morning sitting on the esplanade wall, gazing at the river. The same sense of distance about him. The same sweetness of face. Something fine she could not quite name. Zoe, who can look into wood and see grain. *This is my husband*, she had thought as he looked up, a clear quiet voice in the mind.

He takes her to the back of his truck, unwraps a cabinet two feet by three. Old, she thinks at first as he puts it in her hands. Bird's-Eye maple, deeply figured, dovetail joints in cherry, pale maple drawers. Intricate work. More art than craft. She runs a hand over the finish, holds her breath as he slides out the drawers. Amazing. "I built it," he says. Hint of a smile. Where had he learned? "There was a man in Utah, a Navajo carver. I spent three years with him, the best years of my life. Another year traveling. Have you been West? The Mojave? Beautiful. You should go some time."

Michael was twelve when his mother walked out. One night he woke to the sound of smashing glass, his father's feet running down the stairs, his voice booming "Miriam! Miriam!" A month later, home after hockey practice, Michael walks into his house, drops his bag and his stick, feels the emptiness. A Wednesday, the night his father is on duty at the hospital. Afraid to go into her bedroom and look, afraid to open the coat closet, he waits until midnight to pick up the phone. A week later they find her in Boston. "She's gone and there's nothing we can do," his father explains, takes the boy in his arms. "Don't let this ruin things. It isn't the end of the world." Later it becomes a command. "Did she want to talk to me?" "Not yet," said his father.

When Michael was a senior in high school, he took a bus up to Boston, pretending to look at colleges. Miriam Payne had a job in customer service, some big insurance company, a second-floor apartment, a boyfriend, a married man. "Here's what I remember about her. Even when she was home she was never there. Absent when she was right in front of you. It's history," he said to Zoe who wanted more. Everyone urging her to be careful. Go slow. Common knowledge: Michael Payne had never stayed with a woman longer than half a year. "It's the past," Michael said. "It won't happen with you. I will never walk away. It would be like walking away from myself."

Michael and Zoe go to all the fall parties in Cold Spring that year. Zoe in rose velvet, at home in her beauty. Anyone could see how happy they were. Michael raises his beer, taps it with a knife, "I've come back to Cold Spring to marry Zoe Luedke!"

Love is stronger than history, they tell each other. *Their love.*

Five months later they marry, buy a wreck of a house with a view of the Hudson, sturdy hundred-year-old barn out back for their work. Luedke & Payne Cabinet Makers. The clients love Michael, his careful details, his quickness. (And Zoe so slow.) Their house fills with friends. Michael Payne come into his own. Even his father has hope. It lasts exactly three years.

This isn't happening, she thought, when he left. Unable to bear it, not just her own pain, but his. *History stronger than love.* She puts the purple flyer on the bed table. Every morning there it is. One day Zoe throws some clothes in a duffle, sticks the flyer in her jeans, grabs the tent and a sleeping bag, the red tool box—her first—for luck, takes off in the Nova, not even sure until she is on the Thruway where it is she is going to go. The black dot. The Mojave. Pilgrims Unite.

* * *

In the morning Luz has to be prodded to get out of bed. She eats little breakfast, does not want to get dressed. At least the rose smell is gone, Zoe notes with relief. "You will feel better when you are in school." "No," says Luz. "Take your books," says Zoe, handing Luz her backpack. Luz refuses.

"I didn't eat breakfast," Luz tells Father Bill as he kneels on the steps of the church after Mass, trying to convince her to try summer school—for the morning, at least. He is hollow-eyed, frail in spite of his thickness as if one touch could knock him flat. "I didn't do the homework," Luz pleads.

He looks at Zoe apologetically.

"If she wants to stay home again, I could take her to Twenty-Nine Palms—or the campgrounds."

"The campgrounds? Whose idea was that?" Father Bill says.

"Mine, I think," Zoe says.

"She knows she cannot go there. The campgrounds are not allowed. Mami wants you in school, Luz. You won't be able to talk to her until evening. That's a long time to wait."

"I am patient," Luz says.

The campgrounds are not allowed? Zoe thinks.

"I don't know what to tell you," Father Bill says. "Did she sleep?"

"I slept in the night. I didn't wake up," Luz offers.

"Very good," says Father Bill, "but do you see I am speaking to Zoe?"

"We'll fill up the day. It's okay if she wants to stay home," Zoe says.

"Thank you for understanding." Father Bill clasps Zoe's hands. Then he bends down and embraces Luz and says something that Zoe cannot hear, watches as they walk to the Dart.

"How 'bout we go see how the window is doing? Would you like that?" Zoe asks. "And then we can go to the diner for breakfast. After that maybe you can help me find Michael."

Yes, Luz says to it all and sits back in the seat of the Dart. Father Bill had said try not to worry. Mami is coming home soon. But why can't Luz talk to her until the night? She had not asked. Then they are driving the Dart on the freeway that Luz knows so well and Father Bill is gone.

"You didn't tell me you aren't allowed to go to the campgrounds."

"I know," says Luz. "Because Father Bill and Mami are afraid if I go there."

"Afraid of the campgrounds?"

"Yes," says Luz, "they are still."

Still afraid, all right. "Afraid of what?" When Luz does not answer, Zoe does not press her. "Now how am I going to get my pajamas?"

"Pray, hope, don't worry," says Luz.

"I'll try that," Zoe says, wondering as they get close to the car wash what else Luz might have neglected to tell her. Is she not a reliable child? Well, Zoe will soon see. Up ahead is the blue neon sign, Immaculate Autos, an odd name, she had thought when she first saw it, and thinks once again. Before she has even slowed down for the turn, she sees the window and thinks for a moment that something is wrong with her vision. The window she spent hours measuring so it would be plumb is now crooked. Comically crooked, like the window of a witch's house in a child's drawing.

"Oh no," says Luz.

"Oh no, you're not kidding," Zoe says. She looks in the rearview mirror at Luz's solemn face. "We better go see what this is."

Zoe parks the Dart in the space next to Walt's blue Civic, takes Luz's hand, then goes straight down the black asphalt walk past the office door, hoping to avoid Walt.

"We're not going inside?" Luz asks.

"Not yet."

When they get to the window, Zoe can't help but laugh. "Wow, that's weird."

"What happened?" asks Luz, bending her neck far to the right. One braid slides down her shoulder and the window looks straight.

"I have no idea," Zoe says

"Did you make a mistake?"

Zoe runs her hands along the new stucco at the top edge. It has dried nicely. She will have to remove it in order to look at the header.

"What are you doing here?" Walt Adair asks as he comes down the walkway.

"The window is crooked," says Luz.

"So it seems," Walt says. His expression is dour but he looks very nice nonetheless, Zoe thinks, the blue oxford shirt, the well-pressed chinos. He pats Luz on the head. "You doing okay?" Luz nods.

"The header must have been warped," says Zoe. "I could knock out the stucco and check."

"I can't afford any more of your work."

"Oh, it won't cost you anything."

"Like I said. I can't afford you. I've got someone coming to look at it. The whole thing may have to come out."

"The window?" asks Luz.

"You should have told me you didn't know what the hell you were doing."

"I'll come back when I have some time," Zoe offers.

"You've done quite enough already," says Walt.

"Usually Walt is more nice," says Luz when she and Zoe are back in the Dart.

"It's the window. He didn't want it up there in the first place."

"Yes, he did. That's why he bought it. And She told him to do it."

"Who told him?" asks Zoe.

"Our Lady."

"Luz," says Zoe, laughing now.

But Luz is not laughing. Why would she laugh at the truth?

* * *

The diner is crowded and noisy, the warm breakfast smells rising above the too-frigid air. Luz looks down at the floor tiles as a tall forthright woman with a shock of white hair leads them to a table for two, smack in the middle of the busy dining room. Too exposed, Zoe thinks, as they sit down. Luz needs the shelter of walls, a back booth perhaps. But all the booths are filled.

"How are we doing this morning?" the woman says. "Your mother okay?" She hands Zoe a menu.

"She's still having tests in the hospital," Luz says.

At the table beside them sit two little girls in bright matching short sets, one with striking red curls, their mothers in pastel dresses, bright lipstick, freshly washed hair. The women stop their conversation to look Zoe over. The girls whisper and giggle.

"And this must be the talented window gal from New York."

But before Zoe has a chance to defend herself—and really, what can she say, it's not my fault it is crooked, it's some faulty header or stud?—Bobbie has asked for their orders. "Coffee," says Zoe. "Two scrambled eggs."

"Toast?" says Bobbie.

"Yes."

"What kind?"

"Rye."

"No rye," Bobbie says and waits.

"Any kind is fine."

"Any kind," she writes, amused.

"Luz?" Zoe says.

"I know what she wants," Bobbie says and walks away.

"Bobbie knows me since I am three."

"That's nice."

Zoe sighs and looks around the busy room, heads swivel away. They are being stared at. The window, she thinks, and feels her face flush. The booths are full of people who showed up at the car wash to watch Walt's window go in, the heavyset men wearing baseball caps who are right now peppering her with those humorous looks—they were definitely there. Walt took lots of teasing that day, she remembers, and now look what he is stuck with. Is it her fault? How could it be? She looks at Luz, who appears quite miserable. The whole purpose of going to the diner was to cheer Luz up. Another mistake. At the table beside them, the two little girls lift tall glasses of orange juice, clink them, and laugh.

"Do you know them?" Zoe whispers.

"From my school," whispers Luz, beginning to shiver in the cold of the diner.

"Are you okay?" Zoe asks.

Luz nods. What to do now? Zoe could try warming Luz up by thinking. She can cool down a car with her mind, but she has never tried warming a person, at least not in that way.

"Who are your friends?" Zoe asks. "Maybe we can call one."

"No," says Luz.

Finally, Bobbie returns and slaps down their plates. They are huge. Potatoes and onions and a generous skewer of fruit surround Zoe's two scrambled eggs. Luz's strawberry waffles cover the whole oval plate. Luz looks at it, defeated. We shouldn't have come here, thinks Zoe. She picks up her coffee cup, while Luz reaches for the syrup. Suddenly, the little girls at the table beside them stand up. "One, two, three!" says the red-headed girl as they turn to Luz and begin dancing in place, a foot-shuffling stomp, their feet tapping the floor, faster and faster. "Amanda, sit down!" says one of the mothers, as they start circling the table where Luz and Zoe sit, running and giggling and gasping for breath. One of the little girls' mothers slaps her hand on the tabletop. "Amanda! Ruth!" The plates and the juice glasses rattle. "Sit down right now!"

As quickly as they started, the girls stop their running and clamber noisily onto their seats. There are harsh whispers at their table, giggles, and then silence. No one looks up. No one apologizes to Luz.

The tables around them have grown quiet. Luz is clutching the handle of the syrup bottle, her eyes downcast.

"Luz?" Zoe says, but she does not respond. "Want to go?" Zoe asks after a moment. Luz lets go of the syrup and stands up. Zoe signals for Bobbie. Several slow minutes later Bobbie is back with the bill and white take-out boxes. Luz stands, clutching the back of the chair, her back to the girls.

"Sorry about that," Bobbie says, raising her eyes at the little girls and their mothers. "Take good care of our girl. And you hang in there, Luz. Your mother will be home before you know it."

The heat strikes them hard as Zoe and Luz step outside the diner, the sun glaring off the hoods of the cars in the parking lot, the freeway traffic speeding noisily beyond them.

"Why did they do that?" asks Zoe, taking Luz's hand as they navigate the broad diner steps and go back to the Dart.

"To make fun of my feet."

"By dancing?"

"It wasn't dancing."

"What was it?"

"I don't know."

But Luz does know. She knows very well. But no one believes her, and Luz must not say.

CHAPTER 12

"Are you sure you don't mind?" Zoe asks Luz when they arrive one hour later at the Casita of 29 Palms, the first place where they will try to find Michael.

"I'm sure," Luz says, stepping out of the Dart. "I want to." The Casita is small, only twelve rooms, a dusky pink adobe with owl chimneys and turquoise blue trim and a sign for a swimming pool. If only Luz had a bathing suit. Maybe they would let her go in.

Zoe opens a heavy glass door. A lady behind the counter is talking on the phone. She wears a big silver necklace and bright blue dress and looks up as they enter. "I'm sorry," she says, "we have nothing."

"I'm not here for a room," Zoe says.

"Just a minute," the lady says, turning away, continuing her conversation.

Zoe looks down at Luz and smiles. Already Luz's mood seems to have lifted. She has said that she wants to help Zoe find Michael. She wants to help Zoe however she can. She has even told her not to be sad about the window mistake. Luz wants to tell Zoe it makes no difference if the window is crooked. She wants to say Walt did not tell the truth. No man is coming to take it out. But how she knows this she cannot explain. And now she is eager to hear Zoe ask people about Michael, the questions she'll ask, and what they will say in response. How do you find people who have gone? On the drive to Twenty-Nine Palms

Zoe gave Luz a photo of Michael to hold. Luz had looked at it for a very long time. It made her stop thinking of what the girls did again, Amanda and Ruth, and in public. What they do every time that they see her; they do other things too that are bad. But Luz must not think of the girls. She must think of Michael, whose picture she likes. She likes his crossed arms and his plaid shirt. She likes his smile, which is a little bit like Father Bill's, kind. Behind him is a tree with colors she has not seen, the leaves yellow-gold.

Because of the picture of Michael, she has almost missed seeing the campgrounds. But the Joshua trees start coming, then the big brown sign for the campgrounds. Her heart beats with happiness. Our Lady would never let Luz miss the campgrounds, and just when she thought that, Zoe had spoken.

"I was thinking, maybe on the way back from Twenty-Nine Palms we can just scoot through to my campsite and I'll grab my duffle. Does that qualify as going to the campgrounds? You won't even have to set foot out of the car."

"Okay," Luz says, her voice very soft.

"Don't worry, I'll take all the blame with Father Bill."

When she says this, Luz gets very quiet. The Felangela, thinks Luz, who is doing this help for Our Lady and Luz. She tries very hard not to cry, but the sweet place has opened inside her heart like it does after Mass. Then Zoe says, "Do you want your breakfast? That waffle is doing no-one any good in the box."

"No, thank you," says Luz, though the words come out slow. And then Zoe is quiet too. A little while later Zoe announces it, the first motel where they will stop, the Casita of 29 Palms.

When the lady behind the counter puts down the phone, Zoe says, "I hope you can help me. I am looking for someone." She searches in her big bag for some papers and shows them. She takes Michael's picture from Luz. "I would really appreciate it. I've driven all the way from New York." Then she says something soft to the lady, but Luz does not hear.

"I don't do this kind of the thing," the lady says, looking from Zoe to Luz but not at the papers Zoe has spread on the glass-topped counter,

Michael's picture and a piece of pale purple paper with words. "Maybe you should call the police," says the lady.

"It's nothing for the police. He left me," Zoe says. *Walked away from himself.* "We've been married three years. I'm only asking you to see if his name is in your computer. Or if you remember his face." Zoe picks up Michael's photograph and holds it in front of the lady.

The woman frowns. "We don't get many singles. Especially not in the summer. Usually couples and families." Her skin is very brown, Luz observes, shiny from lotion, and with many deep lines that look like someone has pressed in her skin with the point of a pencil.

"Please," says Zoe, "he is my husband. Michael Payne is his name."

The lady looks at Luz then goes to her computer. Zoe squeezes Luz's hand.

Through a big glass door at the end of a hall Luz sees part of the Casita of 29 Palms swimming pool where a little girl has jumped in with a splash and a faraway yell. People Luz cannot see cheer. "Do it again!" a man's voice calls out, but the girl stays in the water, splashing around near the edge.

"I'm sorry," says the lady after she has looked for a while. "No Michael Payne."

Michael has not stayed at the Casita of 29 Palms.

Three times Luz watches Zoe ask the people in different motels at Twenty-Nine Palms the same things. And three times Zoe takes the photograph of Michael and a piece of light purple paper and shows it. No one has seen Michael Payne. No one knows what the purple paper means.

In the car on the way to the last place where they will look, not a motel but a bar, Zoe says, Luz makes a suggestion. "Maybe Michael was taken."

"Taken?" asks Zoe turning around.

"Escuaderos," says Luz.

"I'm sorry," Zoe says, turning back to the road. "I don't understand."

Luz pauses. She has never spoken these words, words she has only overheard. "Escuaderos take people away in the night, but sometimes even in the day. They take them from anywhere. Even their houses."

"No one took Michael, he left."

Luz does not understand. Why would someone with such a kind face leave Zoe unless, like the family that Luz has lost in El Salvador, he too had been disappeared?

* * *

The Red Palm Bar is dark as a cave after the midday glare of High Desert August. "Can you see?" Zoe asks, taking Luz's hand. The temperature of the bar is downright balmy compared to the frigid air of the Infidelity Diner. Zoe lets out her breath. There is soft country music, sparse conversation, walls lined with booths, the front aisle too narrow for tables.

Poor Luz, Zoe thinks, when she sees that most of the booths are filled. They are going to be talking to lots of people. Over and over the same questions. Maybe she should not be inflicting this on a child. Though each time she had shown Michael's photo and told about him, Luz had been fascinated, standing beside her with her big black eyes, hanging on every word. The last place they went was a dive, the Last Palm Motel. The owner wore a beat-up felt hat, a straggly gray beard, and a bemused expression. He kept asking if Zoe had really come all the way from New York for a man. Zoe showed him Michael's photo. "Good looking," he said, "but I never remember a face." He was getting ready to sell his place, he told them. "I'm pretty sure things have peaked. After thirty years, I can finally cash in." He seemed relieved. "I'm not a people person. I don't know how I ended up here in the first place." He had a hand-written ledger and flipped open the reservation book, turning it so she could read the names, but there had been no barely legible Michael Payne signature at the Last Palm Motel registry. Luz was still studying the names when Zoe said it was time to go. "Woodworker," whispered Luz. Then Zoe told the owner Michael was a woodworker; the man perked up and gave Zoe directions to the Red Palm Bar. "Guys in the wood trade hang there. If your man is looking for work, that's where he might find it." And as they were going out the door he had called, "Good luck to you and your girl."

"My girl?" Zoe said, smiling at Luz in the appalling heat of midday. "Did you hear what he said?"

Luz's stomach is grumbling, but she doesn't care. The bad feeling is gone from remembering Amanda and Ruth, and when she thought about Mami she remembered only the last things Father Bill had said when he bent down and whispered softly, "Try not to worry. Mami is doing very well." And now, soon, before she knows it, the most wonderful thing has come to her: Zoe is going to take her to the campgrounds.

The Red Palm Bar has a long high bar with a string of Christmas lights in the shape of red palms dancing across the mirror. It smells like peanuts and the bad smell of beer.

They stop at every table, men in backwards baseball caps and dark tee shirts, some with beards. A few women who smoke. The tables smell of cold beer, fried food, sweat. Zoe asks over and over about Michael, questions Luz already knows. She says he is a woodworker and that he might have been looking for work. It is nearly too dark to see the photo. And the flyer makes the men laugh, only a few of them curious. No one has seen Michael Payne or his blue and white van. "But that doesn't mean we wouldn't be glad to make room for you girls right here," some friendly men say.

"They are nice," whispers Luz.

"Uh huh," Zoe says. "Let's get something to eat and finish this later."

Zoe helps Luz climb up on a stool.

"That's quite a lovely yellow dress," the bartender observes after he has called in their order. He tells them his name, "Mike Lopez," and shakes their hands, first Luz's then Zoe's. "I didn't know what was going on between you and my customers," Mike Lopez says to Zoe. "Looking for her husband," says Luz. Mike Lopez laughs then puts on a serious face. "Couldn't you just hire someone?" he asks when Zoe explains about Michael all over again. "I feel like I have," she says. Then Luz is digging into a basket of fried onion rings and Zoe has downed two Sierra Nevadas on tap and Luz has a soda, a Sprite, which she is not allowed. They split a big plate of barbecue chicken, finishing it all and using half the bar's napkins. Afterwards, Zoe and Luz go from one person to another at the bar with the picture of Michael and the flyer.

"You forgot to show Mike Lopez the flyer," Luz whispers when they are back in their places eating dessert, a brownie sundae Mike Lopez has said is worth the price of admission. "Yep," he says, when Zoe unfolds the flyer once more. "You are definitely in the right place. That black dot is Infidelity for sure. They've got a good mechanic up there. I've used him myself."

"Bryant Platz," says Luz.

"What do you know? That's him. You know him?" Mike Lopez asks.

"That's where I live," says Luz. "And I used to even live on his property."

"Wait, slow down. You're not from New York?"

"She is," says Luz.

Who is in charge of this day, Zoe thinks. Luz seems to have taken over. "Hang on!" Mike Lopez says then and puts his hand up like he is going to stop traffic. "I just remembered something." He goes back into the kitchen; a minute later he has returned. "Someone tacked this up a while back. Don't ask me who. It's been hanging by the back door for weeks. Hey, a great event might be headed our way after all."

Zoe takes the flyer from his hand. Same wording, same map, same lilac bond, only splotchy with grease. Same dime-sized black dot.

Before they leave, Mike Lopez writes some numbers down on a small yellow paper and hands them to Zoe. "There are a couple of shops around here where they job-in help. If your Michael found his way to them, you might be in luck. You never know."

"Michael and Mike," says Luz.

Mike Lopez throws up his hands. "Small world!" he says.

When they are outside, Zoe makes a noise, somewhere between blowing air and whistling as they are out squinting in the light and looking among the parked cars for the Dart. "Another purple flyer. I don't mind telling you, Luz Reyes, I'm a little bit freaked."

"I'm sorry," says Luz.

"What do you have to be sorry for? It's not your fault. You were a big help. Really. This was my first iota of success." If the flyer has anything to do with Michael, that is, if she has not walked into her own mistake.

"I-o-ta?" says Luz.

"A very small thing. I think. Don't quote me."

When they get to the Dart, Zoe opens all the doors, starts the ignition then the air conditioning, so they can drive without roasting in their own juices.

"Could the Feast be the great event?" Luz asks when the car is cool enough for them to risk sitting down and closing the doors.

"What feast?" Zoe asks, turning back onto the freeway.

Luz explains the Feast of Our Lady's Assumption—the party Father Bill has every year at night outside of his church that everyone goes to.

All roads lead to Our Lady in Luz World, Zoe thinks. "Well, how great an event is it?" Zoe asks.

"To me it's very great. Bingo that lights up, every cookie and cake that you want, dancing if you like it, and the best thing, the ball-jumping game."

"What makes the balls jump?"

"No," says Luz. "Not the balls, the children. It's in a big cage. We go in and jump and fall in the balls, and no one pushes anyone or kicks. Maybe you can come too."

"When is it again?"

"August the fifteenth," says Luz, "the Feast of Our Lady's Assumption. Will you be here?"

"In five days? I may well be. I'll be back at the campgrounds. Unless, of course, a miracle happens and Michael turns up."

* * *

The campgrounds are meant to be a half-hour foray. It is only a ten-minute drive up the curving gray ribbon of Park Boulevard Road to the Hidden Valley Campsite, a five-step sprint to her dark green two-person eastward-tending tent. A quick dash inside—mere seconds when she will have lost sight of Luz before emerging with her duffle bag in hand. And then, and only possibly, on the way out will Zoe stop the car at the Cottonwood Visitor Station, take Luz inside, Luz's feet only briefly making contact with campgrounds soil, so that Zoe can check in with the ranger on duty to see if Michael Payne has suddenly appeared during the two, or is it already three days since Zoe has been gone from the campgrounds. Two days or three days that have the heft of weeks, months, even. Yes, Zoe will tell Father Bill, we went to the campgrounds, but only so I could get my clothes. And Luz mostly stayed in the car.

Zoe knows the roads through the campgrounds. She has been there nearly a week, studied the site map by early light and later by full moon and flashlight. She knows, even without the sign, that ten miles exactly off of Park Boulevard is a spur road to Hidden Valley, a seven-foot brown-painted white-lettered right-pointing marker to her campsite. Park Boulevard on which she drives is the only road possible, and she is checking her mileage gauge at seven miles, at ten miles, then at ten miles-and-a-half, driving even when she sees that Echo Rock Mountain is getting too big, its curved granite face approaching when it should stay away. This is not the way to her campsite, she knows it, but not for five minutes more, having gone over two miles up Park Boulevard and with the sign marker nowhere in sight, does she stop, make a U-turn, cursing loudly as she starts back. The road takes her down and around, nothing to do but follow, and all at once there she is in the vast Joshua Tree Forest, hundreds, thousands of spiky Joshuas all thick-branched and gray, splayed pointing gracelessly up to the sky. "You okay back there?" she says. "I can't find the road to the campsite, but I will, just bear with me."

And, naturally, thinks Zoe, no one to ask, not a hiker in sight, not even a heat-loving German. Meanwhile, Luz in the backseat has gone quiet. So quiet that Zoe thinks for a moment she may have fallen asleep. But Luz is not asleep. She is looking out the window at that bleached landscape, the mounds of dry brush, at the gorgeous endlessness of sky.

"Could Mami die?" says Luz.

"Ah," says Zoe, a soft wind in her voice. "Who would let that happen?"

"God."

And then Zoe pulls to the side of the road and stops the car. "It's all right," she says, getting out and opening Luz's door. Zoe presses her mouth to Luz's forehead, tasting salt, only the faintest aroma of roses, maybe imagined.

"I'm sorry we came here. We'll leave. The heck with my clothes. I'll take you right home."

"No," says Luz, unfastening her seatbelt, "I don't want to leave. Please, help me to stay." Her heart is hurting, and just when she is where she has been praying to be since the spring.

In the spring, when she was brought home from the hospital, Luz had tried to tell Mami how her feet made her run to the campgrounds. When she told the truth, Mami had said the curse then yelled. "No song from your mind makes your feet go. No phantom Madonna tells you to run away from your school." Mami walked fast to the telephone and called. "It is your fault that Luz has done this," she yelled on the phone in the kitchen. "You are turning my daughter fanatic."

Father Bill came to the blue house. He knocked on the door of her room. Her mouth was thick with the white cream that spoiled every taste, her lips hard and heavy from burning. Father Bill sat next to Luz on the edge of her bed in a plain white shirt. Luz watched his chest moving up and down from breathing slow. His face turned away to the window. Then he turned back. Father Bill looked very softly into her eyes, the look so beautiful she did not have the words. "Luz," he said, "don't open yourself so deeply. You are becoming confused." She waited for him to name the Rosary and give the number, but he only put soft hands on her head then closed his eyes.

"Our Lady," Luz said, trying to tell it.

"Shush," says Father Bill, "We can't speak this way anymore. You must promise me now."

"No," Luz said, "I have to."

"You must promise not to think of these things. Will you promise? God doesn't want you running away from school. He doesn't want you lost in the campgrounds."

She touches his cheek. She says to his heart, *don't be afraid.* She prays to Our Lady. She looks into Father Bill's eyes.

"Rest now," he says and stands up.

"Pineapple or guava?" said Mami, like always walking fast into the room with two pitchers. She made the refrescas to cool Luz for sleep, to cool Luz's mouth from burning. She put down the pitchers on the small table next to the bed. The pitchers were full. One was yellow, one gold. Luz said pineapple and guava, both. Then Mami brought three bowls and three spoons. Father Bill put the lamp on the floor so there was room. Mami held one bowl. Father Bill poured the syrup, first yellow, then gold. Then Mami sat down near her pillow and filled a spoon with the gold. Luz opened her mouth. The cool ice went in. At last Luz could eat, not just drink with the straw. Mami fed her like she was a baby.

How patiently Luz has waited for Our Lady to show her the way back to the campgrounds. Now it is here. Now Luz must let Our Lady show her the one tree, the place where Luz can once again hear Her voice. Luz moves slowly, pausing before a wooly trunk to listen, to stand in the quiet and wait for the voice. Zoe follows like a shadow. In summer the trees are more silent, more gray and dry, no white sacks of blossoms in the trunk of the Joshuas, no tiny white moths flying out of the branches like upside-down snow. Everywhere, nothing but Joshuas. Joshuas, desert, and the too-bright sky. Luz walks slow, the quiet so loud it is humming. In the spring she walked fast. Our Lady could make her feet fly.

"What are you doing?" Zoe asks, her words making shapes in the silence of the Joshua forest.

"Finding the tree." Even Luz is too loud to herself, though her voice barely carries.

"There are thousands here, Luz. If you're looking for one tree, you'll be walking the rest of your life."

Now Luz is so still in her body, when she raises her head and looks up, the wooly gray branches grow soft. Now they dissolve into gold.

CHAPTER 13

It is nearly eight when they get back to the blue house. Luz would not leave the campgrounds even after two big horn sheep had come perilously close to where they stood, startling Zoe when they appeared in the distance at the north edge of the Joshua forest. There had been not one single hiker to witness it, the big horn sheep rarely seen and never in flatlands, even a glimpse of them on the mountains considered lucky. She had pointed them out in the distance while Luz was moving from Joshua tree to Joshua tree, her hands on their trunks, her face pressed close as if she were listening for something, sometimes closing her eyes. "Luz!" Zoe cried. "Look at the sheep." Luz had turned and looked, standing quite still, so still that Zoe thought she might be frightened. "Don't worry," Zoe had said, "they won't come down here." But the sheep were moving fast, and Zoe saw she was wrong. For now she could hear their hooves, smell the muttony musk, see their buff-colored coats, three hundred pounds of muscular grace, then the indentations in their enormous curled horns and the softness of their eyes.

"Stay still," whispered Luz when Zoe rushed toward her with her hand outstretched, ready to grab her and run. "Don't be afraid."

The sheep came within five feet of where Luz stood, then Luz held out her hands. Zoe froze. Luz's features relaxed, her expression expectant as the sheep came closer, bent their necks, and one after the other nuzzled her cheek. Luz laughed, allowed it, taking each enormous soft face in her hands. When she dropped her hands the sheep remained for a long while without moving, soundless, right beside Luz, Zoe a little apart. After several moments the sheep turned and galloped off, Luz watching until they were no longer visible, said nothing, and went back to exploring the trees.

What is this child, Zoe had wondered, to whom such a thing happens and who seems to take it in stride? It is Zoe, the witness, who is amazed. Amazed and so moved by what she had seen, almost afraid to break the spell of it by speaking. And there was Luz, feeling her way through a cluster of Joshua trees. "Luz," Zoe said, "those sheep! Do you realize what has just happened?"

"Don't worry. The animals always come to me in the campgrounds."

Zoe had walked up to Luz then, lowering herself so she could look at Luz's face. "What do you mean the animals always come to you? What other animals have done this?"

"The tortoises, shhh," said Luz spreading her fingers on the trunk of the Joshua.

"Luz, how many times have you been to the campgrounds?"

"I don't know. I think three."

The entire drive back to Infidelity Luz had been quiet, leaving Zoe to wonder about what she seen, and the things about Luz that she could not yet grasp.

She can hear the phone ringing from the driveway, as she and Luz run up the walk to the blue house. It is ringing again as Zoe struggles to open the locks.

"Let me answer it," Zoe says, racing to the kitchen. "This is my fault."

"Where have you been?" Father Bill demands. "I've been trying to get you for over an hour."

Zoe takes a breath and leans against the back door of the kitchen. Luz sits down at the table and stares at Zoe with her dark eyes wide. Something has happened, Zoe thinks, she has seen something extraordinary that Father Bill should be told. Still, he had said not to take Luz to the campgrounds, and Zoe has taken her there, let her stay for quite a long time. How can she not tell him this? Don't *tell, don't tell,* Luz mouths. *Please!*

What good will it do to speak of the campgrounds now when Zoe doesn't have time to do it justice? She will wait until after Luz is asleep, and perhaps, by then Luz will have told her why the campgrounds—where the animals come to Luz all the time—are forbidden. "We're just getting back from Twenty-Nine Palms. There was so much traffic." It is a cheap lie, and as she is telling it Zoe does not feel right. Does not like having told it in front of Luz. Still, Father Bill breezes right by it.

"How is Luz?" he asks.

"She is fine," Zoe says. "Here, you can speak with her yourself."

Luz takes the phone, listens then responds in Spanish. The conversation is brief. When she is finished, she hangs up and Zoe is relieved.

"They gave Mami an operation," Luz says.

"When?" Zoe tries not to sound alarmed.

"In the afternoon." Luz says. "We have to make the refrescas. Mami wants us to do it. I'll scrape the ice. You can pour."

She shows Zoe where the big silver bowls are kept, points to the one they need, tells her to put it in the sink, then goes to the freezer and stands on her toes, takes out a loaf pan of ice. "I will show you how we do it," she says. "Do you know how to get the ice out of the pan? I can't do it."

Zoe runs the hot water and taps the loaf pan with a knife. Then she shakes out the ice cake. It slides into the bowl with a clang. "Did they say what the operation was?"

"For her blood," says Luz. Then she goes to the refrigerator again. "Pineapple or guava," asks Luz, struggling toward the table carrying first one then another filled plastic pitcher. "You can have both."

"Oh no, you can't use that knife," says Zoe when Luz goes for the big knife, a nine-inch carver, which Luz explains is used to scrape the ice. "Tell me what to do," Zoe says. She does the best she can to scrape shavings out of the ice block into the big silver bowl, finally giving up on the blade, hacking great chunks of ice with the knife handle. "Now what?" says Zoe looking down at the ice. "Little bowls," says Luz, and hands her two yellow ones.

At the table Luz pours the thick syrup, pineapple, then guava into the ice in their yellow bowls. They eat in silence, the ice block melting slowly in the sink. "We haven't had dinner," says Zoe. "Isn't this dessert?"

Luz ignores the question. She puts down her spoon. "In spring Father Bill moved us to the blue house to be close to the church. I could hear and see everything."

"What do you mean, Luz?"

"I don't know," Luz says. "In the spring I ran all the way to the Joshua trees from my school."

"Where we went today? You ran there?"

Luz hesitates. She must be very careful not to let out the secret, but sometimes her words have a tongue of their own. "Yes."

Zoe stops eating. Then she looks at Luz's face. "Why?"

Again Luz is silent.

"I can't say the reason."

"That's fine. You don't have to tell me. But does it have something to do with animals? Do you love to be around animals?"

"That's not the reason," says Luz.

"Is it far from your school to the campgrounds?"

"Yes." says Luz, "very far."

"Why did you do that?"

"Will you believe me?"

"Of course."

"Our Lady," says Luz. "Because she called me."

"Luz."

"She did."

"How did She manage to do that?"

"She sang."

Zoe puts down her spoon. "What did she sing, 'I am calling you-ou-ou-ou-ou-ou-ou?'"

"That's not her song. That's terrible singing."

"I apologize for my voice."

"You think it's a story, but I am not the only one She calls."

"Oh, really?" Zoe replies.

"She calls other people too," says Luz.

"Name one."

"You won't believe me."

"Does she call Father Bill?"

Luz thinks for a moment. "Yes."

"Does he tell you about it?"

"No. He says don't talk about it. Don't think about it."

Good for him, Zoe thinks. Zoe should probably change the topic, not let Luz go on in this way, but there is something fascinating about this child. And isn't it better for Luz to be making up stories than thinking about Josefina? An operation, Zoe wonders, what could it have been?

"Okay, I'm game," Zoe says. "Who else does She call?"

"She calls Michael." Luz says this looking straight at Zoe, solemn and round-eyed. The picture of truth, the same intent open stare she had given to the sheep.

For a moment, looking into those round black eyes Zoe believes Luz knows things about her, thinks Luz is speaking of Michael, *her* Michael. How *can* she? And for a moment Zoe is frightened in the way she was when Luz touched her and she felt she would pass out. And then Luz opens her mouth and runs her tongue over her bottom teeth, teasing them, teasing Zoe, perhaps. "Oh, I get it!" says Zoe. "Michael is an angel. Remember, you taught me? That's his job to be called."

"I meant your Michael."

"Well, She never called him when I was home."

"Yes," Luz whispers, "she did."

"What do you mean, Luz?"

"She always calls to the souls of hurt children."

"But Michael is not a child."

"To Her."

Zoe can feel the strange silver-fish feeling bubbling around the back of her neck. *What else do you know about Michael?* Zoe almost asks. But she would be afraid to hear Luz's answer. She will not go there. She will stay with the game. "Okay, Luz Reyes, if She called Michael, then did She call me?"

"I don't think so."

"Well, that's not fair," Zoe says, aware of the falsity of her tone and of a certain sober reflection in Luz's face.

"Maybe She called you, but you weren't listening. Why are you smiling?"

"Me? I don't know. What you say makes me smile," Zoe says, looking now into her bowl of refrescas, where the ice has melted into a golden slush.

"You don't believe me."

"Luz."

"But you are still nice, Felangela." Why can the Felangela do all these good things and not know what Luz says is true?

"But I am not an angel."

"I know that!" Luz laughs.

"Then what's this felangela business?"

Luz puts down her spoon and covers her left hand with her right. "It's a mean thing."

"That beautiful word means something mean?"

"Mean mean," Luz says, looking up, delighted.

"Mean, mean. Now tell me."

Luz points to Zoe's missing digit.

"What?"

"Fingertip—in Spanish. Because you lost it, your felangela."

Zoe takes a moment to let it sink in. "You mean little teaser," she says and bursts into laughter. The idea of it delights her. *Felangela*, they call her—Josefina and Luz playing a game. She sits back in her chair and looks at Luz. "Felangela!" Zoe exclaims. Luz smiles. Zoe stretches her legs, gazes down at her dingy white slacks. She had better wash them tonight, Zoe thinks. Walk around wrapped in the pale green sheet because in the morning she will have only these clothes once again. How could she have missed that road to her campsite?

"Ask me one more question about Our Lady," Luz says.

"One question about Our Lady is one question too many! Okay, one more. After that we are changing the subject."

"Make a good question. A very good question."

"Hmmnn, let me think." Zoe stands up and walks to the sink with her bowl, rinses it, then refills the loaf pan with water and replaces it in the freezer, wipes off the big knife and puts it away in the drawer. Shakes the moisture out of the big silver bowl. She turns to Luz Reyes, waiting with solemn dark eyes.

"Why does Our Lady call *you*?" Zoe asks.

Oh no, thinks Luz. The question whose answer she does not yet know. She gets up from her chair and walks, stepping first on a white square and then on a black. She closes her eyes. She will wait. If no answer comes, she will say nothing. She opens her eyes and looks into the Felangela's smiling face, her shining clear yellow-brown eyes, the Felangela who is almost as beautiful when she smiles as Our Lady. Zoe Luedke, Felangela, thinks Luz, who put in the window crooked or straight. A small sun bursts open in Luz Reyes' heart. The words come sailing toward her. From Zoe Luedke, Luz has found something that Our Lady wants her to know.

"I have the reason," says Luz.

"Okay, shoot."

"Our Lady calls me because I am little and I love the world."

"Oh, Luz," Zoe says. If only she could pick up this child and keep her safe from all that awaits her. All Zoe's fears about Luz fall from her then. Luz is only a child, little and loving, surrounded by all kinds of sorrows, and yet look what she knows of herself. Look how she opens to life. Zoe can hardly stand it, such an answer, from such a child, a child whose life is crowded with death.

"Why," says Luz, "don't you love it too?"

* * *

That night, as Luz climbs into bed under the glinting white canopy, Zoe smells the faint aroma of roses once again, rising and falling as if on a gentle spring wind. She is just about to ask Luz if she smells it too when Luz lifts her arms and pulls Zoe down for a kiss.

"I want to tell you the real real secret," Luz whispers.

"About what?" The kiss is delicious, but Zoe is weak, drained in her body and mind. It will be all she can do to put in a wash: the yellow dress, her own three-day-worn clothes.

"Our Lady," Luz whispers.

"Oh no, you promised, remember? No more on this subject. It will have to wait until morning." Zoe reaches out and strokes Luz's hair, heavy and damp from her bath. But at least now she gets it, the obsession is becoming a little bit clearer. Luz has turned to Our Lady for comfort. She has just turned a little too far.

CHAPTER 14

Close to midnight, with her clothes and Luz's tumbling around in the dryer and Zoe dozing on the brown couch, the phone startles her awake. Michael, thinks Zoe, no matter that Michael has no idea where she is, no way to reach her, Michael, who seems in this moment, irretrievably gone.

She goes into the kitchen in darkness and feels her way to the phone, expecting to hear his voice. It is Father Bill calling to apologize. He had no time to speak to her earlier and explain. A surgical procedure was done on Josefina in midafternoon. A small catheter has been implanted in her chest. The surgery took less than an hour. Josefina has come through it okay, although Zoe suspects from his tone that it was not a smooth ride. "Tomorrow afternoon," he explains, "Josefina will have her dialysis, and then, God willing, she will respond, right away, the doctors have said, and be ready to go home."

Zoe wants to get down on her knees right there in the kitchen. "I am so glad," she says, surprised at how grateful she feels for this little bit of good news.

"I think I can catch a few hours of actual sleep tonight," Father Bill says. "Now tell me how are you doing? How's Luz?"

Where to begin? Zoe thinks. She should tell him about the campgrounds. No question. That she has taken Luz there. Maybe she should tell him about the sheep in the campgrounds, what an experience it was to see Luz with them, unafraid, welcoming, even. Amazing, really. But maybe not to Father Bill, maybe to him the whole thing would be nothing but disturbing—the campgrounds off limits to Luz. She should wait to tell it in person, Zoe decides. What else can she tell then—that today Luz had asked if her mother could die?

"What's wrong?' he asks.

Zoe pauses a little bit longer. "It's the window I put in for Walt," she says. "It didn't go in right. I think I made some kind of mistake." But when she goes on to describe what has happened and how Walt reacted, Father Bill only laughs. "I'm sorry," he says. "Anytime else it might not seem funny, but now . . ." Then he tells her a little about Walt. How long it has taken him to put the thing in. How he has obsessed for a year over what to do with his window, afraid he would make a mistake.

And after this she feels better, much lighter, sees the whole thing as funny, Walt's fears coming right home to roost. Then she finds all kinds of encouraging things to say about Luz, that her appetite was excellent, listing all that she ate, how helpful Luz was in 29 Palms, friendly and curious. Now Luz has joined in the search for Michael. Again Father Bill laughed, and Zoe is cheered. Luz took her bath, put on her summer pajamas, read to Zoe, quite well, Zoe adds, told all kinds of stories. Luz has quite an imagination, Zoe adds. "Yes," says Father Bill, "we know about that." Though she wouldn't do her summer school homework, but still Luz did not once complain on the long trip to Twenty-Nine Palms, did not complain about bedtime even. "She's really quite something. She helped me so much, I don't even know what to say except Luz is a beautiful child."

"I am so happy to hear this. So grateful," Father Bill says. "Thank you, Zoe. You are a gift to us all."

A gift! Zoe thinks when she hangs up the phone, feeling less guilty for her evasions, then tremendous relief. Even a little bit celebratory and reckless! All kinds of good things, it turns out, have come of this day, a day that started so poorly, with the window, and Walt, those little girls at the diner who had run circles around Luz, taunting her, Zoe is sure. Even the bartender remembering he had a purple flyer—what a surprise to find another all these thousands of miles from Michael's sock drawer—seems in this moment a reason for hope. She goes to the front door and unbolts all three locks, walks outside the blue house in the quiet, looking at the lights in the little stucco houses up and down Mariposa Lane. Not a soul passes on foot. No car engine sounds. No one is even out walking a dog. Nothing threatens to enter the blue house but the night air. The only intruder the rose scent, which hovers behind her while Zoe takes five bold steps and then ten more. Until she is right in the middle of the street, in the middle of the black dot, the velvet black hulk of the San Jacinto Mountains behind her, the uncountable stars, and the expanding High Desert night sky above.

CHAPTER 15

The day before Josefina's homecoming, Zoe and Luz decide they will make the house perfect, but first they will buy Josefina a gift. They drive past the car wash, see the window still there, still tilting, four or five cars lined up and waiting in front of the light-sparking wash. Tomorrow, Zoe thinks, after she leaves Luz she will try and get Walt to let her take another look. She of all people, whose work is meticulous. Maybe by then Walt will have calmed down.

At the Yucca Valley Mall Luz knows just where to go, just what they'll buy: red lipstick, magazines that are in Spanish. At the cosmetics counter of J. C. Penney, Zoe catches herself in the mirror, wild-eyed and disheveled in those same worn-out whites, the tee shirt, the light cotton pants. She's forgotten her appearance entirely these days. All her focus has been on Luz.

At the A&P they find the magazines and then flowers the size of cantaloupes, three white snowball mums, peppery and cool. At the bakery department Luz picks out a coconut cake from the case.

In the blue house they work together to clean every room. They put fresh sheets on the two beds. They scour the bathroom. Luz colors a welcome-home sign in two languages.

In Josefina's bedroom they mop lightly, dust the little dresser, Luz kisses the photo of her father, Raphael Reyes, then replaces it on the wall, puts the magazines she has bought for her mother on the table, tapes up the welcome home sign outside the front door.

Zoe keeps Luz busy every moment she can. Only one round of Sorrowful Mysteries, a three-day record. Not a mention of the forbidden Lady, Zoe notes with relief. No word of the secret Luz has promised to tell.

In the evening when it's cool, they sit on the back step and eat dinner. Soggy sub sandwiches they have bought at the mall that Luz loves. Right across the drive, the Ottos sit at their umbrella table, talking softly over their dinner. "Why don't you join us, dears?" Emily Otto calls in a velvety voice.

"Would you like that?" asks Zoe.

"We can't," says Luz. "We don't go to the house of a stranger."

"But they are neighbors. And you see Emily Otto at—"

"We can wave," Luz says.

"Thanks," says Zoe, standing up and gathering the remains of their sandwiches, "but we were just going in."

Inside the kitchen, the day's heat persists, and though they have scoured the house, the aroma of roses is undeniable, growing stronger in the living room and in the hall. How will she ever explain it? Could it be her fault, some lapse? Something she has or has not done to Luz that has caused it to erupt from the floorboards or seep through the joists? Something Zoe herself has unknowingly brought into the house?

At bedtime Luz asks to say one prayer only: an out-of-order Joyful Mystery, for Josefina, for Michael, for everyone in Infidelity who may need it. Zoe thinks of Father Bill. Luz names Tommy Platz and Amanda, who threw the most rocks.

"What rocks?" Zoe asks, sitting for the final time on the edge of Luz's bed, with Luz in her summer pajamas looking clean and, yes, Zoe thinks, even relaxed.

"Are you ready to know the secret?" Luz asks. "Did you think I forgot?"

I was hoping, Zoe thinks. "I was just waiting," Zoe says.

It is many long weeks that Luz Reyes, too, has been waiting—for the one who could listen and not say she lies. Waiting to tell of the day that her feet took her fast to the campgrounds—the day of the one tree when the winds moved in quickly and cooled her and brought in the face, then the voice of Our Lady very strong. She must try to speak slowly so Zoe can understand every part, but once she begins she can hardly keep up with her words. Like her feet sometimes, Luz's tongue has a mind of its own.

Luz sits up very straight and looks directly at Zoe. "You're ready?"

"Ready as I'll ever be."

Luz takes a big breath and then she begins. "I was on the high swing at recess and I could finally hear it for the first time in life, Her beautiful voice. Her words were like singing so beautiful. Not the bad song. That is Mozote."

"The bad song is Mozote?" Zoe asks.

"Shhh," says Luz, "wait till the end. I was hearing the voice that is music—Our Lady's voice. Then I was crying from the voice because the children in my country, they need the good song, and I started to say a Rosary for them only. Tommy shouted, 'Look at Luz!' And Amanda ran to the swing and the children came running behind her."

"Wait, who is Amanda? Who is Tommy? I forget."

"You already saw her. Amanda is the one with the face like a doll and hair that is red. She threw the first rock. Tommy Platz is my friend that plays wild. He did not throw one rock. He told me, 'Come down, you'll fall.' When I came down, the children were looking at me with the sun beating so hot. Their words were mean. And rocks came from their hands, small ones and big ones that made the mark." Luz points to the place on her cheek, the faint curl of a scar.

Zoe straightens up, fascinated. So this is what happened in the spring. "Didn't anyone stop them from throwing the rocks? Didn't Tommy?"

"Nobody stopped. I could already see Her up in a cloud. And I felt the shining and I felt the rocks. Then my feet started running too fast."

"That's why you ran to the campgrounds? When the children threw rocks at you at school?" At last, Zoe thinks, it is starting to make sense.

No, Luz thinks, that is not why. "I already told you. I didn't do it. Our Lady gave me the fast feet. She sang Her song. She showed Her face. Our Lady gave me the fast feet to run to the campgrounds."

"It was not a good thing those kids did to you," says Zoe.

"Yes it *was* a good thing. It was the best," Luz puts her hand in the middle of her chest. A strong brown hand against pale blue pajamas. When Zoe takes it in hers it is warm, the palm damp. But Luz is not finished, her voice low and insistent, her face so close Zoe can feel the puffs of breath hitting her cheek as Luz speaks. "Because that was the day I knew Our Lady was coming. For me and for Mami, for my country El Salvador, and for all of Infidelity."

Zoe reaches for Luz's other hand, and holds both between her own. How full of feeling she is for this strange troubled child. "What a beautiful child you are."

CHAPTER 16

Father Bill pushes up from the chrome chair, slowly as if he cannot quite lift his weight, his fingertips touching, his thumbs gripping the underside of Josefina's kitchen table, his face set with barely concealed rage.

Zoe should get up as well, but she can't. She feels stuck to her chair, well she is, she is sweating through her thin cotton pants, as she tries to describe the innocent foray she took with Luz. The thick female smell of her mixing with the sickly sweet undertone of roses, faintest in the kitchen at least. The smell that Father Bill has not yet mentioned.

"You took Luz to the campgrounds, even after you knew that the campgrounds were out of bounds."

Once again she tries to explain. Again, she is speaking of sheep. What does he care about two bighorn sheep? He has reached the refrigerator, leaning against the cool metal. He does not want to hear Zoe's explanation. She has no idea about Luz, the tendencies which had revealed themselves in the campgrounds in late spring. Those mystical gifts he does not believe in that he has succeeded in quelling. There, he has admitted it. He has succeeded in quelling them.

He takes a breath and looks at Zoe. It is better to stand across the room from her. This hapless woman, this Zoe Luedke with the clear wide-set eyes and musical voice, who he had believed was going to be something extraordinary for them, the one who had been sent. Is he a child himself that he still believes such things? She has turned out to have no judgment at all. Not for installing a window or for caring for a child. And who knows where else it is lacking? She is broke. Her husband has fled. Still, he knows he cannot blame Luz on Zoe. If there is blame for Luz it is his. "Did anything happen to Luz in the campgrounds?" he asks. "Did she say or do anything that seemed in any way alarming?"

"Alarming? Not really," Zoe says.

At least it is not what he fears. Neither of the things she had mentioned is cause for alarm. Luz had no dissociative episode in the campgrounds. She did not fall into transport in Zoe's presence. She touched the sheep. She had walked among the Joshua trees.

They can hear her now, her high laugh, Josefina's occasional admonition, the low undertone of their voices at the far end of the house. Josefina is settled in her bed, Luz has not left her side. The house is very clean, Father Bill thinks. And there were lovely flowers, white snowball mums beside Josefina's bed. There is a coconut cake in a box in the refrigerator, which Josefina cannot eat. Zoe has tried, he thinks. She is not a bad person. But Luz has spent hours in prayer in her presence, and the house reeks of roses.

"Why didn't you just follow the list?"

How can Zoe answer? The list did not seem to apply. It seemed to get lost. "I tried," she said. Now she should really get up, make her apology, say good-bye. She has failed, she can see that, failed with Luz. Failed with the window. She had better get up and leave. But there is something she wants to say, what is it? In the face of Father Bill's censure she has seen herself in a way that makes her feel wrong in her thoughts, in her choices. Wrong to the core. He has not said the word "irresponsible," yet that is how she feels now. That is how he thinks of her anyway. Zoe wriggles in the seat, lifts up, pulling the fabric of her pants away from her thighs. She is hot, and she stinks. She can smell herself. She needs a shower. What will she do, now that she is going back to the campgrounds where no showers exist? A shower or a bath, or, even better, a swim. Long Lake is a clear mile across, small sandy inlets, great dark blue-green pines. She used to swim across Long Lake every summer from the time she was twelve. For years there was a law forbidding boats with gas-powered motors and the water was pure and dark, bracing and cold straight through August.

She wishes she could tell Father Bill the way that Luz looked with the sheep, or walking among the Joshuas. But Zoe cannot describe it in a way that will carry the quality of Luz that she has glimpsed, rare and unusual, she believes, Zoe, who can look into wood and see grain. Father Bill does not want to hear it—the beauty that she sees in this little girl, Luz. He is pushing it away; she can feel his resistance as if he has put up his hands. As if he is saying, *don't tell me so much.*

Now the small triumphs of the past twenty-four hours have been spoiled: the way Josefina had responded so quickly to the treatment, the look of relief on Luz's face when Josefina came into the house, in sandals and blue dress, lipstick and freshly washed hair, the neckline of the dress hiding the gauze of her bandage. These small gifts have been spoiled for him and he is back in the pit of his misery. The blue house seems poisoned with the dense smell of roses.

In this light, everything Zoe has done with Luz is wrong. In this light, under Father Bill's questions, in the mirror of his distress Zoe sees all her misjudgments: play-acting with plaster saints, the endless rounds of out-of-order Rosaries. "How many times did you sit with her in prayer?" "In prayer?" she had echoed. *Is that what it was?* "I did what she did. What she seemed to want."

"And she wanted to go to the campgrounds?"

"No, I did. I had no clothes."

She has not done justice to it, not to Luz, not to herself. Something had happened between them, something good, Zoe thinks, even if she can't give it a name. And though she would like to say that she thinks the whole problem with Luz is her obsession with a certain lady, she does not want to betray Luz and whatever serves Luz, this little girl with her life so crowded with death.

He takes out the two hundred dollars and walks to the table and puts the bills down.

"I can't take the money," says Zoe and stands up. "I'm sorry. I really thought I was helping. I'll go in and say good-bye."

CHAPTER 17

Luz lies beside Josefina, worrying her hand above the bandage she cannot touch. A square of gauze lightly taped just over the place on her mother where Luz likes to rest.

Josefina takes Luz's face in her hand. Solemn and guilty, the red lipstick mouth.

"Who let you put on such makeup."

"You know."

"Who gave you that perfume, mi hija? You don't have fever?"

"No," says Luz. "I am cool." Luz reaches to kiss her neck.

"Careful." But already Josefina feels better. Her daughter, that is her medicine. The best of all. The nearness of Luz is beginning to ease the pain. "Now I will tell you a secret," Josefina says, covering the access with a cupped hand. Luz smiles, puts her ear to Josefina's mouth in the customary way, closes her eyes and waits for the secret to start. Her mother tells wonderful secrets, each one taking away sorrow, like bringing in good dreams and sending out bad. "The doctors have discovered something strong in my blood, so now they are going to take from me only to give it to others. Don't worry, the body can quickly make more blood. Can you share me? I must go three, maybe four times a week, and sit with the needle for hours. I will take you to watch it so you will know."

"Yes," says Luz. She doesn't like the word "needle." It spoils the story. But Luz will not dwell on it. She will not tell her mother she does not want to watch it. "They will do it to help make people strong?"

This is a good thing, a big thing. She loves this new piece of her mother, this gift that she has that they have discovered in the hospital. She moves her head slightly from her mother's mouth, puts her head on the clean white pillow; her feet remain on the floor as her mother has said that they must.

"Good-bye, Luz," calls the voice of Zoe. Luz opens her eyes. Zoe is standing in the doorway, very tall, far away.

"Come in," says Josefina. "I want to thank you for Luz."

"Oh, that's all right," Zoe says. "I don't want to . . ." Her voice dies out. She is thinking of Father Bill's accusations.

"My daughter is happy. And my house is so beautiful. You worked so hard. Please, come back."

"Please, come back," says Luz, "And thank you for me."

"You're very welcome," says Zoe.

Luz says her words without moving. She is so still that even before Zoe Luedke-Felangela has left the room she has begun to turn gold.

"What kind of thank-you is that?" says Josefina.

"She knows," says Luz with her red smiling mouth.

"The Felangela was good? She makes you happy from letting you do as you wish? Not like me who makes you do what you hate. You like her better because she lets you stay home from summer school and cover your face with my makeup that you have no doubt ruined? And that perfume! If you don't wash it off, I won't let you return to my bed. But don't worry. I am here for you now to make you go to the summer school and do everything that you hate so you will have a good future."

"And be bossy," Luz says, quite happy now.

"Very bossy. The most bossy."

Luz listens to the words of her mother that make her happy in her heart because of the music. Because of her language that she loves that is so full of songs. The words do not matter. Her mother can say anything. Even crazy things like Luz wears the perfume of Zoe. Zoe has no perfume. Zoe smells the way snow smells, Luz thinks, though she was only a baby when she smelled the snow. But now Luz is happy in two ways. Happy she told Zoe the secret that will stay and maybe grow as Our Lady has grown inside Luz. Happy her mother did not die in the hospital. Now Luz can breathe—all the way in and float with her feet still on the floor. She and her mother are one thing again.

CHAPTER 18

On the morning of his son's play-off game, Walt wakes early, afraid he'll be late. His bedroom is filled with a midday brightness, and right away he knows the worst has happened. He has overslept and missed his son's game. He sits up, heart hammering in panic, leans over and checks the alarm clock, his wrist watch, and the travel alarm lined up on the mission oak table beside him. All three read 6:46. He is fine.

He looks straight ahead at the old six-drawer dresser, the oak closet door beside it, and then turns to the uncurtained sliding glass door at his right where the light is strongest, staring like a man who has locked eyes with the sun and can't pull away. He tries to decide where he's seen light like this, which has presence, as if it weighs something. It is almost opaque. Looking out at his backyard, he sees only dim curves and lines, the Teddy Bear cholla, rock fountain, the trailer for his daughter—all ghosts of themselves in the eerie white light. He thinks of his father and fishing, the shimmering iridescence of trout leaving traces of opal in his mind.

For a moment he considers he is dreaming until he puts his hand on himself, leans back against the pillows and gives himself to the pleasures of his rhythm and his own silken skin. At least he knows he's awake now and not dreaming that light.

He forces himself to get out of bed, slides open the door, and steps naked into his yard. No neighbors for miles. It is beastly hot.

Mid-nineties, he guesses, maybe more. If this keeps up Ryan is in for one hell of a day. Why expect anything less from the dog days of summer? He does. Walt Adair expects the gods to line up for his son. He expects no afternoon smog and an unseasonable seventy-eight degrees, if not here, then in Fullerton. He expects the gentlest of breezes and he lets the sky know this, right there, naked in his own cactus garden, and why not? It's the least they can do. And look what they give him, this impossible light, this soon-to-be-record heat.

In all he has asked of this day, he has overlooked weather. Instead he has talked daily to Ryan after practice, reminded him ad nauseam to hold back with the sinker till he has them expecting the fastball. Assured Gwen three times at least he will be there, let her insults breeze by him. He even managed to get his daughter on the phone, asked if she liked yellow or white gold. "Oh, Dad, please don't buy me anything, we just want to see you." The earrings he bought her are oval with tiny blue sapphires, her birthstone and also the color of her lovely round eyes.

He walks back inside through his bedroom, to the hallway and into the bathroom and turns on the water in the small prefab shower. Amazing what he's grown used to, amenity-wise. Otherwise as well. This place is nine hundred square feet, his custom-built Newport house close to nine thousand. Stepping awkwardly into the small shower, he thinks of his white marble bath (the size of the living room in this house), the steam shower for two, and the ledge where he used to sit and scrub his tennis-calloused feet. No tennis, no calluses, and a small pot belly from no exercise. He will not be appearing naked for inspection before his family, he reminds himself, and is startled to hear his own laugh. Then he pees long and with great satisfaction.

When he has soaped up, he puts his head back and leans into the too-thin flow of the water. He is happy beyond reason this morning. He lets himself bask in it now, the shaking off of sleep, the water like a new skin on his skin, his body's persistent arousal. Today for a whole day and well into the night he will be with his family. And he will be fine.

The night before, he had set out his clothes for the day. Now they wait on a black kitchen stool next to the counter, where the green Newport Tigers cap always sits. The blue oxford (he has gotten pretty good at ironing his shirts now) on a wooden hanger, and on the second stool the polished cordovan loafers that he will transfer to the back of the Civic. He slips on a white tee shirt, then the chinos, which he also had ironed and which hold up quite well even on a two-hour drive, white socks, an old pair of tennis shoes. He has forgotten the socks he will wear with the cordovans. He goes back down to the hall to his bedroom, opens his sock drawer, and picks out a pair of brown silk he has not worn in years. They will feel good. And when his family sees him, he will look like his old self, down to his feet.

He has planned to go early to the car wash, which he usually opens a little before eight. He'll keep it open till ten or ten thirty the latest, and then, for the first time in three years, he will close down on a Friday.

He has prepared for this day for a week, put all of his energy into it, in fact, which helped him get past his window fiasco. The whole thing compounded by the behavior of the one man in Infidelity that Walt considers a genuine friend, Father Bill, who has just disappeared on him. No call to say how Josefina is doing since she's come back, no apology for his part in what has turned out to be quite an expensive mistake for Walt. Father Bill had just left Walt guessing as to whether Josefina was living or dead. Josefina had to walk into his wash herself for him to know she was fine, with the energy he has not seen in weeks and the swollen look gone from her face. There she was eight ten in the morning, in her pink uniform and the heavy white shoes on her way in to work. "I am back from the dead," she had said, "I hope you did not worry too much after seeing me in my condition."

"Don't even think about it. I'm just glad to see you, period." But *what* condition? he had wanted to say. She had acted like he knows it, but he doesn't, not its name or its anything, and he sees very plainly the big square of gauze that pokes through her uniform right over her heart. There she is smiling with those flashing black eyes, throwing him off with that way she has so he can't bring himself to ask, *What condition? You know, you've never really said.*

"And for my daughter's behavior, I am sorry she got wild with you. She was frightened, you know? But still, that is not a reason."

"She was certainly frightened that night," says Walt. "And now how is she?"

"She went back to summer school. Don't ask about the homework. But I made her do everything, all the math worksheets, so she will get credit. We are all back to normal."

"She was well taken care of in your absence? No complaints?" He can't bring himself to say the name Zoe Luedke, though he thinks it. He can't escape thinking it. He hears it enough, *Zoe Luedke, that long-legged beauty, who took Walt for six hundred dollars.*

"Luz was so happy with Sewey. She talks all the time about Sewey this, Sewey that. But you have only disappointment from her, I am sorry to see. Thank you, but I cannot drink coffee. The doctors are changing my diet."

And then she had asked about his children. She always asked about them, and he often spoke of them to her. So he'd told her that Ryan had made starting pitcher and that he was going to Ryan's Little League playoff game. She gave him the smile that could keep him going straight through the morning.

"I wish you every good luck. Let your son be the winner, but the most important thing is that you will be with your family."

"Hey, I've missed you," he said. "Don't be a stranger."

"You will come to my house for eating next week. We will celebrate your boy."

Tactful, too. Only the mildest reference to his window. After seeing Josefina, Walt is immensely relieved. He even changes his mind about Luz. What he thought had happened with her at the blue house he has decided now was all in his mind. The face of that splendid woman overriding Luz's little face when he brought her to look at the window? That too, he must have imagined. No possible way it could be real.

Tonight with his own family at the restaurant after the game, whatever the outcome, they'll celebrate on him. He will waylay the waiter, getting up from the table just after they've ordered, so there's no question as to who gets the bill. He does not want Gwen to insist she will pay, or to argue, nothing that will give his children a moment's unease.

At a little after seven, as he's going outside to turn off his fountain, he reaches for the doorknob and is aware of a peculiar vibration in his hand, both hands, in fact, his feet, his forehead, and even his throat, his body about to do something off—his heart maybe or some arterial event in his brain that will land him in the emergency room of the High Desert Hospital, where, very likely, his body will pick this day to die. That's just guilt, thinks Walt, that's just what Father Bill keeps warning him to watch for—ways he is punishing himself—because the truth is he is happy, pure and simple. The sensation in his body is no doubt excitement, something he's not used to these days, he tells himself as he walks out the door and goes to the side of the house to turn off his fish fountain. He flips the switch. The water ceases running from the mouth of the trout. There is absolute silence and, under the strange morning glare, absolute white. Everything's pearly. He stops to admire, though it hurts his eyes to look: the stones, the water, the trailer, *Jen's trailer*, he thinks. Everything this morning is washed in a light already too bright for him to look at bare-eyed. And he can't find his sunglasses. He hopes they're not lost. He'll need them for driving and then for the game. Maybe he's left them in the car.

After he has locked his front door, he rechecks his pants pocket for the box with Jen's earrings, and with the shirt on the hanger, the shoes and the socks in their case, the green Tigers cap on his head, makes his way to the Civic. When his things are stowed and he is seated, he places the cap on the passenger seat, then feels around the gearshift for his sunglasses and finds them. Not lost at all. There they are, waiting, a very good sign.

CHAPTER 19

On the last day of her stay in the campgrounds, Zoe wakes to the light flooding through the walls of her green tent. When she opens the flap and looks out, she can hardly see through to the mountain; the light is dense and granular as snowfall.

Unnatural, she thinks, and wonders what Luz would think of the campgrounds today. Would the animals still come to her in this light? Zoe was going to stop at the blue house today. She would see Josefina and Luz. A quick good-bye visit. Josefina had insisted. "Come for a little party. She finishes summer school." Zoe was going to have to hang around, kill some time, leave later than she had planned. "I'll bring the cake," Zoe offered. "But you didn't find Michael," said Luz taking the phone from her mother. Zoe held her breath, afraid of what Luz might say. *Don't go, please*. "Bring a coconut cake," said Luz. "Of course," Zoe said.

When Zoe steps outside, she has to don sunglasses just to disassemble the tent. She pulls out an end pole, and the whole thing falls in a heap. A fitting end for her stay in this part of the world. She gathers the tent in her arms, drags it to the Dart and hurls it into the trunk, zips up her duffle, and stows her empty water containers before starting the familiar drive to the ranger station at Cottonwood where she will check out of the campgrounds. Then up to the auto shop for the Nova having earned just enough jobbing in at a shop in Twenty-Nine Palms to pay for her car and an uneventful drive east. As she drives up Park Boulevard, she keeps the windows of the Dart wide open, although it is beastly hot. Zoe has grown used to the noisy desert stillness, the odd humming music that resides in the silence. Grown to welcome the sight of the climbers dotting the mountains in blazing neon spandex and bisecting colored ropes, the endless stretches of desert long and white, the dry brown extrusions that the photos in the visitor center show in spring, risen up in bright colors, orange poppy-covered hillsides, the tall ocotillo with its spiky red blooms, and the Joshuas, Luz's trees.

"*Have you ever been West?" Michael had asked the day he showed up at her shop. "The Mojave? Beautiful. You should go some time.*"

Now she had.

When Zoe gets onto the freeway, the light nearly blinds her. It is worse than the light in the campgrounds, denser, more glaring; it's like looking through midday snow. The sun should be behind her, and yet it seems to be hitting her right in the eyes. She has to drive slowly, barely noting when she has passed Our Lady of Guadalupe—pea green shingles lost behind a scrim—the houses in the hill district all but erased. Less than a half mile beyond them, the traffic in front of her is stalled, a line of red brake lights dimmed in the uncertain distance.

Higher up and farther ahead she sees a blur of blue neon. Immaculate Autos. Walt must have turned on the sign. She has drifted into the slow lane and now sees there's a crowd on the sidewalk facing the window. Walt stands before them holding an oversized umbrella, white and blue, Father Bill in his clerical robe gesturing to the crowd.

Then Walt hands the umbrella to Father Bill, steps forward, and raises his hands as if he is going to push or bless someone. A few people begin to stir, a step or two back, a little apart. Zoe looks through the crowd, sees nothing at first and then she sees perfectly—the sturdy brown legs, the skirt of the yellow dress, the soles of the sandals. Oh, please, Zoe asks, let this not be what it is. Make it another, any other child, not kneeling but fallen—an accident, a trick of the light.

CHAPTER 20

It was just about eight when Walt saw her that morning. She was out there on the sidewalk staring through the window of his office. He had looked up, checking traffic, and there she was. At first he didn't know it was Luz. The light made it hard to discern her face. But one thing he did know, it was a child. He went outside, walked down to the place where she stood, asked how she got there, what she was seeing, where her mother was. She said she was looking at wings, that a lady had sent her. All the stuff that he knew she'd made up.

When he bent to touch her she was hot as a furnace, and there was something about her smell, like someone had doused her in rosewater. *Sun poisoned, maybe*, he thought.

He took her into his office, sat her down on the couch, got the ice, wiped her down. She looked at him straight, her black eyes so intense for a second he felt she could see into his mind. Then she smiled and he relaxed to a place he had no business being, heard himself sigh, felt himself falling, though he was right there beside her on his sofa. Somehow he had sat down. Inside his body he began to feel warmth. Like coming to a warm spot in the cold of the ocean. He relaxed even deeper. They stared into each other's eyes like lovers. The warmth in his body finding spaces to congregate. Little pulses in his throat, in his heart, in his gut. The spaces wheeled and pulsed like tiny new stars. Not a word passed between them. They just sat on the sofa in absolute silence in a heaven of looking, eyes to eyes, the light charging through the crooked new window. It was gorgeous. It lasted for an eon or a moment. And then he was back.

"What the hell," he said, and shot up from the couch. He wanted to walk into the street and thank everything that had ever been and would ever be for giving him this moment, which, when he got right down to it, was simply an immense dose of ordinary love—discounting the little zones whirring in his body. But love for what? Not strictly speaking for Luz, *for himself*, for what he'd just felt. It kept coming at him, or through him, a softness, a rich flooding warmth, growing till he couldn't hold any more. *What the hell is this?* he thought. Whatever it is, it is wonderful.

"How 'bout we call your mother?" he said.

That's when she runs for the door—and him after her. He is right with her when she makes it back to the sidewalk. This time when he reaches for her, she fights him. She kicks out hard when he tries to lift her, the print of her sandal leaving a mark on his chinos just above the groin.

"Shit," he says. Now he is going to have to go home and change for Ryan's game. And he hasn't yet opened the wash.

Then Luz turns her head and looks around. For a moment he thinks it is over, that she is about to stand up, take his hand, ask him to drive her to summer school or wherever she is supposed to be. She looks up at him. A succession of faces begins to eclipse her face, or rise through it, erasing Luz's features completely. He hardly has time to absorb one face when another appears as if someone is flipping the pages of a fine book of portraits—much too fast. They are men's faces mostly, and not one that he recognizes, but he knows they are holy—saints, maybe, faces he has never seen—not in the papers or magazines, not in books, not on TV or in movies, not even faces he had dreamed. He wonders if maybe Gandhi will pop up, or if Gandhi is even a saint, but then comes the woman whose face he had seen the night they discovered the window was crooked—what a beauty—and Walt wants to shout for the flickering to stop, but on it goes. All of the faces are beautiful in ways he can hardly describe. Wise and deep in the way of saints. Then just like that they are gone. He kneels to study her, black eyes on the window, mouth moving, no sound. What is she, anyway, that this stuff can come to him from her? Or is it all hallucination? Is he quite possibly nuts? Can he dare to reveal it—to whom? Father Bill?

Now she is making a sound, low and far back in her throat. "Mmmm." He'd like to close his eyes and stay there beside her, but inside are customers and a schedule for the day—his family, his son. He is already off it.

"Mmmmm," says Luz, like she's dreaming of something delicious.

CHAPTER 21

By the time Father Bill arrives, running down the walk to the window, his black robe trailing behind him, Luz appears light as spun sugar, her color a rich rosy-gold. Father Bill sees the splendor that is Luz and goes straight to the curb, leans dangerously close to the oncoming traffic, and heaves up the remains of his previous night's dinner.

When he looks back, he can see right through her. Luz is a radiant shell—not even living perhaps. She reminds him of a story he had read at seminary, a great Hindu saint who one morning slipped out of his body at prayer. Hours later, a disciple brushed past and the body fell over, light as a husk.

Then a young girl comes toward him, Bobbie's girl, Skye, stepping out of the gold that holds Luz. She is dense with flesh as the living should be, safely anchored in color: purple swath of hair, black tee shirt, pink stripes down her black climber's shorts. She is crying.

"Father Bill," she beseeches, afraid he will leap straight into traffic. She strips off her shirt and reaches out to blot the vomit on the front of his surplice. "You've ruined your beautiful robe!"

"What's wrong with you? Cover yourself." He turns his gaze away from her breasts and shrinks from her hand.

Skye will not remember, and only Father Bill will carry it, how sweetly she came toward him, the tender white cones of her breasts as she lifted her arm to blot the stain that had already ruined the silk.

"Go into the office. Tell Walt to give you his shirt. Get him out here."

Now he sidesteps past Skye and enters the space where the light is most intense and Luz the child is barely to be seen. He will touch Luz's shoulder and bring her back from the illusion of this dangerous light. "Luz," he says softly and kneels.

Up close Luz is vivid and etched with the surpassing sweetness of one of her Madonnas of the Centuries, a nimbus of gold more beautiful than even the Renaissance masters could paint. He squats beside her, places his palm on her shoulder, curls his fingers on the bones, feeling the curve of the scapular. She does not respond to his touch, but neither does she fall. The fabric of her dress is warmly damp. She is living, that much he knows.

Now his eyes start to burn; he can't stop from blinking. Any moment he will look as if he is crying. Yet he feels no sadness, he is emptied of feeling, quite calm and relaxed, the state he achieves when he's deep in his prayers: as if time has quietly stopped. He shifts his position to study her eyes, squatting directly in front of her face, elbows on his knees, hands together, palms barely touching. It is the posture Luz's father, Dr. Raphael Reyes, so often adopted when surrounded by his students or the rapt campesinos he had been teaching in secret for years. Immediately, Luz shuffles past him, keeping her eyes on the window.

"Querida," he whispers, and begs her in Spanish for her mother's sake, for the memory of her father, for the sake of her mother's employment, for the green-winged quetzal and for every living thing that she cherishes, "don't do this to us."

CHAPTER 22

At nine thirty, with Father Bill still on the sidewalk, with Luz encircled by his parishioners, a host of onlookers, twenty, or so, maybe more, Walt's palms start to sweat and things start to fall from his hands. Credit cards slip to the floor, a stack of coupon books slides into the trash, a can of Dr. Pepper spills over his counter, and Chico Platz, whom he's called in to help, has to run to the bathroom for the paper towels that have disappeared from the shelf below. Walt has allowed too many customers into his wash. There is a line from the door to the drink cabinets. People sprawl on the couch, stand at the window, deliberating over Luz. It is nine forty-five. The cars are backed up in the entry lane. Finally, Walt goes back out.

"Would you like me to get Josefina?" Walt asks.

"I can do it."

Walt holds out his hand, an offering, a reminder that his friend must stand up. The smell of vomit is overpowering. It's a wonder it doesn't make Luz sick to her stomach, Luz's hum now deepens to a growl. Father Bill's parishioners perk up their ears and begin to move closer.

Father Bill looks at Walt with alarm as he rises. He turns to the crowd. Expectation rises. Relief. He will speak to them at last. He will tell them what this is.

"For God's sake step back," he says. They don't move.

"Can't you see there is nothing? Go home."

Everyone stunned as much by his demeanor as by what he has said, the harshness in his voice, the priest's complete indifference to their withheld joy. *Nothing?*

"Get back," Walt echoes.

They shuffle a little—small steps to the side, then move a little bit back.

"How can I bring Josefina to this?"

Even now, knowing he will never arrive at the Fullerton College ball field in time to wish his son luck, give his daughter the earrings, settle down in the stands next to the woman he still calls his wife, Walt considers whether he owes it to Father Bill, to himself, to everyone on the sidewalk and perhaps most of all to Luz not to let one more moment pass without trying to convey to his friend what has happened to him. He should take Father Bill into his office, clear out the customers and try to describe it, how those faces came to him through her face, how many there were of those probable saints, how clearly he saw them, the dimensions he senses are waiting, things he has never imagined. The joy this has brought is still anchored within him, a calm, steady sense of the possible largeness of life.

"Father Bill," he says, putting his arm on his friend's shoulder, "Maybe you should take off the robe."

Father Bill looks down at himself as if he has forgotten what he is wearing. "Can you help me?" he asks. "Don't let it touch the ground." When the robe is off, Father Bill stands in his white tee shirt, sweat-stained, ungainly, a derelict who has lost the ability to care for himself.

"Wait," says Walt and races to the back of the wash to his car, opens the door, grabs the blue oxford shirt he had ironed and brings it back to his friend. "Go ahead, put it on. It will be easier for Josefina if she sees you looking nice."

Father Bill looks at the shirt.

"Trust me. Bad news goes down easier in a blue cloth shirt. Good news as well."

"All right."

"Go inside. Wash up."

"I think I will."

"Get some coffee. Take some with you on the drive."

Father Bill nods, hands Walt the umbrella, takes the shirt. "I want you to promise that you'll stay right here until I get back. Don't let anyone touch her, don't let her touch anybody—"

"Don't worry. I won't leave. I'll be her hawk."

Father Bill says nothing to Luz, ignores the throng as he starts down the sidewalk, his steps a little tentative as if he is not sure his own legs will carry him.

A few of his parishioners follow him, "Go down to the church. Get everything ready for tonight. Do what we planned," he tells them. Then Father Bill goes into the car wash office and into the bathroom to wash. The shirt is too small. He does the best he can, does not tuck it into his pants, leaves the bottom three buttons undone.

Seeing the way Father Bill looked, Chico Platz will tell people later, he was afraid for a second that maybe Luz had died.

Once Father Bill drives off, Walt is barraged with questions.

Walt Adair takes a long breath. There are thirty or more standing on the sidewalk, not a one of them he cannot see through, past the thick encrustations of years to the bright hearts of their yearning. He looks into the face of Emily Otto to the girl she still is, shining with life, then looks at Wren, her beloved beside her, ninety-three this fall, and ageless.

Something has come to this sidewalk, Walt thinks, and I do not know its name. He stands before them with his embarrassed tears, the blue and white umbrella, and the unaccustomed weight of a love-heavy heart, the pungent robe of Father Bill over his arm. He raises the umbrella to still their voices, and before him they open like blossoms. *Ah*, he thinks, *it is true*. And in this moment Walt Adair ceased to doubt. Whatever Luz Reyes had brought, or was being brought through her, it was going to be beautiful.

CHAPTER 23

Zoe stands in the back of the crowd holding her breath, her hands on her throat as if she's arrived on the scene of an accident, afraid she will cry out or scream.

"What is she doing?" Zoe asks the man beside her, vaguely familiar, the shock of red hair. She has seen him in that group at a noisy back table in the diner.

"Can't say."

She has only to take a few steps to where Luz kneels beside Walt, slip under the umbrella, put her hands around Luz's face, look in her eyes to pull Luz out of the far place. She knows this child's secrets, the things she imagines that keep her safe. Any moment Luz may do something awful, cry out—fall to the ground. Bring into fulfillment Father Bill's fears. Or someone else might fall, or declare that they're seeing a vision, and then they are in for it. One of those crazy visions, Jesus on a taco shell in El Paso, Texas, the bee-sting savior in a man's beefy chest that she has seen in a photograph somewhere, a billboard-sized Our Lady on a glass-fronted complex in Clearwater, Florida. Our Lady in Walt's single-pane horizontal slider. Her window, her crooked window.

Oh, Luz, thinks Zoe, *you were supposed to be in summer school. You did all the homework. This was your last day.*

What a mess this has become. Better she should slip away now, drive to Platz's garage, swap the Dart for the Nova, leave Infidelity without saying good-bye—leave Luz swirling out of control, the child of this terrible light.

But instead, without thinking, throwing logic to the high desert wind, Zoe starts through the crowd, maneuvering past lawn chairs, ducking her head past the unfurled umbrellas, the parishioners of Our Lady of Guadalupe settling in as if on some invisible beach, while Zoe, on instinct, runs to the shore on a blinding hot day to rescue a child who is drowning.

Walt turns around and meets her gaze, his eyes entirely changed. *Who are you again?* she wonders, his eyes, the light that surrounds them both like a prelude to sleep or enchantment. Soft. Softer, the silence like stepping through fog. Luz's tender back, the black braids like gold in this light, a cocoon of gold so palpable Zoe imagines incipient wings hidden under the folds of Luz's bright yellow dress.

"What happened," whispers Zoe as she kneels behind Luz.

"She walked to me," Walt says, his voice thick and indistinct as if he has just woken up.

Walked on fast feet? Walked like she walked to the campgrounds in spring? Impossibly fast invisible feet. Walked because she was called?

"What do you mean? How do you know she walked?"

"Shhh," says Walt. "Just sit for a moment. Relax. Everything's fine." She believes him, or rather she neither believes nor disbelieves. Belief seems out of the question. What has happened to the man that his face looks so ringingly alive? She sits down on the hot sidewalk right beside Luz, inhales Luz's smell, the faint breath of rose. Through the gold haze that surrounds her, Luz's skin burns a deep orange-pink. Around her a border of tiny gold threads wave like cilia. *What is this child?* Zoe thinks, and reaches her hand through the light. Before Walt can tell her, "Don't touch," she has traced a circle around Luz's left wrist, drawn her finger up Luz's arm.

"Hey, my friend, I was just on my way to the A&P to buy you a coconut cake."

Luz neither moves nor responds.

"Is coconut still your favorite?"

"Ummm," says Luz from a faraway place.

"Yes," says Zoe, "umm. We love coconut cake."

"Did she speak?" someone in the crowd calls out.

"Did she say 'cake'?" asks Emily Otto.

Now Luz begins to shift to the left, her head advancing by quarter inches until her gaze falls directly upon Zoe's. Luz smiles through half-lidded eyes, gives a small nod.

Come out, come out wherever you are Luz, Zoe thinks, and is just about to say it when Luz looks right at her. Something barrels at Zoe with the brightness of a bearable sun, a firestorm of light from the depths of the engine that is Luz. *Turn away*, a voice within Zoe warns: *don't look at her eyes*. Too late. Back Zoe goes falling onto the sidewalk like an upended swan in slow motion, a sound rising out of her, the rich throaty warble that hums out when she is losing herself into pleasure. On and on it goes, rising and falling long after she is downed. A few sitters rise from their chairs for a better look. There lies Zoe Luedke for all to see, sprawled on the sidewalk, those much-noted legs, one sandal kicked off, her whole half-clad length on display. Knocked out by the child.

For a moment no one reacts. Walt appears stunned. He drops the umbrella. Luz continues to nod, as if she approves Zoe's fall. Then the first shouts go up in the crowd and some of the women spontaneously weep. The rest look around as if they're not sure they've actually seen what they've seen and have to confirm it by the shock on a neighboring face.

"I knew it," declares Emily Otto, the first one to rise from her lawn chair. "I knew last week from the smell. This child is bringing great things."

And with that Luz snaps back to herself and scrambles to her feet, puts her hand on her head and pulls off the green baseball cap.

"Who gave me this?" And then she looks down and sees Zoe and lets out a cry.

Zoe opens her eyes onto the piercing blue sky, so beautiful it hurts. Or perhaps it's the back of her head, maybe both. Immediately, she gathers her limbs and sits up, one hand (the one with that finger) cradling the back of her skull, her focus drawn down from the ethers not by the bump she can already feel; not by Luz, standing beside her calling her name; not even by Walt Adair in his wide-shouldered, bare-chested, creamy-skinned nearness kneeling anxiously toward her—but by someone inside Walt's office who is beckoning to her through the off-kilter window. What? Zoe inquires, for now the person seems to be speaking. *Keep going*! Keep going where? Zoe asks in her mind, to what? Zoe's whole body trembles. *It's all right*, says the voice. *No need to worry. Don't strain yourself. You're just fine. In fact you are superb.* There is no one at the window. No one is speaking and yet Zoe can hear it, a voice as clear as her own.

With enormous effort, she turns from the window to the commotion of real voices swirling around her. To Luz Reyes, looking healthy and miserable, her color restored—exactly the child that Zoe has known.

"Come here," Zoe says, as she reaches out to Luz and draws her close.

"Do you have to go to the hospital?" Luz asks. Two times she has seen her own mother taken by ambulance after a fall.

"Oh no. It's nothing. I am fine." Zoe still feels the force drawing her gaze to the window, wanting her (how can she knows this?) to look once again. *Listen! Do you see your own wonderfulness?* Only with great effort is she able to keep her attention on Luz. "Why did you fall?" asks Luz. Zoe cannot answer. What was it that knocked her on her back like that—and in public? Now Luz is caressing Zoe's hair. Zoe winces. "You got a bump!" says Luz. And all of a sudden Zoe begins to laugh. She feels wonderful, unreasonably happy and safe. "You're sure you're okay?" Walt asks, his gaze so acute, his umbrella so wide, his nakedness looming over her so generous and musky she nearly forgets where she is all over again.

"Absolutely. Really, I'm great. How 'bout you, Luz?"

"Good," Luz whispers into Zoe's ear, "but why are the church people here? Why isn't Walt wearing a shirt?"

When Zoe fails to answer, Luz turns to Walt standing up now, the umbrella upside down on the ground, hands in his pockets. "Honey," he says. What can he tell her that will not frighten Luz half to death?

Luz pushes out from Zoe's embrace, grinds the toe of her new red sandal on the sidewalk scuffing out what is left of the shine. "Why is everyone staring at me?"

And before they can figure out what to do next, Luz takes off on visible feet, looking gravely insulted and for all the world like she is about to cry.

CHAPTER 24

Father Bill is lost in a paradise of fan palms and faultless white stucco, the houses, the walls that enclose them. He can't find the one where Josefina works, an address he knows by heart. He drives down the wide, empty streets, not a car or a person in sight, all the streets identical, all the numbers elusive. She has said that the Palms reminds her of the neighborhood in San Salvador where she grew up, San Benito, where the wealthy and the privileged live protected by walls of brick and stone embedded with shards of glass sharp enough to slice off a hand. The Palms is San Benito bleached, lacking character or color, or the mercy of shade.

In the nights in San Benito there was often the clamor of gunfire and in the mornings it was not uncommon to find a body propped outside the gate, the eyes gouged out, limbs missing, the thumbs tied together behind the back when the arms had been spared. In those years the bodies or parts of a body might be found anywhere. No way to escape them. No neighborhood safe.

As Father Bill reaches the end of the street, he sees he has been driving in circles. He tries not to think of Luz on the sidewalk, the gathering crowd. Of Walt waiting for him to return. He continues the Rosary he has been saying on the drive. His prayer remains thin, at a distance, his heart closed down by his fear. The sweat collects under his arms, staining Walt's shirt.

Driving back to the street he has come from, he damns the perfection of fan palms that tower above him, the braided brown trunks, each tree costing thousands, enough to dress and feed a whole village, build a small school in the country. Buy farm equipment and books.

At the corner he turns left when all logic tells him he should have turned right and finds the street that has eluded him, the house he is looking for only a few driveways up. He pulls up to the gate, an imposing obstruction, a golden wood he could not name. The gates of San Benito are iron and intricately forged, with space enough for a hand to slip out a last forbidden gift to a dangerous sister: twice imprisoned, a disappeared husband, her whereabouts tracked.

Now he presses the button on the intercom, then breathes with deliberate slow breaths, reaches once more for the rosary. "Blessed are thou among women," he says. Josefina's voice comes through, formal and cool. "Yes, who is this please?"

By the time the gates have opened and he has driven through them, she is standing on the wide marble steps, the front door open behind her, her hand over her mouth.

She knows instantly by his presence, the restrained, measured step—the walk of bad news—something irrevocable has occurred. By the time he says his first words, the visible world has shifted for Josefina. The courtyard is shaded by the thick, leafy branches of ancient ceibas, the air humid and heavy with dust-laden rain, San Benito in summer. She is home.

"Everything is fine. Luz is all right." He reaches out to touch her arm; the sharp smell of lemon ammonia comes at him. "Walt found her outside the car wash. She is there with him now."

"No," she says, covering her mouth.

"Look at me. Luz is at the car wash with Walt."

Luz has turned up at the wrong place in time. Not desaparecido. Appeared. Appeared at the car wash. Father William in the wrong clothes, tight at the jaw, his color all wrong. She looks into his hooded eyes. She knows that look, the same look whenever he brings them bad news from the prisons, Ilopango for the women, Mariona the men. The look all the priests carry when they come to report the name of another whose body was found.

Her mind breaks cleanly, a shard of glass sliced through the moment as through a hand. Only for an instant does Josefina wonder why her mother has allowed her inside the gates of the home from which she has been banned, or why Father William, dressed in ill-fitting lay clothes, speaks to her in English and of Luz. *Luz lives in a time Josefina has not yet come to. It is years too soon for these words.*

"You have called Tutela Legal?"

"We don't need a lawyer. No one is in jail. Luz your daughter is down at the car wash and Walt is with her. I will take you. You can see for yourself."

From inside the house a woman's voice calls out, "Josefina, who's there?"

"Wait here. Can you do that? Don't go inside. I'll just be a minute," Father Bill says.

He steps inside the cool white entry, white marble floors, high, gleaming staircase—a palace. From where does she find the strength to clean such a palace? Lydia Darrow, a tiny figure the color and texture of oiled bronze, stands at the top of the staircase wrapped in a thick white towel. She gasps when she sees him. Immediately he announces his name.

Ah, she thinks, the plainclothes priest.

"Josefina's daughter has had an accident. I have to bring her right away. Where is her purse?"

"My God, the little girl now?" says Lydia Darrow, hugging her towel to her skeletal body as she pads down the stairs. "Where is she?"

"She is outside waiting. She is very upset."

"No, the child."

"She is with a friend."

"Not the hospital again?"

"Not the hospital yet."

She arrives at the bottom of the stairs. She is older than he thought, her lined face furrowed with concern. "What happened?"

Perhaps he could tell her the truth. Josefina has said she is a woman with heart. But what is the truth about Luz? He does not know.

"She had a bad fall."

"What terrible luck. I'll get her things."

"Thank you. I appreciate that."

Lydia Darrow goes quickly down a white corridor, a corridor longer than the echoing stone one where he walked as a young seminarian—why does he think of this now?—so lit with God's presence, so blessed and blazing with love, so sure of his call. She returns with her arms full: clothes, purse, Josefina's familiar white sandals. He takes the things carefully lest the sleeve of Walt's shirt touch her oiled flesh.

"Make sure Luz gets to a doctor."

He nods, surprised to hear Lydia Darrow pronounce Luz's name.

"I hope it's all right if we leave Josefina's car. Someone will come by and pick it up later."

He leaves before she can answer.

Josefina is on the step exactly as he left her, staring into the blinding light. He grips her around the waist and they hurry to his car.

"You have seen her?" she asks, breathless. "You promise me Luz is alive?"

"I promise you."

She lets herself down onto the front seat, her feet resting on the stones of the driveway. *The courtyard too bright, not a single sheltering tree. Her mother upstairs in her high white bed, Esperanza even now gathering the rosary from the carved silver box on her dresser.*

He has to bend down and lift up her legs, then place them on the floor of the car, tossing her things in the back seat, not caring how they fall.

"You tell me this," she demands, low and accusing as if someone close by is listening: "How can it be that now they take even the children?"

"There has been no one taken. No one has disappeared. I will bring you to Luz. You can see for yourself."

He closes her door.

On the drive Father Bill tries to engage Josefina with small talk, but it is impossible. She is lost in this moment working its way into the ever-present past. *Who did he say was taken? Raphael again? Raphael or Esperanza? Esperanza in her place?*

He reaches once more for the rosary and enters the stillness. Each word of the prayer a stone dropped into water, and he has been parched, each syllable a perfect bead of water on his tongue. "*Hail Mary, full of grace.*" This is the heart of him now, the self he has lost. Grace has come to him although he has forgotten to ask. At a time when he no longer feels worthy of asking. Now, driving, Josefina lost to her demons, Luz on her knees in a state he dare not think of, the air in the Cavalier has grown softer. Perhaps even Josefina can receive it.

He drives without thinking, contemplates the Glorious Mystery. He is risen out of the battle he has been waging with the day. "Blessed are thou among women. And blessed is the fruit of thy womb, Jesus." He reaches the freeway, no idea how he arrived.

"Josefina," he says, but she does not answer.

He drives on in silence, continuing his prayer. Very quickly, it seems, they begin the climb up the steep Infidelity grade, the place where only two weeks before his radiator went straight into red, the steam shooting out in a tremendous explosion of white. Where the stranger Zoe Luedke stopped her car for him and took him to the garage. Zoe Luedke, he thinks, of whose hands he had dreamed. He did not treat her kindly. There will be no time to apologize to Zoe now. She must already be gone.

The light up ahead has softened. And now he can read the first Infidelity sign.

When they are almost in sight of the car wash, Josefina turns from the window and looks straight ahead, not yet toward him, her eyes still closed. He knows not to speak. He must simply wait. She cannot be rushed. Perhaps he should drive right past the car wash and take her home.

"William," says Josefina, "why are you wearing Walt's shirt?"

The question brings him such relief that for a moment he cannot answer.

"Was there blood?" she asks. "Is that the reason?"

"There was no blood. Luz is not hurt."

"I sent her this morning to Mass."

She is not yet clear. She has forgotten they are not allowing Luz Mass.

"Can you tell me what day it is?" he asks.

"I know the day. It is Wednesday. It is the day of the feast of your lady that you love. I know where I am. I have recovered myself. I know what has happened. You came to my work. You are taking me to Luz. Tell me again why is she at the car wash when I sent her this morning to you?"

"You didn't put her on the summer school bus?"

"Don't you hear me? I sent her to Mass."

"But why?"

"To make her happy."

"But why didn't you bring her?"

"She always walks to the church by herself. What's wrong with you?"

"She never came to me. She walked to the car wash."

"No," says Josefina without hesitation, "Luz did not walk."

She grows quiet again, her index finger moving reflexively to the gauze, which covers the access. She is only a week out of the hospital. He wonders again if perhaps he should take her straight home to rest, let Walt look after Luz a while longer. Still, he was counting on Josefina to bring Luz out of the unreachable place where he left her.

Whom does he care for in this moment? Who has the greater need? Josefina? Luz? He feels like a man torn between his wife and his child. And what of his parishioners whom he abandoned on the sidewalk? He is not Dr. Raphael Reyes, the husband of Josefina, the father of Luz. Only moments ago he had been given back his wholeness, through a great gift of grace. How quickly he has lost it. Under the complicated love he bears for this woman, he has forgotten himself—more times than he can count. No wonder he has suffered. No wonder Luz shakes him so deeply. He behaves like a man, not a priest, and an unenlightened one at that, as if by his will he can control things. As if his will can shape what Luz is.

Just up ahead to the right he can see the diner, the curved glass windows fronting the freeway, and beyond it the Infidelity Motel with its pink neon sign. The blind light of morning has begun to disperse and the world is visible again, even the dense sweep of mountain from which he takes strength. Now Josefina leans toward him, straining to see across to the car wash where Luz waits: in what state he does not know. He has not yet prepared her and is a little startled himself by what he sees: the sidewalk is thronged with people, umbrellas, lawn chairs like a popular local beach.

"What are they doing out there with my daughter?"

He checks his rearview mirror and sees that the traffic behind him is clear, quickly swerving two lanes to the right, and drives into the parking lot of the Infidelity Diner where he stops the car and turns his face to Josefina.

"What is wrong? Why are we stopping?" she asks. "I want to go to my daughter."

"You are going see some things that will upset you."

"I knew it!" she cries.

"It's not what you think." He puts his hands lightly on her arms, enfolding his fingers in her flesh, as familiar to him now as his own. "Are you going to be able to hear this, or should I take you home?"

"She is alive? She is not hurt?"

"Not hurt, no."

"Just say what is wrong. You are driving me crazy."

Then he tells Josefina. When he has finished, he looks down at his hands in his lap. Josefina's hands cover them, the aroma of lemon ammonia rising between them.

Anyone seeing them like this, outside the diner in a small gray car, windows rolled up, in late morning—after breakfast, before lunch—might think them lovers. Lovers who have conspired to meet where they won't be recognized and few people will be around.

"You are finished?" she asks. "You have told me everything?"

"Yes."

"Do you think she is a saint?"

He laughs. "No."

"Do you think she is genuine in her prayer?"

"Yes." And suddenly he feels a surpassing calm. "Genuine, yes, but the rest I cannot yet say."

And now he will have to live it. He will truly have to let Luz go. The right love and she is weightless. If only he can remember to release her.

"William," says Josefina, "you are everything to me, but also you are a priest. I know this. I am sorry to tell you. All you priests are a little crazy. Those people on Walt's sidewalk? They are crazy as well. My Luz did not walk. She was taken again. Now I am certain. Someone is stealing my daughter."

CHAPTER 25

It is close to eleven when Father Bill and Josefina arrive on the sidewalk and discover that Luz is not there.

Though the crowd has doubled, it is eerily quiet. Some of the people appear to be napping. Others stare at Walt's window with glazed, sleepy eyes. At what in the window, no one has said. No one has declared that a vision has visited the town of Infidelity. No one claims to see anything at all in that off-kilter window. No one except Zoe Luedke has been knocked flat by the power of spirit or heat or low blood sugar.

The breakfast regulars, the few tourists from the Infidelity Motel, Walt's overflow customers, and the mothers on the summer school phone chain who are huddled in the back in a cluster, bright pastel short sets, expressions of the tenderest inquiry on their faces—everyone is strangely subdued. The rumors fly elsewhere in Infidelity: something has happened that no one can name. Something that started with Luz, the second grade girl with the reclusive mother. The child who gives the other kids nightmares, runs off from school on impossible feet, turning up by herself in the strangest of places: the campgrounds? The car wash? (Maybe she's taken.) No one knows how.

Here, where Luz knelt for nearly two hours, there is nothing but a palpable sweetness hanging over the sidewalk fronting the office of Walt's Immaculate Autos. It reminds Father Bill of the after effect of many prayerful hours on the part of the most faithful souls.

"They're inside," Emily Otto tells them, getting up from her chair as she sees them approach. Josefina, the frightened mother, who clings to the arm of Father Bill as if she has been given bad news. "She's fine. Bobbie brought food from the diner. Your child was starved."

Josefina responds with a nod. *Yes, that is my daughter, what an appetite. Luz is eating? A good sign.* But still, she thinks, as they go from sidewalk to the walkway to the door of the office, past strange men and women (with these strangers so close, she will lose her mind), until she sees Luz with her own eyes no word of assurance can have substance. Only with her eyes, with her own subtle touch will she know what has happened to her child.

CHAPTER 26

There is such turmoil inside Walt's office. Much chatter, many people, and the place smells like the diner, of tuna and roast beef, of Walt's cinnamon coffee. Laughter and noise, and yes, it is true! Even her daughter's unmistakable high cadence, her daughter who sits on the couch between Bobbie (why is she not at the diner?) and the Felangela. Luz on the couch, reclining: a sandwich in one hand, a drink in the other, and not just a drink, Coca-Cola, which is forbidden; Luz knows this. Her child who appears on first glance, at this distance, to be suffering from only an excess of spoiling.

"Mami," Luz cries in surprise, "why didn't you stay at your work?"

Ah, thinks Father Bill with relief. His petition has been answered. Here is Luz. Luz herself. She is back.

Josefina feels a fire from deep in the earth; it moves through her heavy white shoes, through the soles of her feet, through the whole of her body, fanning into her hands. For the first time Josefina understands how a woman is able to strike her own child. She strides through the office and stands before Luz.

"Get up."

"Look! Zoe is here!"

"I see Sewey. I see all your friends. Get up right now."

Never in her life has Luz been asked to stop in the middle of eating, Bobbie's sweet tuna fish, crunchy lettuce, skinny tomato, the untoasted honey bread. She has never known hunger like this. Every part of her wants to eat food and more food. She feels hungry enough to keep eating for the rest of the day. After roast beef and tuna, Bobbie has brought Luz's special dessert: whipped cream on strawberry pie.

And now, without warning, comes her mother. Luz feels hot right away at the neck. Blood floods to her cheeks so they burn. The pee comes sharp in her down parts. She presses her thighs close in case some might spill out on the couch.

Someone has told Josefina that Luz did not get on the summer school bus.

"I did a bad thing," she whispers to Zoe who takes the soda can from her.

"Just go," Zoe says.

But she doesn't. Luz only sits up.

"What are you waiting for? Didn't you hear me?" her mother commands as if there is no one in Walt's office but herself and her impossible daughter.

The happiness of her eating has gone quickly away. Her mother is angry. She had to leave work and lose money. It is all Luz's fault. Luz did not go to Mass. She did not get on the summer school bus.

Bobbie puts the white paper bag with the whipped cream–topped strawberry pie on the floor next to her coffee.

A scramble of voices from the folks at the snack bar, then Father Bill leans over the counter, conferring with Walt. "Folks," Walt says as he comes out from the counter and walks to his entry door, opening it just a crack on account of the heat. "Could you do us a favor, step outside for a minute. We'll have you right back. You too, Chico. If you don't mind. Just wait outside till you're called."

They do as he asks; Chico Platz shuts the door.

It has turned quiet as a grave in the car wash office, only the hum of the refrigerator case and the slow drip of the air conditioning. And still Luz Reyes does not move, the half-eaten tuna fish sandwich held in her upraised right hand.

"You can walk one mile from the house to the car wash and you cannot walk ten steps to me?"

Bobbie takes the sandwich from Luz and whispers, "Go on, honey, Mami is waiting."

"What if I pee?"

"Talk to me, not to Sewey and Bobbie!"

Luz slides off the couch and stands up. She takes one step forward, then two, her legs thick and lazy as if she has been given the body of some heavier child in place of her own. At last like magic she can walk and the pee goes back up where it came from. She moves toward the door where the customers went out, and Father Bill watches and her mother now waits in a barely held rage.

As she walks, Josefina studies Luz's upright posture, the proud little chest thrust out like a pigeon's that threatens to send a lifetime of uncontrolled love careening out of Josefina's fast-beating heart. The yellow dress shows no sign of blood, the limbs intact, the skin unmarked except at the knees, which are chafed red from hours of kneeling. Luz's gait is unnatural. She is ready to cry.

It takes twenty-one steps for Luz Reyes to reach her mother near the door of Walt's office, with Luz standing close enough now to be kissed or slapped. Instead of kissing her or wiping the crumbs off her daughter's face, Josefina sinks to her knees. Father Bill, having just prayed his way to the fourth decade of the Glorious Mystery—*Her body as well as her soul taken up to Heaven*—is blessed by a second bout of realized grace on this day of all days, the fifteenth of August, the day of Our Lady's Assumption, removes his hand from the rosary in his pocket, Esperanza's, he thinks, the one he has taken from Luz, and quickly bends forward in bliss to catch Josefina in case she has fainted. To the dismay of the few who remain in the office, Josefina is running her hands up Luz's legs, then under the skirt of the yellow dress, feeling her way to the warm unbroken thigh flesh. As she reaches the damp cotton underpants Luz flinches, then shuts her eyes. Her thighs tighten. Inside herself Luz pulls back.

"What are you doing?" Father Bill cries. His cry is ignored.

"No one touched you? No one hurt you? You swear to me?"

"No one hurt me. I promise," Luz says in a whisper, and in Spanish. "Nadie."

Now Josefina smells her fingers, finding nothing, no taint of semen. Blind to the shock of those who have witnessed Luz's shame. Father Bill and Walt, Bobbie on the couch, mouth half agape, Zoe feeling more than a little bit sick.

"I am sorry if this insults you," says Josefina then she slowly stands up. "Mejor es mio que los médicos." *Better me than the doctors,* she says and holds up her hands to stop Father Bill from interfering. "Who drove you to the car wash, Luz?"

Luz starts to shiver. She has gone cold as a corpse. Her mother has trespassed her body. It happened. It was real.

"Give me the name of this person."

"Mami, no person, the feet again," Luz says softly, no sense of conviction.

Walt has come out from behind the counter in a blue-blotched white tee shirt, moving as close as he dares. He could reach past her mother. He could bend down and raise Luz with his arms. He sends out a net over Luz, a gentling smile, so much kindness Luz cannot hold it. She has sealed up her body of light.

"I am getting sick from your lies."

"Please, Mami, I have to go to the bathroom very bad."

"You go nowhere until you answer my question."

"No one took me. I swear the truth to you Mami. The feet."

"You walked to the car wash all by yourself? Like you walked to the campgrounds on those feet? Luz, you do this two times to me?"

Now Luz stands silent, dark eyes shining with withheld tears. But her feet, she thinks, and waits for the words to come into her mind. But no words arrive to tell her mother how fast they can go.

"What is your reason this time to do such a dangerous thing that makes me think something has happened to you again?"

How can she speak of the speed that came back to her feet, of the light that came down and came through her heart on the sidewalk when she opened and opened in a floating of gold? Our Lady, thinks Luz, and her heart moves like wings with wild flutters. So much gold she can't understand who could give this to her but Our Lady herself that her mother will not allow.

Father Bill bends down close to Luz as he did on the sidewalk. She remembers his words. *Luz, don't do this to us.* "Can you answer the question for Mami?" he asks. "Can you tell us what made you go to the car wash?"

But Luz does not trust Father Bill.

"Please, Mami, take me into the bathroom. I don't want to tell Father. I will tell you only inside."

Her mother has the face of a demon and fingers like ice, no hands to hold Luz. They are folded to cover her breasts just under the bandage and the tube. "I am waiting for the truth from you," Josefina says, "I am prepared to wait here all day."

Luz prays to Our Lady for help with melting the heart of her mother, for showing that Luz tells the truth.

"Something was going to happen. I knew it from my body. And something did happen, but I don't know the words."

"What did you know from your body?"

"The sweet place came back," Luz says. *The place that got bigger and bigger until Luz was a dark speck, a burned thing, the sweetness so big like a fire of gold blazing out of her heart.* "Please, it was something, not a person. I don't know the name, just the sweetness. You can even ask Walt. Walt knows I'm not lying. He knows I am saying the truth."

CHAPTER 27

He is going to disappoint them, Walt thinks. He is late beyond help now. He will make the third inning if he leaves right now. If he speeds. And he is a mess, wearing a blue-blotched tee shirt he keeps in the office to use as a rag, dirty chinos; he will have no time to change if he wants to get to the Fullerton Stadium. He has missed his son's opening pitch. He stands with his back to the counter having told Josefina all he can about Luz, but his words don't begin to explain what has happened and, anyway, she does not believe them. She has turned her relentless gaze upon him, her relentless questions. She has stupefied Zoe to silence. She has caused even Bobbie to withhold her opinion. There they sit on his sofa, Zoe dozing, Bobbie leaning forward, feet planted, head cocked, taking in every word.

"But what happened?" Josefina demands of him. "What was it, this sweet place? I don't understand."

What can Walt say that will make sense to this woman? He throws up his hands.

Josefina turns back to Luz. "You think this sweet place comes from the Virgin?"

"Maybe," Luz says. "Maybe She sends it. I don't know."

Josefina looks up to the ceiling for patience, the corrugated tiles, very ugly, she thinks, very cheap. Walt can do better than this.

"Luz spoke Our Lady's name on the sidewalk?"

Walt hesitates. "Not exactly. She did say there had been a voice. Isn't that right, Luz, do you remember you told me something called you?"

"You see this girl?" Josefina accuses Father Bill. "You see what this is again?"

Father Bill, leaning against the freezer case, a safe distance. He nods, tries to rise from his bliss, but it hangs on to him like a virus. The truth is, he's so grateful that Luz is herself she can say anything and he won't be fazed. As long as she does not fall into rapture, as long as Josefina is spared this.

"Come here, Luz. You have crumbs on your face." Josefina reaches into her pocket for a tissue and spits on it, wipes her daughter's face. "So that is why you kneel for two hours like a penitent? Our Lady calls you to run with the traffic? After all I have been through with you since the spring, you are still running to Her?"

"I didn't run. I told you it was the feet."

"The feet don't decide for the body. The brain tells the feet!"

"You never believe me!" Luz says.

"Who can believe you with that dirty face? Everyone knows you are lying."

How much easier if Luz had seen Our Lady today, Walt thinks. How much easier if he'd seen the Virgin flashing across Luz's face. He could call it a holy appearance—a vision. Our Lady of Infidelity. Dump the whole thing on Father Bill. Instead, he is stuck with the mystery of those nameless holy faces. Stuck with the mystery of Luz, with Luz's feet, which he may well have seen, or not seen, they were moving so fast they could hardly *be* seen, not this morning but two weeks ago. The night she had scared him silly.

"What time did you see Luz?" Josefina asks Walt with a sigh of disgust.

"Do you want to sit down?" he asks. "This must be exhausting. How 'bout something to drink?" He is never going to get out of this office. *Hold on Ryan*, he prays, *keep on seeing the seams of the ball.*

"What time?" she repeats, waving away his offer. Though her feet are beginning to ache, her ankles to swell, she will stand up. All her strength, she thinks, all the good strength that she woke with this morning is going to disappear any second. She must finally get to the bottom of her daughter's running away.

"I saw Luz a couple of minutes after I opened the wash, eight o'clock, give or take a few minutes."

"Eight o'clock I was kissing Luz good-bye at the door. She was just starting to go for the church. Eight o'clock is impossible for a one-mile walk, even for a child with such talented feet. You must have been sleeping on that couch, Walt. I am telling you, you are wrong."

"I was watching the clock. I have someplace important I need to be."

"Where for the first time since I know you are you needed someplace?" Josefina demands.

"My son has a game. I told you, remember? Little League play-offs."

"He is pitching the game today?"

"Starting pitcher. Yep, it's happening now."

"He invited you to go?" Luz asks.

"Last week."

"You are missing it?" Josefina turns to her daughter with disgust. "Do you see all the problems you are causing? Now you have made Walt late for his son."

"I'm sorry." Luz's voice is muffled. She stares at the floor, her fingers worrying the backs of new teeth.

If he leaves in five minutes and he's lucky with traffic, he will catch the fifth inning and Ryan will still be pitching. "You had us fooled. We really thought you were going to make it today," Gwen had said when he called to say he'd be late. "I intend to be there. Something is going on at the car wash." How could he describe what it was without sounding like he was insane? "Fuck you and your car wash," Gwen had said and hung up the phone.

"Be sorry also for being in two places at once," Josefina chides.

"No, because I wasn't!" Luz looks up at her mother. Now Luz is angry. Her mother is ugly and mean.

"Then Walt and I are crazy. Or maybe you make us crazy."

"Josefina," says Father Bill.

"What?" Her face is hot. She can feel the blood rushing at her temples.

"Have some consideration for Walt. He is already late."

"How 'bout we take a break and figure this all out later?" Walt says. He wants to touch Josefina, wants his touch to reassure her since his words cannot, knows she cannot abide it, cringes when he is too close. But what is this child of hers? What is he? He has just seen the wisdom of the ages on her daughter's shining face. It pains him that he cannot reveal what he saw. Maybe later, he thinks, maybe when the crowd has disappeared and he has come back from the game he will go to the blue house, sit down at her clean kitchen table, and tell Josefina the truth. He will tell it in a way that makes it seem right, this thing that he thinks Luz may bring. Apart from those faces it is just what Luz said—a sweet place, some new geography of feeling. A little off the map, he'll concede, but nonetheless lovely, kind of innocent, deeply sweet. We could all use a place like that, Walt thinks.

"Why don't you two go home? Take it easy for the rest of the day. Okay, Luz? Later we can talk more. When I get back."

CHAPTER 28

Zoe watches Walt leaving the office in a hail of white lights. Something is wrong with all of them. They have turned kind of starry. Everything so bright. Streaks of white light shooting out from Father Bill, from Josefina, from her own arms and legs, and blazing out of the belly of Luz. She has to put a hand over her eyes as Josefina and Luz come toward her, asking if something is wrong.

"Maybe because she fell on the sidewalk," Luz says.

"She fell? What happened? Did you do something, Luz?"

Zoe can't find the words. Was it Luz or was it the force in the window? Force without a face, Zoe thinks. Without a face but with a voice. She hears herself laugh.

"It wasn't my fault," says Luz. "She did it like this," and plops down on the floor then tips her head back and back.

"Did you eat today, Sewey?" Josefina asks.

"Have a tuna sandwich," says Bobbie, who is thinking that she really must get back to the diner.

But Zoe declines it.

"Sewey?" says Josefina, "What day is this?"

"The day I must pick up my car."

It is clear to Josefina: the Felangela is not acting right. In truth she looks dazed, but still she saw Luz on the sidewalk. There may be something she remembers that Josefina should know. "Tell me the truth. You sat close to my daughter before falling? She talked to you?"

"She's a beautiful child," Zoe says. She has said this before, in what context she can't quite pin down.

"Thank you, but right now I have trouble agreeing. I was asking for information. When you saw her on the sidewalk she talked to you then? She was saying those prayers?"

"I don't know what she was doing. I can't remember a thing." *There*, Zoe thinks, *a whole sentence. I said it. I must be okay*. And she moves the ice pack to her other hand, the ice pack she has been holding on the back of her head. Walt gave it to her, running back into the office to tell them that Chico was coming. Chico and friends to the rescue. Walt had decided to keep the wash open. Then he had gone to his refrigerator and reached in and got this for her. An ice pack. Ice blue. And she hadn't even told him there was a bump. She feels like crying just thinking of Walt with his starry blue eyes and his blue-blotched white shirt, his blue ice pack, late for his son. She feels like crying when she thinks of their window fiasco, which she can't look at right now. It's behind her, she knows, she does not want to turn. What if she looks and that voice starts talking again. The voice in the glass. Her window mistake, which has turned on her with a vengeance. Now all those people on the sidewalk staring into it. What do they see? Or maybe hear? That they too are fine? Wonderful? Maybe superb? She doesn't feel fine at all. Can she take an aspirin? she wonders. She feels the beginning of a headache. The lights are coming at her so strongly she must cover her eyes. Luz moving toward her, now creeping behind the couch, slips her hand under the ice pack and cups Zoe's head.

"Ummm," Zoe says, "that feels nice."

"Luz, ask permission to touch," Josefina says.

"I'm just petting the bump."

"Ladies," says Father Bill, "I'm taking you home."

"I'm going home too today," Zoe says.

"I meant all of you," says Father Bill. "Zoe, you are in no condition to drive."

Father Bill taking her home. Luz's hand on the back of Zoe's head. Zoe closes her eyes. Her eyelids flutter. She drifts, rises. There is a shower of gold like oak leaves in autumn. *Don't fall for me, I'm bad news, Michael said. But it was too late.* "Don't close your eyes," Father Bill says. "You can't go to sleep. You might have a concussion. Stay awake."

"Okay," Zoe murmurs. She should really avoid autumn, the season of their love. Just never go back to Cold Spring.

Father Bill says her name. Luz repeats it. The word is irrelevant, efficient. *Zoe, Zoe,* Michael called, like a hoot owl, called from the top of the too-gold old oak. Out of the long golden past.

"Luz, take your hands off of Zoe's head. You are making her sleep."

"I'm awake," Zoe says. She comes to with a jolt. Michael is falling and falling straight through the branches.

"Sewey, you saw Luz kneeling? You sat beside her. What do you remember?"

"Ah," says Zoe who is struggling to subtract Michael from the moment, to attend to Josefina and her important question. Not Michael but Luz. Luz kneeling beside her. Yes, first Luz was kneeling, then she got up. Why not tell them the truth and be rid of it? "I remember the words."

"What words?" Father Bill asks.

"Very nice ones."

"Who said the nice words?"

"The window, I think."

The room grows quiet. What has she said? Luz holds her excitement deep in the pouch of her throat. "Was she so pretty? Was she wearing the cape and the crown?"

"Luz!" Josefina says, "you are impossible. Zoe is not in her mind. She is hurt. She fell. You think Zoe saw Our Lady in the window?"

Be quiet, Luz thinks. "She could."

"Don't do that, Josefina," Father Bill says, "Don't put ideas in Luz's head."

"Just please can she tell me one thing?" Luz says, her finger on Zoe's cheek.

Ah, that little finger, Zoe thinks. Luz close enough for Zoe to feel the gold of her, the sweetness.

"Was she beautiful? What was her hair?"

"No hair at all."

"No," says Luz, "that's not true."

"No face, hardly a voice. Oh, Michael, why did you leave? Don't you know how wonderful I am?"

"The Felangela is not right in her head."

"Does she have to go to the hospital?" cries Luz.

Father Bill curses to himself. They are having a field day with him today. Every last one of these women.

CHAPTER 29

Father Bill feels the tension move through and claim him, the movement in his will that wants to take charge. It is difficult this new way, giving Luz back to God. Now who is the dangerous one? Is it Zoe? Is it Luz?

"We'll take Zoe with us. I'm going out to get Chico and get those people off the sidewalk. Then we will leave."

"Tell them the Virgin has already done her damage for the day. We have one person who cannot think straight," Josefina says. "When you fell down, Sewey, do you think you passed out?"

"Not out. In."

"You are nauseous or dizzy?"

"No. I feel great. Even my headache is already gone."

"Does Zoe have to go to the hospital?" Luz asks.

"I don't think so. Tell me if the headache comes back. Now sit still, Luz," says Josefina, frowning at the flecks of tuna fish and bread still under Luz's lip, the faint stain from the forbidden soda above it.

"Do you know what they do with saints, Zoe?" Josefina asks. "They take them away from their families."

"Saints?"

"They put them to live in a cell. A very small cell. They give them food without taste, no strawberry pie, and to drink only water. And from going crazy in the cell the saints do terrible things to their bodies. Do you know this, Sewey?"

"Why are you saying these bad things?" Luz says.

"Saint Michael takes souls to Heaven. I remember that," says Zoe.

"And who else?" Luz asks.

"I'm not sure."

"Zoe, the one with all the animals . . . remember?"

"The big horn sheep? The Mojave tortoise?" says Zoe.

"No!" Luz laughs.

"Be quiet, Luz, you think it is funny? It is my turn to teach Sewey. The saints beat themselves and make themselves bleed because they are so miserable. That is the life of a saint. You want this for your future, Luz?"

"I am not listening. I am hungry. I want the strawberry pie."

"Saints don't eat pie. Get used to it Luz."

"You just want to be mean. I can't help about my feet. That's not a saint."

"You *can* help your feet." Josefina puts her rough hands around Luz's skull. "Look at me, Luz. Repeat: The brain tells the feet. That is the way the mind works."

Luz narrows her eyes, pulls away from her mother's hands.

"Maybe we send you to the Franciscans down the road. Maybe they give you a cell to be a saint."

"I want to go home with the Felangela," says Luz, and the sound of the word sends a shiver running down Zoe's spine. She has become the Felangela, a creature not quite of this earth. "Zoe knows how to be nice. She is going to buy us a coconut cake."

"Be quiet, Luz," Josefina says. "The Felangela is not driving to the A&P today."

"Why not?" Luz says.

Father Bill opens the door.

"Let's go," he says. "Right now."

"I am ready," says Luz and she stands up. "Zoe?" she asks. "We are going."

"Did the people leave?" asks Zoe.

"I'm afraid not."

"We don't leave either," says Josefina.

"What's wrong?" Father Bill asks.

"You think we are finished?"

"I am finished," says Luz. "I want to go home."

"Tell that to your people that are waiting for you to go back on that cushion."

"They are not my people. They belong to themselves."

"And you belong to me. Don't forget it."

"No," says Luz, "I belong to God."

"Luz," says Father Bill, striding through the office to the couch. "Don't argue with your mother." His prize pupil, his sweet little girl who won't meet his eyes, the one that he must completely let go. He is helpless with these females. They are tearing him apart.

He takes Josefina by the arm, none too gently. He must remind himself she is not a well woman. She seems plenty well to him now—the Josefina of old, fiery reckless, and forceful. "Come with me, please, Josefina." Now he takes her hand and leads her away from Luz, to the window where he can eclipse her from Luz with his own blue-shirted back. He looks down at her and tells her to be quiet. He looks into her eyes. He is roused like a boy. She is glorious. He knows what it's like to inhabit her body, the devastated body of this woman. He simply adores her. Life could be simple, he thinks. He could live as an uncontrolled man. And why not? He is halfway there now. Never with such clarity has he felt this. Could have been simple. No longer. She is sick, he reminds himself, his love. *Her chances of transplant are nil.* And she is stubborn. She does not understand the contagion of the crowd, the infection of hope that these things instill. Luz must be removed from this place. "You cannot let Luz stay," he says.

CHAPTER 30

"Please," says Josefina, "just leave now. Go to the church for your feast day. Those people do not concern me. Only my daughter. I am not through here yet."

"Why aren't you through? Why aren't we going in Father Bill's car?" Luz demands.

"Why do you think?"

"I don't know."

"You want to be a saint on a cushion."

"I don't want to go back on the cushion. I hate the cushion!"

"That is a very good sign. Because saints must always do what they hate. See how I will already help you to become what you wish?"

"You don't help me. You don't even listen. Zoe listens."

"What did you say?" Zoe asks.

"Stop it, both of you," Father Bill says. "Josefina, don't play games with her."

"I am not the one who is playing."

Luz slides off the couch and stands with her hands on her hips. So powerful and defiant Josefina cannot help it. Her heart, looking at this child, it is going to combust with frustration and love. Here is the child her father had warned her would arrive one day, a child like herself. Equal in stubbornness.

"Go ahead," Josefina says, dismissing Father Bill. "Go for your business. We have given you enough trouble. You are free. You can leave."

"You don't have a car."

"I don't need a car. I'm not going anywhere."

"No va," says Zoe. "I still have the Dart."

Chico opens the door and steps into the fray. "Are you ready for me yet?" he asks. "There are customers."

"Just a minute, Chico. We've got a problem," says Father Bill.

"Come in," said Josefina. "Just who I need is Chico Platz."

Father Bill walks wearily to the front of the office, where Chico and two of his black-clad friends whose names he should know now stand blocking the door. He must ask them to move in order to lock it. They peer down at Luz, who has curled next to Zoe on the couch, looking just like a kid settling in for a nice round of morning cartoons.

"How's it going?" Chico asks Father Bill.

"Zoe fell down."

Luz calls out in answer, "But it isn't my fault."

"Is Luz okay?" he asks Josefina, who has left her daughter and is standing uncomfortably close to him now. Too close for the comfort of the friends.

"Look for yourself. Go ahead," Josefina tells Chico. "Go down and look at her. Tell me what do you see? Does she look like a saint?"

The boys swallow and look away. Chico promised there would be zero contact with Luz.

"Leave them out of this," Father Bill says. "Boys, just relax. We'll be done in a minute. Then the car wash is yours."

Josefina is through with Father Bill. She turns her back to him. She puts her hand on Chico's arm. "We are going to need things. Find something to write it all down."

"What are you doing?" Father Bill says.

"Go ahead, Chico!"

Chico glances at his friends who are wishing they were still outside. His friends know all about Luz from Skye, Chico's girlfriend. Know why the priest is wearing Walt Adair's too-small shirt. Luz is a freak who can do things to people. Chico is unfazed, even worse he's intrigued; he has theories, planes of existence he believes in they don't have a clue about. Chico reads things, thick books with hard covers. The English assignments. Science fiction from second-hand stores. Chico believes some new species of kids are being sent down to live on the earth now. Kids with weird psychic powers sent here on missions to save the whole human race. Now Chico goes behind the counter like he already owns the place, reaches for a notepad and pen. Chico can always find what he needs.

"Shoot," Chico says.

"First, call your mother. Please tell her Josefina is asking can she use the nice big umbrella from the patio, or maybe a little tent for our heads. You have a tent, Chico?"

"Sure. You planning to camp out?"

"That depends on my daughter."

"I said, what do you think you are doing?" Father Bill interrupts.

"I am warning you," Josefina says. "If you can't take it, then go. Don't make this more hard for me. Keep writing, Chico. Also we need big hats. Two of them. Sunscreen. Water and ice. I am going too fast? You and your friends go drive and get them. We need it right away."

"Why an umbrella?" asks Luz, who has heard everything by straining.

"So we don't faint from heatstroke from that sun beating down on our heads."

"It's not heatstroke," says Zoe, "I fell."

"Yes, we know," Josefina replies. "Luz, be useful. Make sure Sewey keeps the ice on her head. Chico, tell her also to give you a cheat, a big flat one." Chico looks at her quizzically. "You know, for the bed." "Ah, a sheet." "A cheat and a cooler of ice. Write also three chairs, not two. You are getting all of this? Nice ones that go back. Sewey, you can sit with us. I will make sure you don't fall again," she says, looking to the wall-leaning boys dressed in black. So skinny. So frightened. She must reassure them by smiling.

"I won't allow you to do this," says Father Bill, who is finally beginning to understand.

"Then how do you stop me? Call, Chico, now!"

When Chico makes the call, the boys mumble and go stand outside. Luz crosses the floor to go close to her mother and glare. Her mother glares back. No one can stop her mother when she becomes like this. Even today with her bandage and the hole for the tube. Her mother in her pink uniform and her hair that is a mess because Luz did not go to Father Bill's Mass. Because Luz did not get on the summer school bus.

Luz, the child, with no memory of what awaits her on the sidewalk, of how easily she will slip back into the majesty that she is, Luz the child who has not for a moment forgotten that dented white box with whipped cream on pie still on the floor near the side of the couch, whose mouth fills with saliva just thinking of the taste, whose feet strain to play the ball-jumping game, whose whole body is yearning for the party at Our Lady of Guadalupe, for the games and the noise and the white strings of icicle lights. This Luz does not remember—not now, in the beginning, and for several days to come—this thing that she is. Does not understand why her mother who thinks Luz is lying makes her return to the place where the voice and her feet made her go.

"Why are you crying? You should be happy. With all of those misguided people waiting to watch you, and waiting with patience for the face of Our Lady to come to that window."

"What will it take to get through to you?" Father Bill says. "Do you know what they will think if you take her back out there?"

"That is not my problem what they think. Luz needs a big lesson. I am going to make sure she gets one."

"Give it to her a different way."

"This *is* the way."

"I want to go with Father Bill. I want to help with the Feast of Our Lady."

"You had your feast. Tuna fish from Bobbie from the diner."

"I'm not even going to the feast of Our Lady? I have to. Tommy Platz is my partner for the ball-jumping game."

"No Tommy for you and no Feast of Our Lady. Remember for next year. Today since this morning you chose to be the saint of Infidelity you will stay a saint all day."

"No, I won't. I will be Luz."

“Okay, then be Luz. But whoever you are, you are punished. For frightening me two times nearly to death with running away. For not taking responsibility from your feet. And who knows? After today maybe Lydia Darrow fires me from my work. Then we have two poor saints in one house. I am sorry for your tears, but it will not change my mind for you. We are going to sit on the sidewalk. We will stay for as long as it takes. You will never, do you hear me? You will never want to walk on those feet like this again.”

CHAPTER 31

Father Bill misjudges a step and stumbles onto the walkway, righting himself just in time. Then he hurries to where the crowd waits, moves awkwardly through them, stands with his back to the window, squinting through the light at the faithful, the diner folk, the mothers in their bright summer clothes (some with kids on their laps), the overflow customers from the car wash and the curious, whose faces and names he does not know. And though he knows what he's going to say—*For the sake of the child, I am asking you to leave now*—when he starts to speak, he cannot say the words. He must wait, ask for guidance, say nothing until he is prompted, a course of action his vocation has long accustomed him to.

The words he receives are simple and clear. *Call Hope Merton*, a woman he has not seen or spoken with in nearly six years. These are not the directives he's waiting for. He notes it then closes his eyes, waits some more. The people on the sidewalk hold their breath.

When he opens his eyes, he looks from face to face, meeting the eyes of the thirty-two sitters and standees, looking at them or through them, or deep into their being in a way, they would later exclaim, that was sufficient reward for hours on that sidewalk, even considering the sweetness of the day. There was some place within them Father Bill seemed to touch with that look that made people glad to have lived just to know that they had it. Whatever *it* was. *Beheld,* his people called it.

Seen to the core and then some. The moment he had only intended to ask them to leave he gives them the thing that made many want to remain on that sidewalk to see what else they might get. One hundred degrees on the Joshua Freeway, the fifteenth of August, the day of Our Lady's Assumption, the cars whizzing by, the lunch crowd gathering across the road at the diner, Luz and her mother and Zoe Luedke with the missing felangela and a possible concussion preparing themselves to come out.

Then, after he has looked at his very last face, Father Bill raises his hands no higher than his waist, turns them upward, opening his palms to the impossible blue desert sky, holds them that way a good several minutes, as if he is weighing the air.

Is it a blessing, or an inquiry, or a sign of submission? No one dares ask.

CHAPTER 32

Under Josefina's watchful eye, not a word issues forth from Luz's mouth, not for the six hours they remain on the sidewalk. Until the end. Not a twitch out of Luz or a syllable of joy. No one able to read her expression, concealed as she is by the chair, the umbrella, and that broad brimmed sunhat. The standees report she would rise on the hour and hover a little, inches, no more, off the chair. Others were sure she was snoring, probably fast asleep.

No one knows who gave the order for food, but just around one people start bringing in quantities of it, plates and utensils, and they arrive with their children. And then some go home for the tables. Chico lets the women set them up in back of Walt's office under the awning in sight of the San Jacinto Mountains and the long expanse of summer-white desert. As more people show up, trying to get on the sidewalk, the crowd threatening to spill into the far right lane of east-bound freeway traffic, the overflow folks head back there, parking their cars in the wide open area across from the little white structure that houses the wash. The lights blinking on and off all day as all day those cars go on through. And that's where the confusion came from about the crying. It is the car wash patrons, not the sidewalk folk, in tears.

Without Walt to prepare them, the first-time customers are goners. All kinds of memories and feelings are evoked by the experience of that wash, no way to resist. The pattern of the pinpoint overhead bulbs, their surpassing brightness and quantity, combined with the in-your-face thrust of the wash cycle water, then the slow noiseless balm of the rinse cycle all coming at you in under three minutes. An emotional workout. In the minds of many the wash and the sidewalk seem linked, some people saying to get the sidewalk benefit you had to first buy a car wash.

Once the food tables go up out back, the dancing soon follows. Just an old boom box, upbeat tunes (in respect to the youngest), people moving in public (instead of their cars). Then one of the kids finds the hose and the spigot in back of Walt's office and turns on the water. Mud on the ground like you wouldn't believe. Someone aims the hose at the dancers and no one complains. Lots of people get drenched and happy and stay that way. Nice sounds for a weekday. More laughter than usual. A party kind of day. And the sidewalk vigil continues. In silence, in self-communion, in rapturous sighs. And no one claiming to see anything on that window.

By midafternoon the light has eased, diminishing throughout the High Desert to the normal mid-August glare. Traffic on the freeway thins out as it usually does in the pre–rush-hour lull. Walt in the stands at the stadium of Fullerton College, the game in its final slow inning. Father Bill at the church, getting ready for his favorite feast day. In the middle of all the preparations, all his fears about Luz, he remembers the prompting of guidance that had come to him on the sidewalk, goes into his office to call Hope Merton, knows her number without even checking, surprised that he knows it, six years since he's called, more surprised when she picks up the phone, "My God, Bill, I can't believe it is you. I was thinking about you all morning." Six years since he'd taken Josefina and Luz from the safety of her home. And very quickly, with no idea he is going to do this, he explains Josefina's imminent need. "A relative, any blood relative, or barring that someone who knew her who might be a compatible donor. I'm grasping at straws, but I don't know how else to do this. Do you think," he had said, "there's some way you can help?"

"Give me a few days," she says. "I'll see who I can reach."

Three hours later when he is changing his clothes for the feast she calls back. In three hours she has given him this: Ten cities, fourteen phone numbers. "Not hard at all," she says when he nearly breaks down. "We're all still in touch."

And now he is no longer alone. Hope Merton does not ask him to say why he has not called her in all this time. Others had been driven the four thousand miles from the prisons of El Salvador, Ilopango, Mariona, walked up the back steps of her suburban New Jersey in darkness, some of them unable to walk, had been carried. Unable to remember, once they'd moved on, where it was they had been or the name of the woman who'd saved them. "Can you tell me a little about Luz?" she asks.

"I don't know where to start. She's quite a handful. She looks a lot like Raphael."

"Could you send me a photograph?"

"As soon as I get a chance."

She had started to give him her address. He knew it. Down to the zip code.

After that he hears the truck gears grind and goes out to sign for the ball-jumping game and watch the men set it up in the usual place. Then his committee arrives, fresh from the sidewalk. He explains that they are not to speak of it, or of Luz. Not at Our Lady of Guadalupe. It has nothing to do with the church. As if he had not even been to the sidewalk. As if he has not already blessed them.

They go on with the feast preparations as if nothing had happened that morning, or is happening this very moment. They put up the game tables, get out the electric bingo, eat the traditional egg salad and watermelon lunch that no one really relishes but has become custom, sip politely at Emily Otto's ginger mint tea. Their tasks done quickly and in silence, then everyone leaves. Father Bill does not have to ask where they are going. He simply thanks them, tells them he will see them later at Our Lady's Mass, goes into his office, sits down at the desk, takes the yellow pad on which he has written the names and the numbers Hope Merton has given, and starts his calls.

CHAPTER 33

Zoe settles into the deep-cushioned beach chair, looking at Luz's sturdy brown legs stretched out on the chair beside hers, her scuffed red sandals. Luz should take off her shoes, Zoe thinks. At least open the straps. Let those little feet breathe.

"Front row, look up and stop daydreaming. I have an important announcement."

The commanding tone catches Zoe off guard. She looks to the window. Nothing is there.

"Now pay attention. You won't be in this class forever." She knows she is probably hallucinating. That she is not in her right mind. But what if she is being compelled to attention by some force she does not even believe can exist? She could not endure it, knowing such a thing were true. Coward that she is, she chooses not even to try looking away from the window. If she tries to look away and cannot, she will panic. Easier to let the window make its announcement and hope it's a short one and interesting at least. Zoe squints and waits. Nothing. A pause. Zoe's mind drifts off. She thinks about Luz, who appears to be sleeping. She wonders about Walt and his son. "You are doing very well," someone says. Once again she'd been tricked. That time warp again. And it wasn't even an announcement, just a compliment of sorts. "You are doing very well." There she had heard it again.

I'm what? No, I'm not, Zoe thinks. *Are you kidding?*

"Yes, you are. You are doing wonderfully," the voice replies with great warmth. Now Zoe feels a gentle effusion of adoration coming at her being at a level so deep and so natural that for a moment she wonders whether it is simply one of her own misplaced joys that is flooding through her body. A stored joy knocked loose from her memory, detached from its cause, making her feel very much the way she felt after she and Michael made love. Not quite in her body. Not quite on this earth. She curls her feet and draws up her knees, wishing for a quilt or a sheet. In spite of herself she has a strong desire to melt down into it, drift off, maybe sleep. A joy so persistent and nearly unbearable in its persistence that for a moment Zoe has the uncanny sensation that something is wrong with her. She is simply unable to stop the good feeling, no choice but to bask in it, feeling wonderfully, floatingly well, as if all things and everything were perfect, as if she *is* in fact doing very well. And after some minutes or seconds or maybe even a half hour of basking, her mind returns and starts clicking. Several inches above her, it seems, Zoe can hear her own mind, attempting to figure out in what way anyone might think she is doing very well. There are so many ways in which Zoe judges herself to be doing not at all well in this moment. Marriage-wise, of course. Hers is not well at all. It is ill, perhaps dead. Her husband has left her a month ago now, not a word or a call, just a bunch of random thoughts and dreams. Which most likely are *her* thoughts, her dreams, her wishful thinking, not some mystical messages from Michael saying he is on his way back. *Michael is afraid*, says the voice. *But of what?* Zoe wonders. The voice in the window does not reply. What good is this voice if it won't answer her question about Michael? *A voice in the window?* she thinks. Maybe Luz is not alone in her delusions. Her transport. Zoe herself may have fallen into transport. By no means can a person who falls into transport be judged to be doing well. Nontheless, physically, she feels superb. Her body is in love with itself in this moment, all its swirls and swallows and juicings. Just fantastic how well she feels. Zoe is ripe as a fruit. She is studded with seeds. At any moment she could burst through her skin. But just past this moment is the future, the unbearable beauties of autumn. How will she stand it when she has gone back to Cold Spring and every day has to face the gold, the reds, and across the Hudson the tree line golden and scarlet and orange, more vivid and smoky each day, the cold air on her face as she steps out the back door and walks to her shop? The walk in such air, the smell making her feel so alive in her Michael-less emptiness. A person doing well does not dread the future, does not cringe at anticipated beauties of the fall. If she goes back and Michael remains nowhere-to-be-found, she will expire of longing and beauty.

And in this very moment when she is most self-condemning, most certain of her unwellness on nearly every level of life, she sees it—just for an instant right there in the window, a face so beautiful it brings tears to her eyes, a womanly face, the sweetest, most perfect of features. Now the face breaks into a luminous smile, so deep and golden Zoe is unable to bear it. She hears herself sigh long and luxuriantly as great sounds of pleasure escape from her once again and she can feel herself falling, falling, but this time, already reclining on Patty Platz's white-padded beach chair, there is nowhere to fall.

She sinks deep into the cushions, and after a while feels herself quite pleasantly beginning to rise. Gently lifting until she is nearly sitting up. Now she *is* sitting up, her head making faint nodding motions, inclining itself toward the window like a sun-tending seedling or a person in deep conversation. *Go on, yes, keep talking to me!*

You. Are. Doing. Very. Well. Indeed.

This is a dangerous drug, Zoe thinks. Very dangerous this sidewalk experience.

Zoe tears her gaze from the face in the window and shoots up in the chair with a jolt, startling Josefina out of her own reverie or transportation and startling the two rows of sitters behind her.

Josefina looks up. Even Luz slowly turns toward her. Oh no, Zoe thinks as she sees the big hat on Luz's head start to swivel—all of them ridiculous under the umbrella, under these hats—I won't let those eyes come at me again. And now fully herself, she gets off the chair and runs down the walk toward Walt's office, where the music comes from and the smell of barbecue rushes toward her, the chatter and laughter and smoke, all the people in back of the office who are having a party. Zoe heads toward them, toward the noise and the commotion where life is going on as it should.

CHAPTER 34

All afternoon Josefina reclines on the sidewalk in comfort, enduring the heat and the light. Her sleeping daughter amazes her—such fortitude—no child can remain still for this long, she thinks, certainly not her child. But there Luz lies in a state of great calm, unnatural, confusing, quite beautiful, in fact. She can't help but smile.

Behind her Josefina hears deep sighs of pleasure—indecent—are the old ones making love on their chairs? Now she hears movements, shuffling feet, chairs scraped against asphalt as some people rise and others, the waiting, come to take their places. Indifferent to the heat, the people keep arriving. Her neighbors, their faces familiar, the names she can hardly keep straight. She has been inhospitable these six years. Never one time inviting them for a meal or sharing a coffee (no coffee now, say the doctors, and no real tea). How long since she has thought of what it might mean to be once again friendly, not to be worn down by fears. Yet now, in this moment, her back to a whole host of strangers, she has no apprehension. Her shoulders do not stiffen; the skin on the back of her neck does not turn cold. She has not felt such safety since when? Since she was a child in the home of her parents before she knew her country was at war with itself, the breeding ground of horrors, disappearance, and torture. No home in El Salvador safe.

Another great sigh fills her. Each one seems to release the heaviness she carries and has come to accept in her body, release her from her own history. Nothing to carry, time to dream! And what waking dreams visit Josefina as she lounges like a lady of leisure, like her own mother, in fact. Her mother in her silk suit and pearls in the middle of summer looking cool, not a hair out of place, her long red nails. So surprising, this sidewalk sojourn, Josefina thinks. So much pleasure and ease comes to her from this day of her daughter's great punishment. If only the Felangela could share it, but there she goes jumping out of her chair once again. What is wrong with this Sewey who lacks patience for relaxing? Where does she go this time? To the field where the noise comes from now, music and laughter, the smell of grilled meat. Josefina is starving. What can she eat with that diet they have put her on? Only meat. Chicken, the whites of eggs, beef, rice, and bread. Oil. No salad. Few vegetables. Almost no fruit. Oh, it is the fruit that she misses most of all. The sweet guava, the papaya with its full belly of gleaming black seeds. It is the watery foods she must avoid. Even now she dare not drink water, only put ice in her mouth, letting it melt on her tongue. She takes a cube from Patty's cooler and places it in her mouth. "Are you thirsty, mamita? You want to suck ice? Here, you must drink." She puts a cube in Luz's mouth. "Good, take another. You want to hold it in your hand?"

The ice melts in Josefina's mouth. She used to do this when she was a child. Ice in her mouth. Esperanza as well. Who could hold it the longest, without biting down, chewing it into bits? Esperanza, always the winner, opening her mouth to show it was still there on her little pink tongue. And suddenly she can feel herself as she felt at that time, ten years old. Wiry and strong. *You are still young*, Josefina says, addressing her disobedient body. *You used to be perfect, remember?* The sense of well-being returns in a rush, as if memory itself could command it back. And now she is the one who is sighing and making indecent sounds. And Luz does not even turn to her mother. Her sleepy little saint.

Now Zoe is back, sitting down in her chair. Josefina gives her a questioning look. "Okay?" she asks. Zoe nods, but how annoyed she appears in her Chinese straw hat and her disheveled white dress, squinting at the window, which seems to disturb her. Of course, it is crooked and her fault. Don't look, Josefina thinks. Don't study your mistake.

And to think Luz waits for the Virgin to appear in such a poor receptacle. Josefina cannot help but smile.

And only when she remembers how Luz had walked from the house turning right and not left and onto the freeway in the midst of that light, does the fear that she carries return. A miracle, Josefina thinks, that her daughter was not hit by a car.

"Mamita," she says, leaning toward Luz, testing her forehead, the back of her neck to make sure she is not too warm. "How are you doing? You want to wake up? You need the bathroom? You want a break?"

Luz turns her head slowly and regards Josefina with half-closed eyes, as if she is partly asleep. All at once Josefina feels from her daughter such love, such naked and powerful love that she must turn away. How the shame burns through her then. What is wrong with her that she cannot endure her own daughter's gaze?

"Esperanza is coming for her rosary," Luz says huskily.

It is some minutes before Josefina can recover from the force of that gaze and is able to bring herself to speak. "What do you say, mamita?"

But Luz has turned away, and after several moments Josefina has lapsed back into the familiar well-being. She feels it flood through her, the sense that her body is once again perfect, smooth, unscarred. Filled with incredible energy.

She lets out an enormous breathy sigh and gives the window a cursory glance. In its center a brightness has appeared no larger than a fist. Very quickly it begins to change color from white to indigo to black, burning out like a short-lived star and leaving in its wake an eye, a single eye only, dark and relentless. Like the eye of the dishonored dead.

CHAPTER 35

Just around four, the temperature drops without warning, the sky becoming a rare welcome gray. First the winds, then a brief steady rain. The smoky aftertaste like flakes of blown ash dissolved in the mouth.

And after the rain, the strangers begin arriving in numbers, and the cars and vans continue arriving past evening and long into dark. The next morning, there they were on the field. License plates from all over the map, from far-flung states.

And the one who would come to be called the moon-faced man, who appears in the dark with a brown shopping bag, a small canvas stool, sits himself down, turns his shining white face to the window and remains on the sidewalk all night.

The ones who changed everything.

The ones who would say they'd been waiting.

CHAPTER 36

They had taken Ryan out in the fifth: two innings before Walt even arrived. He found a seat in the section reserved for the Chargers in the top, half-empty row. Gwen had grimaced as he mounted the stadium stairs; his daughter grasped onto her mother and Gwen's arm went around her. Tight. He had tried to focus on the action on the field, to cheer the team back (they were down eight to one). In the shadow of the dugout, his son huddled off by himself, his cap pulled down over his eyes, his face entirely erased. After the last Charger had been called out, Gwen and his daughter had rushed down to the field along with the other parents. "What the hell happened to you?" Gwen asked when he caught up to them.

"There's something going on at the car wash," he said.

"I'm talking about your clothes."

Then Gwen started across to the dugout but was stopped by a group of her friends.

Jen had pulled her face away when he went to kiss her. "Dad," she breathed. Everything he feared contained in that motion. She followed her mother across the field, joining a circle of Charger parents standing in well-groomed splendor. He had become unused to seeing so many people who were good-looking in that way. Walt said his hellos, and they barely gave him a glance. "I'll be right back," he said to Jen, then went to the dugout to let Ryan see he was there. The kids on the benches looked beat. Ryan hunkered down in his green Chargers cap, the coach going on about how lousy they'd played, the insults flying off his tongue like spittle. When he started in on Ryan, Walt walked away.

In the parking lot he managed to slow them down long enough to suggest they go out for a meal. "Give me the keys, Mom," Ryan muttered, as Walt tried to convince them it was still not too late to salvage a piece of the day. "I know you're disappointed in a lot of things right now, but it isn't as bad as you think."

"Fuck you," Ryan said.

"Ryan, try to hear this, buddy. We don't only get one chance in life. We get as many chances as we take."

"Bullshit," said Ryan.

"Oh God, Dad," cried Jen, "Please don't do this. You're just making it worse."

"Don't beat yourself up is all I am telling you."

"You weren't even there. You didn't see it. I folded. I cost us the game."

"Are you drinking again?" Gwen asked. "Is the plan to humiliate us, showing up looking like a derelict?"

"I'm not drinking," Walt said.

"Or do you clean those cars with your shirt?"

And they looked at him then, the three of them standing by the hood of Gwen's red Jag, he having stepped back a little, maybe to show them he wasn't dangerous, but at any rate stepping a little too far out in the lane with the exiting cars, ignoring the drivers and their horns. Suddenly, he was seeing right through their shame to the fear. Their fear for him, for what he had become.

"It's going to be all right," he said.

Then Walt remembered the earrings and fumbled in his pocket. He took out the box and stepped toward Jen, but she shook her head, too much for her even to look at that little white box. "It is not always going to hurt like this," he said, "I promise you. Take the earrings. Just take them, honey, please. I want to give them to you." He placed the box in her palm and closed her fingers around it. She looked at the box, "J. C. Penney?" His daughter had never been in a J. C. Penney.

"It's not a Tiffany year."

And she had laughed. A small delicious sound that went through him like water.

"I like the blue," she said when she looked at the stones.

"Oh, honey, good."

Then he turned to his son, to Gwen who was mercifully silent. "There'll be other games," Walt said. "Other dinners. Times I will look like you like me to look. You had a great season. Don't punish yourself for one loss. I am so sorry I was so late."

"You used to never be late," Ryan said, his breaking voice, bringing to Walt's mind the unbearable limb-split tree.

"I'll do better for you next time. I promise."

"Do you have any idea how hard you are making this for them?" Gwen said, then she put her perfect red polished thumb on the Open button, and the little chirp sounded, and the buttons of the Jag popped up.

"Bye, Dad," said Ryan. As he was getting into the back seat, he paused and looked at Walt and nearly smiled. "See ya."

Watching them drive off as he stood in his blue-blotched rag of a shirt with the mark on his pants from where Luz had kicked him, Walt felt unaccountably calm. He walked to the Civic, just one more thing that made his family ashamed to know him. How did he ever do that—show them that a way to know people is through their cars? What in him agreed to that way of knowing?

All of himself, he realizes. All of him had agreed. And for most of his life. And when it had all fallen from him, he had expected they would understand. It was a minor scandal. Title company kickback. He hadn't even known until the indictment, though now he would have made it his business to know. There had been many deals like that. Kickbacks to the title company, fairly routine. His secretary put the day's Orange County Register on his desk, and halfway down he saw his name. They were all being sued. He called his lawyer. Easy to get out of it. We'll just settle. People lost their shirts. Not him.

"I'm done," he told Gwen. "Good, go retire. Maybe I'll see you once in a while." "No, I'm stepping out of this. I need some time to reassess." "Reassess away," she says, "But know I'm not moving. I'm not moving the kids." "Honey," he said, "we can cut back. We don't need to live like pashas. The kids don't need—"

She brought him his salad. They were in the small dining room, ten-foot French doors open to the garden, pool beyond, shimmering blue. One hundred thousand in palm trees. "Try this. Heirloom tomatoes. The greens are organic. The cheese is trucked down from Sonoma."

Living in the guesthouse of friends, he started going to a gas station with a self-service wash. He'd never even noticed they had one. Cutbacks, he thought. And paid the six bucks and drove through. Something happened to him when that water rushed down. He wept. Every day for a week he went back.

One weekend he tried to take the kids camping. Get them away. Just be together. Somewhere new. A whole different scene. *Camping?* Like he'd suggested they sleep on the street. Alone, he drove out to Joshua Tree, spent three nights in the campgrounds, early spring, the whole place blazing with color. Ended his trip at a diner, sitting in a window booth eating strawberry pie, looking across the freeway at a for sale sign. Twenty acres. Saw, *saw* the thing he would build. A car wash.

Gwen thought he was joking. Then she thought it was the depression talking. And then, when he checked into the Infidelity Motel, though she knew they were pretty much done, she drove down and tried with everything she had to bring him back.

He still can't explain it, what he's doing. But somehow he trusts it will be for their good. He cannot say how. He only knows this, how far he has come in only three years, how much closer to the tenuous filament that is Walt.

He started the Civic and turned on the air conditioning. Seeing his face in the rearview mirror, he was startled. He looked so alive.

The whole drive home he replayed the trip, the way he used to replay Ryan's moves on the mound: how Jen had cried and taken the earrings, the surprise of her laugh. How Ryan had looked at him finally, full in the face with a hint of a smile, the sound of his voice when he told Walt good-bye.

And as he nears Infidelity, Walt allows himself to think again of the morning, of the faces he had seen and the little girl Luz. The joy expands through him once again, the heat and the gentle openings in his body. He grows certain in all that is happening, feels he is being moved past the known boundaries of his life.

Now he approaches the steep Infidelity grade, hoping the Civic won't overheat and strand him, as it has been known to do. He watches the gauge moving a little into the red and laughs, thinking of the first time he hit the Infidelity grade: the Mercedes sailed up the hill effortlessly.

The Civic sputters and balks, having reached the top under protest. Platz's garage on the right then the descent, straight into the bowl of the town. In the pink hazy distance he sees the signs: the motel—lurid pink neon, the diner in white. Across from them, Immaculate Autos, its neon deep blue. Infidelity—a blip on the map, his blip. He is almost there. Before him he sees a long line of cars, steady red brake lights, turn signals flashing. The image Walt's been carrying for three years in his mind's eye. It is here.

CHAPTER 37

When the Feast of the Assumption has ended, the game tables folded and put back in storage, icicle lights boxed, and all his people have gone home, Father Bill walks stiffly in familiar darkness to the rear of his church and lets himself into the rectory. His thighs ache, the long muscles agonizingly tight from contending with Luz on the sidewalk, so far past exhaustion he won't even be able to sleep.

Still, he checks his office in case there's a message, certain there will be none, but he is wrong. A soft-voiced woman, who speaks halting English, in an accent he recognizes immediately as the voice of a Salvadoran, has asked that he call her at 9 a.m. Stockholm time. "In your time, this is midnight," she says. The phone number is fourteen digits long. She repeats the numbers clearly, two times, but does not leave her name.

He sits down slowly in the hardwood desk chair, then leans back and raises his legs out before him, placing his feet on top of his desk, careful not to scatter his papers. He replays the message, copying the number on a new yellow pad. Stockholm, he writes.

He has only just learned from Hope Merton there are Salvadoran exiles in Stockholm, one thousand strong. Many are former guerillas, young boys when they fled eight years earlier, now men. Refugees all. The boys are not likely donors for Josefina, Father Bill knows. But still, there are others, who might have been from the capital, might have known Professor Raphael Reyes, or Josefina herself, someone who brushed elbows with her family, a past patron of her father's toy stores, a friend of a cousin, a student. A stranger with a blessed heart who would agree to be tested, tissue-typed, blood-typed. He has it all written down, what's required, the tests and the forms, the numbers for the transplant center at the High Desert Hospital, the numbers of her physicians. An act against the odds, this kind of search. Act and let go. He has put this entirely in God's hands. All the calls: Seattle; San Antonio; El Paso; Montclair, New Jersey; Berlin; San Jose, Costa Rica. And suddenly this message from Stockholm, a city not yet on his list.

How he will explain his August phone bill to the bishop, he has no idea. Perhaps he will simply tell the truth. He has a parishioner in trouble, indigent and ill. They are trying to locate a family member; her family is scattered all over the globe. A half-truth then, these *are* family, the ones who, like Josefina, had sought asylum and been denied. The ones who could not prove they had been persecuted except by the scars on their bodies, a category of proof not included on the document for seekers of asylum at the embassy or the border. The illegals, driven through Mexico by people like him, avoiding the borders, ferried to churches, hidden in private homes. Hope Merton's.

A Salvadoran from Stockholm. He cannot stop the rush of excitement. The stirring of premature hope. Twenty-five minutes to midnight. In Stockholm, it is morning, twenty-five minutes to nine.

He gets up and goes to the rectory bathroom, leans over the small blue sink, turns on the cold water and bends to it, washing his face several times then letting the water run over his hands and wrists. As he buries his face in the towel, his own smell comes at him and a vague uncleanness. He has not done the laundry since Josefina got sick.

He returns to his desk with time to review his questions, to look through his papers and rearrange them with the most important on top. Time for the necessary moments for prayer.

He cannot deny, as he begins his gratitudes, that the day has been full of gifts, so many that Luz herself has begun to seem at this late hour, muted at least, a part of the day, no longer the whole of it. This call, of course. Those extraordinary moments of realized grace. Yes, even the one that came to him on the sidewalk so insistent and deep that when it was over he was surprised to find himself not in his church, humbled that he had been able to share it and with so many. That there had not been a vision, even for that he is grateful. Especially for that.

When he moves into prayer, he goes deeply and quickly, a thing he has not been able to achieve in months. So deeply he does not hear the rectory door when it is opened. As he so often does, he has forgotten to lock it. When the human sounds work their way through to his senses, he opens his eyes.

"Father?" says Walt. "Are you sleeping at your desk tonight? You should at least lock the door."

Father Bill tries to stand up but is stopped by the burning in his thighs.

"I didn't want to call and disturb your sleep. But here you are, awake." Walt says.

There are folders and papers strewn over Father Bill's old desk, battered mahogany, the surface of worn maroon leather where Walt has so often sat with this man, trying to sort out his life.

"Were you working this late?" Walt asks.

"In fact, yes, I am."

"I have to discuss the situation at my car wash."

"Can't it wait till tomorrow?"

"Do you know what's going on there?"

Suddenly, the morning looms up again, insisting itself through Father Bill's consciousness when he has all but succeeded in shutting it down for the night. His stomach clenches as it did when he first saw Luz in rapture and had vomited.

"Sit down. I only have a few minutes."

A few minutes, Walt thinks, as he pulls up a chair, feeling slapped. Where to begin? With which of his miracles?

"There are people still out there on the sidewalk. And the cars keep coming."

"Really? Still? This late?"

"Still. There may be a hundred parked in the field now. And there are tents."

"A hundred, that many. Are they my people? Our people?"

"Some, but mostly not. Mostly strangers."

"I see. And what did you say, there are tents?" Father Bill asks, trying to picture one hundred tents on a sixteen-by-sixteen-foot sidewalk.

"Out back in the field."

Josefina did not mention tents. She did not mention strangers appearing at the car wash. He had discouraged his parishioners' talk about the sidewalk. Forbidden their questions about Luz. All those silent communings and visions that have lit them like present-day mystics. Even the word is insubstantial and suspect on the tongue. Father Bill picks up his pen and draws a box around the fourteen-digit phone number. "Did you call the highway patrol?"

"No. Do you think I should?"

"I suppose they don't need to be called. They'll see it. Are you afraid you'll be cited?"

"What?"

"Are you worried you'll be fined for the people on your property?"

"A fine? It didn't occur to me."

Walt shifts in the chair. This is not at all the conversation he has intended to have with Father Bill; it has gotten off on the wrong track. He has glories to discuss. Miracles he has witnessed, extraordinary things he has seen and felt within himself.

"Are they peaceful? Are they making any kind of disturbance, these people?" Father Bill asks, not looking up from his pad.

"Quiet. Very quiet. There were flowers and candles burning under my window, though I took them away. No one objected."

Father Bill nods. Now Walt is growing impatient. What is it with that yellow pad? That long line of numbers Father Bill is doodling around, as if this conversation is only mildly important and what happened today at the car wash and is happening still a trivial event. "I told them not to put anything under the window. That I'd throw it away."

"That was good."

Now Walt can hardly get his hands on what it is he really wants and struggles to retrieve it. For a moment the men are silent. Father Bill has managed to distance himself from the whole of it, Walt thinks.

Except, what was it Bryant Platz said? Something Father Bill had done with the crowd after Walt left. Walt had dismissed it as exaggeration. Bryant Platz had been angry. He didn't like Luz sitting out there, the people gathering. He didn't like who he saw there, the strangers with their flyers. He had been over the top with his fears.

"Do you think Josefina and Luz will be back there tomorrow?" Walt asks.

"I know they won't."

"You've discussed this with Josefina?"

"We are in absolute agreement."

Ah, thinks Walt, slammed with disappointment at the finality of it. Again, he feels he should plead for something. For what? For Luz to return? For the beauty of Luz, of the faces which he has not told Father Bill he has seen? Some people were saying that Father Bill had blessed them. Blessed the event. To ask if it's true now seems absurd. It was only a rumor, just as Walt thought.

"Two minutes, Walt, then we have to stop."

With only two minutes what can Walt ask?

"If there's nothing else, let's continue tomorrow. I have someone waiting for my call."

A midnight phone call, Walt thinks. Whom but a lover do you call at midnight? Father Bill has already spoken with Josefina.

Walt stands up, disgusted with himself. How completely the conversation has failed to represent him. If only he could find a way back in. "How was your feast?"

"We did very well. A little quiet this year. Not our usual crowd. The kids had fun."

"I guess I was the competition. The car wash."

Father Bill does not respond to Walt's half-hearted joke. He rises, wincing, and steps around his desk. "And how was the game?"

"Not what I hoped. It was a pretty bad loss. They're done for the season."

"How'd your son he take it?" Father Bill puts his arm under Walt's elbow, guiding Walt to the door. A polite man. Practiced in his professional courtesies, Walt thinks. A man who knows more than anyone how Walt has struggled to find his way back into his children's lives. They have discussed it countless times, in this very room. This man is brushing Walt off. This man Walt considered a friend.

"He took it hard."

"I'm sorry."

"It was a record-breaking day for me business-wise."

"Congratulations. That's a nice benefit." Now Father Bill opens the door. The night sky is breathtakingly black. The stars sharp as cut glass, the air so sweet Walt wants to feed it into his children's lungs.

No, thinks Walt. He will not let it end so easily.

"How did Luz get to me today?"

The question stops Father Bill cold. "I think it's pretty clear that she walked," then he pauses. "It turns out Josefina was mistaken about the time."

"Mistaken how?"

"Luz left the house at seven."

"Left at seven and was headed for eight o'clock Mass?"

"Something wrong with their clocks. A power surge in the night, we figure. Her time was all off this morning."

"And when did she realize this?"

"This evening. When they got home and she looked at her clocks; they were off by an hour."

"Well, I'm glad to know that. I was pretty disturbed. About the time thing. So then she just walked along the freeway to me by herself, in all that traffic in that light?"

"There is a problem with Luz and her walking off. But we all know that. I'm sorry it upset you. I'll let you go now, Walt. You must be exhausted. It's been such a long day for us all. By tomorrow this whole thing will be behind us. I am going to make sure none of my parishioners go back. And thanks once again for your help today with Luz. And for the shirt. I'll get it back to you soon." Father Bill puts a light hand on Walt's shoulder then lets it linger just for an instant, and for an instant Walt thinks he is going to ask him back inside. "Goodnight, Walt," Father Bill says, and lifts his hand and goes into the rectory, closing and locking the door.

I am alone with it now, Walt thinks as he walks to his car. How deftly Father Bill has avoided any discussion of Luz. He has lied too, of course, about Josefina's clocks. Walt is sure of it. They must have decided on that story, Father Bill and Josefina, in a conversation he cannot begin to imagine.

He approaches the Civic, feeling suddenly used, a rawness taking hold in the center of his chest, a tightness in his windpipe as the doubts come with a vengeance. Is he ridiculous? Dangerous or deluded? Had he imagined those faces and Luz? He and the others, all drawn to his sidewalk out of what—the need to connect with something more spacious than their own failed lives? Suddenly he is wrong again, wrong in the old way. How can he trust his experience of this day when he feels himself wrong to the core?

He pauses, turning back to Our Lady of Guadalupe, entirely dark save for the light in the rectory. The wideness of the High Desert night sky devours the last of his pride. He has nothing again. Only these feelings and faces and hunches. Like that, they have been taken away—the joy and the certainty completely dissolved. Even the beauty of the sky—a summer sky with a spectacularly red Antares—seems like a rebuke. He will drive to his sorry little cinderblock house that would make his kids frightened, ashamed. They are wise to avoid it. He'll drink a few beers, or more than a few until his body is numb and his mind is a blur, and then he will sleep off this day.

He gets into the Civic and begins the trip home, taking the back way over unpaved roads, avoiding the freeway, avoiding his car wash. He is bumping over hard dry earth, driving straight into the night sky. He waits to be swallowed, for the stars to stop his thoughts, but even the brilliance of the stars insults him tonight, the stars with their deceptive presence, all those suns that have long ago died that he sees clearly but knows are not there.

CHAPTER 38

From the moment she wakes, even before she looks in the mirror, Josefina Reyes knows something amazing has happened to her. She had felt it even earlier, in the night, as if a great hand has come through her body and scoured her clean.

In the morning she is able to stand at the sink, look at her face in the mirror and not flinch. No swelling distorts her jaw and her cheeks; her color does not bear a hint of the yellowish cast, the whites of her eyes white to the rims. And her skin so taut and shining, she looks just as she did in the years she was healthy and pretty, and Raphael, bending to kiss her, would cover his eyes pretending to be blinded by the sheen of her face.

It was all due to her day on the sidewalk, she thinks. For herself, if not for Luz, she had done such a good thing to stay there. Her daughter chastened, her body rested to the core. That's what it had been. Her face is the proof. So she had forced Luz, well, perhaps that was just what they needed. Perhaps she has worried too much every second for her daughter's opinion and feelings. Perhaps a little forcing of Luz will have been for the best. It does not matter that Luz had hardly eaten dinner, would not speak (not even to demand to be taken to the feast), went straight to bed, refusing her goodnight kiss.

For the first time in memory Josefina had not worried at all about Luz. She herself had been able to stay awake long past midnight, no rushing to the bathroom with every thin stream of urine. Nor did her feet develop the achy bruised swelling that had plagued her for months. There was no need even to elevate them, though she did out of habit, sitting with Zoe on the brown couch, sipping her half cup of tea while Zoe with her bare feet planted firmly on the hard wood floor drank several whiskeys in quick succession, unable herself to relax. Had it not been for Zoe, Josefina would have enjoyed a whole evening's peace.

"I thought the day would never end," Zoe had said. "I thought I'd be stuck on that sidewalk the rest of my life."

"For me, I must tell you, it was just as everyone said. Very peaceful, quite beautiful, really. I am sorry you suffered."

Even the eye that had appeared to her in the window at the end of the day seemed insignificant compared to the delight Josefina felt from being on the sidewalk, among good people, able to feel their goodness. Her daughter was well and close by, dozing lightly, not one complaint. There had been some nice food and that lovely umbrella to shelter them from the sun. Everything perfect, even the silver smell before the rains and the cool air that followed. She could let go of the eye in the window the same way she was able to let go of the question of how Luz had managed the one-mile walk to the car wash. The question floated up through the roof of the blue house that night, where it hovered but did not spoil her peace.

It was Zoe who worried her way through the evening, mostly about Luz. Several times, just to pacify Zoe, Josefina had taken her to look in on Luz as she slept. To bend over the bed with the canopy floating above them and gaze at her child in her summer pajamas, sleeping deeply, her dreamless lids still and delicate as shells, her brow cool. Not a hint of the rose smell, even. How charming, Josefina thought, as she looked at Zoe gazing down on her child, that the Felangela had formed such an attachment to Luz.

Now the Felangela was uncertain whether to go back to her Cold Spring home as she had planned. Because of Luz, she had confessed, when they sat once more on the couch and picked up their drinks, but also because of the influx of strangers. Her husband might soon be among them.

"And why would he come to Infidelity? Because your window has suddenly grown famous?" Josefina had teased as she moved closer and patted the Felangela's strong thigh. The Felangela did not even smile. It was then that she tried to tell Josefina the rumors she had heard, first in Walt's office and then later from the strangers camped on the field, all the places she had run to when she couldn't find peace on the sidewalk. "But there are always rumors in this town," Josefina dismissed them. "Many people stepped out of their lives for a rest and a little fun on a day that my daughter was punished. In one day it will all be forgotten. Of course, you are welcome to stay if you choose. But don't fool yourself that your husband is coming, or that anything amazing is going to happen here." Josefina felt the warmth of friendship spread through her chest in a rush, a feeling so familiar yet so long lost she had nearly forgotten how lovely it was. She wished she had some place comfortable to offer the Felangela, a room with a lovely cool bed, clean linens, a vase of tall flowers. But the Felangela was happy to sleep on the brown couch with only a sheet. "Maybe in the morning when I see that Luz is okay, I'll feel better about everything. Maybe then I'll be ready to go. Unless Michael shows up."

"She is okay, believe me I know my own child. Try not to worry so much. This was an excellent lesson for Luz. You'll see. And don't get your hopes up about that husband of yours. That isn't wise." But now the thought of the Felangela actually leaving made her sad. She drank the last sip of tea and kissed Zoe goodnight. Only the prospect of the four-hour treatment Josefina would have to endure in the morning distressed her that night.

Josefina slept deeply and well, dreaming of Esperanza and Raphael, such a warm pleasant dream, the three of them sitting in the garden of her parents' pink stucco house under the shade of the dark-leafed ceiba. Esperanza no longer a girl but a woman, with full breasts and laughing eyes, had been telling a story. Such an interesting woman she has become, Josefina thought, so intelligent, so full of humor. She was about to say as much to Raphael, who was listening himself, his eyes so keen and alive Josefina woke with a pang of longing such as she had not felt in years. And for several moments she was able to reach into the dream and be happy, her husband and sister living and well, her own life unbroken by loss.

"Why is Luz sleeping?" the Felangela greets her as soon as Josefina comes down the hall. She stands beside the dog-eared Madonnas of the Centuries that Josefina looks at briefly with amusement. "Children sleep, sometimes," says Josefina. "They sometimes surprise us by sleeping late. I am going to make some tea. Would you like some? Or maybe first you will take a chower."

Zoe chooses the shower and Josefina is glad, the dream of her sister and husband is still with her and she wants to hold onto it as long as she can.

Later when Zoe is dressing, Josefina takes her half cup of spearmint tea and looks through the kitchen window and into the light, not even knowing the time, for her clocks are all off, and her telephone as well. Even the temperamental television that came with the house is blaring, and she has to run back from the kitchen to turn it off lest it wake Luz.

Her clinic appointment is for ten o'clock. Father Bill is going to arrive between nine fifteen and nine thirty. Her kitchen clock says 2:22, and the one in her bedroom 4:44. How strange, she thinks, when they had only last night discussed what to tell people about Luz's inexplicable walk to the car wash. "Blame it on a power surge," Father Bill had suggested. Apparently, they have had one.

Then she returns to the kitchen, opens her back door, and steps outside. The blinding white light forces her to shield her eyes. The light is harsh, but the air feels kind. How good, she thinks, and takes a strong breath of the sweet air. Four hours at least she will have to sit on the chair in the clinic for her treatment, and on a day when she feels so thoroughly fine she swears she could run to the car wash herself and still not be tired.

Across the driveway through the scrim of the light she can see Wren Otto sitting in his backyard in business dress, that peacock blue tie, drinking his coffee and reading the paper as he does every morning. He looks up, catches her watching, then waves. Josefina waves back. A great feeling of affection for her neighbor sweeps through her. She walks in her housedress and her soft blue cloth slippers across the driveway and into his bone-dry yard with the little beds of yellow and orange manzanita and says good morning and asks how he is, filled with the simple happiness of morning. "Fine and dandy," he replies, rising in a half bow, the formality of which she finds charming. "How about I fix you some coffee?" "No coffee, thank you. I already have tea." "How 'bout a biscuit at least?" "All right, thank you." And she sits down in the chair opposite Wren Otto's chair under a flowered umbrella with the faded yellow tassels that she has seen from her kitchen window every morning of the four months she has lived on Mariposa Lane. Under the umbrella that, all that time, has seemed as distant as the white peaks of the San Jacinto Mountains.

"Emily's going to be jealous when she comes back from church and I tell her I had my coffee with a beautiful young woman." He has returned with the biscuits on a white and gold plate.

"Thank you," she says, as she takes a biscuit, "but maybe we should not tell your wife."

When Wren Otto smiles, Josefina can see how handsome he must have been in his youth, his fine even features, the light in his eyes. "Oh, Emily will find out some way, I don't think we can keep this a secret. Besides, she'll be glad. She's quite the fan of your daughter, you know." He sits down, slowly, as if his bones were not quite certain of themselves. "Where is Miss Luz this morning? Did she go off to Mass?"

"Sleeping off her punishment, I am afraid."

"Punished? What did she do?"

Josefina makes up a small lie, for she remembers how happy he had been on the sidewalk and does not want to insult him, and Wren Otto does not question her further. He picks up a biscuit, studies it with pleasure, then takes a bite. Then he offers her a section of newspaper and she reads a wonderful small story about the Mojave tortoise, which is returning in strength in their region. She finishes her tea and her delicious lemon biscuit, then says good-bye and goes into the blue house to see if Luz is awake.

Later, after she has gotten Luz ready and the Felangela has left for the day looking lovely and calm in that attractive white dress, and William has arrived to drive them to the clinic for her treatment—the first one that Luz will watch—Josefina remembers the good news about the Mojave tortoise and turns from the passenger seat to look at her daughter, who is seated in the back. Luz looks withdrawn, as she had looked the previous night—the same distant expression she had worn after her dangerous walk to the campgrounds in the spring. "I missed the Feast," Luz says.

Ah, thinks Josefina, now we are in for it.

"And we missed you," William says, cheerfully. "But there will be next year," though the moment he says it he knows in that way that he cannot explain, there will not be.

"Mamita, this is a new day. You have school starting in two weeks and new books, and new friends to think about. And the Felangela has promised to come back tonight with your cake."

"Where did she go?"

"You know what she does. She went to search for her husband. Maybe she will find him this time and bring him to the house in the Nova. Wouldn't that be exciting?"

"But where did she go?"

"I am sure she will tell us when she gets back."

I know where Zoe went, Luz thinks, and she touches her right knee then her left, then reaches down to feel one foot then the other because her body feels strange and far away. And when Father Bill turns just for a second from the driving seat to look down at her, Luz is surprised that he is smiling the old way. As if she had not seen him yesterday frightened and sweating and telling her over and over, "Come back, Luz, you must not do this!" As if he has forgotten the sidewalk already, with Luz far down in the gold of Our Lady where he had not wanted her to go.

The whole ride to the clinic she thinks about the sidewalk and the way she had been called, and her heart bangs hard with excitement. But she cannot remember the feeling of her feet. She thinks of the big green wings she has seen so clearly and of the gold feeling that had come to her and stayed. All day long after her mother had made her go back to the sidewalk, Luz felt the gold rising up and running out, rising up and running out, wider and wider until she had drifted far from her body, becoming part of the ocean of gold. She wonders about the people in the chairs and how so many had come to the sidewalk and wonders if anyone else had the gold ocean feeling. If anyone else had been *called.* But whom could she ask? She had tried the Felangela, but she had said no. Maybe Walt, thinks Luz. And yet, even though the gold was so good, something was missing, in spite of the gold and the rising, in spite of how far Luz could reach, Our Lady had not shown Luz Her face.

And all of a sudden in Father Bill's car with her mother looking so pretty and being so cheerful, Luz's body feels hungry, not for food but for something else. The hunger begins in her body on the Joshua Freeway in the middle of the drive to the clinic, stronger than the hunger for any food. She could tell her mother who likes when she's hungry, but Luz does not know how to say it. She does not know where in her body it comes from. It seems like it comes from everyplace inside her. Every muscle, every part of her skin. Every small cell.

And the hunger does not go away until the nurse, dressed in flowers and sneakers at the clinic, calls her mother back for a second test and, instead of going for the treatment after that, calls her mother a third time. This time her mother has to go to the desk and talk on the phone to the doctor, who is at a different place. Then Luz feels like herself again. She feels her whole body, even the knees and the feet.

That day Luz does not go to the J. C. Penney with Father Bill and twenty-five dollars for anything she wants for school. She does not see the tube near her mother's heart or her mother's blood going around and around in the special dialysis for giving Mami's strong blood to others. Because after Josefina had talked on the phone to the doctor, they had left and gone back to the blue house for lunch.

"Good luck," says the nurse and smiles across the room at Luz, and even the lady at the desk smiles this time.

But first Father Bill says, "I don't believe it," to her mother and walks back to the desk, and the nurse and the lady speak to him but Luz cannot hear. And the whole time both ladies smile and shake their heads as they talk to Father Bill as if something good has happened.

"What's the matter?" asks Luz, getting back into Father Bill's car. "Why are we leaving?"

"Nothing is the matter. The tests are normal."

"Is that good?" Luz asks.

"It is amazing," says Josefina. "But to tell you the truth, I already knew."

Then, in the car driving back to the blue house, Josefina sits in the back next to Luz very close and takes her hand and puts her mouth very close to Luz's ear and tells Luz another amazing thing. How early that morning when Luz was still sleeping and Zoe was taking a very long shower to get ready to look for her husband, Josefina had walked out of the kitchen with tea to visit Wren Otto in his yard where he always drinks coffee and wears the striped tie. And how wonderful a thing this was for her mother, for the first time since Luz was a baby, to walk out of her house without worry and take breakfast with a neighbor.

CHAPTER 39

Walt Adair puts down the phone, rubs his chin, sorry he has not shaved, tells Chico Platz he will be gone for a bit, then excuses himself past the customers waiting on line in his office, lined up on his steps, and walks out to the field to find Zoe.

The light hurts his eyes. He has forgotten his sunglasses and hat. People come up to him, wanting to talk. They praise his wash; they ask about Luz. He smiles and shrugs. Better not to speak now. He could easily say the wrong thing.

He moves through the rows of random parked cars, holding on when he loses his footing. He finds her in a far row out by the tents, in that white dress and the big yellow hat, feeling her way through like she is trying to read each car by hand. When he calls out to her, she turns around, then he stumbles. He stands up, shakes the grit off his hands.

"Could you stand still for a minute? Better yet, come on with me to the office."

"What's going on?" She stops and waits for him to catch up, leaning against the hood of a '66 Mustang. Cream color, a classic, nicely restored, with Missouri plates. Through the thin dress he can see the length of her torso, the delicate curve of her breasts.

He looks around to make sure no one is near. Only the cars, haphazardly parked. "They're coming down to see me."

"To see you?" She looks at him, so lovely, her body, that graceful white dress, the hat throwing shadows on her face. "Are they putting Luz back on the sidewalk?"

He doesn't know what to say. "Don't walk away. I need to ask you something."

"You already did. I said no."

"No," he says, "something else." He hurries behind her. "How are you doing?"

"Lousy."

"How's your head?" Walt asks, "Still got that headache?"

"It's better." She takes off her hat and feels the back of her head, the wisps of hair blowing across her face in the hot wind. "Just a little bump."

"That's good. Is there anything I can do that will help you right now?"

"Help me find my van." Then she puts the hat on again.

"Okay."

"Do you know what you're looking for?" she asks, still moving. She will not slow down.

He pretends to be thinking, scans the landscape, the dark heaviness of mountain beyond them, the bleached expanse of the desert, the light shooting off the hoods of the random parked cars, Zoe's beauty. "White Caravan. 'Luedke and Payne' in blue lettering on the passenger side." Walt smiles.

At last she stops, turns around. "That's right. Because that's why I'm here, Walt. I've got a flyer. I'm just one of the flyer people. Only I'm not looking for transformation and joy. All I want is that van and my husband."

Oh, she is hurting. She is not in good shape. Of all the times and all the places for her to be like this: nicely broken down and open to her sadness. He's reminded of that thing he's hoped for since the first night he saw her when she'd come through his wash, her face covered in tears. "Better yet, I'll tell the kids to look out for your van. And keep looking out. I'll tell everyone who comes through my car wash, Beware of the Luedke and Payne white van. Meanwhile, come on and see Luz." He reaches out and takes her by the arm. She does not recoil.

"I'm not going near the sidewalk."

"They're not going to sit on the sidewalk."

"Of course they are. Why else are they bringing Luz back?"

He leans back against the door of a small white car, feeling the metal hot through his slacks and onto the flesh of his buttocks. He grinds his Nike into the pebbled surface of the earth. "What would be so bad about it?"

"What would be so bad? For starters? Everything."

"Why?" he asks quietly and looks straight at Zoe, her eyes hidden in the shadow of the hat, hands at her sides, the small imperfection of her left hand in view. "What happened to you on that sidewalk? Did something happen with Luz?"

"I'm not going to talk about it," Zoe says.

"No one is talking about it. Why is that?"

"I don't know."

"Well, I think they should. I think they should put Luz back out there, and I think she should be turned."

"What?"

"They should turn Luz around so everyone can see her face."

"You are talking crazy."

"I may *be* crazy. I saw things. Saints, I think. Beautiful men, the kindness just melting out of them." He takes a step toward her, lifts his hand, moves it through the hot, weighted air to where he can feel Zoe's breath. Offering her the coppery heat of his palm, the salt of his sweat. "Saints were this far away from Luz's face."

"Is this some kind of joke?" She takes hold of his wrist and tries to pull his hand away. His own strength surprises him. He wants her to feel it. How he has seen them.

"Different ones. Plenty. One after the other. As close as my hand to your face, all beauties—amazing." Zoe hardly takes a breath. When she does not step away Walt goes for broke. "We are so close to the wisdom. It's just waiting on us. Just a millimeter away, I think."

"You're serious."

"Yes, I most certainly am."

"When did this happen to you?"

"Just after I found Luz on the sidewalk."

"And what did they say, these beautiful faces?" Her tone is half-mocking, but he doesn't care about the part of Zoe that does not believe him. She is listening. She had *asked.*

"Say? They were faces; they looked. They didn't say a word."

"How do you know that you really saw what you saw?"

"I just know it." There, he's said the truth. All night he had wrestled between doubt and certainty, and when he woke he just knew. Zoe lets out a sigh, an enormous sigh that if he could see it, would stretch past her body and into the air. Then she gets quiet; her shoulders go soft. She is struggling. The knowledge of this moves him deeply. "I have never seen anything in my life that filled me with such happiness."

"And what do you think it all means, that they came to you, all those faces that made you so happy?"

"No idea. Not a clue. Aside from how beautiful it was and that Luz gave them to me."

"Luz doesn't give them. If you even really saw what you say. She's seven and a half years old. You can't lay what you saw on a child."

"Okay, then explain it."

"Me? I'm the one who's supposed to explain it?" She laughs and withdraws her hand. "I don't know anything."

"How 'bout the window, maybe that has something to do with my faces."

"Not funny," she says.

"The window you installed, even though I didn't want it."

"Okay, that's enough."

"So tell me, Zoe Luedke, why does Luz ask for you? Because your friend, Father Bill, was very clear when he called, he wants you there—Josefina does too, Luz most of all—in my office and possibly after."

"Father Bill, my friend? I don't think so. And I don't know what they want."

"No idea at all?"

"I just told you I don't."

"Okay, well what shall I say to her?"

"Say you didn't find me. Say, I don't know what."

"She's going to be very disappointed. So am I. You're the only person who knows about my faces."

"Lucky me," Zoe says. "Listen, you are not in a great state right now. I am not in a great state either. And Luz, I'm afraid to think about what kind of state Luz is in. So please forgive me if I can't take your beautiful faces seriously."

"Who would? You think I don't know how crazy my faces sound?"

That's when they laugh. A nice tension-relieving, mood-elevating laugh, and hers so musical it makes him want to bring her down to the dancing—already begun, he can see the far-away dancers out behind his office. He can hear the music now all the way from where they stand, way out in the field, all the cars around them, the heat shining off the hoods, none of them hers. All the people on the field, not the one that she thought she would find. No husband. Only him. And now Luz.

"Come on. Give us a shot and go back."

"Not me," Zoe says. "I'm done. If I decide to hang around, I'm going to stay here with the cars where it's safe. Pitch my tent with the flyer folk and see if my husband shows up. The whole thing is too weird for me. Saints floating over Luz—quite an invention. I have to hand it to your mind."

"Do you think I could invent this stuff? I'm a failed real estate developer. Did you know that about me? I see concrete and steel and revenue. Stuff you can put your hands on. Or I used to." He moves in a little closer to Zoe, his voice low and excited. "What do you think these people would give to know I saw saints here yesterday?"

"It wasn't saints. It was just faces. And don't forget I am one of these people. I've got the flyer to prove it."

"Your choice," says Walt, "but you're going to miss something fantastic."

"That's okay," says Zoe, "I'll pass."

"You can always change your mind," he says, then moves in and holds her just for a moment. Not even a real embrace, just a holding. Still, it knocks off her hat. She doesn't try to pick it up and stands stiffly, while he stays with his hands barely touching the back of her waist, the suggestion of her flesh beneath them, the air between them. Then she slides her hands up his back and rests them lightly on his shoulder blades. It takes everything he has not to pull her to him, just for an instant, so he can feel her body relax into his. But he keeps himself back. He becomes aware of a buzzing in her body as if there are high tension wires running through her chest and her arms, giving off a charge. "I'm betting you'll show up," Walt says, his face grazing hers, dry, warm, not quite real.

"Hang onto your money," she says. Then she bends down and retrieves the hat.

He walks back through the field, nods to a few of the strangers but does not stop to talk. He enjoys the walk and the people, the softening of the light. It absolutely floors him to see the line-up of cars at his wash, his blue neon sign, and the kids, the Infidelity kids, out in droves. Where do they hide in the summer? They are out on the entrance and exit lines with blue rags and sprayers working away for nothing but tips; they are out at the food tables serving, and some of them are dancing—some dancing even with the little kids. And it had been Zoe Luedke whom he told about those glorious faces. Zoe in her buzzing loveliness and that white dress, who had heard him and been afraid and made him so glad.

He knows now that something wonderful is happening, and it seems both his and beyond him at the same time. What he has seen and what is about to show up, Josefina and Luz. Father Bill coming back.

Before he reaches his office, he stops to chat with the Infidelity ladies in their pastel short sets and thin dresses who have set up the tables and the music under his back awning. He smiles at the little kids racing around them, studies the dancers, their ease in their bodies and wishes he could join them. Wishes to be young, to do it all better, all right—all differently. Wishes Ryan and Jen were here with him now. Maybe tonight he'll dance for a little while with Zoe. "Let's get the yellow tape up like we had yesterday," he says to Patty Platz. "Let's open the umbrellas and get it ready just in case."

"I went into your office three times to ask Chico when they'd be here. He thinks I'm crazy. I knew they would be back. Why does it make me so happy?" Patty says.

Oh, thinks Walt, this is going to be tough. Where are we going to put all this happiness?

"It just feels like we're blessed," she says. "Slap me if I say it again." Then she runs from him as if she cannot stand it either. She gets Chico's friends to look out for Tommy then takes a group of the women to the sidewalk to set up the chairs.

Walt goes into his office and announces to all his customers that he is closing but will open in a while, half an hour or so. They'll know when. Sticks his head out the door and repeats his words to the people on line.

"How's Luz getting here today?" Chico asks. "Flying or walking? Or is Father Bill bringing her in on one of those religious float-things?"

"See, that's just what we don't want. That kind of talk can hurt all of us," says Walt.

"I was joking," says Chico, hooking his long fingers into the waist of his black stovepipe jeans.

"Don't. People won't get it. You be quiet. And pick up the damn flowers. It's like somebody died out there." He gives Chico a trash bag, a thirty-gallon heavy-duty black one. "Don't forget to get rid of the candles. Blow them out. And Chico, see if you can get your friends back. I'd like someone outside the door for a while."

"Expecting a break-in?" he asks as he leaves.

Walt locks the door, drinks a quick cup of coffee, and opens up his Yellow Pages and orders the Portosans from the first place he calls. The earliest they can get them to him is just after five. He orders three units at ninety a day for a week, unable to imagine he will need more, or for longer. After that he calls his kids and leaves them a cheerful message. Cheerful but not over the top. And he ends it with love.

Then he tackles the bathroom: washes out the sink and scrubs down the floor with his mop, washes his own face and hands in the lemon-lime soap, and runs his hands through his hair.

And in the last moments when he feels the anxiety coming on—the chill in his shoulders, the tightening in the center of his chest—he spills out the coffee and makes a fresh pot, then sits down on his gray velvet couch to rest. It is missing a back cushion. He hasn't noticed till now. The far right back cushion that Luz had kneeled on, which seems to be gone.

CHAPTER 40

The first thing that strikes Walt when he opens his door is how well they all look, shiny and spiffed. Luz in her yellow dress, not a crease, her red sandals polished. Father Bill well shaved in his green parrot shirt. Josefina in red lipstick, a skirt that shows her legs, curvy, not thick at the ankles, as they have been. It's a bit of a shock. He has not noticed before how pretty she is. He closes and locks his door, relieved to see Chico and his friends outside.

"Who invited you to my party?"

"Me," says Luz. He wonders how much she remembers of the previous day, what she knows now. What *they* know. He can hardly imagine that Josefina would be happy to learn that her daughter can call forth the wisdom of the ages on this earnest brown face. "Because now I'm not punished and I missed the feast."

"My daughter wants to come back and then this one copies!" Josefina declares. She kisses Walt lightly on the cheek, squeezes his hand, walks to the couch, and settles down. She crosses her legs and puts her arm around the back of the sofa and smiles.

"This one?" Father Bill has walked straight to the coffee machine and reached for a mug. It could be any Thursday, Walt thinks. Father Bill could be stopping by for one of their quick midday chats. Maybe Walt should suggest they take down the racquets and play a set of air ball. "Here, Father. You use the Connors," the prize yellow racquet that hangs on the wall behind his counter.

"Yes, this one, I am talking to you," Josefina replies provocatively. "For no reason he says he wants to come to the car wash, too."

"Not for no reason," said Luz skipping down to the window. She glances out, turns, and begins to skip back.

"Sit down with me, Luz," Josefina says and pats a cushion.

"And what is his reason?" Walt asks, not sure what he's supposed to do now. Sit down next to Josefina? Go take a mug and have some coffee with Father Bill?

"I am here for my girls," Father Bill says, "Wherever they go, I go." He puts his mug under the spout, presses the top of the brewer, and pours himself a cup of coffee.

"He follows me everywhere!" Josefina laughs. "Indecent for a priest, don't you think?"

"Do you want to know the real *real* reason?" Luz says, evading her mother's grasp and skipping toward Walt a little too fast.

"Luz, please go sit on the couch!" Father Bill calls.

But Luz ignores him. "Do you want me to tell you why Father Bill copies?" she teases, touching Walt's wrist.

"Luz!" Father Bill says. "Go sit next to your mother."

"But I want to tell Walt the different one. He will like it. Father Bill came back because he loves the world."

Father Bill does not find this amusing. He looks as if loving the world is not a desirable condition.

"Coffee?" Father Bill offers Walt. He has brought two mugs of coffee and come to join Walt. "How 'bout a game of air ball?"

"We're long overdue." Walt picks up the mug, takes a sip of his own good coffee.

"Did you see Zoe?" Father Bill asks.

"I did. She didn't seem to want to join you. Maybe she doesn't love the world."

He takes a swallow of his coffee. "Do you think she's still around?"

"Oh, she's still here. Back on the field."

The men drink their coffee and listen to the singsong Spanish patter that fills the room now. Josefina and Luz playing a game.

"I'd like to apologize for last night."

"Nothing to apologize for," Walt says. "It was late. I intruded. I was upset about my kids."

The excitement is rising in Walt again, the thrill of all this: all of them here, looking so well. Soon, he cannot imagine how, they will be out on that sidewalk.

"I'm not going to be able to do very much."

"Okay," Walt says.

"A lot of it is going to fall to you. Do you understand what I'm telling you? I can't go out there with them."

Walt takes a moment. "All right." He waits for Father Bill to explain. He does not. "So, what's the plan?"

"They are going to sit on the sidewalk for a while and see how things go. Josefina liked it. She liked it very much."

"Lots of people liked it."

"So I've been hearing."

"Their chairs are ready. The things she asked for yesterday are there again."

"I saw that. That's good. Excuse me a minute. I need a refill. You?" Father walks to the coffee machine with his mug. Walt watches him, the bumpy, graceless gait, the still-heavy belly in spite of his drawn face. Walt's heart opens to his friend. Amazing, he thinks. What could have happened to change his mind? Now Walt is able to pick up the chorus of the song Josefina and Luz are singing, *el pequeño quetzal.* What was "*pequeño?*" Walt wondered. "Quetzal" he knows. He has learned it from Luz. It is a bird, perhaps imaginary. *The wings of the quetzal,* that's what Luz had told him yesterday morning, eight o'clock when she looked into the sky. *Big wings,* she had said. Walt hadn't believed her. Maybe they'd been there after all.

Father Bill returns with his refill; drops of it splash on the floor in his wake. He stands opposite Walt this time, on the customer side, a tourist in a green parrot shirt. He is being so careful, Walt thinks, weighing his words.

"You seem to be okay with this," Father Bill says.

"Oh, I am more than okay. I'm very happy about it."

"Well, it's certainly good for your business."

"It has nothing to do with my business." *Go on,* Walt thinks, *go on, William, step up to the plate—ask.*

"Did something happen for you with Luz?"

"Excuse me?" says Walt.

"Have you had any kind of experience?

What kind of experience? Walt wants to ask. But the question would have been disingenuous. For a moment, just before he speaks, Walt feels thrust into darkness. With a single word he is going to put himself into the void.

"Yes," Walt replies.

"Yes?" The priest makes a move as if he is going to take a step back, and it looks as if he has suddenly gone weak in the leg. Walt reaches across the counter and grasps Father Bill on the shoulder.

"I'm fine with it, really," says Walt.

Father Bill looks at Walt, trying to gauge if Walt is telling the truth. "You're full of surprises, my friend."

"Believe me, I'm pretty surprised myself."

"We'll sit together sometime soon."

"No hurry," Walt says.

Father Bill covers Walt's hand with his own, pauses for an instant, and that is that. He walks to his girls, says a few words in Spanish, then goes to the field to get Zoe.

CHAPTER 41

It is midafternoon before Zoe resolves to join Josefina and Luz and the thirty-two people sitting elbow-to-elbow on the sidewalk, slipping under Patty Platz's market umbrella and onto her chair. "Finally!" Josefina exclaims as if Zoe has been caught in bad summer traffic and has just now arrived at the beach. The light has dispersed, the temperature dropped, and the air is blessed once again with the promise of rain. Luz sitting upright, eyes half-closed, looking half asleep.

"Any luck?" Josefina asks, her voice thick and low, her eyes fixed on the window.

Yes, thinks Zoe. The luck is that you are doing very well. And for a moment, in spite of all her doubts, Zoe lets herself believe something wonderful is happening for them. It may already have happened to Josefina. Does the how and the why even matter? "No luck yet," Zoe says. "No Michael. Not a white van in sight."

"I am losing patience with that man," Josefina says. "If I ever meet him in this life, I will give him a piece of my mind."

"Who's Michael?" Wren Otto asks from his chair directly behind Josefina's.

"That husband of Sewey's," Josefina replies.

Zoe is embarrassed. *That husband of Sewey's*, as if everyone knows about Michael. As if she is one of their own.

She turns her attention to Luz, gone to them. Just like yesterday. Worse. Immediately, Zoe is met with a surge of uncontrolled love. Is it *for* Luz or *from* Luz? Zoe can hardly tell which. Under the big white hat Luz's mouth turns up at the corners. She is smiling, now she is nodding, her eyes barely open, the air around her turning grainy and golden, a diaphanous curtain, a gold that intensifies, until there is more gold than air, more gold than Luz. Beautiful, thinks Zoe, beautiful but dangerous.

"Josefina?" Zoe whispers. "Do you see this?"

"Shush," Josefina responds, "no . . . talking . . . now."

"I was waiting a long time for you, Zoe Luedke," says Luz, her voice clear and true.

"What did she say?" asks Emily Otto. "Waiting?"

No one replies, and Emily Otto does not ask her question again. The deepening gold on the sidewalk makes speech superfluous. It is perfection itself. Such eloquent sighs rise up from the sitters, as if a convention of grandmothers has arrived on the sidewalk to balance the sorrows and joys of life on a breath.

"If you go back to the sidewalk, make sure you are doing it for yourself," Father Bill had said to Zoe when he found her at last on the field. "Don't do it for Josefina and Luz. It will be your experience in the end. Yours if you allow it."

He knows, Zoe had thought. He knows what it is. And then he thanked her for what she had done for Luz. What had she done? And what is the experience, Zoe wonders, as she settles back on the beach chair and once again finds herself falling, giving herself up to the gold.

CHAPTER 42

Luz Reyes surfaces, opens her eyes, and pulls off her hat. Her dark braids in disarray, one in the front, the other undone in the back, a bright-eyed little girl just awakened from an afternoon nap. There is her mother who Our Lady already made well. There is the Felangela, taking a rest. "Are you still little, Zoe Luedke? Do you still love the world?"

As she pulls herself up through the gold and turns to face Luz, Zoe can feel a powerful heat emanating not exactly from Luz, more like through her. Bearable now, Zoe realizes, as yesterday it was not. Yesterday it had knocked her flat. What has Luz asked her? *Does she love the world?*

What can she say? If Zoe answers truthfully, Luz is bound to think she has come back to the sidewalk because Zoe too believes she has been called by Our Lady. Who but Our Lady could perform such a reversal of Josefina's hopeless condition?

Luz waits (looking so much like the photo of her father, Dr. Raphael Reyes, that broad forehead, those intense dark eyes). The people seated nearby wait too. Oh, if Luz Reyes would turn and ask them if they loved the world, how happy they would be in this moment to answer.

Zoe hesitates. This ridiculous world, Zoe thinks, and into her mind pops the eastern autumn whose beauty she can hardly endure. Cold Spring, New York, will she ever see it again, the place of her birth, the place she may love perhaps most of all? The smoky cold air, the burnished trees, the unbearable thick-leafed gold of the oaks. And then there is Michael, who has brought her such joy, walking out the back door to their barn full of plans for the day, a white mug in his hand, sloshing coffee onto his boots. Michael, who has run from himself, from her. Can she still love the world when Michael has run from their love?

What is her answer? Her experience of the world is so small, she knows only the smallest piece of it, and yet she loves it sometimes so much that she can hardly stand to carry it within her. Luz is waiting. Luz who might entirely misunderstand. But Zoe has only one answer. Only those two words: *I do,* Michael said, wreathing her hands in babies' breath, holding them up so she would never hide them again. *I do*, said Zoe, marrying him against all good sense, against Michael's own history. *I do,* said Father Bill, standing with her in his green parrot shirt on the field when Zoe had asked if he knew what he was asking—if he had accepted what Luz Reyes is.

No matter what Luz will make of it, how can Zoe say that she does *not* love the world? Who could possibly deny it who had been blessed to feel in even the smallest of ways how beautiful and precious a thing was their experience of the world? And in her entire life, only Luz has asked her such a question, calling forth something Zoe has never dared say.

"Yes, Luz, yes, I still love the world."

Luz nods matter-of-factly, then puts on her sun hat and turns back to the window. The big hat bobs once more, and all is silent on the sidewalk.

There, Zoe thinks, after a few moments have passed. *That's all she needed. Not the big deal I made it at all.*

But a few moments later Luz whispers hoarsely, "Keep on! Keep on because then Our Lady will show us Her face."

"What did she say?" Emily Otto asks, moving to the edge of her chair and reaching over to rest her delicate fingertips on Zoe's shoulder.

Zoe does not answer. Everyone is having a different experience. Hadn't Father Bill said that too? Don't talk about it with Luz or with anyone, he had said. Don't tell what is happening for you. A different experience. It is nearly a prayer. As close to a prayer as Zoe has known.

CHAPTER 43

Her daughter and Zoe have at last finished whispering their nonsense. Ay, what a question. How sweetly has the Felangela answered! But at least Luz asks something. At least she can still think and speak. (Though what were her last words? Josefina was too much in her own world to hear.) Now Luz is dreamy again, her eyes on that window. Josefina too looks, but still there is nothing. Where is the eye already? She was so looking forward to staring it down. To accusing it back. For three hours there is only the window. Was that eye peering out from the window only a phantom of her mind?

Perhaps the great hand that swept through her body has cleansed not just her blood but also her penchant to see what is not. That black smoky eye so much like her own, like her daughter's, the color of mud and smoke. She tries to remember its contours, the shape and the shading, tries to match it with eyes she has known. Who could it belong to? But the eye won't cooperate; it has taken itself away.

Now her stomach is growling. The cooler beside her is already empty except for six bottles of water, two small packs of chocolate-chip cookies. She has been eating constantly. What shall she cook for dinner? Pupusas, Luz's favorite. Josefina's favorite from childhood. A great deal of trouble but worth it. Does she have enough masa harina for the tortillas, the chicharrones to make filling? She has the bacon and garlic, green onions, tomatoes, the queso fresco and a nice log of cheddar, unopened, yes. Even a new jar of curtido for topping that is sour but that she and Luz both adore, but for Josefina curtido is forbidden, it is not on the list. Her mouth waters only thinking of how the pupusas will sizzle, perfuming her kitchen, the whole house! How many to make? How many will be at her table? The Felangela, of course, Father Bill. Maybe she will invite Walt, and the Ottos, so sweet and her neighbors. Won't that be nice? A party for dinner. The first in the blue house. Does she even have enough chairs?

Her stomach is growling, so loudly she is embarrassed. The good smells from the barbecue are drifting to the sidewalk, making it worse. When she can no longer endure one more pang of hunger, she sits up and reaches to Luz. "Mamita, let's go for a snack. The meats are still cooking. It smells so delicious."

But Luz will not be roused. She shakes off the hand of her mother, as if she is stuck to the chair.

"I must get up," Josefina says to the sleepy Felangela. "I am starving. You will watch her?"

"Fine," Zoe replies after a pause, pulling herself forcibly back to the world. What a relief, Zoe thinks as she struggles to sit and face Josefina, whose summons has called a halt to quite an unpleasant argument. *Pay attention*, came that voice, just as Zoe had felt herself most pleasantly at one with the gold. *You, in the first row, there's going to be a test. All eyes on me*! It was all Zoe could do to not get up and pound her fists on that window. And then she was caught, eyes linked once again to the window. *Try someone else. I'm a rotten test taker. I fold under pressure*, Zoe shot back in their perfectly unspoken language. And there it was, an actual face, quite familiar and plain, a maddeningly reassuring smile. *Just make sure to listen, and you will do very well.*

At the moment Josefina called her, Zoe had been trying to make her mind blank, to will it to wipe out the face and that voice. *Try it*, the voice had responded, privy to everything, could Zoe not think one private thought in its presence? *Contemplate the notion of zero. That's just brilliant. In fact, I am putting it right on the test. Extra credit to all who succeed.*

Instead, with Josefina standing beside her and tapping on her knee, Zoe was already thinking of the opposite of zero. *Infinity,* Zoe had thought. But what was infinity? And how did this whole thing end with her thinking of her least favorite, her least successful, her doing-extremely-poor subject?

Josefina has gone quickly down the walk past the line of Walt's customers before Zoe has even managed to take off the big Chinese hat and shake out her flattened hair, what little there is of it, nearly nothing in the heat and the zero humidity of High Desert summer. Even with the cooler temperature, the silvery smell of the almost-rain, there is not an iota of humidity. She must look a mess. *Doing very well hairwise?* Zoe thinks, *I don't think so*, but her eyes are on Luz now, who is still as a small marshmallow boulder. Lucky Josefina, thinks Zoe, escaped to the food tables. To the music and the kids in the mud. Why didn't she think of it? Because she's been otherwise absorbed. Being tested. Quite the experience today, Zoe thinks, reaching into the cooler Patty Platz has placed so considerately between her chair and Luz's. She takes out a cold bottle, beads of water coating it like jewels. The bottle promptly slides from her hand and rolls toward the window, stopped by a vase of red roses.

Luz whimpers. She squirms like a baby who is just waking up from a nap. Her eyes open wide, then without warning she shoots up from the beach chair. She is standing, the hat falling from her head to the chair, the braids tumbling around her. She gives a little cry, then half turns and stares at the crowd. Zoe hears a few gasps as several people teeter in their chairs, falling backward, the lucky ones saved by their quick-acting neighbors. One of the strangers seated close to the freeway is caught just in time before falling into the slow lane.

Zoe navigates the rows of sitters, the chairs crowded together, no space to walk, reaching Luz in the third row. Luz has stopped beside a man with a beaming white face, his eyes closed in rapture, the sweetest smile on his lips. So at peace he seems hardly aware of Luz. It takes all Zoe's strength to pull Luz from his side and guide her back to the beach chair. But the moment she's seated Luz rises again. Her arms start to whirl, her torso to twist, her head whips around, braids shooting out like a spinning black lasso. Zoe steps back to avoid being struck. For a moment everyone is spellbound, wondering if Luz Reyes will spin straight up in flight.

Father Bill has warned his parishioners not to react to what they see on the sidewalk. "No matter what happens, keep silent; don't move. Do not speak of your experience. You don't want to influence others." (Not even tell others of this? How will they keep it?) In less than a moment it's over. Zoe rises. Luz stills and sits down, looking confused. Zoe smoothes Luz's brow, walks the three feet to the window where the familiar face gazes, nonplussed, and picks up the water bottle, gives it to Luz. "Drink." Luz swallows and coughs then settles back in her chair. As quickly as it started the whole thing is done.

But not everyone on the sidewalk is a parishioner or a Hill district resident. These are the ones who stand up in awe, who cry out in wonder and fear. The ones who will tell it in the diner and again and again on the field.

CHAPTER 44

By the time Josefina saunters back to the sidewalk there is only the quiet and the prevailing calm. She is bursting from happiness, not to mention the honey-glazed chicken (smoky and crisp with thin rinds of orange), her mouth sticky and sweet from raspberry tart. Her hair is awry, her face flushed and damp (so many conversations in such a short time, so much laughter), careless and loose-limbed from dancing—how many years since she's danced? Ten at least! And who would have guessed Walt could dance the Merengue? What hips! Luz should go to the field and exult in the fun.

Luz and Zoe hold hands in the space between chairs, lightly dozing. How lovely they look, faintly gilded with afternoon light, this light, which has rendered the whole sidewalk golden: the sitters, the various umbrellas and hats, the coolers, the sidewalk, the shoes! (Ah, thinks Josefina, the sun has returned; we won't have rain.)

Josefina, strong in her breath and her walking, filled not just from food but also from kindness: from the women who insisted on making for her a plate so she could eat first when many were waiting in line. From Walt running out when he saw her so they could dance. And perhaps most of all from the children who kept calling for Luz.

"I want to go," Zoe mouths before Josefina can say a thing.

"You are ready to eat? You must also be ready to dance!" Josefina teases. Then she looks at Luz, who does not stir, who appears hardly to be in her body. Josefina puts a hand on Luz's face, which is warm and alive. Now a kiss, but the kiss does not cause Luz to stir. (Does she smell roses again?) "Mamita, sit up." Luz does not respond. "What is it?" Josefina asks.

"Something happened," says Zoe.

Something has happened in her absence? Right away the chicken churns up from her belly, the gall rising straight to her mouth. Down on the ground where it could so easily be lost she sees the green soapstone rosary, Esperanza's, where Luz must have dropped it or perhaps it fell out of the pocket of her yellow dress. "Is she sick?" Josefina asks Zoe. "What's the matter? What's wrong?"

"She's fine," Emily Otto replies. "She's resting now."

"All right," she tells Zoe as she bends to scoop the dropped rosary from the ground. "Mamita, the children are begging for you. Come now to the field and spend half an hour for play."

And still Luz does not stir.

"Get her up," the Felangela says in a low voice.

"I am trying." There is acid in her mouth and her throat, her arms growing heavy from fear. She removes Luz's feet from the chair, puts her hands behind her back to make her sit. "Please, one more minute," Luz says.

"You can get up?" Josefina asks, grateful for those four little words.

"Yes, Mami, but not right away."

Without thought Josefina's gaze goes to the window. An accidental glance, she is sure. And there is the eye, glaring at her once again. The eye she has waited hours to see that must have been biding its time.

Now you appear? Exactly in the moment when Luz is in trouble and I am preparing to leave? She stares into its glittering center unblinking, mustering all of the strength of her resolute will. "One minute, mamita," she says as she senses Luz trying to sit up. Then Josefina lowers herself to her chair. "Yes, yes," she tells Zoe who is urging her to stand. All morning she has waited for it to appear. How can she leave? She leans forward, the better to face it. And all at once the sparks in the dark smoky iris sizzle out. All life leaves the eye. In a blink it is gone. Immediately two eyes appear, brilliant dark eyes full of passion and force. The eyes hold her spellbound. She takes in their power, feeding it into her heart.

"Josefina, please," the Felangela insists. But Josefina cannot move a muscle. She has nearly forgotten her daughter. She is caught in a marvelous stare.

CHAPTER 45

Josefina throws up her hands and declares that her daughter is out of control. She has been dancing without rest through the blue house for nearly one hour. Her running feet pound the floor, her ceaseless chatter is driving Josefina to consider a whiskey, to enjoy one, then to open a beer. At this rate Josefina won't be able to coax Luz to bed until midnight. Ah, thinks Josefina, bustling from stove to counter with her bowl of risen maseca, her skillet of moist chiccarones, the hill of tomatoes she is just now getting ready to chop (her diet be damned), the scallions, the two kinds of cheese, her three iron skillets, her lovely white bowls. Her daughter is herself, only more so. Such a handful. So much noise in a four-room house. Thank God! Josefina who worries too much, imagines too far, and here is her Luz: alert, much too noisy, spinning and leaping and perfectly fine.

"Luz, go to play in your room; you give me a headache. Sewey wants to talk just with me." Zoe is chopping cilantro at the table, to add to the parsley heaped in a small yellow bowl.

"But I want to talk first. Zoe, you forgot to say you are still little."

"Did you hear me, Luz?"

"But Zoe forgot one part."

"Continue and you will be talking to no one all night!"

"Say it, please, Zoe," Luz pleads, moving backwards to the doorway that leads to the living room, eyes in the back of her head, a loud hopping exit. Luz is no lightweight. On the bare wooden floors her hops resound.

"What should I say? 'I am still little?'" says Zoe, her right temple pulsing, her thoughts running wild.

"Yes, but no question!"

"Luz! Stop trying to be the boss of Sewey."

"But she didn't say it right."

"Wait, please come back for a minute, Luz," says Zoe, putting down the knife. "Josefina, I want you to hear something."

"I can come back?" asks Luz, pausing dramatically in the doorway, one foot in the air.

"If Sewey says yes."

She does.

Luz hops to the table where Zoe is seated, while Josefina fries something sweet and oniony in a big black skillet, the room already steamy, all the rooms of the blue house rich with it, the smell creeping down the halls, through the barely open windows, chiccarones wafting down Mariposa Lane.

"What do you want, my Zoe Felangela?" says Luz flopping down on a chair.

Zoe puts green fingers on Luz's sweaty arm, looks Luz in the eyes. "Tell your mother what you did on the sidewalk today," she says quietly.

"What did you ask?" Josefina calls from the stove.

"Okay." Luz pauses. The answer does not come to her mind. She asks her nose and her eyes and her cheeks. They don't know either. "Maybe take a rest?"

"What was the question?" Josefina asks.

"You got up from your chair and ran right into all those people. Tell your mother about it."

"This is what made her sick?" Josefina is growing concerned.

"She wasn't sick. She ran," Zoe says.

Josefina turns from the stove, her hand automatically cupping the place where the access resides.

"I didn't do anything bad," says Luz.

"You got up and ran into the rows. Some people fell."

"Luz," Josefina says. "This is what you wanted to tell me?"

Zoe nods.

"You don't remember, mamita?"

"You mean when the people turned into lights?"

"What do you mean lights?" Now Josefina turns off the flame under the iron skillet and goes to sit at the table. The chiccarones will absorb too much oil. Seven for dinner and only six chairs and Luz has run once again without her seeing. What can she do? Her child is impossible. The pupusas must wait.

"Luz," Zoe chides. Now Luz stands with her mother's hands on her shoulders—who knows? She may run.

"You didn't see it? Maybe you will see it tomorrow. How the people can turn into lights."

Luz slips away and begins to skip around the table. "People, lights. Lights, people," she recites. She taps her mother on the top of her head. "Now you're a light," she taps her again. "Now you're Josefina." She skips away, this time stopping at Zoe. "You're always a light and a person, Zoe Luedke, Felangela." She taps Zoe on the top of her head. Then she stops and smiles, quite happy with herself. "Can I take Zoe for playing now in my room?"

"Go play alone until I call you."

"I want to stay where Zoe stays."

"Luz," Josefina calls sharply. "I have no more patience with these games. Look at poor Sewey who you have made exhausted. You know what she's talking about, Sewey? You know the lights?"

"No. Of course not."

"Maybe you will see them tomorrow," Luz says. "Maybe everyone will see them."

"Stop it, Luz. People were hurt from her running? She is becoming misbehaved like Tommy Platz?"

"Not hurt," Zoe concedes. How can she tell this? Zoe knows what Luz Reyes can do with a look. "Tell Mami also why you want to go to the sidewalk. Tell her the real real reason."

"What are you asking?" Josefina wonders. She has the cold heavy feeling in her arms, a taste of a new fear, as if something has just slipped right past her. Something that she will not like. "She goes because I ask her to go."

Luz looks at Zoe, perfectly blank. "Everyone goes now to the sidewalk. But not Father Bill."

"Yes, you *do* know the reason. Not everyone—you," Zoe insists.

"Because Mami likes it. And we aren't scared anymore of the people."

"No, we are not afraid now. They are our friends," says Josefina.

Luz hops in place. "Friends. Not friends. Not Friends. Friends." Luz hops away, circling the kitchen near the stove and the counter. Something is bound to fall down.

"Luz! Be careful before you hurt yourself."

"But why can't I look at the people? Why did Zoe tell me, 'Luz, no!'"

"What did she do, Sewey?"

"She ran into the rows."

"Yes, yes, you already said that. What do you think is the problem? You needed exercise, Luz?" Josefina asks.

Luz cozies up to her mother, who encircles her in her arms.

"Zoe tells me always, 'Luz, don't look at the people!'"

"Where do you get such a crazy idea, mamita?"

"Can I look at the children? I'm afraid if I do."

"Why?" says Josefina.

"Maybe I'll hurt them from looking."

Josefina turns to Zoe, "You think Luz will hurt the children?"

Zoe, sinking fast, out of her element, out-Luzed. Is she the only one in the room who knows what has happened? If she does know. If it happened as she thinks. If Luz is what she is. Will Luz or won't Luz hurt children by looking? No idea. Zoe says, "No."

"That is crazy talking, Luz. Sewey doesn't think you will hurt anyone. Come and give me your thumb. The dough is ready. You remember still how to punch holes for our pupusas? Tomorrow no more sleeping all day on the chair. You will play with the children, your friends. On the field you can dance and give no one a headache. You can run like you want to—and take off your shoes to jump in the mud! That is the way the children have fun. Not hopping in a small house to drive people crazy. Not running on the sidewalk when people are quiet."

Luz and her mother stand up, Luz gives Zoe a sidelong glance, her tongue worries the backs of new teeth.

Luz Reyes is insulted, thinks Zoe. She does not understand. *Knows. Doesn't know. Doesn't know. Knows.* What does Luz Reyes know of herself?

"La Felangela está furiosa," Luz says, standing by her mother at the counter, plunging her thumb into the first ball of soft risen dough.

"Sewey just wants to keep you close like I told her to do. Tomorrow you apologize to the people. Do you know who you ran into on the sidewalk?"

"Maybe."

"Think to remember. You are too crazy still with that energy. You can be calm now? We have guests soon coming for dinner. You will promise to behave?"

Luz the vessel, her little cells charged up with gold. "Yes! Now can I stay in the kitchen? Can I chop the long onion? Zoe, watch me. I can use the knife. Pupusas," says Luz, "Chick-a-roans. Do you remember how to say it? Dance to remember. Pa poo-sas. Chick-a-roans. Look, Zoe. Do it like me!"

CHAPTER 46

The meal is memorable, though not without mishap. The pupusas moist and delicious, plentiful enough for a tribe (with four set aside for the latecomer, Walt). All it lacks, in the chef's considered opinion, is a fifth of Espíritu de Cana—her country's sugar cane vodka—and a little less espíritu from Luz would not hurt: two dropped pupusas, one broken plate. A meal in which, before fleeing the kitchen in tears, Luz is finally ordered to eat standing up.

They are six at a four-seater table. Red-and-white checkered napkins, yellow plates, the orange manzanita from the Ottos' sparse garden in a blue water glass. Father Bill has spoken the blessing. Josefina serves the steaming pupusas on a big yellow platter, a bowl of tangy curtido, and the meal has begun—no forks, warm snowy dough, fragrant, savory filling. They struggle to eat without dropping the juicy parts onto their plates. No one mentions the sidewalk or speaks of the ocean of gold. No one suggests Luz Reyes can knock people flat with a look.

Soon the table is littered with empty brown bottles of Negro Modelo, soon their fingers are dripping with pupusa juice. There is chatter in two languages, Luz's wild elbows and slippery hands. Josefina fills their plates once again and Emily Otto starts to describe a man who sat down next to her on the sidewalk. Zoe puts down her beer. Her fourth, her fifth? She has lost count. Emily Otto discussing the sidewalk. In front of Luz. Luz the child.

"Such an interesting man with a big round moon face and a feeling about him that makes the hair stand up on the back of my neck. My arms, too." "Dearie," says Wren, calling her attention to Luz, listening intently. Now it is too late.

"He was big," says Luz with her mouth full. "The biggest of everyone." She chews for a while then looks up at the ceiling, remembering, seeing it now, then looking at those at the table able to see it by feeling, each one a person, a light. "He was the biggest light."

Lights. People. People. Lights.

Emily Otto draws in her breath.

"Lights?" Father Bill says, looking steadily at Luz.

"Sometimes the people turn into lights."

"Is that so?" asks Father Bill.

"Maybe they do."

Josefina snorts. "I have seen people turn to sand. To coffee." She looks at Luz. "I am sorry. That is a terrible thing I just said." Luz and her stories are driving her crazy. Too many stories already from Luz. She feels tired from Luz's stories, yet so alive from the dinner, its great success. From her body that has cured itself as she knew that it would. Now comes the darkness, the excitement of night gathering outside the windows of her kitchen, and William already so happy. Tonight, right now in fact if she had her way, she would take this man straight to bed.

Then Luz's plate falls from the table and shatters, and Luz runs from the kitchen. "Ignore her," says Josefina, "let her go. Don't," she says, her hand on the back of the priest, who is reaching down to pick up the shattered plate. "Más tarde," she says. Her hand tracing the muscle that sheaths it. The Ottos look at each other then turn away. The doorbell is ringing. Josefina forced up from her table after all. "Ah," she says, "at last this is Walt."

"Let me see what I can do with Luz," says Father Bill, getting up from the table.

As soon as they leave the kitchen, Emily Otto turns to Zoe. "I understand this is difficult, but do you see why you're needed? Josefina has no idea of her child. It's why you were sent."

"Emily, don't," whispers Wren.

"Can't you see how she's suffering? She needs to know this. Father Bill knew you were coming to us. He dreamed your hands. We've been waiting for you since the spring."

CHAPTER 47

"Where are you going?" Walt says as Zoe bolts past him out the front door. He follows her into the street, where she wrestles with the Nova's heavy front door, which swings back as she drops into the driver's seat. He catches it just in time. "What's going on?"

She puts her head down on the steering wheel. "I can't stay there anymore. I'm sleeping in my car."

"What happened?" He squats close to her, holds onto the open door so it stays open, the smell of beer wafting toward him.

"Too hard to explain."

"If you need someplace to stay tonight I've got a trailer."

"A bed?"

"A bed already made. Even a bathroom. Clean towels. The works."

"Who else sleeps there?"

"Nobody."

"Okay, let's go."

"I promised Josefina. She wants to feed me. Why don't you come in for a few minutes? Then I'll take you to the trailer."

"No," she says. "I'll be out here resting my brain."

"What happened to your brain?"

She raises her head slightly, tilts, tries to focus her gaze on his face. "I just found out why my husband left me. It's Father Bill's fault."

"I'd like to hear about that."

"Not from me you won't. My backpack. Can you bring it? It's on the floor near the couch."

"Okay, but don't go anywhere."

"I already have."

It is going to happen, Walt thinks as he reenters the house with its rich food smells, the wash of beer. He finds the Ottos alone in the kitchen, quietly arguing, hears Father Bill's voice intoning from Luz's room. No Josefina. No Luz. "Come try one of these unpronounceables," Emily says. He is going to wake in the morning and see Zoe inside the trailer, just as he did in his dream.

* * *

Father Bill sits on the edge of Luz's white canopy bed holding his hand eye-level before her, the thumb and the index finger a quarter inch apart. Luz, propped on four pillows, tries to keep still while she copies his motion, keeping her eyes on his fingers. "That's right. Very good. Just a little bit bigger. That's the size of a flea." Luz breathes hard, feels her mother's hands firm on her shoulders. A gold force moving straight through her body, making her feet want to run. "Good job, mamita," says Josefina, bending to kiss her daughter's moist brow.

"Are you ready for the next part? Concentrate. Pretend this is you way up here." Father Bill raises his fingers a foot above Luz's dark hair. Luz must look up. "Okay," breathes Luz, working hard. Working so hard to make her feet stay. "Now, without moving a muscle, move yourself down."

"Me?"

"Come down just a little. One quarter of an inch. Like a flea. Like this. Did you see the flea move?"

"Yes."

"Now pretend that the flea is you. Close your eyes."

"Okay," says Luz. She closes her eyes. A small door drops open below her. Just enough space for the flea. Now for her. "Okay," she says, "I did it."

"Can you do it again?"

"Come down a very little bit more?"

"Yes, but keep your eyes closed."

"What is this doing for her?" asks Josefina.

"Shhh," says Father Bill, "Luz knows. One more time. One quarter inch more."

"One flea?"

"That's right. Move one flea down. How does that feel?" Father Bill asks, his heart in his mouth. "Is that far enough?"

"Not yet," says Luz.

"You are doing very well, Luz," Father Bill says.

Somewhere inside her Luz begins to drop into herself. This drop is a little bit heavy, different from rising in the ocean of gold. In several long minutes Luz Reyes returns to herself. Long minutes divided by quarter-inch segments. Each minute measured by one patient flea. Now she does not want to run. Her feet are not telling her mind where to go. In this way Luz settles down in her body: peace in the blue house restored.

"Can you stay on your bed if we leave you alone?"

"Yes," says Luz, lifting her arm to work her two fingers in case.

"Maybe you'll sleep for me, mamita?"

Luz closes her eyes and listens to the footsteps of her mother, of Father Bill. How many footsteps to the kitchen? Luz counts twenty-two till she hears only the voices.

"She can't go back to the window," says Father Bill.

"She will play with the children. But I must go back."

"Only you then," says Father Bill.

That night under the canopy sewn for her happiness, to keep in the good dreams and send away bad, Luz dreams Our Lady has come to her bed in the shape of a shadow, tall as the canopy, gray as smoke with a burned smell besides, a sweetness like spoiled meat. "Don't look for the face in the window," says Our Lady, "I will never be there."

No matter how far in the gold Luz can go. No matter how Luz loves the world. Never will Our Lady show Luz Her face.

CHAPTER 48

Several days later Josefina awakens to find the Madonnas of the Centuries have left her walls. The pieces of scotch tape that held them, marking their places with small uneven stains. Josefina, loathe even to mention Our Lady by name, has decided to wait for her daughter to explain. But so far Luz says nothing. Another day Josefina discovers the yellow dress balled on the floor of Luz's closet. She washes and irons it and then places the dress on a high shelf, too fine to be discarded. Josefina will give it away.

Who would believe it is Josefina who goes every day after work to the window to sit on a beach chair (with the traffic whizzing by on the freeway and neighbors and strangers crammed in behind her) to commune with illusory eyes? The eyes, which seem always so urgent, call to her with their dark gleaming presence. How intensely they gaze, as if trying to reach through the glass, to feed their love into her very heart. Never in her life has Josefina felt such yearning, not even in the days when she and Raphael could not bear to be apart for even one hour, as if already they knew how little time they would share on this earth.

Now even more than the love of her neighbors, even more than the joy she gets walking with Luz to the field, seeing Luz welcomed in play by the children, Josefina has come to enjoy, in a way that seems almost perverse, this time that she spends with the eyes.

In the short weeks since Luz walked to the car wash, she has lived such a wonderful change. No more lost days, her mind and her body dissolving, no more mornings when she is scarcely able to get out of bed or care for her child. Gone the fear of strangers, of the least sound or gesture that could, without warning, cause her captors to rise close as her breath: the guards at the Ilopango with their relentless fists, their black masks and razor blade knives. The soft-voiced colonel in his impeccable uniform and high polished shoes who entered her cell in the hours when she had lost count of the time. Under his arm the thing he had said was a radio—"You want to hear musica, Josefina?"—but had wires. Her body still bears the burns.

No longer does she imagine with each passing car on the freeway, the jeeps with blind windshields of bulletproof glass, the plate-less white death cars, impossible to trace. There are sometimes white jeeps on the field behind the car wash, but no one is coming to take her. She and her daughter are safe.

Does she credit the sidewalk for her body's great healing? Does she thank those splendid dark eyes in the window for the peace that has come to her mind? After eight years of suffering, she is too grateful to search after answers; she has simply returned to her life.

Each morning Zoe comes down from Walt's trailer to watch over Luz while Josefina is at work. At two o'clock Zoe drives Luz to the field to meet Josefina after her workday is through. Is it for love of her daughter that Zoe remains in Infidelity, or maybe for her? (Or for Walt?) Or is it the window? What is it Zoe is seeing? Josefina wonders. She dare not ask, nor if Zoe asked her, could she explain. They all have their secrets, Josefina thinks, letting Zoe into the house, kissing Luz good-bye. Then she drives to the Palms to the home of her employer. The long palm-lined streets that never fail to remind her of San Benito, her family, the home where no girl made a bed, swept a floor, her mother, her father, Esperanza at the gate begging her to run for her life, not to come in. The family whose deaths she must carry, even now, in the midst of such goodness, such hard-won peace.

CHAPTER 49

From where he sits, outside on the rock by his fountain, Walt can look straight through the open windows of his house to the far end where Zoe leans at his kitchen counter, making her call.

When she came out the first night she'd got through to Michael, she looked stricken. Like she'd looked when she came to the car wash that day and smashed through his wall. "Michael is back," she said. And then had gone straight to the trailer. Then she came out again and knocked on his door. "Don't say anything to anyone." All that night Walt kept waking up, getting out of bed to see if the trailer's outside light was still on, if the Nova was still parked in the gravel beside it.

Nearly a week and nothing has changed. Zoe keeps to the same routine. Luz in the morning. The window in the afternoon. Dinner with Luz and Josefina, sometimes Father Bill joins them, sometimes Walt. And then they drive back, she follows him on the unmarked road from the hill district, parks the Nova, goes into his house. He turns on the lights. It's a small house. No place to go and not hear every word that is spoken. Walt goes outside and sits by the River Rock fountain, his back against stone. He does not turn it on until she comes back outside.

It is true that each night the call is a little longer, but only by minutes, two, three. But when she comes out to him, it is as if nothing has transpired. She does not speak about Michael, and Walt does not ask. They sit together on the ground wrapped in blankets. They look up at the sky. They talk.

He has Michael to thank for her company, he thinks. The hurt Michael has done to her. Is there another woman involved? She does not say. Michael is another man who has failed his commitments. Maybe Walt is her balm.

Zoe knows now, though he had not intended to tell her the sad story that led him to Infidelity, first the kickbacks to the title company, the indictment, how he'd declined to sue the partner responsible. A friend since college. He just paid the two million plus court costs and walked away. And then walked away some more. "Oh," he said when he watched her face change, "so now you're impressed. Two million in fines impresses you?" "Surprised," she'd said. Her eyes round. "How big was your house?" "My house?" He laughs. "Square footage." "You don't want to know." "Over five thousand? Over six?" she had asked. "Over six under ten," he said, "and let's leave it at that." "There have to be steps," she had said, "between that kind of life and this one."

"Not steps. A steep hill. And I just kept rolling. I'll tell you the strange thing. At the very time I was leaving my wife and my children, I was thinking of them probably more than I ever had. And of myself. In ways I had never had time to think of them. Like, how were they really? How were we? And what was it exactly that I had been contributing besides a vague kind of love and massive infusions of cash?"

She is watching him, a bittersweet smile on her face. Huddling against the cold in her green woven blanket. His blanket. He puts his arm around her. "We don't talk about these kinds of things," he had said. "Who?" "We. Us. Men. At least my buddies never did." "Does that mean I'm your buddy, Walt?" "I guess so," he had said. "And you're certainly mine." "Yes, I am. So that means I can't charge you for the trailer." "You can charge me," she says. "But I can't pay. Not till I finish the Grosvenors' kitchen." "The Grosvenors?" "My clients who are wondering about me right now." "How big?" he asked. She turns to him, their faces close, she tilts her head. "The Grosvenors' kitchen or their house?" "Their kitchen," he says. "A thousand." He whistles, "A thousand square feet of kitchen. Someone's got some highfalutin clients waiting. Be careful. I know those people. I used to be those people. If you're late they'll sue." "He's on it," she says. "Michael?" "Yep. Just like nothing has happened. Hired back the crew. He's doing the prep work right now." "I see," says Walt. Then he waits for her to say more, something, anything. But she has withdrawn. He can feel her shutting down, watch the light go out of her eyes. "So, what is it Michael doesn't talk about?"

She looks at him. Is she going to say it is none of his business? "Michael doesn't talk about the past."

"Does that have anything to do with him going away?"

"I think it has a lot to do with it."

He takes his arm away then and moves off a little. He can't do this, he thinks. He can't start hearing about the life of the man he was hoping would never come back. "That's too bad," he says.

She sighs, covers her mouth with her hand in a way Walt had seen Gwen do when they were in the midst of a fight. And then they sit and listen to the sound of the River Rock fountain, and beyond it to the silence around them, and the humming in the silence comes back to remind them what they have been missing. At his car wash there are a hundred or more people camped in tents on the field, waiting for the excitement of morning at the window. "Maybe we should go in," he says. It comes out wrong. His voice, husky, low. It comes out the way he means it. A seduction. She takes the hand from her mouth and looks at him again. *Maybe we should go in.* Would she go in with him if he asked? It is getting very easy between them, he thinks. He had better be careful.

She leans over and kisses him softly on the cheek, her mouth lingers two seconds, three before she withdraws. She knows his smell now, deeper, less sharp than Michael's. She is happy in this place, sleeping in the little white trailer. Quiet, alone. A single white bed. A small wicker dresser. She likes being outside with Walt, likes the water flowing out of the mouth of the old River Rock fountain, the erasing sky, the dark, far from the life she does not know how to return to.

"I think Luz's vision is coming to me," she says then. Her own words surprise her. This is not what she intended to say. She had intended to tell him the way she cannot feel her husband's presence. When he speaks to her, when he tells her how much he wants her to come home she feels nothing. It is a familiar feeling, this. Her old sense of distance. No love. No anger. Not even the hurt. When she tells Michael where she is, he doesn't believe her. If he doesn't believe that, how will he ever believe the rest of it? She wants to tell this to Walt, but it would be the worst kind of infidelity speaking to a man she wants to sleep with about the husband she cannot face.

But at least she can tell Walt he is not alone. She too has seen faces, a plain face at first but now it has changed. It is beautiful beyond description. A face and voice. Very clear, very strong. She trusts it completely now. Whatever it is the voice is right. She is doing very well.

"Do you think we have any idea how lucky we are to have these things coming to us?" she asks.

"I do," he had said. "I think we know. I think we all do now." Right now, as they sit under the night sky, there are many camped on the field behind his car wash, speaking as they are, perhaps. Waiting to return to the window.

Where will he ever find a woman he can share this with? he thinks. One who, when he speaks of the faces he sees and the places within him they touch, will not think that he has lost his mind.

She smiles, stands for a moment, then says goodnight.

He watches her walk through the cactus garden and down to Jen's trailer and go inside. The lights go on in the trailer. She draws the curtains.

One morning she is going to leave him. The hurt will drop from her and she will want to go back to her life, to her husband. Maybe it wasn't a woman, Walt thinks. Maybe Michael had a moment like he'd had. Only now he's turned back from his moment, realizing his life with Zoe was worth it. What does Walt know? Only that soon she will be gone. She will be everywhere then for Walt. Moving about in the trailer; in the kitchen with her mouth on his phone. She will be beside him at night by the fountain. At the car wash whenever he looks at the window he will think of her face.

CHAPTER 50

"Do you have to go back to your Springs?" Luz had asked when she walked into the kitchen to hear Mami and Zoe talk in low voices about Michael. "Don't bother Sewey," her mother had said. "Are you going?" Luz says again. "Not yet," Zoe says. "Don't ask Sewey questions. She needs to be quiet to think."

There is nothing that Zoe cannot tell her, Josefina says, nothing wrong that she can feel. "He is your great love," Josefina says. "After what he has done either you kill him or you turn to ice."

She is ice. The first time he had answered she couldn't speak. She listened to his voice shape her name. *Zoe?* Three times. The fourth, a demand. "Yes," she had said and quietly hung up the phone.

"You turn to ice and then slowly, you melt."

CHAPTER 51

With each revelation he betrays her. His Stockholm caller asks for the names of her parents. He gives them. She asks for details of appearance. He says Josefina's mother was blond, he remembers her long polished red nails, her upright posture, the elegant suit she wore the day she had gone with him to the prison (without her husband's knowing) to beg for her daughter's release. He knows Josefina's father's was stocky, that his hair was thick and black, that he wore a thin mustache. This Josefina must have described to him. Her sister, on the other hand, he had seen only once, through the gate, on the very last day. Sixteen, so lovely, so much like Josefina, though smaller, thinner. Esperanza, a terrified girl.

He is able to tell his caller the name of the toy stores her father had owned, "El Rey de Juguetes." To describe the exterior of the home of her parents, that gate. He remembers the grillwork as well as the enormous shade tree in the courtyard by the fountain, that the large house was stucco and pink. No detail is too trivial to his caller. From time to time she asks him to pause, and there is only silence between them. Perhaps she is writing down his words. "Here is what I will need from you," she says finally. "A photograph of Josefina and her child, the most recent. A copy of the little girl's certificate of birth and a complete copy of Josefina's medical records."

He had hoped it would be the reverse—she in Stockholm sending records of a possible donor to them, to the High Desert Hospital. When he'd said this, she paused once again. "I am sorry. This is the only way I may be able to help you." And then, just when he was certain the call was at an end, she had asked if he knew how Josefina had arrived in the States.

"We drove out," he answered without hesitation. He had said it deliberately. Nosotros. We.

"You are the one who drove? You are the American priest who helped many escape?"

"Not so many." Not Dr. Raphael Reyes. Not Sister Jean. Not Seguro Montes. S. J., countless others who might have been saved. She asked him for the date and he gave it; after all he had given away everything else, why not this? She had gone silent. The silence lasted so long that this time he thought he had lost her.

"Get the papers to me right away," she said. Then she dictated twice the address where they were to be sent: a post office box. He had thanked her too profusely, he is certain. "When do you think you'll get back to me?"

"I cannot answer."

"You will have good news for me, I know."

"Vamos a ver," she had said.

He sends the photograph from Luz's communion in the spring, the three of them standing on the steps of Our Lady of Guadalupe, Luz in her white dress, tight at the middle, the veil a little crooked on her head, her triumphant smile. Next to her Josefina looked resigned, slightly swollen of face, the symptom he had entirely overlooked. As for himself, the sun must have caught the camera at a bad angle, for his presence in the photo seems tenuous, as if he is not wholly there or the light had begun to digest him.

You steal my papers? You send my address to strangers? How do you know that they don't come kill me? For days afterward he imagines how Josefina would suffer if she knew what he had done. Each time he looks at her, he averts his eyes.

He uses his Durable Power of Attorney for Health Care to obtain and then copy her medical records. If he had not listened to the hospital social worker, he would not be planning to send through the mail to a stranger in Stockholm Josefina's address, the record of her illness, the photograph of Luz, proof that Josefina Reyes still lives, a fact she has tried to conceal from the world for eight years. Lives, has a child. All of this his caller demands.

The next morning, after confession and Mass he will sneak off to the post office and mail them. He must first meet with those who are not of his parish but who nonetheless wait daily in the hall outside his office to discuss their experience at the window. He has found a little phrase that seems to silence their endless questions. "Think of it as the larger love," he says. Heretical. How would he explain if his bishop should hear he had spoken these words?

He has been working to find Josefina a donor. And she believes her body has cured itself. If she knew what he'd been doing, would she fall prey to self-doubt, lose faith in her body and her delicate hold on it, fail? How he can punish himself, Father Bill thinks as he slips into his car. Josephina's voice in his mind stronger at times than his own.

He goes to the clinic to collect her records, has a brief face-to-face meeting with the doctor, who comes out to wish him well, then drives like a madman to Twenty-Nine Palms, stopping first at a drugstore to make copies of the records and then to the crowded post office where he stands on line for close to half an hour. Not till the clerk has dropped his overseas mailer in the bin does Father Bill let out his breath.

When he returns to the rectory, Hope Merton has left a message. She has more phone numbers for him: people coming out of the woodwork to offer to help Josefina in any way they can, some names he recognizes both from El Salvador and from the churches in the States that kept them, one night, two nights, he can hardly remember till they arrived at the yellow house on Oak Street. "I'm going to see about refinancing the house," she said. "It's a quick way to make sure we have the cash on hand."

Just like that—make sure we have the cash on hand—an afterthought, almost. When he leaves the office, walking out into the tremendous heat of the day he realizes what has just happened. The money for Josefina is there. The impossible thing has arrived once again. The faces of those who helped them get into the country when Immigration refused Josefina Reyes entry come to him. Faces he has not seen in eight years. No reliable proof of persecution. "She has been tortured," he pleaded. "She has been jailed twice, the last time for nearly two months. Her husband murdered. Her parents, her sister . . ." There were documents from the Red Cross. There were forms from Tutela Legal supporting her case. Yet Immigration had turned her away. *No reliable proof of persecution.* They drove back to Mexico and days later were met in the night at the border in Tucson, people who gave their first names only, who took them to sleep and to eat in the home of a minister. Illegal entry. Illegal actions. How surprised he had been by the world, in those years. How he has learned.

Once he has mailed his parcel to Stockholm, Father Bill enjoys a series of days of pure happiness. Luck has come to him through Hope Merton. Perhaps, through his Stockholm caller more luck will arrive. And a change has come over Infidelity. He hears of it everywhere. He feels it among his parishioners, a change in the very air of his church. Something beautiful has settled into their lives. *The larger love*, the strangers are saying. Only briefly does he worry about Luz now. There seems little to worry about. She did not complain when they told her she was no longer allowed to sit at the window. Why, when Josefina returns home from work she will go to the window but Luz cannot. Now Luz plays with the children on the field. The mothers watch out for her, no stranger allowed to approach her. "You should see how the children run to Luz when we arrive," Josefina tells him. "My popular daughter!"

He has moved into trust once again. Going lightly in his thoughts, letting go of his fears when they alight: that something is not right with Luz, that Josefina's condition will slip, that his search will not bear fruit, that the beauty will be taken from his people, from the town. He does not dwell in impatience to know who in Stockholm has the photo of Josefina, of Luz, the copies of Josefina's medical records from the High Desert Hospital. He remembers the rightness of things. Hope Merton will refinance her house. He thinks of his dream in the spring, the hands he had seen. He gives thanks for Zoe Luedke, for Walt Adair, for the window.

CHAPTER 52

No one would know how quickly the peace of these days will vanish. How fragile a hold Luz the child has on the thing that's come through her to them. Luz, safe at play on the field, no longer roiling in her ocean of gold.

Each day, hand-to-hand, an object passes in secret from stranger to stranger to one of the children—to Tommy or Ashley who know how to take it so no one can see. From those who crave proof that Luz Reyes the child is the thing they desire and fear.

The children bring earrings, a key ring, a pink stone, a bracelet with links shaped like fish, a heavy gold ring from a man Tommy thinks might be a king. Luz has hidden them all far in the back of her sock drawer inside the socks she no longer wears that are too little now for her feet.

There are many true souls on the sidewalk who have discounted the rumors—the healings Luz grants, the wishes received, the old loves rekindled, the ones who see Luz in their dreams. Many others have forsaken the sidewalk and are not there to witness the act when at last it is done.

Though no one disputes that her feet are still touching the ground, once she appears Luz moves like lightning, no hands can stop her. Suddenly, she is once again among them, muddy and hot from the field. There she goes past the Ottos in a flash, past the moon-faced man looking out from the depths of great silence, stepping nimbly past coolers and chair legs, not even brushing an elbow or a knee. By the time Josefina stands up, struggling to free herself from the two smoky eyes, Luz has stopped at the last row of sitters—eye-to-eye with a big, sturdy woman ruddy of face in a swirl-printed rough amber dress. "Here," says Luz and holds out a gold link fish bracelet. The woman flushes deeply, cries out, cries out again, her ruddy hands flying up from the trough of her lap. "You don't understand." The bracelet in her fist, the child in her arms, "There is no way she could know this was mine!"

CHAPTER 53

So unsettled is Luz by what she has caused, so distressed is Josefina by the lies of her daughter, the gifts kept in secret Luz was warned not to take, that for two days and nights the blue house is wracked with confusion and tears. "You can't tell the truth? So now we ask."

The children are brought to the blue house to be queried by Josefina, by Zoe. To be studied by Father Bill's all-knowing eyes. They crowd on the brown couch or crouch on the floor. The timid stay close to their mothers, the brave on their own.

In a bowl are the objects in question. Luz had emptied her sock drawer, unballed the socks, revealed her treasure: a gold braid hoop earring, a feather pendant, a half-carat fake diamond stud, tiny pink crystal, Tecate key ring. Nothing of value, nothing to rival the jewel-eyed fish bracelet, belonging to the ruddy-faced woman, which at least, Luz reminds Josefina, she'd returned.

"Who gave these for Luz? What person? What do they look like if you don't know the name?" Josefina demands, ignoring the tears of the children, their mothers' appeals.

"I gave Luz the bracelet," Ashley admits, bowing her lovely red curls.

"And when did the lady give it to you?"

"Not a lady. A man." Ashley raises her doll-like face and looks Josefina straight in the eyes. *An old man. A soft hand.*

"What old man? Who gave it to him?

Ashley pulls at a curl and chews the inside of her cheek. "Tell the truth," says her mother (who knows when her daughter is lying). "I am. We never know."

"When you give Luz a present, don't you say who it came from?" asks Zoe.

"We can't," Tommy Platz says. "That's the game."

"But do you, maybe sometimes?" asks Father Bill.

"No!" Tommy booms, proud he can follow a rule.

"Sometimes," says Ashley, "but that's not the one."

"Never," say the rest. "I didn't, I swear."

Father Bill on the floor with his arm around Luz, his poor little novice with her unwelcome gifts. "They never tell you who it belongs to? Not even the bracelet?"

"Maybe," says Luz. If no one has told her, then how did she know? Everyone baffled, the children, the mothers, the Felangela with her wide-open stare. But no one more baffled than Luz.

CHAPTER 54

From her worry over Luz and her lying, from the rumors of her daughter everyplace in Infidelity and other places as well, from all those who gather on Mariposa Lane day and night just for a glimpse of her child (forcing Josefina to cover her windows with sheets), without drinking so much as one sip of tea before bedtime, Josefina starts again to wake in the night. Two times and three times at least she gets up to pee.

And now that she cannot go back to the window, Josefina cannot stop thinking of the eyes. Their impossible yearning burns in her body, in her breasts, in the scars on her breasts, throbs in her watery ankles. She goes to her window for a breath of cool air. And there, outside on the street in the dark, standing vigil, are the strangers, burning holes in the night with their candles.

Luz too is unable to sleep. Her mother is once again sick, going again and again to the bathroom to pee. Hot and cold fears come through Luz's body. The toilet flushes. It flushes again. Luz thinks of her bad deeds, the gifts she had hidden, of her lies. Of the children in trouble for her sake because of their games. Of the strangers on the street. Of school starting soon. Of her running feet. Of Zoe Luedke going away soon never again to be seen. Luz thinks of the bracelet, how it burned her but so beautiful, gold fish with ruby eyes. Of the big ring from Tommy that he put in her hand when they ran wild on the field, a gold ring with strange words that now she can't find. It was not in the bowl.

"It was the feet again," Luz says when they talk every day of the bracelet. Mami and Luz and Father Bill. "The feet took me to the lady." *And the bracelet that burned.*

"I understand," says Father Bill.

"The mind tells the feet," says her mother, who does not want to hear Luz's lies.

"But how did I know the right lady who the bracelet belonged to?"

That no one can say.

"Shhh," says Zoe Luedke, Felangela. "Don't think about it so much Luz. Remember that we are still little. We still love the world."

But how can Luz tell the Felangela Our Lady refused her. *She has lost all the family.* Her mother is once again sick. How can Luz love the world?

"Mami peed two times in the night." Her voice is soft. The softer the words the less they can grow.

"Is Mami a tortoise that must not pee?" the Felangela asks.

Yes, thinks Luz. If you pick up a tortoise it will pee. If it pees it will die. "Is she going again to the clinic?" asks Luz.

"I don't know. If she does, the treatments will help her. Should we look for the ring now?"

But no matter how many times the Felangela looks with her, no matter how many times in the night Luz wakes and gets off her bed and goes to her dresser and opens her sock drawer with barely a sound, unrolls the red socks kept for cold days and Christmas where she's sure that she tucked it, the gold ring stays lost. It cannot be found.

CHAPTER 55

"Make it go away." The bishop's voice is gravelly, his speech tired and slow. And make sure that no one from your parish is being drawn in. If they are, don't tell me, just stop it. Do you know the owner of the car wash?"

"Yes, in fact, I do," Father Bill says.

"Will he listen to you?"

"I think he will."

"Tell him this is dangerous. Tell him these things hurt people and they always end badly. Get him to close for a few days. And don't let that woman bring her child back to the car wash."

"All right," Father Bill says.

"What does she want?"

"I don't know."

"Money?"

"No. There's no money changing hands."

"I'm counting on you. Use your charisma. Here's your chance to take it out of the deep freeze."

"All right."

"Is there anything else I should know?"

"I don't think so."

"And I don't want any more secondhand news. You tell me if something is happening that might hurt us. This has already gone on too long."

"I'm sorry you had to hear it this way."

But what way, Father Bill wonders as he hangs up the phone. *Certain parties are talking*, the bishop had said. *Word is getting around.* The bishop was vague—and careful. There were things he could have asked that he didn't. He did not mention the blue house rented for four hundred dollars a month. He did not ask Father Bill why it has taken him so long to return his calls. All evening and into the night Father Bill has been at the blue house or outside it, speaking with the strangers whose number increases every hour who wait for the next miracle, the next great event. Over and over, he has asked that they leave, told them their presence upsets Luz and her mother, their candles are a hazard. He points out the weed-choked embankments, the dry brush on the hillside beyond. Their only concession is to cross to the opposite side of the street. Now the neighbors are ready to call the police. He relayed none of this to his bishop, nor was he asked.

"No policía in my house," Josefina begs. "Say to them, Josefina is begging them please don't call." He has prevailed on the neighbors to hold off, even revealed Josefina's history, as much as he dared. "How could an innocent woman be tortured?" they ask. "What did she do to be jailed?" "She was a medical student," he says. "She was in college. She taught the poor how to read. The *head of her college was killed.* A priest," he says, wanting so much to say his name. Seguro Montes, S. J. If he names one he will not stop. He will be all night telling horrors. Professor Raphael Reyes, his friend, the husband of Josefina, the father Luz has not seen, his body delivered to the home of his mother in the coffin of a child, arms and legs missing. El Mozote, a whole town minus one, eight hundred souls, children, women, the old. Lined up and shot. Brutalized. Raped. The killings went on all day long. "What kind of country is that?" they asked. "That was El Salvador," he said. "That was what it was."

There are strangers camped on their street waiting for a miracle, a big one this time—the great event. Now they have this, a woman from a part of the world they cannot understand who was tortured and fears the police.

When he returned to the rectory, he went straight to his desk to check on his calls. His bishop had phoned twice, instructing him to call back no matter the hour. The conversation was brief.

Make it go away, that is his charge now. As if he could. Father Bill has been trying and failing since spring. Luz is beyond them. She is in other hands. Heresies of thought, he thinks as he gets up from his desk. Heresies of deed. He thrills to the experiences total strangers relay to him. So many people being opened in ways he has only read about, never seen.

He turns off the light in the office and walks the narrow hall to his bedroom. He does not undress. He has taken to sleeping in his clothes, removing only his shoes, his belt. He is hungry much of the time. He grabs meals out of cans. At least once a night he wakes, throws on a jacket, and walks from the rectory in the chill air to sit with the strangers.

Luz is what you are, what we all are, he tells them. *What so many desire and fear.* One night he had driven to the car wash and sat with the moon-faced man, a holy man, he knows now, and discovered the depth of his own yearning. Deeper than he could imagine. Only fear of being seen made him leave the sidewalk that night. Each day he falls further, committing the acts that place him outside his own doctrine. For the good of the faithful, the bishop will be forced to petition for his dismissal if he does not pull back. It will not be the first time. Heresies of word. He has named it. What gave him the right? Because he answers their questions. *Because he believes it: the larger love*. He always had dangerous tendencies. Too inclusive, disrespectful of boundaries. It is why he gave up his career in the Church. The very reason he went to El Salvador. Across what border will it take him this time? He does not know.

The next morning he goes through his rounds and does not let himself think of the sidewalk. Nearly noon and he has said Mass, heard confession, turned away those who are not of his parish as the bishop has ordered, chided the strangers on Mariposa Lane once again, and once again been rebuffed. The phone rings in the rectory just as he is leaving for the blue house to check on Luz. It is Hope Merton, her voice is full of excitement. She has heard from the bank. The money for Josefina will be in her hands in less than two days. "What will you do if our donor cannot come to Josefina?" she asks. Our donor, she has said, as if one has already been found. Still, he does not hesitate. "We will go wherever we need to go." "You will be able to do that? "I will do it," he says. Now he knows.

At the blue house, Zoe looks at him appraisingly. *What reason has the priest to be happy?* The strangers outside. Them trapped within. Josefina's health failing. Luz, heavy with guilt and with fear. For what has he dreamed her? *For what?*

"Where's Josefina?" he asks.

"She went to work."

"And Luz?"

"Go away," Luz says when Father Bill knocks on her door.

"I miss you," he says. "I need to see you Lucy, Luz. Get dressed and come out. I will wait."

Then he goes into the living room and sits down next to Zoe on the brown couch, her clothes in a heap on the floor. She is back with them now. Since the strangers have come to their street, they cannot be alone. He sighs, puts his hand over hers.

"She's scared," Zoe says.

He nods. "How did Josefina seem?"

Zoe shakes her head. "Not great." Her eyes fill at his question. Zoe turns her face away, bends to pick up a pair of white cotton slacks from the pile of her clothes, smoothing the creases, refolding them, smoothing again.

"Josefina is going back to the clinic."

"When?"

"The end of next week. It's the soonest they can take her."

"Why do they have to suffer like this?" Zoe says and lets the pants fall from her hands.

"I don't know," says Father Bill.

"How will Luz go back to school? She can't sit in a classroom with these things coming through her."

"Shhh," he says. "Control yourself now. Don't jump ahead. Try not to be afraid for them. That will only make it worse. It is going to be all right." He puts his hand briefly over Zoe's, the left one with the missing felangela. "Can you persuade Luz to get dressed?"

She nods but does not get up. "I don't know how to return to my life."

He has nearly forgotten that Zoe has a life outside of Infidelity.

"I've been speaking to my husband."

He tries to disguise his surprise. It is not what he was expecting. What was he expecting, then?

"He's home. Five days already. He just picked up the phone and said hello."

Anyone else and he would have been happy, happy at her good news, at the chance of reconciliation. The sacrament of marriage. Does he not even honor that?

"He was at a friend's cabin in the Adirondacks. It's up in—"

"I know the Adirondacks." It is where he had gone to seminary. He remembers the winters, the starkness of the landscape, the rolling brown hills, the blackened trees, the silence, the white winter sky.

"All that time and he wasn't even very far away. A few hundred miles. He ended up helping these people put in a new kitchen. He told them his wife was home working. That I couldn't get away. Every night he pretended to call me so they'd think . . ." She breaks off.

He wants to ask if she believes this. He doesn't want to ask.

Father Bill leans forward. Is that Luz in the hall? Has she crept out of her room to listen to this? "Luz, is that you?" he calls.

"She knows Michael is back. I already told her."

He shakes his head. Luz, he thinks. His shirt is damp with perspiration. The heat is doing its work on him. Late morning and no ventilation in this house. He needs to leave for the car wash. Still, he turns back to Zoe, prepared to wait as long as she needs if she wants to discuss her next step.

"Right now, I want to be in two places at once."

"I understand."

She swallows, feels something swell and open in her chest. Puts her hand there. Something soft and lovely, the feeling she gets at the window. Here it is, come to her on the brown couch. "He sounds so sad. He keeps saying he is sorry. It was nothing I'd done, it was just him. He's afraid for himself."

"Well, that's good. That's a start. He can't make it right in himself if he doesn't feel pain for what he's done."

"If I tell him about this, us, what I've, we've been doing, he'll think I've lost my mind."

"Well, in a way you have. You've lost your old mind. Michael has no way to understand. He hasn't had our experience." He looks around at the bare living room, the gates on the windows. A laugh escapes from his throat. "This is a very hard thing to explain." She has closed her eyes, her head rests against the back of the couch, her hand over her heart. He sits in the silence, in the hot stuffy house, the faint smell of rose. He turns his head and there she is. He was right. Luz has been standing in the hall.

"I can't leave yet," says Zoe.

"When the time is right, you'll know how to go back. It will be clear." He says it softly, hoping Luz will not hear. Zoe opens her eyes, looks at him with disbelief. "You will see," he says.

Now he reaches out, puts his hand on the top of her head. She could close her eyes and sleep if only he would keep it there. Her eyes fill again. He takes his hand away and stands up. "You're doing very well. Just know that."

"So I've been told."

That night she calls Michael and for the first time her heart quickens with the realness of his voice. He tells her about his day's work, tells her how much he loves her. She can almost feel Michael again, almost believe she has passed through the first of it, at least. She gives him a taste of it now, the barest outlines, an introduction, the flyer, but he does not remember a purple flyer. It must have been something he'd meant to toss out, picked up in a thoughtless moment, something handed to him by someone he cannot remember. "Are you trying to hurt me? Is there a man?" The priest who had dreamed her. She describes Infidelity. She tells him what it feels like to sit at the window.

"I can't listen to this," he says. "Zoe, you are breaking my heart."

"Michael, please. You have to trust me."

"Do you know how you sound? Infidelity? A black dot? You know what this is. I'm not saying it isn't my fault. But you're in your own world, baby. You're in that old place. Just tell me where you really are. Where on the map."

* * *

"Good-bye, my Lucy, Luz," Father Bill says. She is standing where the little calendar Madonnas he had given her used to be, holding a hairbrush. She's still in pajamas, her face unwashed. The skin under her eyes bruised blue from little sleep. "Zoe will help you get dressed now. You have missed breakfast. You need to eat. Mami will be home soon from work." When he bends to her and tries to touch her face, she walks past him to Zoe.

"Thank you," Zoe says just before he goes out the door. Luz is sitting on her lap, Zoe brushing her hair. He looks at Zoe in all her womanly beauty, her beautiful human misery. "Thank *you*," he says back.

Outside he does not acknowledge the people standing across the street in the glaring heat of midday waiting for what—a glimpse of Luz? A great event? He gets into the Cavalier. Michael is back, but Zoe has chosen to stay. He starts the car, forgets for a moment where he is headed, and when he remembers realizes that what he has set out to do he may not be able to do.

Make it go away—this thing he is coming to cherish. That they all are coming to cherish. He had said nothing to his bishop. He had withheld his opinion, muzzled his joy. Lies great and small, he thinks. This is his life. He should be ashamed of his infidelities. He is not. Something large is moving through him, moving through them all. Something he trusts. Zoe will remain. And Hope Merton has refinanced her house. They have money for Josefina. And Luz is protected. She is held in a circle of love. With all these blessings, can their experience be anything but good? Make it go away, said his bishop. Make it go.

He drives down Mariposa Lane, right onto the Joshua Freeway. It is early afternoon. At least there is not much traffic and his car is cool. He tries to let his life fall away and give himself to the landscape, the annihilating blue of the sky. Any day might send him to a place with a narrow gray one, a city with no vista at all. He will not care. Not if Josefina has her chance. He will leave just like that. Overnight. Abandon his parish, his people, whom he truly loves. He will leave everything, he thinks. They will say he did it for a woman. Is this, then, his truth?

Now the traffic has slowed and soon he will be caught in the line that has in three weeks become a familiar feature of the freeway. The sidewalk convocation that the bishop could not help but hear of, the child and her reputed powers. The whole thing is outside his province to dismiss, outside his province to bless.

He looks out the window of his car at the crowd in their bright, casual attire. Several people are standing together, chatting, laughing. The sounds reach him past the sealed windows of the Cavalier, the hum of the air conditioning. A group of tee-shirted men drinking beer, newspapers strewn at their feet. Emily Otto in her polka-dot hat; she has disobeyed him and taken her seat on the sidewalk. A matter of conscience, she said. Good for you, he had thought. Heresy of thought. And behind her the moon-faced man in his nimbus of devotion, the light around him pale. Few faces today that he recognizes. It looks harmless, an open air waiting room, flat. Maybe it is over, he thinks. Luz will not return. Josefina won't bring her back. Amazing, really how Josefina does not see it, what Luz is. When he asks why she goes to the window she says, "I go for the people, to enjoy them. The other you would not understand." "Is that so?" he says, bemused. "You should try it sometime," she urges. "Sit with us." And then she had touched his mouth. "Or are you afraid?"

The entrance line is hardly moving, and he cannot maneuver around it. Now his stomach is growling. He is hollowed out with hunger. Has he even eaten breakfast? Suddenly, he wants to cook. A big meal. A nice bracciole. Arugula with walnuts and seed tomatoes, shaved Parmesan. A fruity olive oil, three cloves of fragrant garlic, and some good semolina. Why is it that nowhere in this state can he find a good semolina bread? Maybe he should skip the talk with Walt and just head for the A&P, though the bread there is cotton and dust. Perhaps he doesn't need to do anything today but cook and eat. Give a little dinner. Perhaps the whole thing will fade away on its own and he won't have to ask Walt to shut down the wash.

At last the cars have moved. He parks the Cavalier next to Walt's Civic. He has not far to walk, just up the stairs past the lines at the entrance to the office. The people he passes are here to buy wash tickets, not paying to sit on Walt's sidewalk and have a dangerous experience. "The priest," he hears. "That one . . ." He has dressed, deliberately, in his collar. This is an official visit. No green parrot shirt to hide what he is.

CHAPTER 56

"You must have known it wouldn't last forever," Father Bill says. Walt has cleared out the office as he'd asked, gone behind the counter where he stands now, eyeing Father Bill. The priest walks casually around it to the wall where the prize Connors racquet hangs and reaches up to take the racquet in his hands. A racquet whose grip he knows well. He will do this slowly, he thinks. Let Walt be his partner in it. Now he pretends to be fascinated by the racquet, looking down to read the writing on the inside rim: Kinetic Stabilizer. Official Racquet of Team Estusa. He looks up at Walt and smiles. "Been a while between matches for us," Father Bill says. "Is the Prince here?"

"Bottom shelf," says Walt.

They will conclude this together, Father Bill thinks. He knows how to reason with Walt. The racquet in his hand cost Walt a thousand dollars, one of the actual four used by the great Jimmy Connors in his last U.S. Open. Connors, 40, versus Krickstein, 21: five hours and forty-four minutes till Jimbo went down. A man who drops a thousand dollars at a charity auction—that's the life Walt Adair left.

"You may be surprised by how much business you end up retaining from this, once the sidewalk production is over."

A slow burn spreads through Walt Adair's chest. He comes around the counter and takes a step toward Father Bill. "Don't insult me."

Father Bill flushes with embarrassment, surprised at Walt's reaction. "I didn't mean to." He bounces the racquet strings against his palm, listening to the ping of the gut. Of course, how could he have forgotten? Walt had had an experience. He had not asked about it, and has never heard exactly what kind of experience it was.

"We need to think of Luz and Josefina, and the children. After that bracelet misunderstanding, all of them are having a difficult time," Father Bill says. "A week, that's all I'm asking. Shut down for a week and give things a chance to get back to normal."

As if Walt were not deluged with calls, with people stopping in to discuss their sleepless kids, their own uncertainties now. Perhaps it would be better for Josefina and Luz if Walt closed down the wash, if the strangers left. If everything came to a halt. "Do you think that hasn't been on my mind?"

At another time, Walt thinks, he might have complied simply because Father Bill had asked it. But something has happened—at *his* place, not at Father Bill's church. It is not Father Bill who decides when it ends. "I'd be happy to help Josefina and Luz any way that I can, but I'm not inclined to shut down my car wash."

Father Bill smiles in spite of himself. "Well, that certainly complicates things."

"Have you discussed this with Luz?" Walt asks.

"With Luz?" Father Bill says, taken aback. "What kind of a question is that?"

"She might have an opinion."

"Walt," says Father Bill.

"You think she doesn't know what's gone on here?"

"I know she doesn't."

"Well, then maybe you should explain it to her."

"Just what do you think I can tell her?"

"You can tell her what she is, for one. She's way out there somewhere all alone. I don't know what to call it, this gift that she has. I am sure she didn't ask for it. Don't you think she has a right to a little understanding of herself?"

Father Bill puts the Connors down on the counter. "Let's be a little careful right now." He looks at Walt. "I'm sorry," he says. "I don't need your advice when it comes to Luz. I'm here on a practical matter. The bishop has asked me to bring this to an end."

"So that's what this is all about," says Walt. For a moment he stands looking at his friend. In a flash Walt sees exactly what he must do. And then he smiles, walks back around the counter, bends down, disappears briefly then comes out with a single yellow tennis ball and the Prince Jr., his son's old racquet, with a cracked frame and a broken main string. "I'll play you for the call. You use the Connors. I win, I stay open. You win, I will shut down the wash."

The priest is dumbfounded. He's got Jimmy Connors' racquet in his hand. Walt might as well have a broom. "I can't do that. Not with such an unfair advantage."

* * *

It is five sets to one, forty-love when Walt serves the final ace that has Father Bill reaching so far back on the return that the tip of the Connors connects with the window. Thin as that single-pane glass is, it does not shatter. The sidewalk crowd gasps and struggles for balance as the ones gathered near the window leap back.

"I could have won with a broom today," Walt says, crossing the office to shake hands with the priest, who is still shaking his head with disbelief.

"How about giving me two out of three?" Father Bill asks, panting. "I'm just warmed up."

"Not on your life. I've got customers waiting."

"I'll remember that for next time."

Then the men down several cups of spring water, ignoring the catcalls on the street, the pounding at the door. "Now what?" Walt asks.

"I'm going to have to rely on my powers of persuasion."

"Can I remind you what happened the last time you did that?"

"No need," says Father Bill, hanging the Connors back on its hook. He goes into the bathroom and washes his face, runs his wet hands through his hair. He stands for a while, and before he steps out he closes his eyes, asks that whatever comes through him when he speaks, he be guided to serve what is highest.

Afterwards he returns to the blue house. He takes Luz's brown hands in his, walks her from the kitchen to her room, sits down on the edge of her bed, looks into her eyes, and tells her what she is.

I don't do bad things?"

"You do very good things."

"But I don't want to be special. I don't want to do special things."

She is right, of course. And he tries to explain it differently. It is not by her but through her that all this has happened. Through them all.

She is quiet for a while. How he wishes he could read her thoughts. "So let me go back one more time. Tell it to Mami. Make her say yes."

CHAPTER 57

"And now I will try to become like Sewey." Josefina says, looking from Zoe to Walt. They have just finished eating. The rest of the blue house is dark, Luz in a dead sleep, too tired from the great exertion of the day even to take off her yellow dress. The kitchen lit only by a small white lamp, the strangers at bay. "I also will become too patient. Three times a week I will sit for the dialysis four hours, maybe five. Don't look so sorry. I will live. It is just till my body gets strength to make itself right again." Josefina takes Walt's hands and squeezes to reassure him. She does not succeed. "Though to tell you the truth after what I have seen from your window I should be like a newborn right now. Please, I am sorry, I have ruined this beautiful meal."

And then Josefina hears a soft cry, faint as a memory. It could be the sound she will hear when she is no longer with Luz on earth. She listens again then makes a move to rise, her hands on the tabletop, beside the dinner plate with the remains of the omelette, the fruit, the tortilla, her feet so heavy she can scarcely feel them. The throbbing in her skull grows sharp when she tries to stand up. But she has known worse pain than this. "Luz," she says and gets to her feet. Walt and Zoe rise as well. "No, please. Stay here. I will go myself." They watch her struggle to stand. "At least no one can accuse Luz of making miracle cures on her mother," Josefina says ruefully, beginning her slow walk. She crosses the black-and-white squares then disappears into the dark living room, where she stops for breath and to turn on a lamp. "I am coming, mamita," she calls. "One more minute."

In the silence of the kitchen they listen to her heavy steps, the sound of Luz's faraway voice, calling.

"Did you know?" Walt asks.

"Yes."

"Did Father Bill tell you?"

"Yes, that first night at the hospital."

He can feel the weight of her, her leg inches from his, her bare arm. And something else, the whole sense of her body. One of them should get up, clear the table. He moves his leg imperceptibly, leans to his left, one quarter inch. How he feels her. She is moving a fork around her plate, making little designs, thin strips of red pepper, a glazed fragment of onion. He would touch her, but it is better if he does not. She will stay in Infidelity but not for him. These nights she is back at the blue house with Josefina and Luz, but once he closes the wash he comes to her. And in the morning, when she is with Luz she calls him to talk. There is a softness between them, something he would kill to hold onto, watch grow, this thing that has opened between them. Look up, he wants to say, just look at me.

They can hear the low voices of Josefina and Luz, the sounds of the people gathered across Mariposa Lane, indistinct. The ones for whom even today's sidewalk experience was not enough. The depth of the light that seemed to blaze through Luz's little body and enter theirs. How much do they want from this child? Sometime in the night a neighbor will get tired of them and call the police, then the police will come to the blue house. What can Josefina say when they question her? *Those people on the street are crazy. I don't know what they are waiting for. I have no idea why they blame their fantasies on Luz.*

"It isn't as simple as she makes it seem, her condition," Zoe says, her voice is hushed.

"I didn't think that it was," Walt says.

"Her chances for transplant are not good. She is low on the list. There is no money. Father Bill is looking for a donor; for money, too, I think. Among people they knew years ago in El Salvador. He hasn't told her. He'll have to tell her now."

Ah, Walt thinks, he broke their silence.

"He was worried about how he would explain his phone bill to the diocese. I guess that is the least of it for him now."

"I should think so." Walt wonders what Father Bill has said to his bishop today. From the length of his meeting, he expects it is a lot. It is nearly nine o'clock. Father Bill has been gone since morning. "And how about your explanations?"

He is asking her about Michael. She does not want to tell him what Michael says. His fears for her. How her staying is breaking Michael's heart. Michael's guilty heart. He thinks she is living in delusion, inventing what she is trying to explain.

"I'm sorry." Walt puts a finger on her arm. A coin of flesh, that is how much of her he has. "I shouldn't be asking you about Michael."

She stands up. "Let's clear."

CHAPTER 58

"You are awake, mamita? Did you get hungry for me?" Josefina makes her slow way into Luz's room. The gold stitches in Luz's canopy winking at her in the dark, the gold thread that she bought not at the sewing department, but at the jewelry department, that small lie she told her daughter.

When Josefina turns on the lamp, Luz tries to sit up but her arms are too weak, cheeks deeply flushed, her black eyes glazed. "Why is the ball-jumping game on the roof?" she asks, her voice husky as if she has suddenly caught croup.

"What are you telling to me?" Josefina sits down on the edge of the bed, leans into the cloying sweet smell, the engine of illness churning its way inside Luz's flesh, her own head pounding now straight across the front of her skull.

"Green ones. Purple ones," croaks Luz, her mother's mouth on her forehead, her mother's cold hand on her cheek.

"You have fever, mamita. Where does it hurt?"

"No, I don't want to be sick."

The red liquid for fever is in the bathroom. The spoon Josefina needs all the way in the kitchen. Once again the effort of walking, her feet weighted and dulled. When she gets to the kitchen, Zoe and Walt are standing at the sink cleaning up, her friends whom she has just shattered with the precipitate truth.

"Luz is sick." Josefina breathing hard now from the exertion of walking.

"Can we do something?" says Walt. "Do you want to call a doctor?"

"First I will try to bring down her fever."

When Josefina returns, Luz is shaking. Something hot makes her freeze in her skin, but they cover her with only a sheet. "I am cold," Luz says. Still, Father Bill's trick makes her laugh. "Why did he send me the ball-jumping game from the feast?"

"First swallow, then tell us about the game."

Josefina and Zoe and Walt on the edge of Luz's bed counting minutes. The liquid Luz swallows does nothing. Her temperature climbs. Her skin remains dry as a tarp. To silence her crazy talk, they tell stories. Josefina sings to Luz in Spanish. "That makes me happy," says Luz. Walt reads out loud from the wall the twenty-seven Tortoise Facts and asks for more. "Butterball shell," says Luz. "They are my friends. They know my name." "That's not a fact, it's a story," says Josefina, her fingers on Luz's wrist. Luz's pulse is too fast. Her skin is too dry. The ball-jumping game comes and goes from the roof, a red one, a green one, a purple one. Luz's lips are burning.

"We must put her in the tub." Josefina says

"Not naked!" cries Luz.

"Can you walk, mamita?"

"I'm not a baby!" says Luz.

Josefina insists they can do it alone. She goes on numb feet, supporting her daughter, the pulse of her blood beating against the frame of her skull. On the way to the bathroom Luz vomits. How thin Luz has become and how suddenly strong. She struggles, "No bath!" she cries. "I am freezing!" Only by guile and by softness does Josefina persuade Luz to step out of the soiled yellow dress and into the lukewarm bath water. "Come, mamita," says Josefina, leaning into the water, her arm a cushion for Luz's head, "So the water can cool you." Luz steps into the tub on unsteady legs. Her teeth chatter. The water is cruel. When she lies back, the shaking goes straight through her body. "Mozote," cries Luz. The girl in the tree, the branches piercing her thighs. She goes high in the tree in her mind singing the notes so sharp the sound breaks like glass in her ears. She pleads with the children to climb with her, higher, and opens her arm, cries out that she is little—that she still loves the world.

Every sound that Luz makes carries out to the street. "What are they doing to that child?"

When Josefina cannot lift Luz from the tub she calls out for help. The people outside cross over, approach the blue house. Wait.

When at last she is carried to bed, Luz calls out for shoes. Josefina grabs Luz's red sandals from the closet floor, puts them on, does not fasten the straps. Luz sinks into her pillows, her summer pajamas unfastened.

Walt, crossing the street, goes person to person, begging each one to leave. "She's got fever. She's sick. It's the last thing they need tonight. Don't wait for the neighbors to call the police, go home."

"I'm going to call the police," he says to Zoe when he returns.

"No police in my house. Not now!" Josefina insists.

When Father Bill finally arrives, it is close to eleven. Mariposa Lane is ablaze with candles. "A child with a gift," he had said to the bishop. "It is nothing but beautiful. You must see her yourself." After that, there was no turning back. He had spoken the words that would shadow his end. When he enters the house, there it is once again that rose smell, the odor of sanctity. Luz in her bed in her summer pajamas and sandals, her face blazing.

All night they attend to her. Walt feeds her ice chips; he washes her face with a wet paper towel, runs ice along her palms and wrists, as he did when she ran to the car wash. Hourly they wrestle her into and out of the tub, urge her to swallow another spoonful of the red liquid for fever. "Where does it hurt you, mamita?" "Nowhere," says Luz, "everywhere."

Luz swallows each mouthful of water, from each hand that gives it, with such wrenching smiles. "I am sorry," she says and each time grows teary. "Why are you sorry?" asks Father Bill. "Nothing is your fault—nothing." It is four in the morning when Luz sleeps at last and, at last, the blessed sweat flows.

Josefina and Zoe, Walt Adair, Father Bill, the late-coming, dissident priest—all of them able to say they were with her, saw her and held her, and watched the fever burn through her all through that night.

CHAPTER 59

The way the desk clerk would tell it, the door did not open. He simply opened his eyes and looked up, 4 a.m. on the round lobby clock. There she was, dressed in her summer pajamas, her left hand upraised in a fist. Before he could even say her name she had sailed right by him, red sandals not quite touching the carpet. He called out to her as she passed, but she did not hear or did not choose to hear, just kept going down the dimly lit hallway, dark braids bobbing, pajama shirt sailing behind her.

Blankenship tried to reach for the phone, but by then he could not move a muscle. His hands remained on the counter as if buried in bedrock. That is how he finally knew her depravity. In her presence he could not lift even his hands. The moment her followers came through the door, twenty out-of-breath strangers who had seen Luz take flight, full movement returned to him, and he leapt off his chair, able to join them as they sped down the hall in her wake. At the end of the hallway Luz stood before room number four—a view room with a trio of Joshuas just outside the plate glass, the cloud-obscured mountains beyond.

After a moment she reached for the door and it opened. Or perhaps it was already open. The night clerk was sure Luz's hand had not even grazed it, she had slipped no card in the slot, had surely not reached for the handle.

When they saw the moon-faced man down on the floor kneeling in prayer at the foot of the bed, heavy brown robe with the cowl at the back, a great *ahhhhh* escaped from the throats of the strangers, nearly in unison. *Ahhhh.* A Franciscan, thought Blankenship, so that's what he is. The night clerk had known all along there was something peculiar in the moon-faced man, who had smiled but not uttered a word to him in the nine nights of his stay.

The monk's eyes were closed, his mouth moving wordlessly. And so he remained even with the sounds of the strangers who knew him but did not till this moment know what he was. Even in the presence of Luz, who at last settled down, feet resting on the carpet like a winged insect alights on a leaf. The monk nodded twice then, as if Luz had spoken. With the slowness of dreams she reached through the air for his hand, opened her fist, revealing a heavy gold ring, which she slid on his finger with ease.

"Thank you," the monk says in a throaty half-whisper. Only then did he open his eyes and look up at Luz, a long adoring moment. Then he reached for her hands, placing them on the crown of his head, the gold ring glinting, that room growing as bright nearly as day.

When Blankenship felt the light begin to pull at him, golden and hot, he lit out like he was on fire, ran down the hall and straight to the street in terror for his life.

At the door of the diner, Bobbie was fiddling with her key. She was unable to sleep that night, not a wink, and had come a half hour early to work. She could not say why.

When Blankenship tells her what he has just seen, she says, "All right, I'm game. Show me." But he refuses to go back. He stands like a wind-addled sapling until Bobbie takes his hand. "Come on, honey," she says. "You show me Luz."

When they get to the room, they are bathed, child, monk, and at least twenty followers, in a cloud of white. A smile on the face of the young Franciscan, Blankenship will later say, like none he has ever seen in his life nor does he wish ever to see on this earth. Reason enough to have lived, others will say, to have witnessed it. Nearly eclipsing the beauty they'd seen at the blue house, when Luz had emerged through the door as if it were smoke, sailed down to the freeway in her summer pajamas and red-sandaled feet, floating one solid mile, trailing a glorious light.

CHAPTER 60

Josefina is in the first phase of sleep when the ringing phone jolts her awake.

"Luz is at the motel," Bobbie says matter-of-factly. "You'd better get down here."

What craziness is this? Perhaps Josefina is dreaming. "Está enferma," Josefina says, her lips grazing the phone.

"What did you say?"

"Luz is sick. She is asleep in her bed."

"Go look. I'll wait. I want to hear you tell me she's where you think."

Josefina sighs loudly. "For you I will look." She puts the phone on the pillow and eases her way to the edge of the bed. When her feet touch the floor she feels nothing. She waits for the pain that precedes sensation, then the faraway sense of the floor, raising and lowering each foot before risking her weight. Finally, she is able to drag herself to the doorway then into the hall, palming the walls for support. Only briefly does it occur to Josefina that her daughter has in fact left the house. Perhaps she is dreaming. How can it be that Bobbie, a sensible woman, has made such a call? When she gets to Luz's room, the faint light of morning has already intruded. There is Luz, right where she should be, asleep under her canopy, and there is Zoe, whom Josefina has nearly forgotten, her long body curled on a thin blanket on the floor beside Luz's bed. Josefina shuffles around to the side, leans down to Luz, whose face appears peaceful and soft, her chest rising and falling with even slow breaths. Luz in the midst of a beautiful sleep. Josefina puts her lips against Luz's broad, stony brow, which is cool and damp. Luz shudders, a deep easeful breath as if expelling the last of her illness.

"Something wrong?" Zoe murmurs. "Shhh," Josefina says, "we are fine. Sleep."

Then Josefina goes slowly out of the room.

"Did someone phone?" William calls from the couch. Josefina pauses in the hall, one hand on the wall for balance, the other on her forehead to contain the throbbing. "No one," she says. "Are you all right?" he asks as he pulls off the sheet and begins to sit up. "Stay, try to sleep. I am returning to bed," she responds. What is wrong with that Bobbie, she thinks, to make such a call and at such an hour?

Now her house is once again quiet. Even from outside the house comes no sound. No low hum of talk from the strangers, whom she trusts must be sleeping. Still, so unusual is the silence that Josefina goes back into the living room and raises the sheet from the near window and looks out. The first light of morning has gilded the fronts of the small stucco houses that face hers and the tops of the tall, graceful weeds, and not one person standing or sitting, not a living soul to be seen anywhere. "What is it now?" says William. "Finally," says Josefina turning to him, "the strangers have gone."

On her way back to bed, she goes to the bathroom, avoiding her face in the mirror, the urine she makes now, scant, alarmingly dark. And though many minutes have passed, when she returns to her room and picks up the phone, Bobbie is still on the other end, waiting. "We had a bad night. Please, leave us in peace." Then without listening to Bobbie's reply, Josefina hangs up, bends down with slowness and care, so as not to add to the pounding in her head, and unplugs the phone from the jack. Returning to bed she sleeps badly and heavily till the light is fierce and the voices on the street jar her awake, till they are ringing her doorbell and pounding their fists on her door.

CHAPTER 61

Dead of joy is the rumor when the young monk is found, his rapturous face pressed down on the rank flowered carpet of room number four, his body smelling faintly of roses.

Hadn't the night clerk predicted that Luz Reyes was dangerous? That the whole sidewalk business would come to no good? Now he had proof. From the moment he first glimpsed the body—from the doorway, no closer; he was afraid to go into the room—to the moment Walt Adair knocked him out, Blankenship kept insisting Luz had killed the moon-faced monk with a look.

"No one was murdered," Bobbie tells the police, tells everyone who gathers outside the motel, all who walk into the diner, each person who phones her, strangers who ask if it's true. "I saw it myself. Saw him living and then saw him dead. That sweet man died of his joy."

Even before the monk's death is confirmed, the rumors, that just days before were considered too wild for belief, are being touted as fact: Luz can run and her feet do not touch the ground. She can know whom an object belongs to without being told—she can find her way to the owner, come hell or high water! And she can knock people flat with a look—maybe worse. Not a parent, that morning, whose heart is not seized with the fear of it. Could our children be right about Luz after all? Have they been telling the truth—and not been believed—since the spring?

Before the crowd descends at the motel, the rescue squad shows up in force. The green EMT van arrives first, then the volunteer fire crew, and then in the midst of the first rush of Labor Day traffic, come the high wailing sirens and red-flashing lights of the Highway Patrol, four black and white squad cars blocking the entrance. Walt Adair, just getting ready to open the car wash, instead leaves his office and drives across in the Civic to see what is wrong.

By eight o'clock people from all over Infidelity are heading to the motel, complaining of the three-digit heat, scared out of their wits about Luz.

The Mariposa Lane watchers who claim to have witnessed the marvel in room number four are called back by the sirens, inciting all kinds of excitement talking freely of what they had seen. Just before dawn, they say, Luz passed through the door of her house as if she were vapor, and sailed right past them on those fast-flying feet. By the time she reached the freeway, they could not even see her. She had turned lustrous. She was nothing but forward-bent light.

Still, they followed her luminous trail (mostly on foot) to the motel front doors, which were shimmering faintly. When they entered they found her looking just like herself, though hovering a bit over the threshold of room number four.

What passed between Luz and the monk in that room, they could not adequately convey, the tenderness of the exchange surpassing anything they had seen, beyond what they'd been given on the sidewalk, far beyond what they might have hoped for when hunger, or instinct, or chance, or something beyond them to know had sent them to Infidelity, a place which appears on no map, a black dot on a small lilac flyer.

Pilgrims unite for a great event. Was this their event? Joy ending in death?

Some time after the ring had been given and the gold air subsided, Luz herself vanished. Not a trace of her remained to be seen. "Don't be alarmed," the monk said, rising to his feet to calm all who had shared in his bliss and witnessed the feats of the child. "She is safe. She has returned to her mother." Then he blessed every one, told them not to seek after Luz and asked for some moments alone.

"Bullshit," said Bobbie, when she heard what the strangers were saying. "Blankenship's a madman, and these people are deluded. No one in this town can trust what we see anymore, let alone blame a child."

* * *

In the one hour that it takes to pronounce his death, the CHP has its officers fanning around the motel to keep the curious at bay.

Dead of joy, everyone is saying by then. The EMT guys have never seen anything like it, a face so blissful, as if the monk has simply slipped out of his skin.

Most of the sidewalk regulars are gathered by then, with Walt Adair saying over and over he was with Luz for most of the night, she was sick, blazing with fever, hardly able to stand on her feet. But he is just one. Too many say differently. Too many too afraid to believe anything but the very thing fueling their fear.

When the monk is brought out, it gets quiet. They carry him out already zipped up. "Take him out of the bag!" someone calls, though many feel the sweetness right through the plastic, embarrassed in public by their uncontrolled tears.

The day clerk arrives. Blankenship comes through the front doors still declaiming about Luz. That's when Walt goes after him—knocks him to the ground with one clean blow to the gut. It takes three CHP officers to pull Walt off Blankenship when he's down. They have to put Walt in a squad car to cool off. By the time they let him out, Blankenship is gone, and Walt leaves in the Civic.

Things quiet down for a while. Bobbie goes back to the diner. Most of the strangers go back to the field, though some head to the hill district, demanding to see Luz. The volunteer fire squad hangs around drinking coffee—in all that heat—talking softly to Patty Platz and her friends, trying to calm them. "Stop crying and listen. No child killed anyone."

The guests clear out of the motel. One death this close is one death too many for any vacation, a few of them say—whatever the cause.

Then over the firemen's phone comes the call for an ambulance: an ambulance needed on Mariposa, stat.

CHAPTER 62

"Stay away!" Josefina cries, "don't come near me." She stands with her back to the front door. Too many voices. Too many people telling her she must step aside, must open the locks. Luz, Father Bill, the Felangela, and an officer in uniform who has been in the house for two hours or more.

How Josefina has managed to return to the front door is a feat of endurance that only Father Bill understands, having seen her walk three times from the Ilopango prison, three times outliving her rumored deaths.

"Mami, please," calls Luz.

She may faint once again. What is the fear and what is the illness? She cannot say. Police at her back door, police at her front door, and another within. No escaudero, this much she knows. When he entered the house, he had right away removed his sunglasses, spoken his name, a name she cannot now remember, nor can she read it on the little black plate on his shirt. "We are here to help you. What do you need?"

"Those people. They want my daughter. Get them away from my door!"

Now Luz comes toward her, Luz who must not see her mother go once again in the ambulance. Her step is hesitant, her face pale from her own bout with fever, her child who had crouched in the hall, cowed by the taunts of the strangers. “Let them take you for your treatment. Go in the ambulance, please.”

“Listen to her, Josefina,” says the officer. He stands with his hands hanging loose past the heavy black belt she cannot look at, stands at a distance, safe, very still, as if it is not outside the bounds of his understanding that a woman who can barely stand up on two feet is refusing the ambulance she herself called. “All those people are gone. We did as you asked. Even your neighbors have gone into their houses,” he says.

“No one will get near your daughter or you. I promise you that. What do you say?” he asks.

“How can you promise? They have ways of returning you don’t even know.”

“Josefina,” says Father Bill.

“I know what he says.” She looks past the officer to William, wavering slightly as if he is beckoning from a very far place. William who knows very well that once she steps out of the blue house she may never come back.

“I do not want to be carried. I must walk.”

The officer nods. “Good girl,” he says under his breath. His phone crackles as he brings it to his mouth. “Put the stretcher away. Then come on back. We’ll walk her out.”

Luz runs to embrace her mother, bites hard on her lower lip so she will not cry, bites harder, tastes her own blood. Josefina puts her hands on Luz’s cheeks, looks into her face, two daughters, three daughters, all of them frightened. Where are the eyes of her sister that she has lost once again, those beautiful eyes of her lost Esperanza that she needs for her daughter to salve Luz’s pain with their inexhaustible love?

CHAPTER 63

Luz opens her eyes, sees the Joshua trees with their ragged gray up-pointing branches speeding before her. She lifts her head. "Why am I in Walt's car? Why did you bring me to the campgrounds? I want to go home."

"Shhh, try to go back to sleep. You'll see Mami soon." The police had been vehement. You never know with these people, they had explained. *Fanatics, notoriously unstable. You don't want to risk it. Better keep Luz away.*

She had gone to the campgrounds, the place that Luz loves.

What stranger would search for Luz here? But now Zoe wonders if she's made a mistake.

Luz tries to drift back to sleep. Tries not to know where she is.

"Is it your girl who was lost in the campgrounds last spring?" the policeman asked Mami. Then Father Bill had taken Luz into the kitchen and poured her juice. "Sip slowly. I'll be right back," he said.

From the kitchen Luz could not hear the policeman. Sometimes his voice was too soft. "Did you take Luz to the motel?" "No," said Mami. "No," said Zoe. "What do you think we are?" said Father Bill. "William," said her mother, so much love in her voice. "Tell me what's been going on here," the policeman said. Everyone talked soft. No one said "sidewalk." She only heard *Luz, Luz.* "Could Luz have gone out when you were sleeping?" asked the policeman. Then murmurs, and only one word clear, *motel, motel, motel.*

But Luz heard what Walt said when he came to the house. Someone died at the motel, Walt had told Zoe—a man whose name Walt did not know.

Did Luz see the man? she wonders. *Did he sit on the sidewalk?*

"Did I walk in the night?" Luz asks suddenly. Zoe startles at the wheel, thrown by the sudden intrusion of Luz's voice. She pulls the Civic to the side of the road, takes off her seatbelt and turns around. "What did you say?"

"Did I walk to the motel?"

"Why are you asking?"

Luz sits up. "Did I?"

"Do you think that you did?" Zoe says softly.

"I don't know. The people say—"

"What people?" Zoe gets out of the car and slides in the back beside Luz, lifting her feet and holding them in her lap. "You were sick last night, remember? Father Bill was there and Walt and Mami."

"Yes, but after," says Luz, "then what did I do?"

"You took your medicine, took a couple of nice cold baths, you told a lot of amazing stories. Oh, you told us some doozies. . . . Then at long last you fell asleep."

"Then who walked?" asks Luz.

Zoe leans into the front seat, grabs a bottle of water. "No one. The strangers. Drink."

"Did the man that died go to the sidewalk?"

Zoe is silent.

"Do we know who he is?"

"Yes," says Zoe. "He used to come to the sidewalk. But you did not walk. Now drink."

Luz drinks the water while Zoe looks past her. A couple of hikers are moving among the Joshua trees across the road from where they have stopped. No cars on Park Boulevard except the faraway parked ones. Two more hours, she thinks, until they can go to the hospital.

"What did he look like?" says Luz.
"Luz," says Zoe. "It has nothing to do with you!"
"Yes," says Luz. "Maybe it could."
"The one with the very white face."
And tan hands?" says Luz.
"Yes,"
Luz hurls the bottle of water at Zoe then bolts from the car.

CHAPTER 64

That they are only one hour late is a miracle. Zoe was afraid there would be no Luz to bring to the High Desert Hospital. In the two hours that Luz was lost in the campgrounds, she was certain that she would never see Luz again.

Now the shaking that wracked her has subsided. Her teeth have stopped chattering, but there is a constant sensation of cold running down Zoe's neck, down her back. Her mouth is dry. Nausea remains in the pit of her stomach. *A mother's fear*, she thinks. Though she is not Luz's mother. She parks the car as close as she can to the hospital, lifts Luz from the back seat and manages to carry her into the lobby. Luz whimpering softly, her face hidden in Zoe's shoulder, her injured foot wrapped in a cold pack, the pain sharp and constant, the worst pain Luz has known.

"It's all right," Zoe says. "We're here."

The cold air of the hospital lobby threatens to set off Zoe's trembling. She clasps Luz tightly in her arms.

"Emergency is back through those doors," the receptionist says. "No," says Zoe. "We're here for Josefina Reyes, a patient." The receptionist checks the computer. "Third floor," she says. "You won't be able to bring a child there." Zoe starts for the elevators and is called back. She has forgotten to fill out the pass.

When they get to the third floor, Father Bill is standing just outside the closed green glass doors of Intensive Care, his face drained of color.

He rushes toward the elevator to meet them. "Just Luz," he says to Zoe. "She had a fall, her foot," Zoe says. She does not say what else. Does not speak of the way that Luz ran, or the way she had nearly lost her. No time to tell Father Bill what she has seen Luz do. Or how the rangers and hikers fanned out through the Joshua Tree Forest at Covington Flats searching for nearly an hour before they found Luz, down on the hard pan, her foot lodged in a crevice at an impossible angle. "You'd better have that looked at," the ranger said, after they'd packed it in ice at the First Aid Center. "An X-ray, probably. This is some lucky girl. How did you get so far away from your mother so fast?"

"She's not my mother," said Luz.

The ranger had laughed.

"Poor Luz," says Father Bill, leaning into the doors of Intensive Care. "What a bad time you are having."

CHAPTER 65

The elevator is empty. They step in. Zoe and Father Bill, unkempt beyond caring. *We are those people you see in hospitals and don't want to acknowledge*, Zoe thinks. *The ones you never want to be.*

"It's not good," Father Bill says as the doors close and the elevator starts down. He speaks of numbers, the results of her tests, Josefina's BUN, her astronomical blood pressure. "She's got a shitload of complications, right now it's the blood pressure they are most worried about; she could stroke out, as they say. Lovely phrase. She is in the fight of her life."

The elevator stops and they get out. "We're going to talk to social services," he says. "Follow me." The corridors are long, and they have to make several turns. Zoe cannot shake the feeling that Luz is gone, disappeared, the sensation she had looking across Park Boulevard and seeing Luz in flight, far off among the Joshuas. Luz and Josefina, together right now in Intensive Care. She has not quite absorbed it, she thinks. It is coming at her too fast. Father Bill opens a door to a small office where a woman in a tan suit and a serious demeanor sits behind a desk, whose surface is covered with files. The woman is talking into a phone. She points to the chairs, acknowledges Zoe with a nod and continues talking. On the desk is a blue glass vase with enormous white crepe paper flowers that seem to be eating the air.

"How are you holding up?" the woman says to Father Bill as soon as she hangs up the phone.

"Okay," he says.

"Luz is with her?"

He nods.

The woman holds out her hand, greets Zoe by name, explains that she is handling Josefina's case. "Josefina and Luz," she says and sighs. "We're old friends from the spring. Have I met you before?"

"No," says Zoe.

"I didn't think so."

The woman has enormous white teeth, absolute choppers. "This must be very hard for you," she says to Zoe.

For me? Zoe thinks, but says yes, not wanting to disagree.

The woman takes a breath, glances from Zoe to Father Bill, as if she's not sure how to begin. "Do you speak Spanish?" she says to Zoe.

"No," says Zoe.

"Are there children of Hispanic background in your district?"

"My district?"

"In your school district."

"I don't know," Zoe says.

The social worker looks quizzically at Father Bill. He turns to Zoe. "Has Father Bill told you what this about?"

"Not yet."

"Would you like me to . . . ?"

"Let me do it," he says.

Father Bill turns his chair to Zoe, and the moment he does her eyes start to burn, even before he speaks she is fighting to control the part of her that knows what he is about to say. Zoe's breath is coming fast. Her mouth has turned dry. She looks into Father Bill's tired gray eyes, at the silver black stubble of his unshaven face. He smiles at her, she smiles back, her bottom lip trembles. She hates herself for it. He takes her hands in his. They have spent so little time together, have spoken so little. How can that be, she wonders, with all that they have shared, Zoe Luedke and Father Bill Esposito? Bill Esposito in truth, though even after he has gathered his parish for the announcement, it will be days before he can bring himself to say it. Bill Esposito, the man. No longer a man of his calling. No longer a priest.

"Josefina is in stage five—failure. They don't know if she can be brought back. She will need to be dialyzed three or four times a day. It is going to be touch and go for . . . we don't know how long. Someone needs to be there for Luz. Josefina has asked that you be the one."

"Okay," Zoe murmurs dream-like, an acknowledgement only that she has heard these words. She has nearly lost Luz today. How can she possibly take her after that? And then she thinks right away of Michael at work on the Grosvenors' river-view kitchen. What a terrible thought, Zoe chastises herself. But then again, maybe it is not so terrible. Maybe, Zoe thinks, she can take Luz with her for a while, away from Infidelity, away from the campgrounds, the places where Luz walks, take Luz to her house in Cold Spring and Michael. Where no one sits on a sidewalk losing themselves in the gold. And so when Father Bill says it, she is already picturing it, Luz in the big house, the one she and Michael had hoped to fill with their children. How will she explain it to him? She is returning. She is bringing a child.

"Josefina wants you to have legal custody of Luz."

He looks at Zoe, who has turned her face away. And in that small office a silence takes over that seems not to know its own end.

"Will you need time to think about this?" asks the social worker.

Legal custody, thinks Zoe. Permanent custody? Are they telling her this is it, Josefina will die? She turns to Father Bill again. *Why not you?* she does not say. *Why has she bypassed you?* "Are you sure this is right?"

"I am sure," he says.

"Can you tell me how it works?" Zoe asks. The social worker reaches for a stack of papers, half stands, then leans across her desk and places them in front of Zoe. "Power of Attorney for Care of a Child" printed over the top in large black type.

"Read through the document," she says, "It's pretty clear. If you have any questions, I'll try to answer. Understand that this might only be temporary. The mother retains the right to revoke it at any time. So if she is again able to care for her, Luz will come back. You'll bring her back. And in the event of her death you can decide whether you want to make a permanent commitment. If you decide against it, we will have to make other arrangements."

"Other?" asks Zoe.

"Foster care."

Zoe glances again at the papers to anchor herself. "Know all men by these presents," it begins. What presents? Zoe wonders. What men? Father Bill? Walt Adair? The moon-faced-man? Why is it not Father Bill who will get Luz? Is it because he's a priest? Know all men by these presents, Zoe reads it again. Josefina in stage five kidney failure. Will two deaths have come from the sidewalk, then? The moon-faced man, and now Josefina's. Why did Josefina not go back to the clinic? Did no one know that her symptoms had returned? Were they all asleep? What was everyone doing, sitting out there in some kind of dream world? Seeing visions, ignoring the truth. *Awe-struck, deluded,* the officer had described the strangers outside the blue house. Awe and hate are not far from each other, he had explained, his voice low so Luz would not hear. *We don't know what kind of maniac will turn up. Best if you take Luz away. Well, maybe we do,* Zoe thinks. Two deaths, and now this. Zoe being asked to take Power of Attorney for Care of a Child. They are giving her Luz.

Before she has read another word, before she has taken the moment, several moments, the rest of her life to read this document and consider what it could possibly mean, she thinks of Michael, solid, undependable Michael who is waiting for her, who will not in any way understand what Zoe has done, will not understand the sidewalk experience, even if she could explain it, even if she herself did not doubt it, as she does right now.

I went into in the home of a stranger, she will tell him, *and she gave me her child.*

Zoe flips the page. She is supposed to be reading. Here it is, her new list. Her list of instructions for Luz.

Father Bill watches Zoe read, smiling an unfathomable smile, as if he is already beyond this moment, as if he finds something about it beautiful. He has been watching Zoe's hands as she holds the document, her long fingers, the missing felangela. What did he think when he dreamed of her hands in spring? He thought she was going to help them, widen the parish, bring new people to his flock, perhaps. He had thought he himself might be changed in some way he was not yet aware of. But his thinking was vague, and he was arrogant, not sure how he could be changed any more than he already had been, ground to a powder, barely reconstituted, even now. After El Salvador. After Josefina. He did not think this person he had dreamed was going to take Luz. He could never have imagined that these were the hands that would take Luz from him.

"You'll need two witnesses and a notary," says the social worker.

Father Bill nods. He looks again at Zoe, his whole face softens. *Don't worry,* his look says. *Don't let this scare you. Everything is all right.* "Walt is on his way."

"There's a notary ten minutes from here in the Palms. If you call, he will meet you. I'll give you his information. I know you'll have questions. You can call me at home tonight." She hands Zoe a card and stands up. "Sit here a few minutes. Catch your breath. I'll go upstairs and get the list from Luz."

"The list?" Zoe asks.

"The things that she wants to bring with her."

"Why can't I take her back to the house?" Zoe asks.

"Not a good idea. You'll go yourself."

CHAPTER 66

"Why do they have the big tube in your body?"

"Don't look, mamita. Look at my face." Josefina says slowly, raising her right hand in a futile attempt to cover the access.

"Why are you talking so soft?"

"Shhh, only listen. I have important things I must tell you, and I am so tired."

"Open your eyes, Mami."

"Luz," says the nurse who is standing behind the wheelchair where Luz sits, her right leg elevated, the foot wrapped in a package of ice. She hardly feels it. "Remember what we said? Your mother is doing the best that she can." The nurse had explained it as she was looking at Luz's foot. Her mother was sleeping. They would wake her to talk to Luz. There was a tube in Josefina's heart, the blood going around, there were screens with numbers and lights and a big plastic bag high up on a pole with her food that looks like water, there were needles under the tape on her left arm. Talking will not be easy, the nurse had said. If her mother grows quiet, Luz must patiently wait.

Now, even with her eyes closed, Josefina can see Luz's face shimmering before her, a wondrous gold. "My beautiful Luz, are you frightened by all this? You are so good, mamita. Do you know how much I love you?"

"Yes."

"How everyone loves you? How the children loved you again? Tell me the names of our neighbor again."

"The Ottos?"

"Remember I went to them for the first time? Remember how good all the people were to us every day?"

"I can't hear you."

"Come closer. Go to the other side of the bed. All right, stay. It was good, mamita. I want you to remember your sidewalk was good. Will you? Forgive me that I . . ."

"I don't know what she's talking about." Luz says to the nurse.

"Do you want to leave?" says the nurse. "We can try later."

"No," says Luz.

"Then be patient. Let her talk."

Josefina resumes. Luz tries to look at her face, to find the parts of her mother that the sickness has not yet claimed. "There are many people waiting to love you. And many more people you are going to love." Josefina is smiling. Can she already see this? The life Luz will have in the future? "You will see. You are only just beginning."

"Why are you telling me this?"

"You are going away now."

"I don't want to go."

"With the Felangela."

"Where will she take me?"

"To her home."

"For a long or a short time?"

"We don't know."

"A short or a long time?" Luz shudders. The heat comes to her arms and her shoulders. The heat then the cold.

Josefina makes a great effort. She opens her eyes. She sees Luz's features forming themselves through the gold. "Long."

"And then I'll come back," Luz says.

"We don't know."

"Don't let it happen, please, Mami."

"It is not up to us." Now, she has lost Luz again, seeing only the light, only the gold, her daughter who has turned into light. "Come here, mamita. Give me your hand. I will tell you a secret. This is the most important secret I have ever told you."

Luz looks at the nurse who stands right behind her. "All right," whispers the nurse. "I'm right here."

Luz leans toward her mother, bending out of the wheelchair, into the space where the rail of the bed has been lowered. Josefina slowly raises her unencumbered hand to cup Luz's face, thin, not the face she is used to, the bones too close to the skin. "You will always have me. Even if you don't have me like this. Do you know what I am saying?"

"No."

"Yes, you do know."

"You will be feeling me always. You will be seeing me, even when I am not here."

"Don't tell me this, Mami. Don't talk."

"Shhhh. Listen. It is important. Even if one goes away, the love between two people can grow. Even if only one stays living. Do you know how I know this? Because of your window. Esperanza was there. She came to me. You brought her back."

"This is a bad story."

"It is the truth. This is a very big truth."

"I don't want to hear. I don't want the Felangela."

"For now. Just for now, take her."

"Because you could die?"

"Because I could die." Josefina hears Luz's voiceless sobs, the quick in and out of her breath, then the tears of her daughter run into the palm of her hand. "Cry, mamita," Josefina says, "you can cry. Don't be ashamed. Just remember you will always have me. You will see how I come to you."

"I won't see anything. I won't see you. I won't have anything. Please, don't let it happen, Mami. If you die, I don't want to be alive anymore."

"Shhh, mamita. We don't decide these things."

Yes, thinks Luz. It is Our Lady. She is the one who does this to us. With a bad smell and only a shadow for a face. And Father Bill who tells lies. "God has given you a gift," he had said, "and you have brought it to us." "No!" Luz shouts, startling Josefina awake. "If you can't live, then

I'm not going to stay in life either. Please, Mami, don't go to sleep. Try, try not to die."

Josefina drops into darkness. Her daughter's face slips from her hand.

And just as she feared, worse, when they come to her bed to take Luz, Luz refuses to go. She clings to the rails; she screams. One nurse. Two nurses. And then William. Josefina in darkness can do nothing but listen, every voice urging Luz to let go. Every one of her daughter's last cries.

CHAPTER 67

There is a single police car outside the motel when Walt arrives back in Infidelity, but none at the wash, not for hours, no customers either. No one to sell them a ticket. In his haste to get to the notary he had locked his office but left the wash open, the little white structure looking small and abandoned against the brilliant purples and blues, the great pink expanse of nightfall. He walks out to the wash to give it a cursory look before shutting the doors, sees that the floor of the wash is covered with glass all the way to the rinse line. A deep unease settles through him as he goes to the light box and turns on the lights. All day he had swallowed his grief over Josefina, reassuring people that things were okay. Nothing was going to happen to anyone, he had said a hundred times, maybe more. Infidelity would not be inundated because someone had died at the motel, not by seekers or maniacs. Not for a moment had he thought that his wash would be anything but safe. He looks up at the lights. Now he can see the damage, half of the delicate ceiling bulbs have been smashed, lopped off like upside-down boiled breakfast eggs, filaments exposed. Blankenship, probably, Walt thinks as he tries to gauge the state of the overhead piping, his shoes crackling on shards as he steps onto the conveyor and looks up.

Or perhaps not Blankenship. Others were afraid and looking for something or someone to blame, maybe kids, maybe a stranger, one nut, someone convinced of the purity of his intentions. The pipes appear untouched, but he won't know until he turns on the water. He walks slowly to the valve, releases it, waits, then watches the water spurt from the pipes sending pockets of needle-thin spray up to the ceiling and out to the air. It is going to cost him a bundle to fix this.

Still, it seems minor. Nothing like what is transpiring right now with Josefina and Luz. Only weeks ago this would have felt catastrophic. Now it seems small. Fixable, he thinks. He sighs, turns off the valve and the light switch. Pulls down the doors. They will use this, he thinks, those who need to, as proof. What they'd all done on the sidewalk had led to no good. But nothing that's happened, even the tragedy of Josefina and Luz can lead him to doubt his experience. He had even defended the strangers camped on his field. *Why had he ever allowed it?* the CHP officers asked. "Because their hunger is real," he had said.

Our hunger *is* real, Walt thinks as he walks back to the office under the darkening sky. He had said this to those who came to his office full of doubt for the whole thing that day. It's all right to want what we wanted. Nothing is wrong in this town. The fear that Walt harbors is for Luz. For in spite of what he has told others, Walt does not disbelieve what the strangers have said. He has seen those feet not quite touching the ground, is prepared to believe there are things he may not quite be able to fathom, in their own way as real as the ground holding him now. Why must Luz, not even eight years old, be made to bear them?

He enters his office, sighs with relief, locks the door, grabs a beer, settles down on the couch. One cushion missing.

Walt lies back, puts his feet up, sips at the beer, thinks of Josefina in her hospital bed, the Civic piled with Luz's things. "We'll work it out later," he had said to Zoe, insisting she take it for the drive east. "I want you to have a good car." In a minute he has to leave for the hospital to see them off. He hopes that the traffic has cleared and he makes good time. He gets up and walks through the office to the phone. Before he leaves, he wants to call his kids. He is going to drive up to Newport and take them to dinner. Wait till they see what he's driving. He smiles as he picks up the phone. If only the monk hadn't died. If only he could have lived with his joy.

CHAPTER 68

"Don't get out of the car!" Father Bill calls as Zoe stops the Civic in the hospital parking lot where he and Walt wait in the glare of white lights, Luz in his arms, struggling against him. "No!" shouts Luz when Walt opens the back door and the men try to ease her into the seat. Pillows and quilts in a heap, two black plastic sacks with her toys on the floor, everything Luz owns packed in the car for the trip. "I'm not going! You can't make me!" They pull her back up. Father Bill rocks her, crooning softly, "You'll be okay."

Walt hands Zoe a yellow pad, the map of her route, that Father Bill has prepared, places where Zoe must stop. "At every stop you'll be met," Father Bill half shouts over Luz's cries.

"I'll be met?" Zoe says.

"You'll have help on the drive." The route lists cities and churches where someone will be waiting to join her, take over the wheel, three hours or four, so she can sleep. "Don't worry. It has all been worked out." How? Zoe wonders. Who are these people? She sees Unitarian, Catholic, Presbyterian. All kinds of churches. How will she find them? She watches Father Bill and Walt struggle with Luz, who is hitting out now with her fists, kicking with her good foot. When they put her on the seat, belt her in, finally close the back door she is sobbing weakly, begging them now to let her stay with her mother. When Zoe hears the door close, she starts up the car, afraid Luz will rip off the seat belt, leap out, run in spite of her foot. She does not say good-bye, does not look back, drives off leaving Father Bill and Walt standing in the parking lot, watching.

Sixty miles later, Luz stops crying, slides down on the seat in defeat, turning her back. Zoe lets out a long sigh, tries to picture Cold Spring, her home, Michael waiting, a continent away, a world away, the big house where Luz will be safe. She lets herself see the late summer flowers, the ragged back lawn, Michael standing at the front door, "A child?" he had said. "You're bringing a child? Zoe, I don't understand."

It is nearly midnight, the roads heavy with holiday traffic. The sky black and starless. Not until they get across the state line to Arizona does Luz stop crying, her anger and sorrow given over to sleep. Their first stop is Flagstaff, but once Luz gets quiet exhaustion overtakes Zoe. She may have to pull over and rest, leave whoever is waiting at St. Paul the Apostle on North Velez Street waiting longer, but at least Luz is quiet. Zoe opens the windows to the chill air and keeps driving.

"I have to go to the bathroom," says Luz. Zoe looks into the rearview mirror. She is pale and drawn, the tension etched into her face. "Okay, honey," she says. At the rest stop, Luz leans at the sink, trying to wash her hands. "Does it hurt?" Zoe says. She bends down to touch the foot, loosely strapped into a sandal. Luz winces. The sole of her foot has ballooned. Zoe's heartbeat quickens. When Zoe calls Michael, Luz stands close and listens, looks up when she hears Zoe say her name. "There's a very nice doctor where we are going," Zoe says. "Michael's father. "Michael?" says Luz. "Yes, Michael. He is waiting for us right now."

"You forgot my toothbrush," says Luz.

Zoe had packed it, but where had she put it? She had packed nearly everything of Luz's, pulling things down from her closet, emptying Luz's drawers. She had torn through the house, found no suitcase, used trash bags. She could not get out of there fast enough.

Just after dawn they arrive in Flagstaff, a smoky white sky, low buildings still holding their gray. Luz has woken but only briefly, whimpered, refused water, gone back to sleep. St. Paul's is two miles off the I 40, only one wrong turn before Zoe finds it—a plain granite building flanked by a laundromat and a small apartment house. A car is parked in front of the church, a woman behind the wheel reading a book. Zoe slows down, opens the window. The woman looks up, says Zoe's name, smiles. "You made good time."

There will be many stops like this one, in Albuquerque, Houston, Kansas City, Columbus, Ohio, Wilkes Barre, Pennsylvania. Men and women who are happy to give up their Labor Day weekend for the privilege of this, not disposed to talk, reminding Zoe she needs to sleep. "Are you trained to do this?" she asks. "Do you know each other?" They reveal nothing. Only the driver who meets them in Albuquerque, a gray-haired woman in a pink sweatshirt who speaks with a brogue, tells Zoe that she knew Raphael Reyes, had no idea he had lived to have a child.

"Did you go to my country?" Luz will say, startling them both. "Yes, I was there many years, sweetheart." And for a little while the woman and Luz will speak, but the conversation is in Spanish, and Zoe drifts off. When Zoe wakes, there is Luz sitting up, looking out at the road, her dark eyes shining. "Tell Father Bill Sister Anne says hello," she says when four hours later in the clear morning light Zoe drops her at a bus station in Amarillo, then checks in by phone with Father Bill. "Who are these people?" she asks.

"Sanctuary," he says. "Another time I will explain." He tells her Josefina is hanging on. He's got the nursing staff praying for her and all of Infidelity.

The driver who meets them in Columbus is surprised at how well Luz understands English. "Did she get hurt running the border?" he had asked. "Is that where she lost her parents?" "I'm not lost," says Luz. "I'm on a short trip." "And her mother's alive," Zoe says.

Luz begins eating, cries only when she is asleep. She sits looking out the window, drawn into the shell of silence in a way that makes Zoe question every moment she had sat at the window, seduced by the gold.

Ten hours from Cold Spring it rains, a hard rain drums on the roof of the car, pelts the windshield, makes the road dissolve into gray. Zoe slows down, looks longingly at every motel sign, thinks of turning off the interstate and checking them in. How good it will be to stretch out in her bed. Her knees have been aching since Ohio. She longs for sleep, long and deep. How will she ever sleep now that she has Luz?

By dawn the rain has stopped and the world has turned green, drenched, the air thickly sweet. Just ahead a school bus has stopped, flashing its red lights. They wait behind it. Clean, well-groomed children with new shoes and backpacks are bidding their parents good-bye, walking solemnly onto the bus. The bus starts up, the parents wave, keep waving. The car behind Zoe honks loudly, twice. "Is it the first day?" asks Luz. "I think so," says Zoe. They have entered the world of the living, a country where they have no place.

"Smell," Zoe says as she rolls down the window. "Nice, isn't it? We're almost there."

Now they can see the Hudson. A faint mist rises up over the water, gray and soft, the tree line a little indistinct, exhausted by summer. Too early for the oaks to turn gold.

"Okay," says Zoe, "we are going to turn up a hill, and then you will see a big gray house. That is the house I told you about where I live. We are almost there." Luz is all eyes. Nothing of her voice seems to have survived the trip. They start the climb; Zoe's heart beats fast. She loves everything her eyes touch, the old stone walls lining the drive, dark from the night's rain, the towering white pines and the deep green of low-growing hosta. Now they can see the house, the gray-painted shingles, immaculate white window trim, side porches, the wide, shaded lawn, Cosmos and black-eyed Susans along the brick walk, droopy with rain. And there is the car she has been tracking for weeks, searching the field behind Walt's office, searching parking lots up and down the Joshua Freeway, Michael and Zoe's white van parked in the driveway next to the kitchen door. She pulls up beside it, seeing her name in blue letters on the side panel, Michael's name, their Cold Spring address. And for a moment Zoe can almost believe she has never gone anywhere, Michael has never gone anywhere; she had only driven up to a friend's house for the Labor Day weekend and waited till Tuesday, *this* day, to make the trip home.

CHAPTER 69

He must have been at the living room window watching for her, for he is out the front door in an instant, running down the flower-rimmed walk in bare feet and jeans, an olive green tee shirt, all quick aliveness and agile gait, unruly dark hair. And before Zoe can turn off the engine he is beside her, reaching through the open window to clasp her bare arm, the familiar heat and weight of his hand against her skin, his fingertips resting on her wrist. Once she opens the door and gets out, they will speak. If they are lucky, the improbable truth. But right now they have only this: Michael's hand on her arm, the way he does not let it go.

CHAPTER 70

Luz awakens to hear Zoe's strange cry in the room next to hers, where earlier the soft voices were rising and falling behind the gray wall. The voices, and then Zoe's cries, each night the same.

Soon Zoe will return to Luz, to sleep beside her in the high wooden bed just as she has every night since they came to the green place, which is how Luz thinks of it, green of the grass, green leaves that make strange rustling noises in the night, the strong sound that is wind when it rains, three nights, maybe four, Zoe's smell like an animal, something wild that might come from the trees that are everywhere, behind every road, trees that shut out the sunlight with many branches, heavy with leaves and many secret homes.

Zoe comes back to the bed and sleeps beside Luz until morning, but Luz does not move near to Zoe or let Zoe touch her, only listens to her breath, waiting for the long ones before she lets herself fall into her dreams.

A doctor has looked at her foot. Each day he wraps it in a brown bandage; he has given her small crutches so she can walk by herself without being carried. They hurt, digging into the skin under her arms. She cannot use them for long. She cannot go down the stairs by herself, there are too many, the staircase too steep, a long way to fall, the wood dark and slippery. She can sit on the seat in the resting place with her foot on the cushion, and look at the window, very big, full of diamond-shaped glass where the light comes through in colors like Father Bill's church. An old house, says Zoe. Hundreds of years old, she says. Hallways Luz has not walked, rooms she is afraid to see. Turns she could take and never be found.

Each night since she and Zoe arrived, when she is first put into bed Luz hears the voices from the big room where they eat dinner, chicken and corn, tomatoes as large as Zoe's hand. Luz and Zoe and Michael. Michael at last, the first one in life Luz has known who could disappear and come back. Handsome as she had thought he would be, with a soft voice that turns sharp when he and Zoe talk in the night and a way of looking at Luz that makes her ashamed for even now, here, she remembers how she has wanted to have her own father.

In the night when she is alone in the room that smells like old things and wood, Luz looks at the small lights outside that fly in the dark. Fireflies, Zoe has said, that come only in summer. If only Luz could step on that foot they could catch some. Instead, Luz catches voices, the ones in this house, angry and deep; they go back and forth with no rising, not like her mother's and Father Bill's went, ending always in laughter. Then Zoe and Michael climb the stairs, talking softly so they will not wake her, stand in the doorway of her room in the dark: Zoe a light and a person, Michael whose light flies up to the ceiling like the fireflies, as if it has not learned where in his body it belongs.

Soon Luz will not look at these things. She will not listen for the back and forth voices or the sound of her name. When the call comes and she is helped to the phone to hear Father Bill say the words that Luz begs not to hear, begs even Our Lady who hates Luz, who Luz also hates, that the word of her mother's death will never be spoken, she will be ready. Luz will already know how to do it, let go of each thing, each voice, each color, every strange smell and taste so she will not be in life like her mother.

CHAPTER 71

He touches her so perfectly, this man who hurts her, the husband who runs. Each night Michael enters her, Zoe feels him a little bit differently, touching a different place, a different current of gold. Now she is molten. A furnace of gold burns between them. Why is it only the body that brings them to such a place? Why doesn't it last?

Sometimes now when she looks at Michael, even here in their bed in the dark, Zoe sees his face dissolve into light. After that happens, she is filled with peace. How can she explain this new way she sees? How she has been changed? He did not sit at the window in the High Desert, did not go out in search of a great event. Michael, who does not know what Luz is.

Over and over Michael tries to assure her. "It's not you. It's me. It was nothing you did or did not do." Then what? "The past is the past," he says. But it lives on, lays down its print in our grain. "I came back, didn't I? I'm here." "But what if it happens again?" What if it does? It is not enough for him to love her and then to leave. Leave and come back. That she will have to decide frightens her. She puts her hand on his neck, resting her fingers on the spaces between the bones. "I love your face," he says.

Not enough.

Each morning, looking out through the maples she watches their leaves break into fragments gold and green, a pattern of light emerging, a grid of light beautiful beyond telling, like the face she saw floating over the window. How can she keep this from her husband? The beautiful world within?

She used to feel something at the core of herself was missing, an absence that could be seen. Now she feels whole, bruised, cracked open, ringingly alive.

Tonight it is her face she sees when she looks at Michael. Seeing hers, does he see his? "Something is different," he says and smoothes back her hair, buries her mouth with his. "You feel different." She puts her mouth on his, closes her eyes, breathes in the heat of their bodies, trying to erase the thought of their end.

He has heard her talking to the priest, or the one who is no longer a priest. She has tried to explain why she stayed in that place. The people she grew to love in such a short time. Now it has made him suspicious.

"Who is Walt?" he asks as she shifts from him, making a move to get up, as she does every night, going to Luz. He pulls her back.

"You know. The one who lent me the Civic."

"Who is he to you?"

She reaches for his hand. "Michael, I have to go." She is moving out of his arms, into the night air.

He watches her get out of bed in the dark, the long line of her back, the delicate curve of her breasts as she reaches for the nightgown, which had slipped to the floor. She has not spent one full night beside him. She says it is Luz. He sees it as punishment, leaving him after such lovemaking. She leaves so he will have only her absence beside him. As he has done to her.

"All she has to do is call out to you."

"I'm afraid she'll run."

"Run where? Zoe, she can't even manage the stairs."

"I'm sorry," says Zoe as she opens the door, steps into the hall, her heart hammering, afraid when she gets to the room where Luz sleeps, Luz will be gone.

CHAPTER 72

"Could I die?" Luz asks Zoe. The doctor has shown her the X-ray, and explained she must have an operation.

"Of course not. It is only to fix a very small bone in your foot."

Maybe I could, Luz Reyes thinks, wondering how she could make it happen, she and Mami, their souls floating out at the very same time, on powerful wings, returned to the place of the light.

CHAPTER 73

"Sit down, Josefina," says Maria Teresa, the mother of Raphael, as she pulls out a chair. "You are going to a party with your husband."

In the dream Josefina understands. Her mother-in-law has come to invite her into the country of death. Josefina sits down in the chair. The room is empty, without a ceiling, without visible walls. Now the old woman is dragging a second chair toward her. She places it opposite Josefina, walks behind it, folds her arms across her chest, waits.

What kind of party is this? Josefina wonders, but still, even if the party is to be her own death, the excitement runs through her. She is going to see him at last. The longing is so powerful she can barely remain in the chair. Josefina sits several minutes, Maria Theresa watching, the empty chair before her. And then without warning Raphael is there, seated with his legs crossed and his eyes closed, his mother gone.

Josefina is overjoyed. Here he is and in one piece again. His body has found itself, dressed itself finely, in a formal blue suit, polished shoes, even a tie. If only he would open his eyes, Josefina thinks, for his lids are shut in a way that suggests he is still thinking.

And then they are open. If she could run from the chair she would do it. If she could move herself down to the floor, she would crawl on all fours to touch even his feet. But she cannot move, cannot tear her gaze from the eyes of her husband. Never has she imagined one human being to carry such pain. And yet she must pay attention. He is showing her something with his eyes, the agony of the return, the effort he has made, is making at every moment, and only for her sake, for the love that he feels to give her this gift, himself in his body once more, all he has done to bring himself back.

"You have a daughter!" Josefina cries. "A wonderful child who looks just like you. So bright and so stubborn. She lived, Raphael. I was able to bring her to life."

But he does not react. Is not cheered by the news of his child, his eyes fixed on hers, a monumental effort being enacted before her. And now she understands, she is not to say anything. He is the one who has come here to speak. She must listen.

Without warning she explodes into love, a quality of love she has never before known, every cell of her being charged with it, every part of her pulsing as if she herself has become the earth's sun.

"You will live," Raphael says at last. "You will live, Josefina." And then right away he falls silent, slipping from her sight even as he remains on the chair looking at her with such longing she cannot endure it. If he does not close his eyes, in spite of what he has told her, Josefina believes in this moment, she is certain to die.

CHAPTER 74

Father Bill enters his office, checking the red message light on the phone. The rectory has a hollow feel. The bookcases empty, only a single yellow pad on the desktop. His personal papers are packed in boxes stored in Walt's trailer. His few clothes and possessions still in the trunk of the Cavalier, which shortly he will have to return to the Diocese. No idea how he will pay for another. He sits down, hits the red button, ready to copy his final messages. A few from the Diocese, several from his parishioners, *former* parishioners, asking him to dinner, inquiries about Josefina, offers of help, a call from Zoe with the results of the X-ray on Luz's foot. Not good. When he hears the voice, he is already so surrendered he does not move. Not a blip. He hears the name with such equanimity that he wonders if perhaps he has grown numb. "This is Esperanza Guerra, Father Bill. I have good news." Is it true that no miracle will surprise him now, no tragedy? Will he have lived to know both?

One month, they had told him at the center. That is how long it will take to schedule a transplant, in the unlikely event that a donor is found. A donor has surely been found. She has already purchased a plane ticket. She is flying in less than a week with her mother. Her mother. How will he ever explain this? How will Josefina bear it? Her mother and her sister alive. Flying in one week from Stockholm with the results of the tests.

He is in a battle now. He will have to move mountains to make this happen before the month is out. He will have to allow the mountains to be moved for him. He closes his eyes, asks for help. A month will be too long to wait. Let the center open up for her, the surgeon, the schedule. Let it be done quickly.

His Stockholm caller, he thinks. No wonder she could barely speak to him. Her sister was dead, she was certain. Esperanza had believed for eight years that her sister Josefina was somewhere in the coffee fields, a body dump in the countryside, her unborn child, impossible to imagine what they had done to Josefina. She has no sister. Surely not a living one in the States. The child could not have been born.

CHAPTER 75

The call comes in the night just as Luz knew that it would. First three rings then four, then Zoe's faraway voice calling, "Luz! Luz!" Then her long *ohhhhh* of joy, loud enough to excite a whole house, excite even a child keeping vigil in a strange bed, letting go of the beautiful things of the world, waiting for her mother to die.

CHAPTER 76

The blue house is a confusion of flowers and languages, English and Spanish. Two sisters who look so much alike when Luz turns away and looks back she does not know, for a moment, who is her mother Josefina, who Esperanza, her aunt. The one with the pain in the back, who walks slow, Esperanza. The one who cannot laugh yet, who covers her stomach and walks fast and is bossy in Spanish and English, Josefina. And there on the couch in a gray suit, long red nails and white pearls, the grandmother who looks like no one, too beautiful for anything but stories, who with everyone laughing and crying is right now shaking her small golden head at the noise.

CHAPTER 77

Sometimes in the night when Zoe is asleep, her hands search the bed for her children, one and then two, waking in panic when she discovers Luz is not there. Even with all of them crowded together in the family bed, Walt hanging onto the edge for dear life, Zoe thinks she has come up short. It is Luz who is missing, Luz Reyes, the first child of her heart.

How strange, Zoe says, and even William cannot help but agree, strange that Luz and Josefina are living in Stockholm, the country of Zoe's ancestors, a place she and Walt plan to visit, as William does every year in his travels. But with two kids under four and unruly ones, minds of their own from day one, two stepkids in college nearby, Walt's business, hers—Zoe Luedke Fine Furniture—right there on the property, Zoe and Walt can barely get to the A&P let alone off to Europe, at least not now.

If she worries about Luz, it is not without cause. Five surgeries to repair the delicate bone, which took years to heal, bouts of pain, the right foot curled at the toes, hard for the foot to lay flat. Then the Swedish, her shyness, sleepless nights filled with strange vivid dreams. Still, in Stockholm Luz lives surrounded by family: cousins, her aunt, and her grandmother, who all adore her. Not to mention her adoring mother. And, too, there is a close-knit community, exiles, all. Salvadorans who found safety in a distant land and in spite of the crazy cold climate decided to stay. Now she has only a limp, and a faint one. It is Luz's fears that trouble Josefina most. And now that she's older, Luz keeps them to herself.

On his last visit to Stockholm, William was able to convince Josefina to let him spend a little time with her. For years Josefina refused to allow it and Luz avoided him, off with her cousins for most of his visit.

He took her to Berzelii Park, bribed her with the coffee Josefina forbade Luz to drink as they left the apartment. They find an empty table, sit down opposite each other under a white market umbrella, people filing by. "Here is my big secret. I just want to be normal for once. Is that too much to ask?" Then she fixes him in a stare, the same dark eyes, her features softer, hair cut short, framing her face. She is growing more to look like her mother, he thinks. What a miracle she is. He wants to stand up in triumph for Rafael Reyes and Josefina Guerra. "You are going to have a beautiful life."

"Right. With this foot? You're just saying that. My mother told you to say it."

"No one told me. I see it as clearly as I see your face."

"What do you do, actually, for a living I mean?"

He had laughed. A renegade priest, a storefront congregation. He barely gets by. "I guess you could call me a teacher."

"Are you glad you aren't still a priest?"

"Yes and no."

She sips the coffee, puts it down on the table, cradling the cup. "Is it my fault?"

"No. It had nothing to do with you. It was me." She doesn't believe him and says so. Blunt. Her mother's daughter. "I would not lie to you, Luz."

"Oh, really."

"Is there anything you would like to ask me?"

"About what?"

"Infidelity."

"I don't remember it."

"You don't remember anything?"

"It was hot. My mother was always sick. And you filled me with a lot of crap."

"What do you mean?" he asks gently.

"I don't remember."

"You were a beautiful child."

"I was a beautiful child. I'm going to have a beautiful life. Only right now my life sucks."

"Well, you're fourteen. This is the time to be miserable. Try to enjoy it!"

"Thanks," she says, picking up the coffee and concealing her smile behind the cup, "that's a big help."

She's fine, he told Josefina. Try not to worry so much. Fine with those moods and that foot, she had said. He understands nothing. The worries of a mother are endless. She shares them with her sister, with her mother, and with Zoe, who has always understood.

Luz will come back to her gifts, William thinks. It is right that for now they lie fallow. He will wait to see how she carries them as she moves into the world. He leaves Stockholm happy. Though it is always hard saying good-bye. He does not need much these days to be happy. In the States he has no lack of students. All he had to let go of seems worth it now, even Josefina. He sees it all around him, every day, as clearly as he did at the window, the way the world is opening. All of them who come to him opening as he was opened that summer in Infidelity, through Luz, to the larger love.

EPILOGUE

When we finally learned that the monk had been fasting, hadn't eaten in days, nine, maybe ten, maybe more, pretty much all of us let out our collective breath. Starving to death being a whole lot more acceptable here than dying of joy.

No one goes around anymore claiming the miraculous had chosen to settle in Infidelity, unfurling its great golden wings. (Or were they green?) No more gift-bearing children wandering among us, not a single one this year changed into forward-bent light.

No holy visions remained in Luz's wake. Hardly anyone pointing to things not humanly possible to be seen.

The sidewalk's still hot. Mostly empty. (No chairs allowed now that Platz owns the car wash.) And if people feel better for having put themselves out there in public for reasons too deep to talk of, more power to them.

Sometimes in the diner an argument will start that gets everyone going—how we handled the great event (if it was great), or if maybe we failed. Simpler to say what Bobbie still says—*something happened to a child here and we let it*—a child who was little and loved the world—than admit to the change few dare speak of but every soul living in Infidelity has come to know. Something amazing happened to us. At any moment it may happen again. May be happening now, as we speak. Who among us can say for sure?

ACKNOWLEDGMENTS

The author gratefully acknowledges the MacDowell Colony for time and space in which to write.

Endless thanks to Catherine W. Swan, Michelle Rapkin, Bruce Joel Rubin, Blanche Rubin, Lenore Smith-Aman, Rosa Lowinger, Susan Buckley, Robert E. Mellman, and Andrew Wagner. For your love and support, Jonathan Parker, Brandon Parker, Rosalind Till, Donna Lee Michaels, Madeline Till, and Amos Kamil.

And to Kimberly Beck Clark, Anna Termine, and Cal Barksdale, deepest gratitude for bringing this book into the world.